STATE OF SHOCK

FIRST FAMILY SERIES, BOOK 4

MARIE FORCE

State of Shock
First Family Series, Book 4
By: Marie Force

Published by HTJB, Inc.
Copyright 2022. HTJB, Inc.
Cover design by Kristina Brinton
Cover photography by Regina Wamba
Models: Robert John and Ellie Dulac
Print Layout: E-book Formatting Fairies
ISBN: 978-1958035092

The First Family Series

Book 1: State of Affairs
Book 2: State of Grace
Book 3: State of the Union
Book 4: State of Shock

More new books are always in the works. For the most up-to-date list of what's available from the First Family Series, go to *marieforce.com/firstfamily*

For Kevin

CHAPTER ONE

A full minute passed before Angela's words registered with Sam.

Spencer won't wake up.

Dr. Harry Flynn bolted from the table, yelling for his fiancée, Lilia, to contact the Camp David medical team and get them to Birch, which was Angela and Spencer's cabin. "Tell them to hurry."

Sam's husband, Nick, and brother-in-law Mike ran after Harry. Her sister Tracy went to Angela, who was hysterical.

"What's going on?" Sam's son, Scotty, asked.

"We aren't sure," Sam said. "Stay with the twins, okay?"

"I will."

"I need to be with him," Angela said.

"Let's go, then." Tracy glanced over her shoulder at Sam as she led their middle sister to the door. "Sam."

Sam tried to shake off the shock. Spencer was young and strong. He'd be fine. Her sister needed her. *Shake it off*, she told herself. "Where're your kids?"

"With Celia," Angela said. "She took them for a walk so we could sleep in."

"What can I do for you?" Lilia asked. At work, she was Sam's chief of staff. Here, she was a close friend.

"Pray," Sam said, even though she wasn't particularly religious. What else could they do at a time like this?

Sam followed her sisters out the door and ran to Birch, a short distance from their cabin. The Camp David ambulance and fire department were already there. "Wait," Sam said to her sisters as her training kicked in. "Ang shouldn't go in there."

"I want to be with him," Angela said pleadingly. Her pretty face was red and puffy, her belly round with her third pregnancy.

"Let me go in and see what's happening first."

"Sam, *please.*"

"You don't want to see things that can't be unseen. Trust me on this."

"Wait with me." Tracy kept her arms around Angela. "Let Sam check first. Go, Sam. Hurry."

Sam went up the stairs and stepped into chaos.

Spencer was on the floor of the living room. The first thing she noticed was that his face was gray. Sam recognized the automated external defibrillator from a training they'd had at work. The AED was hooked to Spencer as Harry performed CPR.

"Did you give him Narcan?" Sam asked, knowing it was routine to give the overdose drug in cases when an otherwise-healthy patient was unresponsive, even if the victim wasn't a known drug user.

"Twice," one of the EMTs said as they worked frantically.

That he hadn't responded to the drug that quickly reversed an overdose could mean any number of things. Besides, there's no way this was drug related. Spencer didn't have a drug problem.

"Ask Angela when she last spoke to him and if he was taking meds," Harry said, doing chest compressions as the EMTs worked on intubating him.

Sam ran outside to ask Angela the questions.

"Earlier this morning," Angela said, her voice shaky. "He got up to use the bathroom and then went back to bed. Celia said she'd get up with our kids. He... He said to wake him up for breakfast."

"Was he taking anything?"

"Just some pain meds."

Sam went back inside. "She talked to him earlier this morning, and he was on pain meds."

"We've got a faint heartbeat," one of the EMTs said.

"We need to get him to GW Trauma ASAP," Harry said, as he stopped compressions. "Get the chopper ready."

"It's standing by, Dr. Flynn."

Working together, they got Spencer loaded onto a gurney.

Spencer's heart might be beating, but he looked dead to Sam. How could this be happening? He'd been fine the night before. They'd played Pictionary. He'd drawn the funniest giraffe.

She went out ahead of the EMTs.

"They've got a heartbeat, and they're taking him to GW," Sam told her sisters.

"I want to go with him," Angela said.

"There may not be room in the chopper."

Nick came outside, looking pale and shocked. "We'll take her on *Marine One*. Tell Elijah he's in charge of the kids. Let's move quickly."

While Tracy took off to do that, Sam stopped Captain Tisha Martin, the Camp David commanding officer.

"Please keep everyone out of the cabin until I can get back here." She glanced at their FBI agent friend, Avery Hill, who had an arm around his wife, Shelby, as they watched the drama unfold. "Especially him."

"I will," Captain Martin said. "No one will get in there except for you."

Sam squeezed her arm. "I appreciate that. I want to protect their privacy."

"I understand."

Within minutes, they'd arranged for the kids to stay behind with Eli and Candace in charge while Celia had Angela's kids and Tracy's. They boarded *Marine One* with Angela, Tracy and Mike.

The Secret Service agents who protected Sam and Nick entered through the rear doorway.

Taco, the Marine colonel who flew the helicopter, had them airborne within seconds and headed for DC.

Sam could tell they were flying much faster than they normally did.

Angela was crying so hard she could barely breathe.

Brant, Nick's lead agent, came into their cabin, whispered something in Nick's ear and then returned to the aft cabin.

"What?" Angela said. "Tell me."

"He crashed again," Nick said. "They're trying to resuscitate him."

Sam wanted to scream at someone to tell her how this was possible. Spencer was thirty-six and in perfect health as far as she knew. What could've happened between last night and this morning? The detective in her wanted answers, and she wanted them now. But her sister needed her, so she kept her focus on Angela.

"The kids..." Angela said.

"They're with Celia and Shelby," Tracy reminded her. "They're fine."

"I can't lose him," Angela said. "I can't."

"You won't," Tracy said. "He's young and strong. Harry is with him, along with the rest of the presidential medical team. They're the best."

"She's right," Nick said. "The medical helicopter has all the state-of-the-art equipment."

That seemed to pacify Angela ever so slightly, but it did nothing to calm Sam's nerves after having seen for herself that Spencer's condition was dire.

Nick took hold of her hand and gave it a squeeze.

When Sam glanced at him, she saw the truth in his blank stare. He was far more worried than he'd let on to Angela.

God, what would Angela do if Spencer died? Jack was seven, Ella not even two and a third baby was due in June.

"I need him," Angela said. "I need him to be okay."

"He will be," Tracy said again.

"Has he had any medical issues recently?" Sam asked because she couldn't help herself.

Angela glanced at her, in obvious torment that went beyond the current emergency. "He's been struggling."

"With what?" Sam asked sharply, earning her a glare from Tracy.

"He hurt his back playing football with his college friends about a year ago," Angela said haltingly.

"I remember that. What about it?"

"He didn't want anyone to know. He said he was handling it."

Sam couldn't help but go into detective mode. "Know what? Handling what?"

Angela took a deep breath. When she released it, she choked on a sob. "He got hooked on the meds they gave him for the pain."

"Was it Oxy?" Sam asked.

Angela nodded as she wiped her face. "And Percocet."

Sam looked at Nick. "We need to get word to Harry to order a tox screen immediately."

Nick pulled his phone from his pocket and put through a call. As the personal physician to the president, Harry would make sure someone took that call. "Tell Dr. Flynn that Sam said to order a tox screen. He was on Oxy and Percocet." Nick listened for a second. "Was it prescribed by a doctor?"

Angela stared at him as if she was uncertain how to reply.

"Angela!" Sam immediately regretted her tone, but this was no time to worry about whether Spencer had obtained illegal drugs. "Tell them what they need to know to save him."

"The doctors wouldn't give him anymore. He was getting it somewhere else."

"Jesus," Sam whispered. "Tell them it could be fentanyl poisoning."

"He didn't take that!" Angela cried.

"The pills he bought might've been laced with it." To Nick, she said, "Tell them."

He relayed the information to Harry and the others.

Spencer must've taken something when he got up earlier that morning, Sam thought, her mind racing.

Angela broke down again into heartbroken sobs. "He was trying so hard to quit taking them. You don't know what he's been through."

"He seemed fine when we saw him," Sam said. "He was riding Jack around on his back on Christmas."

"He was medicated then. They cut him off in January, and it got really bad then."

"Why didn't you tell us, honey?" Tracy asked tearfully.

"He wouldn't let me. He didn't want it to blow back on Nick."

"Oh God, come on," Nick said, sounding agonized. "I don't care about that."

"That's what I said, but he was embarrassed. Last year when the Secret Service took us all to that bunker? I said he was away on business, but he was in rehab."

"Ang," Sam said, battling tears. "I'm so sorry you guys were going through such a difficult thing all by yourselves. We would've been there for you."

"He was adamant. He didn't want anyone to know."

And now he might pay for that decision with his life, Sam

thought. If he'd taken pills laced with fentanyl, it might be too late to save him.

THE NEXT FEW hours played out like a horror movie, with bad news on top of more bad news. Despite the heroic efforts of Harry and the EMTs in restarting his heart, Spencer's brain had been deprived of oxygen long enough that the doctors could find no activity. They would have to test that several more times before they declared him brain dead, but they said it was unlikely that he would recover.

Angela's heartbreak was utterly devastating.

While she supported her sister, Sam was overcome with rage. Someone had done this to him, to them, and she was going to find out who as soon as she possibly could. She would make them pay for taking Spencer from his wife and children. The need for justice for Spencer and Angela was so intense, Sam had to fight it back so she could be there for her sister in her time of need.

Sam and Tracy never left Angela's side during that long, hellish day, physically holding her up more than once as it sank in that Spencer was gone and not coming back.

"What will I do?" Angela asked between sobs as she paced the ICU waiting room while the doctors tended to him. The room had been closed to everyone else by the Secret Service, who stood watch outside the door. "I don't know what to do."

Sam couldn't think of a single thing to say in response to that as she paced along with Angela, wanting to stay close to her. What would she do with three little kids and no husband? Spencer was also the primary breadwinner for their family, and his loss would be a huge economic blow on top of the emotional one. So many thoughts ran through Sam's head that she was nearly dizzy from the spiral.

"You need to sit for a minute," Nick said at one point.

"I don't want to."

"Sam, your hip is still healing. You should get off your feet for a bit."

"Angela needs me."

"You're right here for her. Come sit with me. Just for a minute."

Sam felt almost guilty taking comfort from her husband while Angela was losing hers. It felt wrong to have Nick's arm around her when Spencer could never again put his arm around Angela. He would miss the birth of their third child and everything else with their kids. It was beyond belief. "How can this be happening?"

"I keep asking myself that," Nick said. "He was fine last night, and now... I feel sick that they felt they had to keep this from us because of me."

"That was their choice. You can't take that on."

"Still..."

"Yeah. I don't know what's more shocking—what happened today or that this had been going on right in front of us and we had no idea. I mean, I knew he hurt his back playing football, but not the rest."

Dr. Anderson entered the room. "I came in when I heard something was up with your family. Can I help?"

"I wish you could," Sam said. "But thank you for coming."

"Do you know what happened?"

"We just found out he was battling a pain med addiction and had turned to acquiring them illegally."

"Ah, damn. If I had a nickel for every time I've seen that in the ER lately."

"It's happening a lot?"

"Huge uptick in recent months."

That information made Sam only more determined to find out who was dealing poisonous pills and get them off the streets before this tragedy happened to another family. And why in the hell hadn't the Narcotics squad sounded an alarm about a surge in overdose deaths? She'd be asking that question as soon as possible.

"I guess if you heard about this, that means the word is out," Nick said, overhearing the conversation with Dr. Anderson.

"It's all over the news that a member of your family suffered a medical emergency at Camp David," Anderson said.

"Angela," Nick said, "I hate to ask you this, but we might have to issue a statement because the press has caught wind of an emergency at Camp David."

"Do whatever you need to," she said.

What did she care about a statement when her husband was brain dead?

"Are you all right with us saying who it is?"

Angela nodded.

"Before that happens, you need to notify anyone who shouldn't hear it from the news."

"I'll help you with that," Tracy said. "Give me your phone and tell me who to call or text, and I'll take care of it."

While they did that, Nick called Trevor, his communications director, speaking softly into the phone as he conveyed the news to him and the American people, through his team. "For now, just say his condition is grave and his family is with him," Nick said. "Give us an hour to notify everyone who needs to know before you release it."

Spencer's parents and sisters arrived, compounding the heartbreak with their agony. His brother's family was in Italy but had been notified.

Celia called Sam, looking for an update. "Jack is asking for them. I don't know what to say."

"It's not good."

"Oh God, Sam. Really? How is that possible?"

"Angela told us he's been battling a painkiller addiction. After the doctors cut him off, he turned to acquiring them illegally. We think he might've gotten laced meds."

"*What?*" Celia asked on a gasp. "How long had that been going on?"

"Awhile. They kept it private."

"Oh my Lord. Poor Angela. And the kids..."

"I'm going to talk to Nick about getting you guys home." As she said the words, he stood and went to confer with his lead agent. "Nick is talking to Brant. Just bring everyone to the White House, and we'll be there when we can."

"I can't believe this is happening."

"None of us can."

"Angela..."

"Is destroyed. I don't know, Celia. I just don't know."

"Tell her I'm taking good care of her babies and not to worry."

"That'll help. Thank you." Sam realized they needed to tell their mother what was happening. This surreal day brought back so many memories of the morning last October when her dad passed.

"If there's anything else I can do, please don't hesitate to let me know."

"Thank you."

"Tell Angela I love her."

"I will. Love you."

"Love you, too."

"Ang," Sam said. "Celia said she loves you and she's taking good care of Jack and Ella."

"That's good."

"Do you want me to call Mom?"

"Yeah, I guess we should."

Sam placed the call to her mother, Brenda.

"Hi there. How're things at Camp David?"

Sam realized she hadn't seen the news. "Mom."

"What?"

"Something's happened to Spencer. He's at GW, and it's not good. He's... They're saying he's brain dead."

"No. Sam. My God!"

"We thought you'd want to know."

"I'm coming."

"We're in the ICU waiting room."

"Okay. Tell Angela... I'm coming."

The line went dead, and Sam closed her phone, wishing there was something she could do to turn back the clock, to keep this from happening to her sister, niece and nephew. "Mom is coming."

As tears ran down her face, Angela stared blankly at the wall. What did she care who was coming when the only one she wanted was gone forever?

CHAPTER TWO

At seven o'clock that evening, the doctors asked to speak to Angela and Spencer's family in a private conference room. Angela asked Brenda, Tracy, Mike, Sam, Nick and Harry to come with her and Spencer's family.

When they were seated at the large table, the doctor who'd been with them all day turned to Angela. "Mrs. Radcliffe, I'm very sorry to have to tell you that your husband has suffered a catastrophic injury to his brain due to oxygen deprivation. We've run extensive tests and have confirmed there's no brain activity, which means he's unable to sustain life on his own without the advanced measures currently being taken to keep him alive. We believe the damage to his brain had already been done when he was found unresponsive."

Spencer's mother broke down into sobs as his father tried to comfort her.

Sam wiped away tears as she attempted to wrap her head around the fact that Spencer was all but dead.

"What do we do now?" Angela asked, looking to Harry.

"If he was my family member," Harry said gently, "I would stop life support and allow him to pass away peacefully, but that has to be your decision."

Angela looked to Sam and Tracy, her eyes wild. "I can't decide that. How do I decide that?"

How did anyone make such a decision? Sam tried to imagine

herself in the same situation and couldn't. She simply couldn't go there. "What would Spencer want you to do?"

Angela buried her face in her hands. "I don't know. I just don't know."

"He'd never want to be kept alive artificially," Mr. Radcliffe, Spencer's dad, said. "Remember when my brother was on life support, and we had to make this same decision? Spence said then that being attached to machines is no way to live."

"He said that?" Angela asked, seeming to brighten a bit at hearing that Spencer had expressed an opinion on the matter.

"He did, honey."

Angela's face was red and swollen, her brown eyes puffy from crying for hours, her light brown hair a mess of tangles. "If that's what he would've wanted, then I suppose we have to let him go. I just don't know how I'm supposed to do that."

"We'll be right there with you," Tracy said as tears slid down her cheeks. "Every step of the way."

Angela looked to the doctor, who awaited her decision, and nodded.

There was paperwork to be signed and formalities to be seen to.

"Can we donate his organs?" Angela asked. "I think he'd want to do that if he could."

"I'm sorry, but he was without oxygen too long for them to be viable," the doctor said.

"Oh. Okay."

Heartbreak on top of heartbreak. That was how Sam would remember this dreadful day.

"Should I bring the kids in?" Angela asked.

"No," Tracy said emphatically. "They shouldn't see him like this. They need to remember him the way he was."

"I agree," Sam said. "It would be too much for them to understand." She couldn't think about Jack without wanting to wail at the injustice of it all. Spencer and Jack were inseparable. Her sweet nephew would be crushed by the loss of his dad. "Ang."

Angela turned to Sam, her face ravaged with heartbreak.

"You need to request an autopsy, and I'd like to ask Lindsey to do it. Would that be all right?"

"Whatever you think is best."

"It may not matter now, but you'll want answers. She and I will get them for you."

"Okay."

Sam made the call to her close friend, Dr. Lindsey McNamara, the District's chief medical examiner.

"Hey, Sam. How is he?"

"We're about to remove him from life support."

"Oh my God."

"I'd like you to handle the autopsy. Can you come?"

"Yes, of course. I'll be there shortly."

"Thank you."

"If there's anything else I can do..."

"I need you on this, and I appreciate you handling it."

"Please tell Angela..." Lindsey's voice caught. "Tell her we're praying for her, Spencer and the kids."

"I will."

Sam ended the call and conveyed the update as well as Lindsey's message to Angela, who received it without seeming to understand a word that Sam said.

When the medical team was ready for them, they went to Spencer's room and surrounded his bed with loved ones.

Sam noticed he'd been extubated but was still attached to other machines.

"Would you like to hold him?" the nurse asked Angela.

"Yes. Please."

The nurse helped Angela get settled on the bed next to Spencer.

This was the saddest thing Sam had ever experienced in her life, and she wasn't sure she could bear to watch it happen.

As if he knew that, Nick's arms encircled her, propping her up when she needed him most.

"Are you ready?" the doctor asked Angela.

"How long will it take?"

"Not long."

Angela kissed Spencer's face and then his lips. "I love you forever," she whispered.

Watching his parents kiss their son goodbye had Sam turning into Nick's embrace as she broke down.

"I'm ready now," Angela said.

As the nurses shut off the last of the machines keeping

Spencer alive, Sam forced herself to turn back toward the bed, to be fully present for Angela. She'd never been prouder of her sister than she was as she let her beloved husband go peacefully.

With most of his loved ones by his side, Spencer passed at five after eight.

Sam insisted they wait to ensure that Lindsey and her team were there to remove Spencer's body from the hospital before she felt comfortable leaving.

With Spencer safe with Lindsey, Nick and Mike kept their arms around Angela as the Secret Service escorted them to an exit they'd secured ahead of time.

"I'm so sorry, Mr. President, Mrs. Cappuano," Brant said as he stood by the door to one of the many black SUVs they used to transport the first family.

"Thank you, Brant," Nick said for all of them.

Angela sat between Sam and Tracy. They kept Angela in tissues while dealing with their own tears.

"What am I going to do?" Angela asked.

"Take things one minute at a time," Tracy said. "You have to take care of yourself and the baby."

"The baby won't ever know him," Angela said, as if that was just now occurring to her. "There won't be any pictures…"

"The baby will know him through us," Sam said. "We'll make sure of it."

Nick took a call from Terry. "We'll be back shortly, and I'll review it then. I understand."

"People are clamoring for info?" Sam asked him.

He nodded. "I want to review the statement before they release it." He glanced at Angela. "I'm sorry. Work shouldn't be intruding at a time like this."

"Do whatever you need to and don't be sorry," Angela said. "I understand the press is all over you."

"We hate that most of the time, but never more so than at times like this."

"It's okay. Everyone who needs to know already does."

"We'll release the statement as soon as I approve it."

Sam sent a text to Freddie and Gonzo, asking them to notify the squad so they wouldn't hear about Spencer's death on the news.

Oh my God, Freddie replied. *I'm so, so sorry.*

Heartbroken, Gonzo said.

"Trace," Sam said. "You need to call Brooke." Sam's niece was in college in Charlottesville.

"I will as soon as we get there," Tracy said.

When they arrived at the White House, they were met by Gideon Lawson, the chief usher. "Please accept the condolences of the entire staff on the loss of your brother-in-law."

"Thank you, Gideon," Nick said.

"All the guest rooms on the second and third floor are ready for occupancy, and if you'd like, we can send up some food to the residence."

"That'd be good," Nick said. "Thank you so much."

"We wish there was more we could do."

"We all do. It's... unbelievable."

"I'm sure. He was so young."

"Two years younger than I am."

Sam listened to them, feeling detached from the entire situation, as if she were watching it happen from a distance rather than being smack in the middle of it. She'd experienced that feeling only two other times in her life. The day after Detective Arnold was gunned down and then again when her father had died just as suddenly as Spencer had.

The group trooped up the red-carpeted stairs to the residence.

Eli and Candace were in the hallway and came to hug them.

"We're so sorry," Eli said.

"Thank you."

"Unless you need us to stay, we have to go back to Princeton." Eli seemed pained to be inflicting logistics into the situation. "I have a class I can't miss in the morning. We'll be back for the service."

"Go ahead," Sam said. "Thank you for stepping up with Scotty and the kids today."

"Of course."

Sam hugged them both again. "Be safe."

While Nick walked them out, Sam turned to Angela.

"I'd like to see the kids," she said.

"Let's go up to Celia's room. They're with her." Sam led the way to the third floor and knocked softly on her stepmother's door.

Celia came to the door looking as ravaged as the rest of them. She hugged Angela. "I'm so, so sorry, sweetheart."

"Thank you. Could I see the kids?"

"Of course. Ella is asleep, but Jack is still up. He knows something is terribly wrong, but I didn't say too much."

"Thank you for taking care of them today."

"I wish I could've done more."

Angela squeezed Celia's arm. "There was nothing any of us could've done."

Angela, Tracy and Sam followed Celia into her suite.

Jack was curled up on the sofa, under a blanket.

Angela sat next to him and held out her arms.

He clung to her, as if he already knew what she was going to tell him. He'd always been too smart for his own good.

"Where's Daddy?" Jack asked in a tremulous voice.

"He got very sick this morning, and the doctors tried so hard to help him, but there was nothing they could do."

"Did he have to go to heaven like Grandpa did?"

"Yes, baby, he did, and I'm sure Grandpa was there to welcome him."

"When can he come back?"

"He can't come back. Remember how we talked about that when Grandpa died?"

Jack's little chin trembled. "Why did Daddy have to leave us?"

"I don't know. But he'd want you to remember how much he loved you and how much fun you guys had together. He wouldn't want you to be sad."

"Can't Uncle Nick fix this? He's the president of the whole country."

Sam dropped to her knees in front of her precious nephew. "Uncle Nick would fix this for you and your mommy and Ella in a second if he could, buddy."

Jack reached for her, and Sam hugged him. "I'm so, so sorry."

"Will we still have the new baby?" Jack asked.

"Yes, we will, and I'm going to need you to be such a great big brother to Ella and our new baby." A steady stream of tears fell down Angela's face as she tended to her son. "They'll need us to be strong for them."

"I'll be strong."

Sam's heart shattered for the little boy who'd adored his father. This was all so unfair and so fucking unnecessary.

The minute she was able to break free for a second, she ducked into the bathroom and called Sergeant Tommy "Gonzo" Gonzales, her second-in-command at work.

"Sam. My God. I'm so sorry. How's Ang?" Angela had cared for Gonzo's son, Alex, for most of his life.

"Not good at all."

"Do they have any idea what happened?"

"He took something he bought illegally, and I suspect it was probably laced."

"Oh fuck. No way."

"I want to find the person who did this to him. Anderson says there's been a huge increase in ODs coming into the ER. It might be related."

"Son of a bitch."

"I want to track these motherfuckers down and make them pay for what they've done to my sister and her family—and all the others who've lost their lives because of this crap."

"I'm with you," he said. "There but for the grace of God go I." He'd fought his own battle with painkiller addiction after the murder of his partner and had procured Oxy illegally.

"I thought of that earlier. You got so lucky."

"And I know it. I'll do what I can to help figure out what happened to Spencer. He was a good guy. I hate this for Angela and her kids. Poor Jack."

"She just had to tell him. It was dreadful."

"I can't even imagine. It's all so shocking and devastating."

"Yes, it is."

"I'm really sorry, Sam, for you and your whole family."

"Thank you. Is it all over the news?"

"Nonstop coverage on every network that your brother-in-law is critically ill. Tons of speculation on what happened."

"God. Just what Angela needs. Nick will release a statement soon." And eventually people would learn that Spencer's death was drug related, which would start a second firestorm. Sam would do whatever she could to protect her sister from that blowback.

"Is there any way you can get his phone to me?" Gonzo asked. "That's the best place to start."

"I'll see what I can do to track it down."

"Keep me posted. I'm here and will do whatever I can."

"Thanks, Gonzo. Don't say anything to anyone about the drug thing for now. We need more info before that gets out."

"You got it."

"I'll be in touch when I have the phone. Another thing you can do for me is some gentle digging into why Narcotics hadn't alerted us to the upswing in overdose deaths that Dr. Anderson told me he's seen in the ER."

"I'll do that."

"Try not to ruffle any feathers. Maybe start with Malone?" Even though he was still suspended following the incident that led to the death of Sergeant Ramsey's son, Malone would have the inside scoop.

"Yeah, I will. Take care of yourself and give Ang our love. We're all heartbroken for her."

"Will do. Thanks again."

Sam closed her phone and took one more minute to herself before she rejoined her sister's unbearable tragedy.

CHAPTER THREE

"**M**r. President," Terry said. "If I could have a minute, please?"

"I'll be right there," Nick said to Sam as she headed for their suite to change her clothes.

Terry handed Nick a sheet of paper. "We've drafted a statement from you and the first lady."

Nick scanned the words, still in disbelief that this was necessary. *The President and First Lady regret to announce the death of their beloved brother-in-law, Spencer Radcliffe, at five after eight o'clock this evening. Spencer, the husband of the First Lady's sister Angela, passed away at the George Washington University Hospital, surrounded by his wife, parents, the First Couple and other loved ones. "Our hearts are broken for Angela, Jack, Ella and the Radcliffe family," the President said. "We will support them in every way that we can in the days to come. We ask for privacy as we grieve the tremendous loss of a husband, father, son and friend we loved very much."*

"That's perfect, Terry. Thank you."

"Of course, Mr. President. And on a personal note, I'm heartbroken for Angela and the kids. Spencer was a nice guy."

"Yes, he was. It's so hard to believe."

"You never know what's coming."

"That's a fact. I'm going to check on Sam. Thank you for taking care of the statement."

"Please let me know if there's anything else I can do."

"Thank you."

When Sam emerged from the bathroom in their suite, Nick was waiting for her. "I'd ask if you were all right, but..."

"My phone is blowing up. Everyone is so upset."

"I thought we should spend a few minutes with Scotty. I called him earlier, so he'd hear the news from us."

"Yes, for sure. Thanks for thinking of that. This whole day is just a blur. Was it only this morning that we woke up at Camp David?"

"It was, but it feels like a lifetime ago."

"Gonzo said it's getting nonstop coverage on every network."

"What can they have to say to give it that kind of airtime?" Nick asked.

"I guess it's a big story when a member of the president's family suffers a medical emergency at Camp David. It'll become an even bigger story when we're forced to release his cause of death."

He reached for her and drew her into a hug. "One thing at a time."

Sam wrapped her arms around him. "I feel guilty taking this from you when Angela's love is gone."

"Don't feel guilty. She wouldn't want that."

"I thought it was horrible when Dad died, but this..."

"It's a whole other level of tragic because he's so young."

"Yeah," Sam said. "Poor Jack. He broke my heart."

"Mine, too."

"Let's go see our own boy and try to make some sense of this for him." How would they do that when it didn't make sense to them? "What will we tell him?"

"I think we say it's possible he had a bad reaction to some medication for now," Nick said. "Until the cause of death is confirmed, there's no sense talking about drugs to him or anyone."

"That's true." Sam took a deep breath and blew it out, searching for some inner calm that wasn't going to appear any time soon. "I never imagined we'd need the sudden-death chapter of the parental handbook twice in six months."

"No kidding."

When they emerged from their suite, they nodded to the Secret Service agents in the hallway.

"We're very sorry, Mr. President, Mrs. Cappuano," Vernon said.

Sam took a second to hug her lead agent. "Thank you, Vernon. It's a shock to say the least."

"Our hearts are with you all."

"Appreciate it."

Outside of Scotty's room, they encountered Melinda, another of the agents, whom Sam had referred to in the past as Secret Service Barbie. "I'm so sorry for your loss."

"Thank you, Melinda," Sam said.

Nick knocked on the door to Scotty's room.

"Enter."

They stepped inside and closed the door.

Scotty got up off his bed and came to them, followed by Skippy the dog. Sam noticed his eyes were red from crying. "I'm so, so sorry for Angela, Jack, Ella, everyone."

"Thanks, pal," Sam said, breathing in the familiar, comforting scent of his hair.

"How's Angela?"

"Terrible and in shock, which is to be expected."

"I didn't know what to do. I sort of gave Jack and Ella some space to hang with Celia. I figured if everyone was all over them, they'd know something was up."

"That was probably a good call," Nick said. "Angela just told Jack."

"That poor kid. They were so close. They were always together."

"I know, but we'll all be there for him as best we can," Sam said.

"Do they know what happened to Spencer?"

"They think it had something to do with medication," Nick said, "but we won't know anything definite for a while yet."

"This is a lot on top of losing Gramps," Scotty said.

"It sure is," Sam said, "but I'd like to think Gramps is up there welcoming Spencer and introducing him to everyone and making him feel at home."

"That's a cool way to look at it. It'd be just like Gramps to throw a party."

"I love that you know that about him even though you met him after his injury," Sam said, smiling for the first time in hours.

"The stories were legendary," Scotty said.

"Yes, they were. Your Gramps loved a good party, and he'll

throw a heck of a party for Spencer, even though he'll be devastated to see him there far too soon."

"I hate that people have to die," Scotty said, his eyes filling. He'd had far too much experience with death at a young age, having lost his mother and grandfather before he landed in state custody.

Sam hugged him. "Life is a fatal illness for all of us, which is why we have to enjoy every minute while we can. You just never know."

"It scares me that something like this might happen to you guys," Scotty said.

"I'd like to tell you that could never happen," Nick said, "but we all know it can. There're no guarantees for any of us, but if we love each other the best we can every day, then there'll be no regrets."

"That's all well and good, but I'd really appreciate it if neither of you went and died on me," Scotty said. "It took me a long time to have parents, and I kinda hit the jackpot with you guys. I need to keep you around for many years to come."

"We're not going anywhere, buddy," Sam said, hugging him tighter.

He clung to her like he hadn't since they lost her dad. "Would it be okay if I went up to see Angela?"

"Of course. She'd love to see you."

"Will you come with me?"

"We'll be right there with you through all of this," Nick said.

"Is it weird that I'm so sad?"

"Not at all," Sam said. "He was your uncle, and he died way too young. And you're sad for Angela and the kids."

"So sad."

As they went upstairs with Scotty, it was difficult for Sam to put her thirst for vengeance on behalf of Spencer, Angela and their family on the back burner to tend to her family's grief. The minute she could, she'd be figuring out where he'd gotten those pills. She didn't need to wait for a full toxicity report that'd arrive weeks from now to tell her what'd probably happened. Unfortunately, they'd seen far too much of it in recent years, and why in the hell hadn't Narcotics issued an alert about a sudden increase in overdoses? If only they had, maybe this wouldn't have happened.

Scotty hugged Angela and sat next to Jack, taking his cousin's hand as he spoke softly to him.

Sam kept her gaze fixed on her devastated sister, determined to get answers for her, even if the answers wouldn't bring Spencer back.

THE NEXT DAY was one of the most torturous Sam had ever lived through. As bad as losing her father had been, there'd been relief in that loss, that he was free from the constraints of his terrible injury. And even though they'd lost him too soon, he would've said he'd lived a good life and was content to go.

None of those things was true for Spencer. There was no relief in losing a young husband and father, especially with another child due to arrive in a few months who would never know him.

Angela had asked to go home that morning. Five minutes after they arrived, she wanted to leave. So, Sam and Tracy packed up Ang and the kids and brought them back to the White House to stay indefinitely. At least there they'd be surrounded by family who wanted to help.

Angela had spent the rest of the day in bed.

"I can't stand this for her," Tracy said after she and Sam had tucked Jack into bed and then gone to the sitting room in Sam's suite.

"It's the worst thing ever," Sam replied.

"What's she going to do?"

"I don't know."

"She told me he lost his job two months ago."

"*What?*"

"Yeah, along with all their benefits, including his health and life insurance."

Sam felt like she'd been punched. "Oh my God, Trace."

"Yeah, so…"

"I feel like I'm going to be sick," Sam said, hand on her belly.

"I know. Me, too. Thus, my question. What's she going to do with two little kids, a newborn and no source of income or insurance?"

"I don't know." Angela provided daycare for several children so she could be at home with her own kids, but that didn't generate enough to live on while supporting three young children. "She can stay here as long as she needs to. We'll take care of her and the kids."

"That's a generous short-term solution to a long-term problem."

"How could all this have been happening to her and them and we had no idea? We were with them at Christmas and several times after, and there wasn't the slightest clue."

"We weren't looking for it. We figured she'd tell us if something was wrong."

"It's because of what we were going through, with Nick becoming president and moving here and all that. She should've known we wouldn't care about anything other than getting them whatever help they needed."

"I'm sure she tried to convince him of that," Tracy said. "You know how stubborn he could be sometimes."

"Yeah, but to hide something like this from the people who might've been able to help... It makes no sense."

"I'm sure it made sense to him at the time, and honestly, I might've done the same thing. With everything you guys have had going on, none of us want to add to your load."

"Don't ever keep things from me out of fear of Nick's career or whatever. You heard his State of the Union speech. He doesn't give a rat's ass about his career."

"Still... It would give me pause when you're already so up against it. And I'm sure Angela begged Spencer to come to us, to ask for help."

"No one knows what goes on inside a marriage except the two people in it," Sam said.

"We're all pretty sure about what goes on inside yours," Tracy said with a teasing grin that made Sam laugh even harder when Tracy whistled the "My Humps" tune that had plagued Sam since *Saturday Night Live* had debuted its first skit about her and Nick.

"Shut up."

"Truth hurts."

It felt wrong to laugh or joke or do anything that wasn't focused on Angela and her kids. "I keep thinking about what I'd do if something like this happened to me. I honestly don't think I could go on without him, Trace."

"You could and you would for your kids."

"I don't know about that. I'd want to die, too." Sam looked to her older sister for guidance, as she had her entire life. "Angela loved Spencer like I love Nick and you love Mike."

"She loves her kids just as much. She'll rally for them, and you would, too. What choice does she have?"

"What if she can't?"

"She will. We'll make sure of it."

Sam's phone rang with a call from her friend and communications director, Roni Connolly. "Hey, Roni."

"Sam... I'm so, so sorry about Spencer. How's your sister?"

"Not good. You know how it goes."

"I do, unfortunately. I wanted to call to remind you of my Wild Widows group for when you think Angela might be ready for some support from people who've been where she is and understand the journey."

"I'll let her know when the time is right. She'll appreciate the invite, I'm sure."

"These early days are the worst, especially when it's sudden like it was for her and for me. If there's anything she needs, please don't hesitate to ask. I'll do whatever I can for her."

"She may want to see you. I'll ask her. Thank you for the offer, Roni. It means a lot. It's just been..."

"Horrible."

"Yeah," Sam said with a sigh. "I still can't believe this has happened. He was fine on Saturday."

"Do they have any idea what happened?"

"Not yet." Sam was determined to protect Angela's privacy and Spencer's legacy by keeping suspicions of an overdose quiet for as long as she possibly could. With the story of their brother-in-law's death making the national news, they'd probably be forced to eventually release a cause of death. But they didn't have to think about that today. "Thanks for checking in. I really appreciate it, and Angela will, too."

"Of course. We jokingly refer to the Wild Widows as a club no one ever wants to join, but the support I've found with them has been lifesaving and life-affirming."

"I'm sure Angela will take you up on the offer when she's ready."

"How are you holding up?"

"I don't even know. It's all so shocking, and with Ang expecting her third baby in June... It's too much to process."

"She and I are due the same month, so we have that in common, too."

"She'll take comfort from you when she's ready to. I'm sure of that. It means a lot that you reached out, Roni."

"I wish there was more I could do."

"I feel the same way. I'll talk to you soon."

"Sounds good. Let me know if I can help with anything at all."

"I will. Thanks again." Sam closed her phone and turned to Tracy, who was checking her own phone. "That was my friend Roni, who was widowed in October. She wanted to remind me about her Wild Widows group of young widows for when Angela is ready."

"I love the name of that group."

"It's taken from the Mary Oliver quote... 'What is it you plan to do with your one wild and precious life?'"

"Ah, that's great, and it's a good reminder to live life to the fullest. You never know when the clock will run out. When you think about it, how do any of us function knowing we could kick it at any second?"

"The odds are pretty good that it's not going to happen until we're old and gray, which is how we function."

"I worry so much about something happening to you on the job," Tracy said tearfully.

Sam turned to her. "You do? Really?"

"So much."

"Since when?"

"Always, but even more so since that creep Stahl tried to kill you—twice."

"All this time, almost sixteen years, you've been worried sick about me?"

"Not every minute of every day, but a lot of the time. Yes."

"I don't want that for you. I'm fine. I'm going to be fine."

"Arnold thought he'd be fine. Dad and Steven Coyne did, too. The crap with Stahl freaked me out, and then the thing with Ramsey's son, which makes Ramsey even more dangerous than he was before. It's a lot on top of my brother-in-law being the president and people hating him just because of the job he has."

Sam was shocked to hear how anxious Tracy was. "Has it gotten worse since Dad died and Nick became president?"

Tracy shrugged. "I guess. Maybe a little."

"Would you consider asking your doctor for anxiety meds? I hear they work wonders."

"I've talked about it with the doctor. After this with Spence, I might be desperate enough to do it."

"You should, Trace. Why suffer needlessly?"

"All the medication in the world won't keep me from worrying about my baby sister out there chasing murderers, especially now that the whole world knows who she is."

"I don't want you to worry about me. I'm very good at what I do, and I have Secret Service with me all the time. Vernon and Jimmy won't let anything happen to me, and neither will Freddie."

"That brings me some comfort, but I can't help but worry about you. You were my first baby."

Sam leaned into her sister's embrace and let her squeeze her the way she had her entire life. Tracy had been like a second mother to Sam. She and Angela were her closest friends. That such a disaster had befallen one of them was almost too much to bear. "You're going to have to keep the closest eye on Ang," Sam said.

"I know."

What neither of them had to say was that when Angela eventually returned to her own home, it would be easier for Tracy to keep tabs on her.

"And you have to keep me in the loop on what she needs," Sam added.

"I will."

"We'll get her through this. One way or the other."

"Yes, we will."

CHAPTER FOUR

W hile her sisters talked about how they would support
Angela through the most devastating loss of her life—and
that was saying something after losing her beloved father—Angela
lay awake in the fancy White House guestroom trying to picture
life without Spencer.

Try as she might, two days after he died, she still couldn't
conceive of going forward with three little kids and no Spencer
there to make it all work.

He'd been the glue that held them together—that was, until
the last year, when his life spun off the tracks, taking her down
with him. It'd been a massive shock to realize he'd become
addicted to the pain medication he'd taken after his back injury
and that he was breaking the law to acquire them after multiple
doctors cut him off.

That wasn't the man she'd fallen desperately in love with after
reconnecting with him at the same party where Sam first met
Nick. She'd dated Spencer for a short time after breaking up with
her longtime boyfriend and then made the huge mistake of going
back to Johnny. Thank God she'd gotten a second chance with
Spencer when he came into the office where she worked at the
time for a meeting and asked her to come to the party.

What a consequential night that had been for Angela, Spencer,
Sam and Nick. It had taken six years for Sam and Nick to
reconnect after that night, but Angela had been with Spencer ever
since. Eight years in total, the eight best years of her life.

Well, seven of them had been great.

The last one had been terrifying as they tried to figure out how to get him off the meds that had screwed up their wonderful lives. Somewhere during all that stress and worry, she'd gotten pregnant again with the third child Spencer thought would put things back on track for their family.

And now... she was left sitting in the ashes of her once-beautiful life, wondering how it had all gone so very wrong.

Her eyes ached from crying, her heart was shattered into a million pieces, and her anxiety was through the roof as she tried to fathom how she'd raise three children without Spencer's salary, without health insurance or a life insurance payout that would've made things easier.

They were already behind on their mortgage and other bills due to the outrageous expenses incurred from two trips to rehab. Spencer hadn't wanted to run that through insurance because he didn't want his company to know he was in rehab. He told them he was having medical issues but didn't elaborate. Two months out of work without a doctor's note had been the straw that broke the situation after nearly a year of sketchy performance and frequent absences.

Angela was terrified of what would happen to her and her children now that he was gone along with the income that had supported their family. While she should be mourning the loss of her true love, money was her primary concern, which was infuriating. How could he have let this happen to them?

She no sooner had that thought than she hated herself for it. He'd fought so hard to get free of the addiction. It wasn't fair to blame him for any of this, and yet... She did. She blamed him. The day he'd first gotten hurt, she'd told him not to play football with his always-rough college friends. *What if you get hurt?* she'd asked him. *I won't,* he'd said. *It's just for fun.*

If only he'd listened to her, he would still be there, still have his job, still have his life and the chance to raise the children he loved so much.

And then she was crying again, devastated by the loss of the man who'd been the center of her life. He'd had his flaws. Who didn't? But he'd loved her with his whole heart and soul and was crushed to have brought his addiction into their blessed lives. He'd apologized to her a hundred times, had sworn he was going to beat it no matter what it took, but even as he fought with everything he had, it had only gotten worse.

Losing his job had been the blow that ruined him. He'd spun completely out of control after that, disappearing for days on end and resurfacing looking and smelling like a skid-row bum. Angela had suspected he'd moved on to heroin, which was cheaper and easier to get than Oxy.

Two days before they left for Camp David, she'd given him an ultimatum—her or the drugs. He'd fallen on his knees, sobbing as he wrapped his arms around her and promised to get clean, saying he couldn't lose her or their kids, that he'd die without them. He'd begged her to give him one more chance and promised he would put his life—and hers—back together starting right after the weekend with her family. He'd wanted a couple more days with her and the kids before he left again for rehab.

He'd been due to fly to a clinic in Minnesota right after the weekend at Camp David.

Angela wanted to know when he'd acquired the drugs that had probably killed him. Was it before he begged her for one more chance, or after? She'd like to know that, not that it mattered much now.

If there was one silver lining to the shocking events of the last few days, it was that her sisters now knew what she'd been going through. Keeping it from them had been almost as difficult as the war they'd been waging with his addiction. Spencer had been adamant that no one know. He didn't want his struggles to reflect negatively on the brother- and sister-in-law he loved, admired and respected. It had been hell for Angela to keep it from Tracy and Sam. At times, she'd felt like they had to know, because how could she possibly hide that level of torment from the two people who knew her as well as Spencer did?

The door to her room opened and then closed.

Jack tiptoed toward her bedside, looking to see if she was awake.

Angela held out her arms to him, and he climbed up on the bed with her. "How's my sweet boy?"

"I'm so sad."

"I know, baby. So am I."

"How can Daddy just be gone and never coming back?"

"I don't know. I wish I had answers that would explain it for you. The one thing you should know forever and ever is how much Daddy loved you. He loved Ella, too, but you were his special buddy."

"I miss him so much," Jack said on a soft sob.

"Me, too."

While Angela held her sobbing child, she seethed with rage directed at Spencer, the doctors who'd prescribed addictive pain medicine in the first place—and then cut him off from it—and the person who'd sold him the fatal dose.

Sam was determined to track down the dealer, and Angela hoped her sister found them. That wouldn't bring Spencer back or solve the myriad other problems his death left her with, but if they were caught, at least they wouldn't be able to devastate another family like hers had been.

ON TUESDAY, when Sam felt confident that she could leave Angela with Tracy for a few hours, she took another day of bereavement leave and asked Vernon and Jimmy to drive her to Camp David so she could retrieve the items left behind in their haste to depart. She also planned to do a thorough search of the cabin where Angela and Spencer had stayed. She'd asked Lilia to inform Captain Martin that she'd be coming up.

Traffic made the hour-and-twenty-minute ride even longer.

"We can use the lights, ma'am," Vernon said.

Sam checked her watch and saw it was inching closer to noon. "Go ahead," she said, eager to get this done so she could try to figure out what'd happened to Spencer. She was treating this like she would any murder investigation, for as long as she could. Hopefully, she'd have tracked down his dealer before she got pulled off a case that struck far too close to home.

She'd have to call in some favors from coworkers to keep this investigation off the grid, but she was confident that the people she needed would do it for her.

Using the flashing lights helped to move things along, and they arrived at the mountaintop presidential retreat at Catoctin Mountain Park at just after one o'clock.

Captain Martin greeted her when she stepped out of the SUV. "Welcome back, Mrs. Cappuano."

"Thank you, Captain Martin."

She led Sam into her office and closed the door. "We've been praying for your family and your sister, in particular."

"We appreciate that."

"Per your request, no one has been in Birch since Mr. Radcliffe was taken out by EMS on Sunday morning. And just so you know, I would've immediately secured the cabin even if you hadn't asked me to."

Sam was pleasantly surprised by the CEO's action.

"I was a police officer for two years before I joined the Navy," Captain Martin added.

"Ah, there it is," Sam said, smiling. "Thank you very much for preserving what may be a crime scene."

"If a crime was committed here, we'll need to follow official protocol."

"The crime wasn't committed here," Sam said. "I believe it occurred in my jurisdiction, and the result of that crime occurred here."

"How so?"

"I've learned that my brother-in-law became addicted to pain medication after an injury he sustained more than a year ago. After the doctors refused to prescribe more meds for him, he bought them illegally. I believe he was sold laced pills."

"Fentanyl?"

"That's the most likely culprit, but we won't know for certain until we get the results of the toxicology report, but we're keeping that private for now."

"I understand." Captain Martin handed Sam a set of keys. "That'll get you into Birch."

"Thank you again for your quick thinking and your cooperation. That can be hard to come by in my line of work."

"You're the first lady. I work for you—not to mention I admire your career and accomplishments. I love that you're keeping your job while your husband is president."

"That's nice to hear. Sometimes I wonder if everyone thinks I'm insane for trying to do three jobs."

"If they do, who cares?"

"I like you, Captain Martin, and my friends would tell you I don't like anyone."

The captain laughed as she came around her desk to walk Sam out. "That's the best compliment I've received in a long time. You should know that Agent Hill and several of the Secret Service officers asked for access to the cabin after you left on Sunday. I denied their requests without explanation. If asked, my justification would be there was no reason—at that time—to allow law enforcement to search a private space occupied by the first family."

"Thank you for that."

"Of course. Let me know if I can be of any further assistance to you or your family. I took the liberty of asking the kitchen to prepare lunch for you and your detail. It'll be ready whenever you'd like to have it."

"You're the best. Thanks again for everything." Sam stepped out into air that was much colder on the mountaintop than it had been at home. Vernon and Jimmy waited to accompany her to the cabin where Spencer's life had come to a tragic end. Even though Harry and the EMTs had briefly restarted his heart, it'd already been too late.

"Vernon, I need a favor," Sam said, knowing that if she wanted to maintain control of this investigation, she couldn't bring others into it—at least not there. The minute word got out of a possible crime occurring at Camp David, the Feds would swoop in and take over.

"Whatever I can do, ma'am."

"I need you to witness whatever I take from the cabin for the chain of custody."

"No problem."

Sam glanced at the older man who'd become a friend under the most unlikely of circumstances. "This is way outside your job description."

"I'm aware."

"Thank you."

"I'm happy to do whatever I can to help you figure out what caused this terrible tragedy."

"How did you know that's what I'm doing?"

He gave her a "duh" look that made her laugh. "I'd like to think we've gotten to know each other a little bit over these last couple of months, and I knew as soon as your brother-in-law turned up unresponsive that you'd be all over figuring out what happened to him."

"You figured right, and PS, as I say to Nick, quit knowing me so well."

Vernon's warm smile helped to soothe the ache inside her. They were surrounded by people who'd do anything for them, Angela and her children, which was comforting to realize. "In case you're wondering, I would've been disappointed if you didn't do exactly what you're doing."

"That helps me feel better about it," Sam said. "Technically, I should turn this over to other people, but I want to protect his privacy—and ours—for as long as I can."

"I get it, and Jimmy does, too," Vernon said, giving his partner a look that left no doubt as to what Vernon expected from him.

"I do," Jimmy said. "I get it."

Sam zipped her coat to ward off the chill as they walked to Birch. She used the key Captain Martin had given her and stepped into the cabin, noting that Jack's and Ella's toys were still scattered on the floor. Spencer's leather jacket tossed over a chair gave her a pang as she noticed the diaper bag Tracy had given Angela before Ella's birth sitting by the door.

"You sure you're up for this, Sam?" Vernon asked softly, calling her by her name for the first time ever.

"Not really," she said as she pulled on gloves, "but it needs to be done."

Over the next hour, she took dozens of photos and then did a thorough search of the cabin. She hit paydirt when she found an envelope zipped into Spencer's suitcase that contained three small white pills with S20 stamped on them. On the outside of the envelope was a label that said Therapeutic Oxycodone. "Here it is," Sam said to Vernon, holding up the packet for him to see before she slipped it into an evidence bag.

Sam put Spencer's cell phone into another bag and his suitcase into yet another large plastic bag she'd brought for that purpose. She bagged everything that belonged to him as well as the sheets on the bed and the towels hanging in the bathroom.

And when she'd gathered all the evidence she could find, she packed up the belongings of her sister's family into suitcases and other bags. Thankfully, Celia and Shelby had packed their things and brought them back to the White House on Sunday. "When Angela was packing for this weekend, she had no idea of the bomb about to go off in her life and ours."

Vernon squatted to gather Legos and return them to the bin. "You just never know, do you?"

"No, you don't, and you don't have to do that."

"I know." He kept gathering toys and had them all packed by the time Sam finished with the clothes that she took from dresser drawers and closets.

As she folded her niece's tiny clothes, a wave of emotion came over her at realizing Ella would have no memories of her late father. She propped her hands on the dresser and closed her eyes as tears slid down her cheeks.

"Sam?" Vernon said from behind her. "Are you okay?"

She wiped her face. "It's just so fucking sad."

"Yes, it is. And so senseless, too."

"Jack will remember him, but Ella won't."

"You all will keep him alive for them and the new baby, too."

"We were just getting our legs back under us after losing my dad, and now this. It's too much."

"Way too much, and it's worse when it's someone so young."

"Yeah." Sam wiped her face again. "Sorry to dump my crap on you."

"Don't apologize. We spend a lot of time together. I'd like to think we're friends by now."

"We are." Sam turned and offered him a small smile as she recalled Freddie saying that Vernon already loved her like a daughter. Skip Holland had left a void in her life that no one could ever fill, but she'd come to appreciate Vernon's dry sense of humor, good nature and occasional input into her cases. "Thank you."

"No thanks necessary."

"Captain Martin said they had lunch for us, and I'm sure Jimmy is ravenous by now." They'd commiserated over their young partners' appetites and unfair metabolisms.

"He's probably chewing on tree bark out there."

Just when she wouldn't have thought it possible, Sam laughed.

CHAPTER FIVE

W hen they returned to the District, Vernon delivered her to the morgue entrance at HQ and helped her carry in the evidence bags she'd brought from the cabin. Thanks to Captain Martin's assistance, there would be no jurisdictional headaches to contend with, and for that, Sam was thankful. No one else knew—yet—that Sam would be investigating her brother-in-law's case as a potential homicide.

"Cruz, Gonzo, my office," Sam said when she entered the pit with Vernon and the bags. "Thank you again, Vernon."

"My pleasure, ma'am."

"Close the door," Sam said to Freddie.

"What's all this?" Gonzo asked.

"The stuff from Angela and Spencer's cabin at Camp David." She held up the plastic evidence bag containing the small packet of pills. "Including the pills that probably killed him."

"They let you take this?" Freddie asked.

"The CEO was a cop before she joined the Navy. She was very cooperative and understanding when I explained to her that the actual crime, if there was one, took place in my jurisdiction, not hers. Vernon was with me to assert the chain of custody."

"We would've gone with you," Freddie said.

"I know, but I wanted to do this myself in case there's any blowback. Then the story will be I went rogue, not *we* went rogue. Can you guys take care of logging it in and getting it to the lab?"

She handed the bag containing the pills to Gonzo, knowing it was critical that her name not be anywhere on the reports for this case.

He took a long look at the innocuous white envelope. "We'll take care of it."

"Thank you. Obviously, I want a rush on all of it."

"We'll let them know."

After they left the room, Sam withdrew the bag containing Spencer's cell phone from her pocket and placed it on her desk. Then she picked up the receiver on her desk phone and called Lieutenant Archelotta in IT.

"Archie," he said, sounding rushed as always. His was one of the busiest divisions in the department.

"It's Sam."

"Oh, hey. I didn't notice the extension. How are you?"

"Never been better."

"I'm so sorry. It's such a tragedy."

"Yes, it is."

"How's your sister?"

"Awful—and pregnant."

"Jeez... I forgot about that."

"I need a favor."

"Anything."

"Can you come down?"

"Sure, I'll be right there."

"Thanks, Archie." Sam didn't want to risk going upstairs to IT and running into Sergeant Ramsey, who worked across the hall from IT in Special Victims. Things were extra tense with Ramsey since his son was shot and killed after taking a woman hostage in Rock Creek Park.

Captain Malone, who'd ordered the shot, was still on leave, as was sharpshooter Officer Offenbach. It'd been a clean shot, and Sam had every confidence they'd both be back on the job soon. They'd taken out a rapist/murderer who was threatening the life of an innocent woman. That he also happened to be Sergeant Ramsey's son had turned it into a nightmare for everyone involved. Ramsey was threatening legal action against the department, even though he'd heard his son's confession on numerous rapes and murders the same way the rest of them had. Despite that, Sergeant Ramsey had gone to the media with his rants, and the local and national press was eating up the connection to the first lady and her squad.

Sam would rather think about that than wonder what Archie might find on Spencer's phone. She was tempted to look herself, but this had to be done by the book to preserve evidence and the integrity of the investigation.

She texted Tracy, who'd stayed with Angela while Sam went to Camp David. *Will you please ask Ang for the code to Spencer's phone?*

Yep.

Sam stared at her phone, waiting for Tracy's reply.

Ang says she thinks it's her birthday.

Thanks.

Archie appeared at her door, and Sam waved him in.

"What're you even doing here? Aren't you on bereavement leave?"

"I had some stuff to do, which is what I need to talk to you about." She gestured for him to shut the door.

"What's up?"

"I think someone sold my brother-in-law bad shit."

"As in bad shit drugs?"

"Yeah."

"Did he have an issue?"

"Yes, but I didn't know that until this happened."

"Damn. Okay, so what's the plan?"

"I returned to Camp David today, did a full recon of his room and brought back a ton of evidence and a packet of pills that's been sent to the lab. I also have his phone, and that's where you come in."

"Is this an official investigation?"

"Not technically. Would you be willing to dump the phone for me as a favor to a friend?"

Archie eyed the phone on Sam's desk. "We need a warrant."

"What if I have his next of kin sign the permission form?"

He ran his hand over the back of his neck. "I suppose that would suffice. We need a paper trail, Sam, so this doesn't bite us in the asses."

"I'll get the form signed and forward it to you."

"I'll take the phone and get started while I wait for the form. Do you have the code?"

"We believe it's zero-four-zero-five."

"Got it."

"Thank you."

"Sure. I'm glad there's something I can do to help."

"I'll try not to get us both in trouble for this."

"That'd be good."

After he left with the phone, Sam called Lilia at the White House. "Hey, it's Sam."

"How are you?"

"Hanging in there, but I need a favor that's outside the purview of your chief-of-staff-to-the-first-lady duties."

"Nothing is outside that purview."

Much to her dismay, Sam teared up when Lilia said that. Having such good friends and colleagues at a time like this made all the difference.

"What can I do?"

"I'm going to send over a form via email that I need Angela to sign. She's upstairs with Tracy. Can you take it to her and then scan it back to me?"

"No problem."

"Thank you so much, Lilia."

"Of course. Please don't hesitate to ask if there's anything else I can do."

"I will. Watch for the email."

"I'm ready."

Sam ended that call and made another to Tracy. "How is she?"

"About the same. She stares off into space for hours at a time. I tried to get her to eat something, but she's not interested."

"We have to stay on top of that."

"I know. I'm worried about the baby."

"Maybe we need to get her doctor over there."

"Let's see how she is tomorrow."

"Lilia is bringing up a form that will give us permission to examine Spencer's phone. Will you ask her to sign it for me? Tell her I'd never ask if it wasn't incredibly important."

"I'll take care of it."

"Thanks, Trace. I'll be home after a bit."

"No worries. I have friends covering my kids after school so I can stay with her, and Celia has Jack and Ella."

"Thank goodness for family and friends, huh?"

"No kidding."

"I'll see you soon."

"No rush. I'm here."

"I'm never not thankful for that."

"Love you."

"Love you, too."

Sam slapped her phone closed and was surprised to see the chief of police standing in her doorway. She rose to greet him. "Come in."

Chief Joe Farnsworth came in and shut the door. "How's Angela?"

"Not good."

"What are you doing here? I thought you took today off."

"I had some things to do."

He took a seat in her visitor chair, seeming exhausted and overwhelmed. Sam and her sisters were nieces to him, and he was surely devastated for Angela and the rest of the Holland family. "What kind of things?" The look he gave her said he knew exactly what she was up to, and there was no point in trying to hide it from him.

She looked him in the eyes when she said, "The sort where I went to Camp David, collected evidence from my sister's cabin and brought it back here to be processed along with Spencer's phone, which has gone to Archie along with a form from Angela giving us permission to dump it."

"What're you looking for?"

"Someone sold him laced pills. I want to know who."

"Back up and start from the beginning."

A headache forming between her eyebrows had her reaching for Motrin and a half-full bottle of water. "He'd been battling an opioid addiction following a back injury more than a year ago. It had gotten bad enough for two trips to rehab that didn't work and an ultimatum from his pregnant wife to get clean or get gone. He was due to return to rehab this week. As a result of his addiction, he'd lost his job, his benefits, his life insurance and was on the verge of losing his family."

The chief's expression registered shock. "Dear God, Sam, and you had no idea?"

"They told no one. Spencer didn't want it to blow back on Nick."

His deep sigh said it all. "I can't believe this."

"None of us can. Other than Nick, who am I closer to than my sisters? I had no clue this was happening to them. Have I been so caught up in my own life that I missed this?"

"No, you haven't. They intentionally kept it from everyone. Don't do that to yourself."

"It's hard not to."

"What's your plan?"

"I want to know who sold him the pills that killed him."

"We don't know for sure that's what it was."

"Yes, we do, and I'm not waiting around for proof while someone is out there selling fentanyl-laced drugs to other unsuspecting addicts. This is a homicide investigation, sir."

"That needs to be led by someone other than you."

"Gonzo will sign the reports."

He held her gaze for a long moment before he blinked. "Don't let this turn into another scandal for the department."

"I won't."

"Find the guy who took him from us."

"I will." After a long pause, she said, "There's something else."

"What?"

"When we were in the ER with Spence, Dr. Anderson came in. He mentioned there's been a big increase in OD deaths recently, which I've heard nothing about as a police officer."

"I haven't heard that either."

"Why isn't that on Cooper's radar? Why isn't Narcotics making noise about this? If they had..." Her voice faltered when she thought about how a warning might've saved Spencer's life.

"I'll investigate it personally. You have my word on that."

"Thank you. How's the captain doing?" Sam had gotten a text from Malone after Spencer's death was announced but hadn't talked to him since he was suspended.

"He's okay, riding out the suspension by trying to find former Captain Rosa." Malone was tracking all the captains who'd been active at the time former Lieutenant Stahl had been filing bogus reports about investigations that weren't being done.

"Is he having any luck?"

"Not yet, but if anyone can find him, Jake can."

"I know you haven't considered Conklin because he hated Stahl as much as everyone else did, but if Rosa checks out, we need to look at him for this," Sam said. "Who knows what Stahl had on him? We know for sure it wasn't my dad, and if everyone else checks out, Conklin is the only one left."

"If it was Conklin, I'm going to stab him through the heart," Farnsworth said.

"I'll loan you my rusty steak knife."

CHAPTER SIX

J ake Malone rode to Annapolis in his personal SUV, with the
windows down to let the cold air in. He was that rare bird who
enjoyed the winter. The cold air made him feel alive, whereas
heat sucked the life out of him. In the days since he'd given the
order to take out Shane Ramsey, he'd needed everything he could
get to feel better about himself.

He hated Jim Ramsey's guts and had for years, long before he
began to show his ass on the regular. The guy was just one of those
officers who could never go along and get along. He had a gripe
every other day and was a royal pain in the ass to supervise. Lately,
he'd escalated, going so far as to openly harass Sam and ransack
her office. After they'd nailed him for that with his fingerprints all
over her things, they'd thought they'd seen the last of him before
the union intervened to put him back on the job.

And then the recent rape/murder investigation had led directly
to Ramsey's son, Shane, forcing Jake to make the call to kill the son
of one of his detectives to save the woman he'd taken hostage.
Nowhere in the academy or all the training he'd received since
then was that potential scenario covered.

He'd had nightmares almost every night since that dreadful
day. They ranged from him ordering the shooting of other cops,
people he loved, even his own wife. Nothing he'd encountered on
the job had rattled him the way this had, and that was saying
something. He'd be haunted for the rest of his life by those two
minutes in Rock Creek Park.

To keep from going mad while on the mandatory ten-day suspension while the shooting was investigated, he was working to find retired Captain Tom Rosa, who'd disappeared off the face of the earth, or so it seemed. No one had seen or heard from him in years, and he was one of three people not yet interviewed who'd held the rank of captain at the time that now-disgraced former Lieutenant Leonard Stahl had been faking investigatory reports.

One of the three was Skip Holland, who was now deceased, but never would've done it for any reason, and the other was Paul Conklin, their former deputy chief, who'd also left the department in disgrace when it was discovered he knew who'd shot Skip and sat on the info for years. Conklin had sworn he had no other secrets, but Jake didn't believe a word that rat bastard said anymore. Jake was trying to find Rosa, mostly to eliminate him as a suspect.

Someone had archived those reports, and Jake had a feeling the trail would lead straight back to Paul Conklin. Before he talked to Conklin, though, he wanted to find Rosa. He was on his way to see retired medical examiner Dr. Norman Morganthau, who'd once been one of Rosa's closest friends on the job. If anyone would know where to find Rosa, Norm would.

Norm had been happy to hear from Jake and had invited him to come out for a chat when Jake said he had something he wanted to discuss with him. He hadn't told him what because he wanted to see Norm's reaction when he mentioned Rosa's name.

The pleasant ride to Annapolis served as a reminder of how nice it was to occasionally get out of DC. He and Skip used to joke about why anyone would want to live outside their beloved District. God, he missed that son of a bitch. Even after suffering a devastating injury, Skip had been larger than life. Losing him had been a blow Jake had yet to recover from.

And now the Holland family had lost Spencer, as well.

Jake was feeling philosophical in the wake of the shooting and the losses of people such as Skip and Detective Arnold and now Spencer Radcliffe. He hadn't known Spencer well, but he had spent time with him at various events involving the Holland family. As one of Skip's closest friends, he'd attended Spencer and Angela's wedding and felt a deep sense of grief for Angela and her kids.

As he rolled onto the long dirt road that led to Norm's place,

Jake recalled being there once for a cookout years ago. *Damn*, he thought. That was more than twenty years ago. Decades had passed in the blink of an eye.

Norm's sprawling ranch house sat at the end of the road, on a scenic wooded lot. When he was still working for the department, his colleagues had teased Norm about commuting from Annapolis. He would say that when you lived in paradise, the commute was no bother.

That commute would've been a bother for Jake, who would've found the hideous traffic between Annapolis and DC unbearable.

Jake parked in the driveway and headed for the front door, where Norm waited to greet him with a handshake and a welcoming smile.

"This is a nice surprise, my friend." Norm led him into a warm, cozy space with a fire in the hearth and jazzy music playing. "What can I get you?"

"I'm good, and it's nice to see you. Been too long."

"Sure has. You know we're getting old when we only see each other at funerals."

Jake laughed. "Ain't that the truth? How's the family?"

"Everyone's good," Norm said. "Just had my twelfth grandchild. That's where the missus is now. Helping with our daughter's older kids while the new parents tend to the baby."

"I'm still waiting on my kids to get me some grandkids. They're not in any hurry."

"Mine were in their thirties before they got serious about having kids. I gotta say... I was so sorry to hear about Skip's son-in-law. What a tragedy."

"It sure is, especially since Angela is expecting their third child in June."

"Goodness. That's terrible. Do they have any idea what happened?"

"Not yet. It's early days. You know what that's like."

"I sure do. People want answers, and they want them now. They don't want to hear that answers take time."

"Exactly."

"Any suppositions with Spencer?"

"Not that I'm aware of, but I'm currently out of the loop."

"Ah, right, the thing with Ramsey's kid. That was a clean shot, Jake. Any of us would've done the same thing to save that girl."

"My conscience is clear on it, even if I wish it hadn't happened. Taking out the son of one of my officers isn't something I thought I'd ever do."

"The job comes with all sorts of things we never could've imagined for ourselves."

"Indeed, it does. Including cleaning up the messes of officers now doing time for attempted murder."

"I wondered if Stahl and his messes were bringing you to see me. I didn't have a ton of contact with him. He moved into Homicide around the time I was retiring, but I do remember him being a unique sort of guy."

"He was unique all right," Jake said with a scowl. "Uniquely unpleasant."

Norm laughed. "Which is how I recall him. Always beefing over something."

"Just like Ramsey. They're the ones who make the rest of us look bad."

"Always a few like that on any team, and they get all the attention while the rest of us are doing a job most people couldn't handle."

"Truth."

"What can I do to help with the Stahl stuff?"

"We've discovered reports pertaining to the Worthington and Deasly cases, detailing in-depth investigations that never happened, were archived."

Norm's white brows furrowed. "That'd be captain or above, right?"

"Yes, and we've eliminated almost everyone from that time. I'd like to talk to Tom Rosa about it, but I can't find him. I was hoping you might be able to help me with that."

"He'd never have done it," Norm said emphatically. "He was as by-the-book as anyone I ever worked with."

"That's my recollection of him as well, but we'd like to talk to him, and we've had no luck tracking him down. I was hoping you might know where he is."

"I haven't heard from him in a couple of years. The last time he was in touch, he was living in New Orleans. In the French Quarter, I believe."

"That's helpful, thank you."

Norm tipped his head and smiled as he said, "You didn't have to drive all this way for that info, Jake."

"No, I didn't, but it's nice to see an old friend, especially right now when I'm having a bit of an existential crisis."

"And you don't have Skip to tell you what you need to hear."

"That, too."

"You must miss him."

"So much."

"I used to envy the deep bond you, Skip and Joe shared."

"We always considered you a friend."

"I know, but you three were brothers. We all knew that."

"We were—and we are."

"How's Joe doing?"

"He's good, all things considered. It's been a lot lately."

"I've been following the coverage of the cold cases and was relieved when the FBI report wasn't as bad as feared."

"We were, too. I was afraid they were going to suggest a change in leadership, which would be the worst idea right now. We need Joe leading us through these tough times."

"Agreed. There's no one better than him. I was delighted to see Detective McBride elevated to deputy chief, although I'm sure there was pushback in-house."

"It's been pretty fierce from what I've heard, but the mayor wanted a woman, and after the great work Detective McBride did on the Deasly case, she earned the promotion."

"I couldn't agree more. I had the pleasure of meeting her some time ago and was impressed by her professionalism and thoroughness. And the Deasly case is a BFD."

"Getting bigger by the day from what we hear from the U.S. Marshals."

"The scourge of human trafficking is the vilest thing I encountered on the job."

"Indeed. Sam says it's the only crime worse than murder."

"That it is. How's she holding up since her husband became president?"

"She's making it work, remarkably enough. She's the exact same person she was before his promotion, as she refers to it."

Norm laughed. "That sounds about right. She's a superstar. I was surprised the mayor didn't want her for the deputy chief's job."

"She did. Sam wanted nothing to do with it, said she'd quit if that was the only job she was allowed to do."

"If that don't beat all," he said, laughing. "She's a firecracker, that one."

"She certainly is, and she's damned good at what she does. Joe and I both felt it'd be a crying shame to move her from Homicide, even if we worry about her raised profile."

"Does she have a detail?"

"Two agents."

"Well, that's something, anyway, but I agree it's a worry."

"Add supervising the nation's first lady to the things they never taught me at the academy."

Norm laughed again. "That must come with some unique challenges."

"You'd be surprised. On the job, it honestly feels like nothing has changed, when everything has changed for her and Nick. Or I guess I should refer to him as Mr. President."

"What would he want you to call him?"

"Nick. He's very down-to-earth and unaffected by it all. I admire the way they've both handled this extraordinary situation."

"I loved his State of the Union speech. What a refreshing approach he's taking."

"For sure. I don't blame him for wanting to skip all the campaigning to be home with his kids. Time goes by in a blink, and their son, Scotty, is already fourteen. He'll be off to college in no time."

"Our president has got his priorities straight. He'll never regret that."

"No, he won't. Well, I won't take any more of your time, Norm. It's been great to see you and catch up."

"I'm always here if I can help with anything."

Jake shook his hand at the door. "I appreciate that, my friend." When he was back on the road to home, he called Joe.

"What's up?" Joe asked.

"I just left Norm's place. He says Rosa was in New Orleans the last time he talked to him a couple of years ago. I was thinking I might take a quick trip and see if I can track him down."

"That sounds like a good plan."

"What's new there? Any word from Internal Affairs?"

"Just that they're thoroughly reviewing the body cam footage from the incident and hope to have a determination in the next few days."

"I guess it was too much to hope they'd move it along."

"You want them to be thorough. You and I both know this was a clean shot. Let them come to that determination in the time it takes."

"That's so much easier to do when it's someone else twisting in the wind."

Joe's bark of laughter drew a laugh from Jake, too. "I still can't believe this is your first suspension."

"I was the well-behaved one of our trio, and look at where that got me—a lowly captain while you guys were chief and deputy chief."

"I'm sorry if McBride's promotion was a bitter pill for you, Jake. Monique was adamant that she wanted a woman."

"I get it, and it's fine. I like what I'm doing overseeing the detectives. I wouldn't want to move to admin any more than Holland would've."

"And I knew that, or I would've gone to bat with Monique for you. I hope you know that."

"I do, but thanks for telling me. It's nice to know I wasn't completely overlooked."

"You're my deputy chief in every way that matters, and you know that, too."

"I do. Thank you. What're you hearing from Sam and the family?"

"She's here after a trip to Camp David to collect evidence."

"Evidence of what?"

"They believe Spencer overdosed after acquiring pain medication illegally."

"*What?*" Malone asked on a long exhale.

"I know."

"And Sam had no idea?"

"Spencer wanted it kept private so it wouldn't blow back on Nick."

"Oh my God, Joe. And now Sam is intent on finding the person who sold it to him."

"Yep."

"How do we feel about that?"

"Conflicted, but if we try to stop her, she'll do it anyway. I'd prefer to be involved than to have her go rogue."

"True, and I can't say I blame her. I'd do the same thing."

"As would I. I'll keep an eye on it."

"What's the latest with Ramsey?"

"He's still spewing about lawsuits and whatnot, but no one is paying any attention. Everyone knows it was a clean shot after his son all but confessed. You and Offenbach saved that woman's life. Full stop. End of story."

"I keep telling myself that."

"That's what matters here, Jake. You did your job."

"Sometimes I hate my job."

"Me, too, but I'd rather have us doing it than the Ramseys and Stahls of the world."

"Ain't that the truth?" Jake said on a huff of laughter.

"We're the good guys. Remember that when you're fretting over whether you did the right thing giving that order. That young woman is alive today because you did your job."

"I know, but taking out Ramsey's son... I remember him as a little kid."

"Who grew up to be a monster. Stay focused on what he did."

"Thanks for the reminder."

"I'm here any time you need another one. Don't let this screw you up to the point where you can't do the job anymore."

"I'm trying not to."

"Have you sat with Trulo yet?"

"God, no."

"I want you to do that, and I'm not asking."

"Pulling rank on me now, old friend?" Jake asked, smiling.

"If that's what it takes to get you through this."

"I'll call him."

"Today."

"All right already."

"I need you by my side for whatever time I've got left in this place."

"I hear you."

"Check in later and keep me posted about New Orleans."

"You got it. And Joe?"

"Yes?"

"Thank you."

"You got it, pal."

Jake ended the call and sat for a long time at a traffic light, thinking about how much he missed Skip. What would he have to say about the situation with Shane Ramsey? Probably the same things Joe had said. He'd done his job, and he'd saved a life even if he'd ordered the end of another. If he had it to do over again, would he have done anything different?

No, he wouldn't.

Now he just had to find a way to live with that decision. With that in mind, he picked up the phone and called Tony Trulo, the department psychiatrist.

"Hello, my friend," Tony said. "I was wondering when I might hear from you."

"The boss made me call you."

Tony laughed. "I love how no one ever comes to me without an order, as if my wit and charm aren't enough to bring you in."

"Haha," Jake said. "What wit and charm?"

Tony chuckled. "How're you holding up?"

"Good minutes. Bad minutes. Everything in between."

"This is a tough one, Jake. No way around it. You did your job. Ordering the death of a colleague's son will haunt a good man like you."

"It does, even knowing we saved an innocent life by taking his."

"There's a lot to unpack here. Since you can't come here while suspended, how about we meet for coffee in the next day or two and dig into this some more?"

"I've got to make a quick trip to New Orleans, but I'll be back in a couple of days. I'll reach out then?"

"I'll be here, and we'll get you through this."

"Thanks, Tony."

CHAPTER SEVEN

While she waited for the dump of Spencer's phone, Sam reviewed the final reports on the Shane Ramsey case. The words ran together in a mishmash of symbols that made no sense to her. Damned dyslexia. She closed her eyes, took a deep breath and released it slowly. Then she opened her eyes, blinked a few times and took another look at the computer screen.

Still a maze of nothingness.

"Cruz!"

Her handsome, dark-haired partner came to the door, brow raised. "You bellowed?"

"What's that app you told me about that can read for me?"

"What are you trying to read?"

"These stupid reports, and the dyslexia is being a bitch."

He came into the office, stepped around her desk and clicked around on her computer. "The text-to-speech thing is included in the program. All you do is click right here."

"Huh. How come I never knew that?"

"Because you refuse to attend any of the required training."

"That's a waste of my time."

"There's so much I could say to that."

"Go away. I have listening to do."

"Yes, ma'am. Just bellow again if I can be of any further assistance to you."

"Thank you. I'll do that."

Sam pressed the button he'd indicated and sat back to listen to the reports her team had compiled to summarize the Ramsey case. Gonzo had gathered input from all the officers involved and put it into one cohesive narrative that told the story of Shane Ramsey's murdering, raping rampage and how it had ended in gunfire in Rock Creek Park.

As she listened, Sam's mind wandered to Angela, Spencer, Jack, Ella, Angela's unborn child, Spencer's lost job and the benefits his family relied upon. Her anxiety spiked into the red zone as she tried to get her head around the mess her sister was in and how she could fix it for her. Not that it was her job to fix it, but that was what she did. She fixed things. She got answers. She figured things out.

But this... What the hell was Angela going to do?

Sam pressed Pause on the recording because she wasn't any more capable of listening than she was of reading. Her brain wasn't having it. *Shit, fuck, damn, hell.*

"Cruz!"

He came to the door again. "I'm not your beck-and-call girl, you know."

Sam smiled, pleased by the predictable reply. "I need you."

Freddie stepped into the office and closed the door. "What can I do?"

"I can't concentrate on anything."

"You shouldn't even be here."

"I don't know what else to do but try to figure out who did this to my sister's family."

"You've got people who could do that for you."

"I need to be involved."

"I get that, but if it's too much..."

"It's all too much," she said, mortified when her eyes filled with tears. "Sometimes I didn't even like him because he could be so insufferable, but oh, how he loved my Angela."

"Yes, he did."

"He lost his job—and all his insurance—a couple of months ago."

"Oh God. Sam..."

"What's she going to do?"

He took a seat in her visitor chair.

Sam wiped away tears. She'd tried so hard to be strong for

Angela that she'd barely taken five seconds to tend to her own grief over the brother-in-law she'd loved, even if at times he annoyed her.

"Someone should do a GoFundMe for her," Freddie said.

"What's that?"

He rolled his eyes. "It's an online fundraising site."

"I don't know if she would want that."

"She needs the money, Sam, and it's not like the rest of you are rolling in it to the point that you can support her and her kids, too."

"We have some money," she said. "Especially since we moved to the White House and can't shop or spend money on much of anything. And they can move to our place on Ninth Street." Sam brightened at the idea. "I can't believe I didn't think of that before now."

"That's a great idea, but it's just the start of what she'll need going forward. Why don't you give Tracy a call and see what she thinks of the idea?"

"Okay." She made the call to Tracy and put the phone on speaker.

"Hey," Tracy said. "How's it going?"

"It's going. What about there?"

"She still won't eat. We have a call into the doctor."

"That's good."

"She's stressing out about how she's going to pay for an appointment, let alone the birth."

"Freddie has an idea about that. He thinks we ought to do a GoFundMe thing for her and the kids."

"Mike said the same thing, but I wasn't sure if she'd be into that."

"Like Freddie said, she needs the money. It can't hurt anything."

"I suppose not, but the media will go crazy over a fundraiser for the first lady's sister."

"I don't care about that. Let them. I was also thinking that she and the kids can move to Ninth Street. That place is paid for, and she could sell their place to get rid of that debt."

"That's an amazing idea. Do you think Nick would be okay with that?"

"Of course he would. They're family. Should we just do the

GoFundMe and not tell her? It's not like she's capable of deciding anything right now."

"I'm okay with it if you are, but it should come from me, not you."

"Agreed." Sam glanced at her partner. "Is it okay if I have Freddie set it up for us?"

He gave a thumbs-up.

"Yeah, that's fine."

"He'll take care of it. It will probably raise a lot of money because she's related to me. Do you think that'll cause an issue?"

"You probably should run it by Nick, Terry, Lilia and the communications people before you make it live."

"I'll do that."

"Thanks for thinking about the practicalities while I tend to the broken heart."

"We'll get her through this," Sam said with more certainty of that now that some of the most urgent needs were being seen to. "I keep asking myself, how did this even happen?"

"I know. Mike and I were talking about that last night. How can Spencer be *dead*?"

"I'm going to find the person who did this to him—to them—and make them pay."

"If anyone can do it," Tracy said, "you can."

Sam sure as hell hoped so.

WHEN ARCHIE TOLD her that the dump on Spencer's phone would take until the morning due to the amount of business activity he had on it, Sam decided to go home. Her concentration was nonexistent, so there was no point sticking around. After her father died, she'd been on fire with the need to finally solve his shooting. That had powered her through those first weeks.

As horrible as it had been to lose her dad, at least they'd known for the entire four years since his shooting that they could lose him at any time. This was different. Spencer was young, and most of them hadn't had the first clue that he was juggling with dynamite by procuring pain pills illegally. The shock this time was even more so than when Skip died, and the heartbreak of knowing his young children would barely remember him, and his unborn child would never know him, overwhelmed her.

"I'm going home," Sam said to Freddie, who was alone in the pit. It hadn't occurred to her to ask where the others were, and she couldn't be bothered to ask now. Gonzo was in charge, and he'd take care of things while she couldn't.

"Is Vernon still driving you?"

"Yeah. Another week or so before I'm back to driving myself." It'd been days since she'd given a thought to her still-recovering hip fracture.

"The GoFundMe is all set to go. I sent you a link to approve it before I make it live."

"I'll talk to Nick and his team to make sure they're okay with it and text you later. Thanks for the very good idea."

"I wish there was more I could do."

"If this works the way you think it will, it's the very best thing you could do for her."

He stood and came over to Sam. "I'm here for you and her and all of you. I hope you know that."

Sam hugged him. "Thank you. I appreciate that more than you'll ever know." She walked slowly through the winding corridors that led to the morgue exit, the ache in her hip making its presence known after the long day. Normally, she'd stop in the morgue to say good night to Lindsey, but right now, all she wanted was home.

She emerged into the gloomy late-afternoon winter darkness and paid careful attention to every step, as she couldn't afford another fall right when she was finally off the cane and getting back to normal after the hip catastrophe.

Vernon saw her coming and jumped out of the SUV to get the door for her. "How'd it go today?"

"Not great, but I guess that's to be expected."

"You went back too soon."

"I have stuff to do."

"It's too soon."

Sam loved that he felt free to speak his mind to her. "Yeah, I suppose."

When she was settled, he closed the door and got into the driver's seat.

She stared out the window, not seeing anything as they took the familiar ride home. "Freddie wants to start a GoFundMe for Angela and the kids. How do you think that'll play in Peoria?"

"People are pretty used to that sort of thing these days," Vernon said. "I don't think anyone would be surprised."

"But a GoFundMe for the first lady's sister?"

"Are you guys able to care for your sister and her three children indefinitely?"

"I mean, we have money, but I'm not sure Angela would take it from us—or if she'll take it from others."

"She's going to need it, and when she emerges from the fog of early grief, she'll appreciate it, no matter where it comes from."

"I suppose so. I'll run it up the flagpole at La Casa Blanca before I do anything."

"That's always a good plan."

"I had the idea to move them to Ninth Street. That's something we can do right now."

"That's a great idea," Jimmy said.

"That house is sitting empty, so it would make sense for us to have someone there anyway."

"You're doing all the right things for her," Vernon said.

"It feels so inadequate."

He glanced at her in the mirror. "It won't always be this bad. Remember that."

She nodded. He was right. She'd found that out after her dad died and life had gone on, even if she'd expected the world to stop turning without him in her daily life.

When they arrived at the White House, they were waved through the checkpoint. Vernon helped her out of the SUV.

"Thank you for everything today."

"Wish it could be more."

Sam gave him a small smile. "It's more than enough."

"Have a nice evening."

"You do the same."

It occurred to her that she knew next to nothing about the two men who protected her, and soon she would have to rectify that. But for now, she wanted time with Nick and the kids and to check on her sister, nephew and niece. As she headed up the red-carpeted stairs to the residence, she moved slowly in deference to the stupid hip that had kept her off stairs for weeks now.

Tracy was coming down as Sam made her way up. "Why didn't you take the elevator?" Tracy asked.

"It's time to get back to normal."

"Who says?"

"I say. How is she?"

"About the same. The doctor gave her a stern talking-to about the importance of maintaining her strength for the baby's sake and her own. She recommended protein drinks that'll sustain her when food is unappealing."

"I guess that's something. What'd Angela say about the GoFundMe?"

"If we think she should do it, she says it's fine."

"I need to run it by Nick. If he and his team have no objections, we'll make it live. I'll also check with Nick about the Ninth Street house, but I'm sure it's fine. The money from selling her place will help."

"If it's not mortgaged to the hilt."

"Ugh, I didn't think of that."

"I didn't want to ask how they paid for rehab, but I suspect they might've tapped into the equity in their house."

"What a mess."

"I want to be empathetic toward him because I believe addiction is a disease, but how could he have let this happen, Sam? How could he, who was always so caught up in his career, have let it get to this point?"

"I wondered the same thing when it happened to Gonzo. All I can say is that addiction makes sane people do crazy things."

"Angela told me a few months ago that Spence really wanted a third kid when she was happy with two. In the end, the pregnancy came as somewhat of a surprise, but she got excited because he was. Now I wonder if he thought that new baby might save him or something."

"I suppose that's possible."

"I feel guilty leaving her, but I need to get home. I haven't done laundry in days or grocery shopped or anything. My family needs me."

"Go ahead. I'll be here."

Tracy hugged Sam. "I'll be back in the morning."

"See you then. Love you."

"Love you, too."

As Sam continued up the stairs, she felt guilty going home to her beloved husband when her sister would never see hers again. And the poor kids who'd grow up without their dad. Nick and Mike and Spencer's brother and father would be there for Angela's kids every step of the way, but no one could replace the father who'd adored them, and the sadness of that loss made Sam's entire body ache.

Knowing the kids were still upstairs with Celia, Sam went into their suite to stash her gun, badge and cuffs in the locked bedside table drawer and changed into sweats and a long-sleeved T-shirt. Then she sat on the side of the bed to gather herself before she went to see Ang and the kids.

That's where Nick found her a few minutes later. "I heard the first lady was home and came to see for myself." He sat next to her, put his arm around her and kissed the top of her head. "Rough day?"

Sam nodded and turned into his loving embrace, taking the comfort she needed so badly from the one person who always made her feel better. As she breathed in the warm scent of home, she knew without a doubt that while she could handle just about anything, she would never survive losing him. "Don't you dare ever do this to me. Do you hear me?"

"I won't. I promise."

She didn't remind him that was a promise he might not be able to keep, because she couldn't stand to think about a day without him in it, let alone the rest of her life.

"What can I do?"

"How would you feel about Angela and the kids living at Ninth?"

"That's fine with me."

"It might be indefinitely."

"Also fine with me."

"What do you think about a GoFundMe for her and the kids, organized by Tracy and set up by Freddie?"

"That's a great idea."

"The press might make a thing of it."

"So? She needs money. That could solve some of her most immediate problems."

"Will people think it's weird that there's a fundraiser for the sister-in-law of the president?"

"Just because I'm president doesn't mean I'm sitting on countless millions. I could take care of her, if need be, but I sense that she'd prefer the fundraiser to us supporting her and the kids."

"That's what Tracy and I thought, too. You're likely to be asked about it."

"Okay."

"Should we check with Terry, Lilia and the others?"

"Why?"

"In case there's something we need to be worried about."

"I'm not worried about anything other than getting Angela and the kids the help they need. If I wasn't president, we'd be the ones organizing this for her. Tell Freddie to make it live, and I'll post a link to it from my personal account."

"Wow, that'd be amazing."

"We have these huge platforms that are mostly pains in our asses. But occasionally we can use them to help someone we love."

"Thank you for being awesome, even when you're president."

"I do what I can for my people."

"And we love you for it, but that saying is trademarked."

Grinning, he said, "I knew you'd say that."

"I'm nothing if not predictable. Where are the kids?"

"Getting ready for dinner. Are you hungry?"

"Not really."

"You need to eat, and so does Angela."

"I'll go see if I can convince her."

Nick tightened his hold on her. "Before you go, I just want to make sure you're taking care of my Samantha as you take care of everyone else."

"I am."

"This is a lot on top of a lot, as we like to say, and so soon after your dad."

"Yeah, it is, but I'm okay. I'm just worried about Ang and the kids."

"You're doing everything you can for her, and then some. Go tell her about the GoFundMe and Ninth Street and everything else you did today to get justice for her and Spence."

"Thank you for being my biggest supporter. I love you endlessly."

"I love you more than endlessly."

"There is nothing more than endlessly."

"There's eternity."

Sam scowled at him. "Do you win every debate, or does it just seem that way?"

His smile was positively lethal. "It just seems that way."

"Right. Whatever you say, Mr. President."

CHAPTER EIGHT

S am went to see to her sister, heading for the third-floor guestroom next door to Celia's. More freaking stairs. She missed the elevator but was determined to get back to normal even if her hip wasn't quite as determined. She knocked softly on Angela's door before poking her head in. "Can I come in?"

"Sure."

With that one word, Sam heard a world of despair from the sister she knew as well as she knew herself—or so she'd thought. She stepped into the room, closed the door and gave her eyes a second to adjust to the murky darkness. She went to sit on the edge of the bed. "It's almost dinnertime. Can I convince you to join us?"

"I'm not hungry."

"I know, but the baby is."

"The baby would be better off not being born into this nightmare."

Angela's hopelessness alarmed Sam. "You don't mean that, Ang."

"How do you know what I mean?"

"I know you and how much you love your kids, even the one who isn't here yet."

"How will I take care of an infant and two little kids alone, Sam? How will I do that while working full time to pay for everything?"

"You will never be alone, and I have news that might ease your mind a little."

"What news?"

"First of all, Nick and I want to offer you and the kids Ninth Street, to live there as long as you need to. You could sell your place, which would give you a cushion, and live for free in our house. There's no sense having it sit empty if you could be using it."

"That's an amazing offer, even if the thought of moving is so overwhelming, I can't process it."

"We'd help you with everything."

"Thank you for that. It's very good of you guys to offer that."

"Our home is your home."

"You said that was first of all. What's second of all?"

"Tracy told you that Freddie suggested a GoFundMe for you and the kids?"

"She did."

"The rest of us think it's a wonderful idea."

"The rest of who?"

"Me, Trace, Mike and Nick."

"Nick thinks it's a good idea to have people fundraising for the president's sister-in-law?"

"He said he'd post a link to the GoFundMe from his personal accounts."

Angela seemed to consider that. "I don't feel right taking charity."

"It's not charity, Ang. People love you, they loved Spence, and they want to help. If our higher profiles make it more successful, then so be it." She paused before she added, "Trace told me Spencer lost his job. This will solve many of your most pressing problems."

"It's fine if you guys think it's a good idea."

"We do."

"I just don't care about anything, even my kids. I haven't seen Ella all day, but I can hear her crying. I can't make myself do anything about it."

"She's safe with Celia, who's happy to have her for as long as you need to be alone."

"I don't know what I need. No, wait. I do. I need my husband, but he's gone and never coming back." Her voice caught on a sob. "What am I going to *do* without him, Sam? I don't know what to do."

Sam held out her arms to her sister, who sat up and fell into Sam's embrace. "You'll figure it out one step at a time."

"What if I don't want to figure it out?"

"You have to do it for your kids, Ang. When the fog of early grief lifts, you'll still care very much about them and the baby. I know you will."

"I don't feel anything but despair."

"That won't last forever. Remember how we felt when Dad died, and we wondered how we'd possibly go on without him? Somehow, we found a way, and you will, too."

"What if I don't want to?"

"Don't want to what?"

"Find a way forward without him."

"Angela... Come on. Don't talk like that. What choice do you have?"

"Could you do it? If this happened to Nick, could you pick up and go on as if the worst possible thing hadn't happened?"

"I don't know," Sam said, determined to be honest even if her sister's words had rattled her. "And I hope I never have to find out. But I'd like to think I'd try for the sake of my kids, who'd be depending on me to show them the way forward."

"I'm not strong like you are. I never have been."

"Yes, you are. You're Skip Holland's daughter."

"I'm not the same daughter to him that you were."

"His strength runs through all of us, and that'll help you find the light you need to keep going."

"I just don't know if I can, Sam. I loved him so much. Even when things were horrible this last year, I still loved him."

"I know, and what happened is terrible and tragic. But he would want you to carry on for the kids, and he would want you to find joy again and to somehow be happy. He loved you that much."

"I can't be happy without him."

"It won't be the same kind of happy, but your kids will bring you joy the way they always have."

Angela shrugged, seeming unconvinced, and who could blame her? "I guess."

"Will you please come to dinner and at least try to eat something? Jack needs to see you trying, Ang. It'll scare him if you give up."

She blew out another deep breath. "Give me a minute to make myself presentable."

"Take whatever time you need. We'll wait for you."

"Thank you for all you're doing. You and Trace..." Her voice caught on another sob. "What would I do without you guys?"

Sam hugged her again. "You'll never have to find out."

"I hope not."

"Go take a nice hot shower. You'll feel better after."

"No, I won't, but at least I won't stink."

Sam laughed as relief flooded through her. If Angela could make a joke, there was hope she might emerge from this nightmare somewhat intact.

AFTER SHE LEFT Angela to shower, Sam took a second to text Freddie, giving him the green light to make the GoFundMe live. Then she knocked on Celia's door and stepped into chaos. Ella was crying, and Jack was yelling to be heard over Ella's loud wails. Poor Celia looked more stressed than Sam had seen her in a while.

Sam took Jack by the hand and led him into Celia's tiny kitchen. "What's the matter?"

"Ella won't stop crying, and Celia promised I could watch *The Lion King*." Jack's little chin quivered with the outrage of it all. He was the spitting image of his father, with dark hair and green eyes. "And I want Mommy. Where is she?"

"She was resting, but now she's in the shower and going to join us for dinner. Are you hungry?"

Jack shrugged. "I guess."

Sam hugged him. "I'm sorry you've had a rough day."

"It's not your fault."

Sam breathed in the sweet scent of shampoo and little boy. He'd held a special place in her heart from the day he was born, and she ached for his terrible loss. The tight bond between Jack and Spencer had been obvious to everyone who knew them. "I know this is so hard, buddy, and I'd give anything to fix it for you."

"I know."

"Do you want to come with me and see what Scotty and the twins are doing?"

"Sure."

"We can watch *The Lion King* after dinner."

"Okay."

"Go wash your hands so you're ready to eat."

While he took off to do that, Sam went to relieve Celia with Ella. "What's this all about, young lady?"

"I think she might be teething." Celia shook her arms as if to get the blood flowing again. "She's been upset all day."

"Poor baby." Sam rubbed the baby's back as she pressed her cheek to her forehead. Her soft blonde curls brushed against Sam's chin. "I can't tell if she's feverish or worked up."

"Maybe a little of both."

"Perhaps some time with Mama will help what ails you, sweet girl."

"I gave her some Tylenol a few minutes ago. I think she might've swallowed some of it."

Ella rested her head on Sam's shoulder as sobs hiccupped through her tiny body.

She ached for Ella, for Jack, for Angela and everyone who'd loved Spencer. Nothing in her life had prepared her to guide her sister, niece and nephew through such a dreadful loss. Still holding Ella, Sam took Jack by the hand when he returned from the bathroom.

"Take five before dinner," Sam said to her stepmother. "You've earned it."

"I'll be right there."

Sam emerged into the hallway to find Nick coming up the stairs. "We need to get some help for Celia. Today was rough."

"Why don't you ask your mom to come over? She and Celia are cool with each other, right?"

"Yes, I suppose so. That's a good idea. I'll text her after dinner."

"Would Miss Ella like to see Uncle Nick?" he asked, making a face that drew a reluctant chuckle from the little girl.

Sam handed her over to him and was struck by a pang of longing for a baby of their own for the first time in ages. Cripes, where in the hell had that come from? As if she didn't have enough to contend with. That ship had sailed, and she'd made her peace with it. She had Ella and would soon have Angela's new baby to love, as well as Shelby's babies. That was more than enough. But watching Nick rub Ella's back as he whispered sweet nothings to her gave Sam an ache that had nothing to do with grief.

Shit, fuck, damn, hell with that, she thought. *I don't have time to breathe, let alone have a baby. Go away, baby longings, and leave me alone. I'm done with you.*

If only Nick wasn't so adorable as he tried to charm Ella out of her funk. It was his fault she was having those pangs.

Nick raised a brow in her direction as if to ask what was wrong. Figures he'd see it. He saw everything where she was concerned.

Scotty and the twins appeared in the hallway and rushed to hug Sam. As she loved on each of them, she was so grateful to have them in her life. They had filled the gaping void that had once existed inside her after years of fertility struggles and miscarriages. They had also filled her life with love and laughter and were far more than enough for her.

"What's wrong?" Nick asked after he'd turned Ella over to Angela, who'd gotten a tight hug from Jack when she stepped into the hallway.

"Nothing."

"Don't lie to me."

"I'm not."

"Yes, you are, and we'll take this up again later." To the others, he said, "Let's eat."

Thanks to Scotty and the twins, dinner was a lively affair. Sam even saw Angela smile once when Scotty teased Jack about whether Spider-Man or Iron Man had better powers. Scotty was on Team Iron Man, while Jack was all for Spider-Man.

"Spider-Man can cast webs," Jack said. "There's nothing cooler than that."

"Iron Man can shoot rays, and his suit can do *everything*," Scotty said.

"The suit is cooler," Jack said. "I'll give you that, but Spider-Man is still the coolest."

"If you say so," Scotty said.

"What about Batman?" Alden asked. "His suit is the coolest, and he doesn't need any gimmicks to get things done. My dad told me that. He said a superhero is someone like Batman, who relies on his own smarts and body to take care of business."

"That's a very good point, Alden," Nick said. "I agree with your dad."

"I like Wonder Woman myself," Angela said.

Everyone turned to her, thrilled to hear her contribute.

"She's super smart, has incredible healing abilities and she's semi-immortal."

"I want you to be Wonder Woman, Mommy, so you feel better," Jack said.

The statement brought tears to Sam's eyes, and everyone else's, for that matter.

"I'm working on it, sweetie," Angela said.

After dinner, the kids took bowls of ice cream upstairs to the conservatory to watch *The Lion King*, as promised. Scotty had been put in charge of the Littles and Jack.

"We'll be up after a bit," Nick told him as he took Ella for another snuggle.

"Don't worry," Scotty said. "I've got them covered."

"He's so grown up all of a sudden," Angela said of Scotty as she sipped from a cup of hot tea that Sam had made for her. She'd mostly picked at the roasted chicken dinner but had taken a few bites of chicken and stuffing.

"Yes, he is," Nick said. "We want it to slow down. We haven't had enough time with him."

"You'll have lots of time with him," Angela said.

"It'll never be enough," Sam said. "He's so fun to have around."

"Jack adores him. I'm very thankful for Scotty and all of you right now."

"We're here for you, Ang," Nick said. "For as long as you need us."

"That could be a while."

"We're here," Nick said again, more forcefully this time.

"Thank you. I'm thankful for you guys and Tracy, Mike, Celia and Mom, too."

"People want to help," Sam said.

"I know," Angela said with a sigh. "I just don't know how to accommodate that."

"You don't have to accommodate anything. Just know that people care. That's enough for now." Sam's phone dinged with a text from Freddie. "Holy. *Shit*. The GoFundMe is already up to twenty-five thousand."

"No way," Angela said, her eyes going wide.

"And we haven't even promoted it yet," Nick said as he withdrew his phone from his pocket and started typing something. "There," he said a few minutes later. "I've posted it to my accounts. Let's see what that gets us."

"You guys…" Angela's eyes flooded with tears. "This means so much. I've been in a panic over what we were going to do. The fundraiser and the offer of Ninth Street… It feels like a miracle."

"It's family helping family," Sam said.

"Please tell Freddie thank you for me."

"I will." Sam responded to the text with *WOW. That's amazing. Angela says thank you, and Nick just plugged it through his accounts.*

That's awesome, Freddie replied. *It'll raise millions.*

You think so??

I know so.

Holy crap.

"Freddie says that you promoting it will raise millions," Sam said, astonished.

"Duh," Nick replied with a cocky grin.

"What?" Angela said, gasping. "*Millions?*"

"My people will show up for you," Nick said.

"I don't need millions," Angela said, seeming shocked and amazed at the same time.

"You can use what's left over to help other widowed single moms or something like that," Sam said.

"I'd love to be able to do that, but wow. I'm so overwhelmed and thankful. All I've been able to think about is how would I support us while taking care of three little kids."

"Now you can breathe a little easier," Nick said.

"A lot easier." Angela teared up and dabbed her eyes with a napkin.

"It's okay, Mommy," Jack said, taking them by surprise when he appeared in the doorway to the dining room. "Don't cry."

"I'll try not to, baby."

He went to sit with her, wiping away her tears and tucking her hair behind her ear the way he'd probably seen his father do many times.

His sweetness broke Sam's heart.

"I'll take care of you and Ella," Jack said. "Daddy told me to take good care of you in case he couldn't. I promised him I would."

Angela gasped. "He said that?"

Jack nodded, his expression solemn.

"You don't have to take care of me, honey. We'll take care of each other, okay?"

"Daddy wanted me to look out for you and Ella and the baby."

"You're an amazing big brother, but we're not your responsibility, okay? Your job is to play and have fun and do well in school."

"And take care of you guys. I promised Daddy I would."

"Daddy never should've asked you to do that, Jack. It's too much to put on a seven-year-old."

"I'm a big boy now. I can handle it."

"We'll talk about that later. I thought you were watching *The Lion King*."

"We are, but I wanted to check on you."

"You can go back to the movie. I'm fine. I swear. We'll be up soon."

"Are you sure?"

"Very sure." She kissed him. "Thanks for checking on me."

After they heard him run off to join the other kids upstairs, Angela's expression turned thunderous. "How could he ask such a thing of a *child*? Did he know he was going to die? What the hell?"

"He knew he was playing with fire buying street drugs," Sam said.

"But how could he ask Jack for that? He's *seven*!"

"I don't know," Sam said, feeling as horrified by this as Angela was.

"If he wasn't already dead," Angela said, "I'd kill him for doing this to Jack. How could he?"

"We need to get him a therapist," Sam said. "ASAP."

"Yeah, I'm realizing that." Angela shook her head. "I keep wondering what happened to my lovely life. Just over a year ago, everything was fine, and look at us now." She wiped away more tears. "I'm a widow with a traumatized kid, another who won't remember her dad and another who'll never even meet him. And even when everything was awful, and it's been awful for a long time, Spencer always loved me and treated me like I was the most important thing in his life. What am I supposed to do without that? Without him?"

Sam got up and went to her, putting her arms around her sister while she cried it out. "I don't know the answers to any of those questions, but I do know you, and I have faith you're going to find a way through this."

"How?"

"One day and one minute at a time."

"I don't want to do it without him, even if I'm angry with him right now."

"The anger will pass, and you'll remember the good times."

"I don't know if I will. The bad times have been pretty terrible, and now this with Jack…"

"You *will* remember the good. There was so much good, Ang. Anyone could see how happy you guys were together."

"That's what I'll remember," Nick said. "How much he loved you and how cute you guys were, always holding hands and laughing at your inside jokes. I'll remember the way Spencer was so creative in the games he made up for him and Jack to play. I'll remember how he went weak in the knees over his little girl and how excited he was for the baby. I'll remember how hard he worked so you could be home with the kids and how he supported your daycare business by taking time off to cover you when you had an appointment. I'll remember lots of family dinners, weekends and holidays together. I'll remember the good times."

Both Angela and Sam were mopping up tears by the time he was finished.

"And you should, too," Nick said. "The struggles of the last year shouldn't summarize who he was. He was so much more than that to all of us. When he asked what he did of Jack, he wasn't himself. The Spencer I knew never would've asked such a thing of his little boy."

"You're right," Angela said softly. "He wouldn't have. Thank you for that, Nick. I needed to hear it."

"Spencer was a good guy, Angela," Nick said. "A very good guy, who loved his wife and kids more than anything in this world. No matter what else happened or what else we learn about how it happened, that's the thing you must hold on to."

"I'm trying but thank you for the reminder."

"Let's get some ice cream and spend some time with the kids," Sam suggested.

"That sounds good," Angela said as she got up to help clear the table.

"Well done, my love," Sam whispered to Nick. "Very well done."

CHAPTER NINE

Much later, Sam snuggled up to Nick in bed and let him wrap her in his love. Tomorrow would be another difficult day, but for now, she could forget all that and wallow in the comfort only he could provide. And that, of course, made her feel guilty, because who would comfort Angela the way Spencer once had?

"When are you going to tell me what happened in the hallway earlier?"

Knowing it was pointless to try to keep anything from him, she said, "A little baby pang seeing you holding Ella."

"I wondered if that was it."

She poked his belly. "Quit reading my mind."

Chuckling, he said, "I speak Samantha fluently. It's been a while since there was a baby pang, huh?"

"Yeah. Caught me by surprise. It's your fault because you were so damned cute with her."

"She's adorable."

"Yes, she is. And what you said to Ang about Spence was perfect. She needed to be reminded of the good times."

"There were a lot of them."

"I feel so sick inside for Ang and the kids," she said.

"I know. I do, too."

"What you said was all true, but I'm so *angry* with him for putting her through this. And yes, I know that's irrational. It's not like he could help that he got addicted."

"There're a lot of complicated emotions at a time like this."

"Yeah, for sure."

Sam's phone rang, and she rolled toward her bedside table to check the caller ID. "It's Lindsey. I have to take this."

"Go ahead."

"Hey, Linds. What's up?"

"Sorry to call so late, but I thought you'd want to know that we completed Spencer's autopsy, and you were right about opioid overdose. The peripheral blood morphine concentrations were consistent with fatal intoxications that could've come from fentanyl or heroin. We won't know for sure which until we get the full tox screen back, but I thought you'd want to know this much."

"I'm surprised you're able to know that so quickly."

"Morphine in the brain is a telltale marker for opioids."

"I see."

"We also determined that he asphyxiated on vomit because he was lying on his back when he was found. That's what actually killed him."

"Not the drugs?"

"He wouldn't have asphyxiated without the drugs."

"Thanks for the info. This helps."

"How's Angela?"

"Not good at all."

"I saw the GoFundMe. That's a great idea. Terry and I donated."

"Thank you. That'll mean a lot to her."

"We wish there was more we could do."

"I know. Same here. But she's getting through it one minute at a time."

"She's in our thoughts and prayers. You all are. I'll let you get some sleep."

"Thanks for the update. I'll see you in the morning."

"See you then."

Sam closed her phone, put it back on the table and then returned to Nick's embrace to update him on what Lindsey had told her. "I'm going to hunt down the person who gave him those pills and make them pay for taking him from my sister and her kids."

Nick ran his hand up and down her arm. "Try to put it out of your mind for now so you can get some rest."

Sam took a deep breath and blew it out slowly but didn't feel even slightly relaxed.

"I can see I'm going to have to employ a special effort to ensure you get some sleep."

"What sort of special effort?"

"The most special kind."

Nick shifted them so she was on her back, looking up at him gazing down at her with love and concern in his gorgeous hazel eyes.

"I feel guilty having this when Angela doesn't anymore."

He kissed her. "Don't feel guilty. She wouldn't want that."

"Can't help it."

"I know, babe, but we're still here, and we still have each other. We have to celebrate every second we have together. Spencer's death is a reminder of how quickly things can change."

"I don't want anything to change. Ever."

"I don't either. I've got everything I could ever want or need as long as I have you and our family."

Since there was nothing more she could do for her sister that night, Sam decided to take what Nick was offering and try not to feel guilty about it. Being with him this way always made her feel better, even when she was heartbroken.

He rendered her defenseless with soft kisses and softer caresses that cleared her mind of everything that wasn't him and them and the magical connection that never failed to amaze her. As he kissed her neck, he worked her T-shirt up and over her head.

The cool air over her stimulated flesh had her nipples standing up at full attention as anticipation curled through her.

Nick never disappointed, giving both her nipples his full attention as he pressed his hard cock against her core. He knew all her secrets and had her straining toward release in a matter of seconds. She wouldn't have thought that possible with her heart and mind in such turmoil but leave it to him to thoroughly distract her.

When he moved even lower, removing her pajama pants and underwear and nudging her legs apart with his broad shoulders, she was so ready that it took only one stroke of his tongue to send her soaring. Every part of her was fully engaged in the waves of pleasure that rolled through her one after the other. And then he pressed into her, stretching her to the absolute limit as he filled her so perfectly.

After the emotional overload of grief that had marked her day, Nick had shown her once again that together, they could get through anything. He proved that again as she climbed toward a second release, this time with him.

He came down on top of her, and Sam wrapped her arms around him, wanting to keep him there for as long as she could. Breathing in the familiar scent of him, she knew a moment of peace for the first time since Sunday morning. "Thank you for this."

"Always my pleasure."

"I don't mean the sex, although that's great, too. I mean *this*. Us. All of it. I love my kids and my family and my squad, but you... You're the one who makes everything else possible. Please don't ever leave me." Before Nick Cappuano, she'd never said such a thing to any man. Before him, she'd never felt this way about anyone.

"I'm not going anywhere, love, and I should be thanking you. I had nothing until I had you, and now I have everything. It amazes me that I thought my life was great before I reconnected with you. That was just okay. This is exceptional."

"I wonder sometimes what we did to get so lucky and how long our luck can hold."

"Don't think that way. We're going to grow old and cranky together. Or I should say crankier for you."

She poked his side and made him laugh. "That's hurtful but true."

"I try to imagine you as an old lady, and I see you wearing your rusty steak knife in a holster attached to your belt, so you always have it ready, and me jumping between you and whomever you're trying to stab. My number one job will be keeping you out of trouble."

Sam rocked with silent laughter.

"You laugh because you can picture it as easily as I do. You're hell on wheels now. I can't wait to see what you're like at eighty."

"I'm a police officer, Nicholas. Down to my bone marrow. I only *talk* about stabbing people. I've never actually *done* it."

"Yet. After you retire, you'll be a menace to society."

"I told you I'm never retiring. I'd be bored senseless."

"I'd keep you busy."

"We can't screw all day every day."

"Why not? It's our favorite hobby."

"Because we'd get bored."

His expression conveyed horror. "I will never get bored with screwing my gorgeous, sexy wife."

"Even when she's eighty and wrinkled and packing a rusty steak knife on her hip that she doesn't remove even for sex?"

He slipped a hand under her to squeeze her ass. "Even then."

"This helps."

"What does?"

"Being silly with you."

"Who's being silly? I'm dead serious about you and the steak knife and me spending all my days keeping you from stabbing someone in the produce aisle—when we're not screwing, that is."

"It'd be more likely to happen in the ice cream aisle."

"True."

"By then, I won't give a flying fuck how big my ass is. You might have to grease my hips to get me through the doorways."

"I'm all for more of you to love."

She yawned, and her eyes closed as exhaustion overwhelmed her.

"My baby is tired," Nick said, withdrawing from her.

While he got up to use the bathroom, Sam turned on her side, ignoring the ache coming from her hip—and the other coming from her heart—as she tried to let it all go so she could sleep.

Nick returned and snuggled up to her, his hand resting just above the scar on her hip. "I can picture it so clearly," he whispered. "You and me at eighty, living the dream."

"You'll be eighty-two," she whispered back.

She fell asleep to the sound of his laughter, comforted that he could see them growing old together.

IN THE MORNING, Sam helped get the twins up and ready for school and made eggs and toast for them and Scotty, who was extra grumpy.

"What's up with you?" she asked him.

"Big math test today."

"Oh, okay. That explains the grumpiness."

"Why do they have to ruin a day we'll never get back with stupid tests?"

"I used to feel the same way."

"Exactly."

"Are you ready for the stupid test?" Sam asked just as Nick joined them, fresh from the shower and dressed for a day as the leader of the free world.

He raised a brow when he overheard her question.

"As ready as I ever am to be tortured," Scotty replied.

"I like math," Alden said between bites of egg.

Scotty stared at him. "We can't be friends if you like math."

"Yes, we can," Alden said, smiling.

"No, we can't."

"You're our brother now," Aubrey said. "That means we're friends."

"Yes, it does." Nick poured himself a cup of coffee. "Friends forever, math or no math."

"I'll make an exception for you," Scotty said to Alden, "but don't gloat about loving math in front of me."

"What does gloat mean?" Alden asked, his eyebrows coming together in the cutest expression ever.

"It means talk about how much you love it around me."

"Oh. Okay. Maybe I can help with your math homework."

Scotty laughed. "I'll take all the help I can get, pal."

Scotty's detail arrived a short time later to transport him to school. He left with hugs and kisses for all of them. "Have a good day, people, and pray to the math gods that Scott Cappuano passes this test today."

"We're praying," Sam said.

Angela appeared in the kitchen with Jack, dressed for school. "He wants to go today."

"I'll take him on my way in," Sam said.

"That'll cause a huge stir at the school."

"Better me than you," Sam said. "They'll be all over you if you do it. We'll be fine, right Jack Black?"

He grinned as she picked up their tradition of giving each

other nicknames. "Do we get to ride with the Secret Service, Samuel?"

Smiling, she said, "Sure do."

"That's awesome." He glanced at Angela. "We'll be fine, Mom."

Sam served up a plate of eggs and toast to her nephew.

"Are you sure you're ready to go back, buddy?" Nick asked.

"I have to go sometime, and I miss my friends."

"Plus, he'll miss a day next week for the funeral," Angela said as she took a cup of tea from Sam.

"That's true."

After the twins left with their detail, Sam asked Jack if he was ready to go.

"Just gotta brush my fangs," Jack said as he rushed off.

Angela rubbed a spot on her chest. "That's one of Spence's things with him. Brush your fangs."

Sam hugged her sister. "Go hang out with Ella. She'll make you feel better."

"I will."

Sam went to grab her coat and unlocked her bedside table to grab the tools of her trade.

Jack returned, dragging his coat and backpack.

Angela helped him into the coat and handed the backpack to Sam. "If you get there and it doesn't feel right," Angela said to Jack, "ask the nurse to call me. I'll come get you."

"I'll be okay."

Angela hugged him tightly. "Love you."

"Love you, too, Mom. Will you be okay?"

"I am if you are."

Sam took Jack by the hand. "Let's go to work, my friend."

"I'm going to school, silly."

"I thought you said you had a job now."

"I'm seven, Sam!"

"Oh! That's right. I forgot. I thought you were a lawyer."

He wrinkled his cute little nose as they made their way downstairs to meet Vernon and Jimmy. "I want to be a baseball player, not a lawyer."

"Ah, got it. Have you got an agent yet?"

"Still seven, Sam."

His giggle made her feel lighter and more hopeful than she

had since disaster struck. If he could still laugh and joke, she could, too.

Vernon and Jimmy were waiting for her in the foyer.

"We have a young deputy today."

Vernon and Jimmy shook hands with Jack.

"He needs a lift to school."

"We can do that," Jimmy said.

Sam nodded to Reginald, the usher who held the door for them. "Morning."

"Morning, ma'am."

While Jimmy held the door for them, Sam helped Jack into the back of the SUV. "Buckle up, my man."

She followed him in and gave Vernon directions to the Capitol Hill neighborhood school.

"It's weird," Jack said after a long pause.

"What is?"

"Daddy usually drives me to school. He says it's our buddy time."

His words hit Sam like a punch to the chest. She had no idea what to say to that.

"Everything will be different now," he added, compounding the pain.

"Yes, it will," she said.

He looked over at her, his eyes big and shiny. "Why do people have to die?"

"It's part of life, sweetheart. If you have the honor of living, you know the whole time that it will end someday. Some people get more time than others. That's why you have to live each day to the fullest because you just never know."

"Am I going to die?"

"Sometime in the very far-off future when you're an old man."

"Daddy wasn't an old man."

"No, he wasn't, and it's unfair that he was taken so soon when he had lots more to do here with you and Mommy and Ella and the baby."

"Mommy is very sad."

"Yes, she is."

"I don't like when she's sad."

"I don't either, but she will be for a while. But the good news is eventually she'll laugh and smile again like she used to, even if she'll always miss your daddy."

"Will I see him again?"

"Someday, a very long time from now, when you're an old man and go to heaven, you'll see him. He'll be waiting for you, and in the meantime, he'll watch over you and be so proud of you all the time."

"I don't want to wait that long to see him," Jack said, his chin quivering.

"Any time you close your eyes, you can see him in your memories. He's always right there, waiting for you."

Jack nodded, seeming satisfied with that. For now. She had no doubt there would be more hard questions as he tried to understand what'd happened.

"Are you sure you're up for school?"

"Yeah, it's fine."

"Your mom meant it when she said to call her if it's not good once you get there."

"I will."

Vernon pulled up to the school and parked in the lot. "Would you like us to walk Mr. Jack in for you, ma'am?"

"No, thank you. I've got it."

"Um, ma'am..."

"I know there'll be a stir, but Jack will protect me, won't you?"

He grinned, as she'd hoped he would. "Still seven."

"Vernon and Jimmy will come, too. Just in case."

Vernon helped her out and then gave Jack a hand getting down before turning him over to Sam.

As predicted, a ripple of excitement went through the parents gathered on the sidewalk when they realized who was delivering Jack. Windows went down in SUVs and minivans, and people gawked like they'd never seen the first lady before. Cell phone cameras were directed at her while she kept her head down and focused on her nephew.

"You're famous," Jack whispered.

"Nah, Nick is. I'm just along for the ride."

"You're *famous*."

"If I am, then you are, too."

"Sick," he said with another grin. "All the kids will want to sit with me at lunch."

If that happened, Sam thought, it was worth exposing herself to the stares of stunned parents and teachers as they made their way to Jack's classroom, where she intended to have a quick word with his teacher.

Jack led the way as Vernon and Jimmy stayed close in case anyone decided they needed a word with her.

"Does every school smell like paste, or is that just me? Like, do they have paste-scented air fresheners or something?"

Jack giggled madly. "You're so weird."

"You knew that about me before today. Don't forget to introduce me to your teacher."

"Duh, she knows who you are. Everyone does."

"That doesn't mean we forget our manners, young man." She felt nine hundred years old saying that, and Jack's eye roll told her what he thought of it.

In the second-grade classroom, Mrs. Ellington nearly had a stroke when she saw who'd accompanied young Jack Radcliffe to school. She stood so fast she spilled water all over her desk and clothes.

"Mrs. Cap-Cappuano."

"Told ya," Jack said, delighted and looking more like his old self.

The teacher rubbed her hands on her pants before sticking out her hand. "It's such a pleasure to meet you."

"Likewise." Sam shook the woman's clammy hand. "Jack was very eager to get back to school. His mom told him to call her if it turns into a rough day. I'm sure you understand how difficult this is for him."

"I do, and we'll keep a close eye on him today and over the next few weeks."

"We'd appreciate that." Sam squatted and put her hands on Jack's shoulders. "You good?"

"I'm good. Thanks for the ride."

Sam kissed and hugged him. "Any time, rock star."

"I'm not the rock star. You are."

"Whatever you say. Love you, Jack-o-Lantern."

He laughed. "Love you, too, Samwich."

"Oh, good one!"

At the doorway, she glanced back at him, her heart breaking all over again at how small and vulnerable he looked. She experienced yet another white-hot burst of anger at Spencer for doing this to his son and the rest of their family. As quickly as the anger hit, it morphed into empathy. Spencer in his right mind never would've done anything to hurt his family.

Sam would spend the rest of this day seeking justice for her late brother-in-law, but what would justice mean to Jack? He would still be without his beloved father for the rest of his life.

CHAPTER TEN

S am waited until she was sure Jack was all right before she
signaled to Vernon that she was ready to go. He and Jimmy
walked on either side of her as they escorted her from the
building. Every person they passed stopped and stared, their
mouths falling open in disbelief. Sam ignored them all, intent on
getting to work.

As Vernon helped her back into the SUV, he paused. "That was
exceptionally well done just now with Jack. You answered some
hard questions beautifully."

"You really think so?"

"I do. It was all I could do not to lose my composure listening
to you two."

"Same," Jimmy said from the passenger seat.

"Well, thank you both. It's hard to know what to say to a child
at a time like this."

"You handled it just right. You told him the truth without
making it scary. That's what he needs. I lost my grandfather when I
was ten. People were vague with me about what happened to him,
and that made it worse."

"I'm so sorry, Vernon."

"Thanks." He closed her door and got into the driver's seat.
"Bottom line is the truth matters to everyone, especially a grieving
seven-year-old."

"You're right. I was just hoping I wasn't being too real with
him."

"You were spot-on. And you've been where he is, having lost your dad."

"When I was much older, thank goodness." Sam couldn't imagine what her life would've been like without Skip Holland at the center of it for thirty-six years. That thought made her even sadder for Jack than she already was.

"It's a big loss no matter how old you are."

"Yes, it is," Sam said with a sigh. "I'm glad my dad isn't here for this. He really loved Spencer and respected how good he was to Angela. This would break his heart for her and the kids—and for Spence."

"He's here, and he knows," Vernon said. "He's also there with Spence."

"I'd like to think both those things are true."

"They are. I promise."

"Thank you both for all your support. I feel like I'm saying that a lot lately."

"We're not so bad, are we?" Vernon said, grinning at her in the mirror.

Sam smiled back at him. "Not bad at all."

When they delivered her to the morgue entrance at HQ, she stopped in to see Lindsey. As always, the antiseptic smell of the morgue creeped her out. Lindsey wasn't in her office, so Sam made the mistake of looking in the lab, which was how she saw her dead brother-in-law laid out on the autopsy table.

As she gasped, Lindsey looked up from what she was doing. She quickly covered Spencer's face but not before Sam took a good long look at his waxy remains.

Lindsey came to her and directed her out of the lab. "I'm sorry. You shouldn't have seen that."

Sam felt the way she had the few times she'd had the breath knocked out of her. She tried to shake it off, but that was easier said than done. "I thought you said the autopsy was finished," she said when she could speak again.

"It is. The funeral home is coming to get him shortly."

"Oh. Okay."

"Can you sit for a minute?"

"I kind of need to." She took the seat that Lindsey produced for her. "It's already been a rough morning."

"How so?"

She told Lindsey about taking Jack to school and the conversation they'd had. By the time she finished the story, Lindsey was dabbing at tears.

"He's such a sweetie. I hate this for him. For all of them."

"I do, too. I thought losing my dad was rough at thirty-six, but I had twenty-nine years with Skip that Jack won't get with Spencer. It's not even comparable."

"Of course it is. It was worse for you because you had all that time, and it's worse for him because he didn't get that."

"How can both those things be true?"

Lindsey shrugged. "They just are."

"Yes, I suppose you're right."

"As you would say, I usually am."

"That's one of my trademarked lines, but I'll allow you to use it."

"Gee, thanks," Lindsey said with a grin. "I'm sorry you saw what you did. I came in early and lost track of the time."

"It's okay. I'll see him soon enough at the wake."

"How's Angela doing?"

"It's hard to say. She's in shock. We all are. But she's sort of functioning for the kids."

"That's something, I guess. Did you see the GoFundMe this morning?"

"Not yet."

"Three million."

Sam's mouth fell open in utter shock. "Are you kidding me?"

"Nope."

And then Sam was crying from the kindness of people she'd never know. "Wow. That'll fix a lot of problems for Ang and others. She's already thinking about how she can use some of the money to help other widows."

"Good for her. That's a sign she's looking ahead."

"Yeah, I guess so." Sam wiped away tears and tried to pull herself together to go to work. "Did you send me your full report?"

"I did."

"Thanks. I'll see you later."

"I'll be here."

Sam left the morgue thinking about how much she relied on

people like Lindsey to be there every day and how much she'd miss her if she wasn't there anymore. She'd miss a lot of people if they were no longer part of her life. Once upon a time, that list would've been very short, and now...

She sighed. There were a ton of people she couldn't bear to live without, many of them right here in this building.

She'd no sooner had that thought than she ran into the one person she could happily live without, and in a matter of seconds, he had her backed into a wall, his face an inch from hers.

"I bet you're walking around feeling rather pleased with yourself after taking out my son."

"I haven't given that much thought, to be honest. Got a few other things going on."

Ramsey's beady eyes got beadier as he moved even closer to her. "I'm going to sue you and Malone and Offenbach and every other officer who was there that day and didn't stop the murder of my son."

"Go right ahead and waste your money. It was a clean shot, and everyone who was there knows it."

He cocked his arm back as if he was going to hit her, and Sam lifted her chin defiantly, prepared to take the hit if it meant adding an assault charge to his record. Whatever it took to permanently rid them of him. But before he could get off the punch, someone tackled him, taking him down hard and cuffing him while Ramsey screamed and fought back against the cuffs.

Gonzo looked up at Sam. "Are you okay?"

"Yes."

"Go get Andrews." Captain Andrews from Explosives was covering for Malone during his suspension.

Sam walked toward the pit, her legs feeling rubbery under her and her hip aching from the weird move she'd made to get away from him.

Freddie saw her coming and came over to her. "What's wrong?"

"Get Andrews, will you?"

"What happened?"

"Get the captain, Freddie. Please."

He took off toward the captain's office and returned a minute later with the senior officer.

Sam used her thumb to point toward the opposite hallway. "By the morgue."

Andrews took off at a jog.

"Now tell me what happened," Freddie said.

"Ramsey got in my face about the shooting. Gonzo took him down a second before he was going to punch me. He's got him cuffed on the floor."

"Oh my God, Sam. Are you hurt?"

"Twinged my hip when I backed away from him, but it's fine."

"What did he say?"

"That he's going to sue me, Malone, Offenbach and everyone who was there the day his son was murdered."

"Unreal. He can waste his money suing, but that was a clean shot. Everyone knows that but him."

"That's what I said, too."

They heard Ramsey before they saw him being dragged by Gonzo and Andrews, screaming about his son being murdered and suing the city, the department and everyone involved.

"We're putting him downstairs until he cools off," Andrews said.

"I have rights! You can't lock me up!"

"Wanna bet?" Andrews said as he and Gonzo hauled him away.

He screamed all the way down the stairs to the city jail.

"What's it going to take to get rid of him?" Freddie asked, hands on hips, eyes shooting fire. "Is he going to have to actually kill you or someone else?"

"Let's hope it doesn't come to that," Sam said.

"I'm not joking around here. He could kill you with one well-placed punch, Sam. Don't act like he couldn't. He's twice your size."

"I know. You're right, and I was stupid to stand there and take it from him. I should've kicked him in the balls or something, but I don't trust the hip quite yet for ball kicking."

"All the more reason why this is so outrageous. You're still on desk duty. You shouldn't have to worry about defending yourself in our own house."

"I'm all right, Freddie."

"This time. I want him out of here once and for all."

"Right there with you, Detective," Andrews said when he returned from the basement. "Lieutenant, please give me a written statement of what occurred immediately. I'll take it directly to the chief. We've all had enough of this guy."

"Will do, sir."

After Andrews walked away, Freddie said, "Do you need help with it?"

"I've got it, but if you could proof me, that'd help."

"You got it."

"Any word from Archie with the dump of Spencer's phone?"

"I'll go check on that while you write the report."

"Thanks."

Sam went into her office, ran her hands through her hair and then twisted it into a clip to keep it out of her way. She fired up her computer and called up the report template and began typing. With the incident still fresh in her mind, it flowed quickly.

"What happened?" Joe Farnsworth asked from the doorway, his expression thunderous.

Sam gave him the gist.

"Honest to God. I've completely had it with that guy." Turning toward the pit, he said, "Sergeant Gonzales, can you confirm that Sergeant Ramsey intended to punch Lieutenant Holland?"

"Yes, sir. His arm was cocked backward, and he was winding up when I stopped him."

"I'll have him charged with attempted assault and battery and put the union on notice that they can take me to court if they'd like, but that guy isn't welcome in this building going forward."

After he stormed off, Gonzo came to Sam's office. "Whoa. Never seen him so wound up."

"He's had enough. We all have."

Freddie came in with a massive stack of paper. "The dump on Spencer's phone."

"Holy crap." Sam eyed the stack. "That's got to be one of the biggest we've ever seen."

"He used it for work, so I'm sure a lot of it is that. We'll get started on this while you finish the report."

"It's done. I sent it to you. If it's okay, you can submit it."

Freddie handed the pages to Gonzo. "I'll meet you in the conference room."

Sam got up to follow Gonzo and the phone dump to the conference room, trying to ignore the ache in her hip that had intensified while she was seated. If Ramsey had caused a setback in her recovery, she would stab him.

"What's wrong?" Gonzo asked. "Other than the obvious."

"Did something to the recovering hip while I was trying to get away from him."

"Goddamn it. Seriously?"

"It's fine. Let's get busy. I need some freaking threads to pull, and I need them now."

Gonzo gave her a big chunk of pages and a highlighter while he took another chunk and saved a third stack for Freddie, who joined them ten minutes later.

"Report submitted."

"Thanks."

"No problem."

It made her feel better to know someone was checking her work since the dyslexia made her insecure about anything written. "Was it okay?"

"A perfect description of an asshole who belongs in jail."

Sam hoped the incident would finally get Ramsey out of her life once and for all.

NICK ARRIVED at the reception area outside the Oval Office to find Terry, Derek, Christina and Trevor waiting for him. "What brings out the brain trust?" he asked as they followed him into the most famous office in the world.

"A little thing called GoFundMe," Terry said.

Nick turned to face them. "What about it?"

"The press is going wild over you promoting the fundraiser for your sister-in-law," Terry said.

"How so?"

"Abuse of power, ethical lapses and other such things," Trevor said.

"Okay," Nick replied as he sat behind his desk.

"Just okay?" Terry asked.

"I used my personal accounts."

"Mr. President, this could blow up into a big deal and a big distraction," Terry said.

"That's fine. She needs the money."

"It's up to four million dollars, Mr. President," Derek said.

"We think you need to end the fundraiser and issue a

statement thanking everyone who generously donated," Christina said.

Nick thought about that for a second before reaching for the BlackBerry he used to communicate with Sam, making a call to her.

"Hi there," she said. "Didn't I just see you?"

"You did, but I'm here with Terry, Derek, Christina and Trevor who think we need to take down the fundraiser. It's hit four million, and there's some pushback from the press about me promoting it. We're thinking we should take it down, thank everyone and hope the controversy goes away."

"I'll tell Freddie to take it down with a note of thanks from Angela and her family."

"Can he do it now?"

"Yeah."

"Thanks, babe."

"Four million, though. Wow."

"I know. It's amazing. Angela will be astounded. I've got to run. Have a great day."

"You, too. Love you."

"Love you, too."

Nick ended the call. "They're taking it down with a note of thanks from Angela and her family."

"When?" Derek asked, checking his phone. "It's up to four point five million."

"Sam said she'd ask Freddie to do it now."

They waited in silence until Derek said, "It's been paused, and the note added." He sounded relieved.

"Hopefully, that'll get people off our backs," Terry said.

"They're always going to be on our backs about something," Nick said. "We can't overreact every time they come for us. I did what I did, and I'd do it again to help my family. The media can't have it both ways—a days-long feeding frenzy over my brother-in-law's death and then outrage when we try to help his widow and children."

"That's a good point," Christina said. "They've all experienced a ratings hike from covering Spencer's death. You should also know there's mad speculation about what killed him. We're getting bombed with requests for a cause of death."

"You can tell them his death is a private family matter and no further information will be released by the first couple," Nick said.

"Eventually, you have to tell them what happened," Christina said.

"No, I won't. Spencer and Angela aren't public figures and have a right to privacy."

"It's like osmosis," Derek said. "Their proximity to you makes them public."

"I'm not changing my mind about this. No cause of death or any other details of his passing will be released by the first couple now or in the future unless Angela decides to make it public." Some things had to remain sacrosanct, regardless of what office Nick held.

"We'll put out a statement to that effect." Terry glanced at Trevor, who took notes. "We'll say the first lady's sister is deeply grateful for the outpouring of support after her tragic loss, and that the first couple won't be releasing any further information about their brother-in-law's death as they feel that information should remain private."

"If I could play devil's advocate for a second," Derek said.

Nick looked to his longtime friend. "Sure."

"I think the statement will make them more ravenous, not less. When you say there won't be any further info released, you're almost asking them to go digging for it. Can we say he had an allergic reaction or something?"

"We're not saying anything. Spencer was a private citizen, and he will remain a private citizen in death. You can quote me on that. Can we please move on to pleasant things such as the dreaded security briefing?"

"Yes, Mr. President," Terry said. "We'll be ready for you in ten minutes."

"Thank you all for your advice and input. It's always appreciated even when I don't agree with it."

"Thank you, Mr. President," Derek said for all of them as they departed.

After they left, he pulled an iPad from his desk drawer and logged on to check the headlines. The GoFundMe story was top of the page on most of the major sites, along with speculation about how the president's brother-in-law had died.

Nick understood the curiosity. A thirty-six-year-old man didn't just die for no reason, but Nick would remain firm in his resolve to protect Spencer's privacy. He saw it as one last thing he could do for Spence in addition to being there for Jack, Ella and the new baby as they grew up.

And he would be there for them and for Angela as they moved forward from their tragic loss.

CHAPTER ELEVEN

S am and her detectives spent the rest of the day poring over
the printouts, highlighting things they wanted to investigate,
identifying frequently called numbers and looking for anything
that stood out as suspicious. After a while, the words and numbers
began to run together the way they always did when she got tired.

She sat back to rub her eyes. "Gonzo."

"What?"

"Do you still know dealers?"

"Not sure if the ones I knew are still in the racket."

"I want to talk to them."

"If I send cops to them, they'll come for me and my family."

"Even if you tell them we're on a factfinding mission and not
out to bust anyone's balls?"

"Even if."

"What if we were to 'encounter' them organically?"

He raised a brow, his expression skeptical. "How so?"

"You tell us where we might find them, and we happen upon
them in a way that doesn't look planned."

"You don't think they'd see right through that?"

"I need to find this guy before someone else dies!"

"I understand the urgency, but I have to protect myself and my
family."

Sam's friend Officer Charles came to the conference room
door. "Could I have a moment, Lieutenant?"

"Sure."

When Sam started to get up, her hip wasn't having it. "Ugh," she said as she sat back down. "Let's try that again."

Freddie stood and offered her a hand, which Sam gratefully took, wincing as the worst pain she'd felt in weeks radiated from her hip. If she had to take time out of her life to get that checked, she would be even more furious than she already was with Ramsey.

She made her way out of the conference room and headed to her office.

Officer Charles closed the door behind her and then handed Sam a printed report that she prayed she'd be able to read.

She blinked the words into focus. A twenty-nine-year-old wife and mother of two had been found unresponsive in her Brentwood home. Despite a quick EMS response, they were unable to revive her.

"My partner and I took the call," Officer Charles said. "There were similarities to your brother-in-law, so I thought you might be interested."

"You thought right." Sam eyed the pretty young woman. "What're you doing right now?"

"I'm off duty at three."

"How do you feel about a little overtime?"

"I feel good about it."

"Let's go to Brentwood."

"Now?"

"Right now."

"Um, sure. I can do that."

Sam went back to the conference room. "Keep digging until the end of your tour. I'm taking a ride with Officer Charles."

"To where?" Freddie asked, sounding perturbed.

"Brentwood to talk to the family of a woman who died in a similar scenario to Spencer."

"I can help with that," he said.

"I want the chance to talk to Officer Charles. It's all good. I'll see you back here in the morning."

Freddie nodded, but she could see he was pissed. She'd smooth things over with him later.

"Let's go," she said to Officer Charles. "If my detail takes us, can you get yourself back here or home after?"

"Yes, no problem."

"Great."

As they walked toward the morgue entrance, Sam tried to ignore the increasingly painful situation in her hip.

"What happened with Ramsey?" Officer Charles asked. "Everyone is buzzing about it."

Sam filled her in.

"Wow. He never learns, does he?"

"Nope."

"From everything I've read about the incident at Rock Creek Park, that shot was completely justified."

"It was."

"How's Captain Malone holding up?"

"As well as can be expected, from what I hear. No one comes to work thinking they'll have to give an order to kill a colleague's son. He's upset to have been put in that position, but he did the right thing."

"I feel bad for him."

"I do, too, but he's tough. He'll be okay."

"There's no chance they'll find him at fault, is there?"

"None. Shane Ramsey admitted his guilt and was certainly going to kill the hostage."

"Sometimes this job sucks," Officer Charles said.

Sam liked this young woman. "Most of the time, it sucks." Outside, Sam walked over to the Secret Service SUV. "Vernon, this is Officer Charles."

They shook hands.

"We'd like to go to Brentwood, please."

"I have the address," Officer Charles added.

They got into the vehicle and headed toward the address she provided.

"I don't know your first name," Sam said when they were on the way.

"It's Neveah."

"How do you spell that?"

She spelled it for Sam.

"That's pretty. Is it a family name?"

"My paternal grandmother's mother was Neveah."

"That's cool, Neveah."

"Thank you, Lieutenant."

"Let me tell you how this works. I call you by your first name and then you call me by mine."

"Ma'am."

"That's not gonna fly with her," Vernon said.

"What he said," Sam said, pointing to him. "I'm Sam. S-a-m."

"I can't do it."

"Yes, you can. Let's say it together. Ready? *Sam*."

Officer Charles cringed as she said it with Sam.

"See? Was that so hard?"

"It was, ma'am."

Sam rolled her eyes as Vernon and Jimmy laughed. "It's very important to me in this circus I find myself in to keep things real."

"By circus, do you mean being the nation's first lady while leading the MPD's Homicide division?"

"Yeah, that. Everyone is ma'am-ing the crap out of me, and it drives me crazy. I'm *Sam*."

"It's called respect, Sam," Officer Charles said. "And we respect you and the positions you hold."

"And I appreciate that, but in the fishbowl in which I live and work, I need the people closest to me to keep things real."

"I'll do my best, ma—"

Sam glared at her.

"Sam."

"Did you apply for the opening in my squad like I asked you to?"

"I did."

"If you want the job, you're hired."

"What? Come on... Just like that?"

"Just like that. I like your style. You wowed me with your mad organizational skills when you planned my father's funeral, and I want you on my team. If you'd like to join us, that is."

The young officer's eyes filled, and her lashes fluttered.

"Detectives *do not cry*," Sam said sternly.

"This one might."

"Nope. There're no tears in Homicide."

She dabbed at her eyes with the back of her hand. "I'd be honored to work for you in Homicide."

"You'd work *with* me, not for me, and we'd be honored to have you."

"There're probably more senior officers who'll apply."

"I want you."

"Because I'm Black and female like Deputy Chief McBride," she said, nodding. "I get it."

"Neither of those things has anything to do with why I want you to fill the opening created by her promotion. This is all about merit. You've repeatedly shown me that I can count on you to do your job with no drama. That's gold to me, because I need people I can count on, especially due to the aforementioned circus."

"You can count on me."

"And I know that, which is why I want you on my team."

"I'm incredibly honored to be asked."

"We'll see if you're still honored after a couple of weeks with us."

"I will be."

"I hope so. Give me the highlights on this woman in Brentwood."

Neveah cleared her throat and pulled out her notebook. "Mary Alice Albright was found unresponsive this morning by her husband, Brad. He called 911, and EMS tried to resuscitate her to no avail."

"Do we have any information about whether she had a drug problem?"

"There's nothing in the report about that. I noted the similarities to what I'd learned about the circumstances of your brother-in-law's death."

"We believe he was killed by pills laced with fentanyl."

"I wondered if that's what it was." She glanced at Sam. "Did you know he had a problem?"

"No clue. They chose to keep it private because of Nick. If someone is selling laced pills in this town, we need to find them. Quickly." She sent a text to Gonzo. *Anything standing out?*

A few things that'll give us some threads. We're going to give it another hour and then pick it up in the morning.

Thank you.

Shock had Sam feeling like she was wading through quicksand in this case, but they would keep up the momentum now that they had some leads. When they arrived at the house in Brentwood, numerous cars were parked in the driveway and in the street.

"I hate to do this to them when they're grieving," Sam said, eyeing the house where disaster had struck, "but we need to get the info while it's fresh."

They got out before Vernon could open the door for them and were halfway up the sidewalk when the front door opened, and a man stepped out. "We're not seeing anyone right now."

Sam showed him her badge and saw recognition come over him. "Lieutenant Holland, Officer Charles to see Mr. Albright."

"He's not seeing anyone."

"I understand, and we're sorry to intrude at such a difficult time," Sam said. "We wouldn't be here if we didn't have urgent business with him."

"Wait here."

"Are people always so happy to see you?" Officer Charles asked.

"That was a welcome party compared to what I'm accustomed to. This is the worst part of what we do. Intruding on people's grief or having to tell them news that'll change them forever."

The young woman shuddered. "That's got to be awful."

"It is, and it's not for everyone. I'd understand if you give this some thought and decide to take a pass. There'd be no hard feelings."

"I'm not taking a pass on the opportunity to work with you."

"Don't do that hero-worship thing with me. I'm a red-hot mess ninety-nine percent of the time."

"Whatever you say."

"No, really. It's true. Ask anyone."

"I'll take my chances."

"It's your funeral."

"Is that a Homicide squad joke?"

"Nah, that's my own original material, and I have a lot of that, which is fully trademarked and copyrighted."

"Good to know."

Sam glanced at her. "We joke around to cope with the fact that we have to go into the worst day in this family's life and make it worse. You get that, right?"

"I do."

"Didn't want you to think I'm heartless."

"I know the opposite is true."

"Knock that crap off."

"Yes, ma'am."

"That crap, too."

"Got it."

The man who'd greeted them returned to the door. "Come in."

They followed him into a tidy home with pictures of a happy family on the walls. The people gathered around the family's tragedy stopped what they were doing to stare at Sam as they made their way to the kitchen. "This is Brad, Mary Alice's husband." He was seated at the table with a cup of coffee in front of him.

"Thank you for seeing us at this difficult time." Sam eyed the disheveled young man with messy blond hair, scruff on his jaw and haunted eyes rimmed with red. To the others in the room, she said, "Could we please speak privately?"

"Brad?"

"It's fine."

What did he care? His wife was dead, and he was now a single father to young children. Talking to her was probably the least of his concerns.

After the others had filed out of the room, Sam and Neveah sat at the table. "I'm Lieutenant Holland, and this is Officer Charles."

He looked at Sam. "I know who you are."

"We're very sorry for your loss," Sam said.

"Thank you."

Sam put her notebook on the table and pulled out a pen. "Can you walk us through the events of this morning?"

He glanced at Neveah. "I already told your colleague everything that happened."

"Could you please go through it one more time for me?"

He didn't want to, and who could blame him? "I, um, got up early with the kids so Mary Alice could sleep in. They're six and three and run her ragged. I try to give her a break on my days off."

"What do you do?"

"I'm a DC firefighter and paramedic." He rubbed at the stubble on his face. "When she wasn't up by ten, I went to check on her. It's unusual for her to sleep past nine. The kids are loud even when I try to keep them quiet. When I saw her there, I knew something was wrong. She looked..."

Dead, Sam thought. She looked dead, but he didn't want to say that.

"I tried to wake her, but I couldn't, so I called 911 and

started CPR. They came and tried to resuscitate her, but they said... They said she was gone. The, um, medical examiner came and took her." He glanced at her with ravaged eyes. "I still can't believe it. She was fine last night, laughing and talking with friends who came over to play cards. The kids... They were hysterical. I just... I don't know what to do now. What do I do?"

Sam wished she had the answers he needed.

He perked up a bit and glanced at Sam. "Aren't you a Homicide detective?"

"I am."

"Why are you here?"

"I'll get to that in a minute. Can you tell me if your wife had any health problems?"

"She had a knee surgery that went very wrong about eighteen months ago."

Bingo, Sam thought.

"She's been through hell ever since."

"How so?"

"Two additional surgeries failed to solve the issue, and her pain level was intense. It totally changed her, diminished her. It's hard to explain the ordeal we've been through."

"Was she on medication for the pain?"

He nodded. "Oxy for a while, until the doctors cut her off. That's when things got really bad. She could barely function because she was in so much pain all the time."

"I'm going to ask you something that might seem outrageous and even offensive, but is it possible that she was acquiring Oxy illegally?"

"What? No, that's not possible. She'd never do something like that."

"Are you certain?"

"Yes! Mary Alice followed the rules. She was a good person, a wonderful mother and wife. She'd never do that."

"In the days before she died, did she seem different than she'd been during her ordeal?"

"How so?"

"Was she in less pain than she'd been? Functioning better?"

As he considered that, his entire body went still. "Now that I think about it, she did seem better."

"Mr. Albright, I need you to consider the possibility that desperation led her to acquire the meds she needed illegally."

"No," he said softly. "She'd never do that."

"If I was in the kind of pain you've described, I might be driven to do whatever it took to find relief, too. That wouldn't make me a bad person, and it doesn't make her one either."

Sam paused to give him a second to process that before she added, "If we determine her death was caused by illegally acquired medication, there may be more of it in your home that would put others at risk."

"She wouldn't..." His eyes filled with tears. "She'd never endanger our kids or me. She loved us."

"She wouldn't have known what she was taking was lethal, Mr. Albright. And we won't know anything for sure until after the autopsy, but in the meantime, I'd recommend you allow our team to do a full search of your house."

"When?"

"Right now."

He dropped his head into his hands.

"Is there somewhere you could go while we do the search?"

"My parents live nearby. They've got my kids."

"Could we have your permission to conduct a search? I'll make sure our people are respectful of your home and privacy."

"And if you find something? Will it be blasted all over the news that my wife acquired illegal drugs that led to her death?"

"That won't come from us."

He broke down into heartbroken sobs. "How can this be happening? How can she be gone? She was just here."

"We're so sorry you and your family are going through such an awful tragedy. But if she died because of laced pills, we need to move fast to figure out where they came from so we can stop this from happening to others."

He lifted his head from his hands. "Didn't you just lose your brother-in-law suddenly?"

"I did, and the circumstances are similar. We haven't released this to the public, but his autopsy showed morphine in his brain that could only have come from opioids."

"Oh God," he whispered. "You think Mary Alice died from the same thing as your brother-in-law?"

"We believe it's possible their deaths could be connected, but we won't know anything for certain until after we search your house, examine her phone and complete the autopsy. Do you give us permission to review her phone and to search your home?"

"Yeah."

"Will you please ask the others to vacate immediately and keep the details of our investigation private? If word gets out what we're looking for, the people dealing these drugs will be long gone."

"I get it. No one will hear that from me. I want to protect her."

Sam slid her notebook across the table. "Write down your full name, the address where you'll be staying and your phone number."

He did as she asked and pushed the pad back to her.

Sam turned the page to write *I, Brad Albright, give the Metropolitan Police Department permission to search my home and the phone of my deceased wife, Mary Alice Albright, as part of an investigation.* "Will you please sign this and get her phone for me?"

He read the statement and signed it. Then he got up and left the room.

CHAPTER TWELVE

"Brutal," Neveah said.

"Always is."

"Watching you work, though..."

"Knock it off."

"Just sayin'."

"Make yourself useful and go outside to contact Lieutenant Haggerty with Crime Scene. Ask him to get his team over here ASAP."

She got up to see to Sam's order, seeming relieved to have a reason to exit Brad Albright's nightmare.

Brad returned with Mary Alice's phone, which he handed to Sam. "There're photos and videos on there that're even more precious to me now."

"None of that will be disturbed, but is it backed up to the cloud, just in case?"

"I believe so."

"I'll ask our people to make sure of that. What's the passcode?"

"Ten seventeen, our anniversary." He glanced toward the front of the house. "What do I tell the others when I ask them to leave?"

"Just say it's a routine search that we do whenever someone dies suddenly. Have them meet you at your parents' home."

"Okay."

Neveah returned. "They're on their way."

"Call Patrol for a ride, take this back to the house and turn it over to Lieutenant Archelotta." Sam handed her the phone. "Protect it with your life. Not literally, but you know what I mean."

"I do, and I'll take care of it. Should I come back here after?"

"You're off duty."

"I'd like to see this through. I'm invested."

"You can come back." Before she let her leave, Sam put a hand on the younger woman's arm. "I hope it goes without saying that everything you witnessed here is top secret. We don't need it getting out that we're looking for someone dealing laced pills, because we'll never find them if that happens."

"Understood."

"Thank you for the help."

"Such a pleasure to work with you, Lieutenant."

"For fuck's sake. *Go.*"

"I'm gone."

After Neveah left, Sam waited in the kitchen for Brad to clear the others out of the house. Then he returned to let her know everyone was gone.

"Thank you. Please know how sorry we are to disrupt you at such a difficult time."

"Do you really think Mary Alice might've been buying pills illegally?"

"I think it's possible. We won't know anything for certain until we complete the search and the autopsy."

He ran a shaking hand through his hair. "What do I tell my kids if that's what happened?"

"You tell them their mother loved them. That's the only thing that'll matter to them."

"I suppose. I, um, I'm going to my parents' house. You'll keep me informed?"

"I will. Thank you again for your cooperation."

Shrugging, he said, "What choice do I have about any of this?"

Since there was no good answer to that question, Sam didn't offer him one.

After he left, she walked through the home, looking at photos of the happy couple with their blond children, a girl of six and a boy who was three. A deep feeling of sadness overtook her when she viewed wedding pictures and other scenes from a normal life now upended by immense tragedy.

She removed the BlackBerry from her pocket and called Nick,

using the ridiculous star sixty-nine code he'd programmed it with. How many inside jokes had Brad and Mary Alice shared that were now gone forever?

"Hey," Nick said, the sound of his voice calming her as it always did.

"Hey."

"What's up?"

"I'm at the scene of another possible OD. A young mother with knee trouble who died in her sleep."

"Oh God, Sam. Just like Spencer."

"Yep. Someone is selling laced pills and killing people. We've got some leads to pursue from Spencer's phone, and we'll see what transpires with this latest development. I'm waiting for Crime Scene to get here to search the house. I wanted to let you know I'll be a little late getting home."

"Do what you need to. We'll be here."

"Thank you for always understanding."

His soft laughter made her smile. "I owe you a lifetime of understanding after these last couple of months."

"Yes, you certainly do."

"Be safe out there. We love you."

"Love you, too."

She ended the call and made another to Lindsey.

"Hi there," Lindsey said. "Are you still working?"

"I am. Do you have Mary Alice Albright?"

"Yes, I was just about to get started."

"I think this could be related to Spencer."

"I wondered if that was a possibility."

"She had bad knee trouble, multiple surgeries and the doctors cut off the pain meds, which makes me wonder if she went looking for them elsewhere."

Lindsey's deep sigh said it all. "I'll get on it and let you know."

"Thank you."

As she slapped her phone closed, Sam heard voices outside and walked to the door to admit Haggerty and his team.

"What've you got?" Haggerty asked.

"Mary Alice Albright, age twenty-nine, wife and mother of two young children, found deceased in her bed this morning. I'm looking for pills, possibly in a white packet, but any medication you find will need to be analyzed."

"We'll get going, and I'll tag you with anything we find."

"Thanks. Officer Charles will be back in a bit. She's with me now."

"Got it."

Sam took a last look at Mary Alice and Brad's former happily ever after before she zipped her coat and headed out to where Vernon waited for her.

He held the door for her. "Where to?"

"Back to HQ, please."

She wanted to see what Gonzo and Freddie had gotten from Spencer's phone and make a plan for the next day before she headed home.

JAKE MALONE TOUCHED down in NOLA at six o'clock local time and took a cab to his hotel in the French Quarter. According to Norm, Tom Rosa worked in a bar in the Quarter and was there most nights. This being his first time in N'awlins, Jake was determined to see some of the sights while he was there and try to enjoy his forced break from the grind.

Joe said he had nothing to worry about with the IA investigation, so Jake was doing his best to relax while he could. His wife, Valerie, had declined his invitation to join him because she was scheduled to volunteer at the local hospital the next day, and it was too late to change her plans. They'd have to come back here together sometime. They had a long list of places they wanted to visit if he ever got around to retiring. Val had retired two years ago after twenty-five years in a first-grade classroom and was after him to join her in retirement.

He'd said he wasn't ready yet, but the Ramsey shooting had him questioning everything, including his desire to keep working for a few more years when he could retire at any time. If he were being honest, he was bloody sick of it all—and even more so after the last year of shocking revelations about longtime colleagues. They'd known for years that Len Stahl was a bad cop, but to find out that Paul Conklin had sat on info that could've solved Skip's case years ago was something Jake still struggled with months later.

They'd considered Conklin a friend as well as a colleague. Then they'd found out that Captain Hernandez had somehow known Conklin was involved and hadn't told anyone. Now to learn that someone had been aiding and abetting Stahl as he lied about investigations and the recent goings on with Ramsey—even before his son turned into a violent criminal—threatened to push Jake right into retirement. Being a cop in the current climate was harder than it had ever been. Their biggest problems shouldn't be coming from inside their own house.

The one thing that kept him going, even when he'd rather quit, was his decades-long close friendship with Joe Farnsworth. The chief needed Jake watching his back, so he would stay for as long as Joe was chief. If Joe left, he would, too. Looking out for Joe was the number one reason he was in New Orleans. If he could find Tom Rosa, hopefully he could get some answers about how Stahl had managed to convince his superior officers that he was fully investigating cases when in fact he was doing the bare minimum —and sometimes not even that.

The Worthington and Deasly cases had been solved in a matter of days after being reopened by Sam and Jeannie, which had led them to wonder what else Stahl had barely bothered to investigate. U.S. Attorney Tom Forrester had ordered a full investigation into all the cases Stahl worked on, including the ones that had led to successful prosecution. If he'd failed to do even the most rudimentary investigation in some cases, what was the likelihood he'd manufactured evidence in other cases?

High.

Jake shuddered to think of how many convictions might be overturned due to these revelations. All because one man had decided to collect a paycheck while cutting every imaginable corner on the job and being a son of a bitch to work with. Stahl would spend the rest of his life in prison for twice trying to kill Sam, and the rest of them were left to clean up his mess.

After Jake checked in and dropped his bags in his room, he headed out into thick, swampy heat that had him sweating immediately. He took in the sights in the Quarter—live jazz, revelry, architecture, people on balconies, sex shops on every block, bars, mimes and an overall party atmosphere.

He was glad not to be a cop in this town.

Behind him, loud music seemed to be getting closer to him. He turned to find a band leading a bride and groom through the streets with the wedding party bringing up the rear. Smiling, he stepped back to watch the joyful group go by, singing and dancing their way through the Quarter.

Two blocks in, he found Sully's Bar right where Norman had told him to look and ducked inside, seeking an older version of Tom Rosa. Jake hadn't seen him in more than ten years, and Norm wasn't sure if he even still worked there. Sully's was the most recent place Norm had known him to work, so Jake had decided to start there.

He took a seat at the bar next to an older couple drinking tall blue concoctions. "What's that?" he asked the bartender, pointing to their drinks.

"That's a famous NOLA Hurricane."

When in Rome... "I'll try one of those."

The bartender served up the drink. "First-timer?"

"How'd you guess?"

"You gotta look to ya."

Jake laughed. "I suppose I do. Hey, do you know a guy named Tom Rosa? I think he works here, or he used to."

The guy's expression immediately sobered. "He used to work here. He's got a bad cancer. Not expected to live much longer."

That news shocked Jake. "Oh no. I hadn't heard."

"Yeah, came on outta nowhere, and next thing we knew, he's in hospice."

"He's an old friend. Do you know where I might find him?"

"I'll ask the manager if he has his address."

"I'd appreciate that."

While the bartender went to find the manager, Jake sat back to absorb the news about Tom. He sent off a text to Joe. *I'm at the bar Norm sent me to in NOLA, looking for Tom. Just heard he's dying of cancer. Going to try to see him tomorrow.*

Oh no. That's terrible. He can't even be 65, right?

Yeah, about that. He was a couple years older than us.

I'll say a prayer for him and his family.

Joe was a good man. Perhaps the best man Jake had ever known, and that was saying something with Skip Holland in the mix. But even Skip would've said that Joe was the best of them all. That was why Jake would have Joe's back for as long as he needed a wingman watching out for him, especially now that Skip was gone.

Jake took comfort in Jeannie McBride being elevated to deputy chief. She was an outstanding cop and a great person. She'd make for an excellent partner to Joe in the chief's suite. But Jake would stick around to keep an eye on things from the lower ranks, where he served as the chief's eyes and ears.

He sipped the sweet, strong drink and perused the menu while he waited for the bartender to return.

"The manager says he's not comfortable giving Tom's address to a stranger."

Jake looked up at the young man. "I understand." He removed his badge from his pocket and put it on the bar. "We worked together at the Metro PD in Washington, DC. Could you tell your manager I'm an old friend looking to see Tom before he passes?"

"Sure, I'll tell him."

While the young man went off to deliver the message, Jake took another sip of his drink. If this was the drink of NOLA, no wonder everyone had such a good time here. The stuff was potent.

"You're a cop in DC?" the lady sitting next to him asked.

"That's right."

"Do you know the first lady?"

"I'm her boss."

"Oh my gosh! No way! Larry, he's the first lady's *boss*! What's she like? Is she as cool as she seems on TV?"

"She's very cool and a great cop. We're lucky to have her on our team."

The woman leaned in and whispered, "I think her husband is *very* handsome."

"I heard that, Myrna," Larry said. "She's got a thing for him. I tell her she's a dirty cougar. The president is young enough to be her son."

"But he's *not* my son, and I'm allowed to say he's a sexy devil."

"Honestly," Larry said with exasperation. "Do you see what I live with?"

"I do," Jake said, amused by them. "Where're you folks from?"

"Wisconsin," Myrna said. "Milwaukee area. Have you met him? The president?"

"Many times."

"You're so lucky," she said with a sigh. "I'd love to meet them both."

"I hope you get the chance sometime." Jake wondered where his bartender had gotten off to. "They're great people."

Another guy approached him from behind the bar. "You the one asking for Tom Rosa?"

"That's me."

"You're not looking to harass him or anything, are you? He's very sick."

"Not at all. I'd just like the chance to see him."

He put a piece of paper on the bar that had Tom's address and phone number. "Don't make me sorry I gave you this."

"I won't. Thank you."

"Tom's good people. We miss him around here."

"I just want to see an old friend."

The man nodded, his jaw pulsing. "It's hard to believe how fast it came on. One day he was fine, and the next..."

"It's been quick, then?"

"Like three months."

"Damn."

"You just never know what's coming around the next corner."

Jake nodded in agreement. "No, you don't."

He wiped down the bar and then glanced up at Jake. "It's kind of changed how I live. Does that make sense?"

"Sure, it does. Someone you're close to gets stricken with a fatal illness... That'd make anyone think twice about their life."

"You ever think that maybe you did everything wrong?"

"Every day," Jake said with a laugh. "Sometimes I wish I'd gone into accounting or business or something a little more predictable."

"Nothing is predictable. Not one damned thing. That's kinda my point."

"You're right," Myrna chimed in. "Life is unpredictable, which is why you have to do your best to be a good person and take care of the people you love. If you've done that, your life is a success no matter how much money is in your bank account."

The bar manager's eyes filled. "That's lovely, ma'am. Thank you. Can I buy you a drink?"

"These Hurricanes are quite tasty," Myrna said.

"I recommend you only have one if you're not used to them," the bartender said. "They tend to deliver a bit of a kick after the fact that a lot of tourists don't see coming until they're good and drunk."

Jake could attest to the kick. He was already buzzed after only a few sips of his drink.

"I'll have a glass of Chardonnay, then," Myrna said.

"Good call," the bartender said. "Top you off?"

"No, thank you," Jake said. "I'm going to take your advice and go slow."

"How about some dinner? Our jambalaya is the best in the Quarter."

"That sounds great," Jake said.

Tomorrow, he would try to see Tom. He hoped he wasn't too late.

CHAPTER THIRTEEN

"Talk to me about threads," Sam said when she entered the conference room.

"We're focusing on the last seven days in particular," Gonzo said, "and there're several calls and texts to the one number we can't trace." He held up a sheet that had long lists of numbers printed on it to show her how they'd highlighted all the instances of that number in yellow.

"Do you think it's a burner?" Sam asked.

"Possibly," Freddie said. "We were waiting to see if you want us to call it."

"Do you know how to make it so they can't see where the call is coming from?" Sam asked.

"I can do that on my cell," Gonzo said. "Let me make the call. I speak the language, unfortunately."

"Go ahead."

He punched a few things on his iPhone and then made the call, putting it on speaker.

"What?" a gruff voice said.

"I got your name from a friend," Gonzo said. "Looking for some pills."

"Oxy?"

"Yeah."

"Ain't got none left."

"What else you got?"

"H."

"I'd take that over nothing. Where can we meet?"

"Give me your number. I'll call you with a place."

"When will you call me?"

"When I want to."

Gonzo gave him his number. "I really need to score, man."

"I hear you. I'll be in touch."

The line went dead.

"Is your number traceable to you?" Sam asked, immediately concerned.

"No, I have it scrubbed. No one can tie that number to me."

"How do you scrub a number?" Sam asked.

"Archie can do it for you. Might be a good idea in your case."

"I'll ask him about that. What do we do now?"

"We wait," Gonzo said.

AFTER HEARING that Haggerty's team had found a white packet of pills at Mary Alice's home with the same S20 marking as the ones Spencer had, Sam told him to call in HazMat to get them to the lab since they might be laced with fentanyl. She was about to head home when FBI Special Agent-in-Charge Avery Hill appeared in her doorway. "Hey. What brings you here? I thought the proctology exam was completed." The FBI had issued their report on the internal investigation of the department the week before.

Hill's sinfully handsome face lifted into a half grin. "Does that mean I'm not allowed to come by anymore?"

"It means we've all seen enough of you around here."

"I'm hurt."

Sam rolled her eyes. "Whatever. What can I do for you, Agent Hill? I need to get home."

"I'm wondering if you've heard anything about what caused your brother-in-law's death."

Avery Hill wasn't just a colleague to her. He was also a close friend now that he was married to Shelby. They'd been with them at Camp David the previous weekend when disaster had struck. Sam didn't want to lie to him, but she also didn't want him butting into her investigation. "Not yet."

"Wow, did it really take you a full minute to come up with that two-word answer?"

"No, it didn't."

"I'd like to remind you that if you suspect something nefarious happened at Camp David, that makes this a federal investigation."

"Duly noted."

"Did something nefarious happen at Camp David, Sam?"

"Not that I'm aware of." That wasn't exactly a lie. She believed the pills were acquired locally and transported to Camp David, where they'd been ingested. The jurisdictional lines were murky, but she still felt justified handling the investigation based on what she knew so far. And that another person in her city might've died the same way Spencer did was information she wasn't compelled to share with him.

"I could help, you know."

"I do know, and I appreciate that. But I don't need help. If I do, you'll be the first to know."

"Then I'll just say this… If you're running an investigation that would be better handled by people not related to the deceased, you might be jeopardizing a future prosecution."

"I appreciate the lecture on law enforcement and how it works, as I was previously unaware before you came in and mansplained it to me."

"That's not what I'm doing, Sam."

"No? Then what's this about? Proving you have bigger balls than I do?"

He released an exasperated sigh. "Not at all."

"Your balls will always be bigger than mine since you're a guy and a Fed, but I know what I'm doing when I'm inside this building. I don't need anyone to tell me how it works here. Everywhere else besides here? If you have a road map on how to deal with that, I'm all ears."

"I don't have any road maps."

"Then I think our work here is finished, Agent Hill. I need to get home and see to my sister and my family."

"How's she doing?"

"Terrible."

"I can't stop thinking about her and the kids."

"Same." She glanced up at him. "I've been meaning to ask if you've got any news about my revolting mother-in-law. You'd mentioned a while back that you were on to something, but I haven't heard any more."

"We're still digging into a few things there, but I'm not ready to report to you yet."

"I keep waiting for her to rear her ugly head again, especially now that Nick is president."

"I'll let you know as soon as I have anything solid."

"Have a good night, Avery."

"You do the same."

She waited until he walked away and then locked her office and made for the morgue exit, eager to get out of there while she could.

AVERY LEFT Sam's office feeling more concerned than he'd been going in. A perfectly healthy thirtysomething man didn't just die in his sleep. He knew he ought to leave it alone, but he'd been doing this too long not to sound alarms when he saw a friend wading into risky waters. Sam would be pissed with him, but he still made his way to the chief's suite to ask Helen if he could have a minute with Joe Farnsworth.

"Only a minute," Helen said. "He's due home for dinner."

"I won't keep him."

"Please don't. He's had a long day already."

"Yes, ma'am." Avery knocked on Joe's door and stuck his head in. "Could I have a minute?"

"Sure, come in."

Thankfully, their investigation hadn't led to any sort of corruption at the top of the department, or he'd not be welcome there. Their recommendations had been received with professionalism and an admirable desire to right the wrongs of the past.

Joe stood to shake Avery's hand. "What's up?"

"I'm in a bit of a bind."

"How so?"

"I was there when Spencer Radcliffe was found dead at Camp David."

"Such an awful tragedy."

"Yes, it is, but you and I both know Sam, and it occurred to me that she might be trying to get to the bottom of what happened and that it might not be appropriate for her to be the one leading the investigation."

"That's in the hands of the ME."

"Has she reported yet?"

"I'm not sure."

"Do you have a way to check?"

Joe gave him a side-eyed look before he sat down with a sigh and booted up his computer. After a few silent minutes of typing, he turned his monitor toward Avery.

He got up for a closer look, scanning the report, looking for keywords and stopping short at the words *morphine* and *brain*. Just as he'd suspected. "You see that there?" He pointed to the words.

"What about it?"

"The only way morphine is found in the brain postmortem is through opioid overdose, and Holland would know that. If she didn't already know it, Lindsey would've clued her in. She's investigating his death."

"So what if she is?"

"He overdosed on federal property, Joe. This should be a federal investigation."

"Well, it's not, and it's not going to be."

Avery raised a brow in surprise. "Does that mean you're fine with her investigating the death of her own brother-in-law? What if it leads to charges?"

"I've already consulted with my lieutenant, and we're handling this in-house. Thank you for bringing it to my attention, Agent Hill. You've done your due diligence. You can go home now feeling good about yourself."

"That's not what this is about, Joe, and you know it. If a crime has been committed, she's the last person who should be investigating it. What would Forrester say about it if he knew?"

"If you go to him with this, you'll no longer be welcome around here. You got me?"

"I see how it is," Avery said.

"If you see that we protect our own in their times of grief, then you've got the full picture. Have a nice evening, Agent Hill."

Avery stared him down for a long moment, but Joe never blinked. He turned and left the office, feeling unsettled about what he'd learned at HQ. He hoped that whatever Sam was up to didn't blow up into a scandal the department could ill afford.

. . .

ON THE WAY out of the building, Sam poked her head into the morgue looking for Lindsey, but she wasn't there. When she was in the car, she put through a call to her friend.

"Hey," Sam said, hearing music playing in the background.

"What's up?" Lindsey asked.

"Just wondering if you had anything yet on Mary Alice Albright."

"I should know more in the morning."

"Have you had any others like her and Spence recently? People who died suddenly for no apparent reason?"

"No, we haven't, but that doesn't mean it hasn't happened. If the family and responding EMS don't suspect a crime has been committed, then we might not see them."

"So, it's entirely possible there've been others, but we wouldn't know it."

"Yes, I suppose it is."

"This helps, Linds. Thanks."

"How're you holding up?"

"I'm okay. I'll be glad when we get past the funeral and stuff early next week. His brother's family was in Italy, so we're waiting for them to get home."

"What an awful call to get when you're away like that."

"Yeah, for sure."

"Can I do anything for you or Angela?"

"Nah, we're okay. But thanks for asking. Everyone has been amazing through this."

"We all wish there was more we could do."

"I know. Me, too. I'll talk to you tomorrow."

"Sounds good."

They arrived at the White House a short time later, and Vernon helped her out of the car. "Sam," he said quietly so as not to be overheard.

She turned to him.

"While you're busy taking care of everyone else, make sure you're taking care of yourself, okay?"

His concern touched her deeply. "I will. Thank you."

Nodding, he stepped aside for her to go inside, where she was greeted by Harold, one of the ushers. "Evening, ma'am."

"Evening, Harold. How goes it?"

"Very well, ma'am. Hope you had a good day."

"It wasn't completely awful, so that's something, in light of current events."

"Yes, ma'am," he said.

She headed up the stairs, despite the protest coming from her hip. When she arrived in their suite, she went straight to her laptop on the desk and called up the *Washington Star* website to scan the obituaries, looking for people who'd died young in recent weeks. She found two that stood out. Morgan Newell, age thirty-two, had died unexpectedly two weeks ago at her home in Glover Park.

Sam pulled out her notebook and wrote down the woman's name and other pertinent details, such as her parents' names.

The other, Angelo Diaz, was twenty-three and had been found dead ten days ago in his bedroom at the home he shared with his mother. Sam wrote down his mother's name and noted that Angelo had graduated from Wilson High School five years ago.

She called Gonzo.

"Hey, what's up?"

"Have you heard back from the dealer?"

"Not yet."

"Is that unusual?"

"Not entirely."

"I had a thought about other recent deaths of younger people and scanned the obits. I found two from the last couple of weeks that I'll look into in the morning. But that made me wonder if all the deaths would make the paper."

"Not necessarily. They charge for obits these days, so a lot of people don't bother with them. I can check the local funeral homes tonight if that would help."

"That would help. Thanks."

"I'll let you know what I find."

"Great, thanks. We need to pick up the pace on this investigation."

"We'll get back on it in the AM."

"See you then."

Sam slapped her phone closed and was lost in thought when it rang with a call from Farnsworth. Surprised to see his name on her caller ID after hours, she took the call. "Is this my chief or my uncle?"

"It's both."

"Uh-oh."

"I know we already talked about this, but do I need to be concerned about you investigating Spencer's death?"

Goddamned Avery Hill. "Not at all. I may be on the trail of a dealer who's selling laced drugs. So far, I'm aware of four suspicious local deaths in the last two weeks, including Spence, and I expect to possibly uncover more by tomorrow."

"I spoke with Cooper in Narcotics and asked why an alert hadn't been made with an increase in OD deaths. He said they were a couple of weeks behind on gathering reports from local hospitals due to being short-staffed. He's had two officers out on leave. One had surgery, and the other took a few weeks off after having his first baby."

Sam took a second to process that information. "So you're telling me that one of the most important jobs they have—to notify the public if there's an increase in overdoses—wasn't done because they were shorthanded? Why didn't they ask for help?"

"I raised that question with Cooper, and he said everyone is overworked and understaffed."

"That alert might've saved Spencer. It might've saved Mary Alice Albright and who knows how many others?" Sam's heart broke all over again to know that the tragedy of Spencer's death might've been prevented if her own colleagues had done their jobs. "We need to issue that alert now. We've got at least two people who've died from laced pills." That might make finding the dealer or dealers harder, but it could also save some lives.

"I'll get Public Affairs on that now and have them take care of it."

"Thank you."

"I'm sorry if we let you and your family down—again."

"It's very upsetting to me to know this might've been prevented."

"It is to me as well, and I told Cooper not to let that happen again or else."

"I feel like I might be sick."

"Why don't you take some time off, Sam? Be with your sister and the kids. Take care of yourself and your family."

"I'd rather be hunting the person who killed Spence. And that's what Ang would want me to do, too."

"The offer of time off is on the table if you need it."

"Thank you."

"You're on a slippery slope here, Lieutenant."

"When am I not on a slippery slope, sir?"

"All kidding aside, this one is slipperier than usual due to your personal connection to one of the victims."

"I understand your concern, but you should know... As devastated as I am for Ang and her kids, I didn't feel particularly close to Spencer. Not like I am to Mike, who's always been like a big brother to me. I never reached that level with Spence. My relationship with him was based solely around my sister and their children, so I feel confident that I can maintain a professional distance in this case. If I didn't, I'd turn it over to someone else."

"I appreciate that insight and hear what you're saying. However, make sure Sergeant Gonzales signs the reports."

"That's the plan. Thank you for understanding that I need to do what I can to get justice for Ang and the kids. Not that it will bring Spencer back, but it might give her some closure."

"I know I don't have to tell you this, but you need to deliver a case that the USA can prosecute without prejudice."

"Understood. I may need to authorize overtime this weekend to keep up the momentum."

"I'll authorize that."

"What are you hearing from the captain?"

"He's in New Orleans looking for Tom Rosa. He's learned that Rosa is in hospice with cancer."

"Oh damn. I hope he's able to see him in time."

"Me, too."

"Keep me posted every step on this one."

"Will do."

CHAPTER FOURTEEN

S am slapped her phone shut just as Nick came into the suite and closed the door behind him.

"I heard a rumor that my lovely wife had arrived at home, but when she didn't come to find me, I decided to come find her."

"You heard correctly," she said, smiling up at him as he bent to kiss her.

"How's my love?"

"I'm upset."

"Because of Spence?"

"Indirectly. I found out that Narcotics, whose job it is to track overdose deaths in the District, had dropped the ball on that in recent weeks because they were short-staffed."

"Oh no."

"If they'd just done their jobs and alerted the public to an increase in OD deaths associated with Oxy, that might've saved Spencer and others."

"And now you're struggling to cope with that information."

"The chief just told me what he found out from Narcotics, and I'm enraged to know this awful tragedy might've been avoided— for our family and others."

"That's horrible, Sam. I'm sorry."

"How many times can this department let me down before I can't bear to work there anymore?"

Nick sat on the bed and put his arm around her. "No one would blame you if this took you over the edge."

"Except I have no idea what I'd do with myself without the job."

"You could be a full-time first lady."

"No, I really couldn't," she said with a laugh. "Thanks for reminding me of what's waiting for me if I up and quit. This helped."

"Glad to be of service," he said with a smile.

"I'm all yours until zero seven hundred."

He checked his watch. "That's ten whole hours. We can get a lot done in ten whole hours."

"I need to see the kids and Ang and eat something."

"I can make all that happen." He held out a hand to help her up and then wrapped his arms around her. "But I need this first."

"I need it, too. More than ever tonight. How did Scotty's math test go?"

"He said it was fine and we're not discussing it any further."

"Fair enough."

"What's the latest with the case?"

"Numerous people expiring before their time in the last few weeks, which leads us to believe we've got a dealer selling laced drugs. Unfortunately, finding that person will be like looking for a needle in a haystack."

"You'll find him—or her. You always do."

"Gonzo says it'll be tough because they go to great lengths to stay below the radar. He's working his channels, but nothing is happening as fast as we need it to."

"What is it you always tell me? Slow and steady wins the race?"

"That's not one of mine. I'm all about fast and reckless, not slow and steady."

His low rumble of laughter along with the unmistakable scent of home soothed her after a difficult day.

"I wish we could have a night in our loft," she said, "but it's too close to Angela's room."

"We can re-create the magic right here. Meet me back here after dinner and family time?"

"I'll be here."

. . .

SAM WENT FIRST to check on Angela, who was sitting on her bed with Ella sleeping in her arms and Jack curled up to her as he watched *Iron Man*. Her sister looked exhausted and overwhelmed.

"Let me take her," Sam whispered, reaching for Ella.

Angela kissed the top of her daughter's head and released her hold on her so Sam could carry her to bed in the portable crib they'd put in the room's walk-in closet. As she laid Ella down, Sam ached for the loss the little girl was too young now to process but that would mark the rest of her life. There would always be someone important missing, someone she wouldn't remember, but would love anyway.

The wallop of emotion caught Sam off guard. Though she hadn't felt particularly close to Spencer, she was to Angela and her kids. Their pain was her pain, which meant she was too close to the victim to conduct an impartial investigation. She would rely on Gonzo and the rest of her team to bring the objectivity, because there was no way she was taking a step back from it.

She left the closet door propped open when she returned to the bedroom.

"Did you catch any bad guys today, Sam?" Jack asked.

"Not today, Jack in the Box, but we're after a few of them."

"You'll catch them, Sammy Wammy. You always do."

Smiling, Sam cuddled up to him and kissed his cheek. "Thanks, buddy. That means a lot. How was school?"

"Fine," Jack said. "The other kids said they were sorry about my daddy."

"That's nice of them." To Angela, she said, "How are you?"

Angela shrugged. "I'm still waiting for him to come breezing in and tell me it was all a big mistake."

"Daddy would come if he could, Mommy. He'd never want us to be sad."

"No, he wouldn't, baby."

"Did you get some ice cream tonight, Jack Frost?"

Giggling at the name, he said, "Not yet."

"Why don't you go find Uncle Nick and tell him you need some?"

"Okay." He took off like a shot.

"The poor kid has been plastered to me since he got home from school. I think he's worried I'm going to die, too."

With Jack gone, Sam snuggled in closer to Angela, putting her arm around her sister. "Do you want me to talk to him?"

Angela leaned her head on Sam's shoulder. "I suppose it couldn't hurt."

"I'll handle bedtime and have a chat with him."

"Thanks."

"What else do you need?"

"I can't think of anything. Trace went to my house today and got the clothes we'll need for the wake and funeral. Spencer's brother, Jed, and his family got back from Italy finally. They ended up with their original flight when they couldn't get anything sooner."

"That must've been rough for them."

"He sounded incredibly stressed on the phone."

"I wish there was something more I could do, Ang. It breaks my heart that I can't make this right for you."

"I know and being here with you guys is a huge help. I just hope it won't always hurt this bad."

"My friend Roni mentioned the widow group she's part of. She says they've made a huge difference for her. Derek is part of the group, too."

"I don't think I'm ready for anything like that."

"No, but maybe you could talk to Roni? It might help to talk to someone who's been there."

"I'll think about it."

"Roni would want me to tell you the offer is on the table indefinitely."

"Thank you, and please thank her, too."

"I will. Did you eat something?"

"I had some soup earlier."

"Is that enough for you and the baby?"

"Probably not, but it was all I could keep down. I'm so nauseated, I can't bear to eat anything."

"You need to keep checking in with your doctor."

"I have another appointment on Thursday."

"Should you wait that long?"

"It was her first available."

"And she knows what you're going through?"

"She does."

"Hmmm, how would you feel if I asked Harry to come see you? He might be able to help."

"No, I don't want that. He's a friend. It's too weird. I'm fine. I promise."

Sam didn't believe she was fine at all, but she didn't want to add to Angela's stress by insisting she see their doctor friend. "Is there anything I can get you?"

"No, thanks."

The dull, flat tone of Angela's voice was in stark contrast to her usual animation. "I'll leave you to get some rest. Text me if you need anything at all."

"I'll be out of your hair soon. The kids and I have to get back to a normal routine."

"There's no rush on any of that. You're welcome here indefinitely."

"Thank you, but you've got enough on your plate without worrying about me and my kids."

"Ang, do you honestly think I'm going to worry about you less when you're not staying with us anymore? It's easier for me to have you here with us, so please stay as long as you'd like to."

"Jack is getting too comfortable here."

"Jack is welcome to get comfortable in my home."

Angela sighed and sank back into her pillows. "We'll fight about this tomorrow."

Sam smiled and kissed her sister's cheek. "I'll look forward to that." She got up to leave Angela to get some rest and headed for the door.

"Hey, Sam?"

She turned back. "Yes?"

"As horrible as this is, having you and Trace by my side makes it more bearable than it would be without you."

"We're here for the long haul. Just like you'd be for us."

"I hope neither of you ever knows what this is like."

"We'd do anything we could to make it so this never happened."

"I know. Love you."

"Love you, too. Call if you need anything."

"I will."

Sam walked out of Angela's room, bringing the heavy weight of her sister's grief with her. Nick was in the hallway with Jack, Aubrey and Alden.

"We're heading for ice cream and then story time," Nick said. "Would you like to join us?"

"I'd love to."

After the kids had their dessert and brushed their teeth, they snuggled into the bed the twins shared, with Jack pressed against Sam while Nick read three stories, using voices for each character that delighted the kids. He was such a wonderful father and uncle, and it made her heart swell with love for him to see him in both roles. She loved that while the whole world knew who he was, no one else ever got to see him like this.

"And now," Nick said, "it's time for all kiddos to go to sleep."

"I'm not tired," Aubrey said, even though her eyes were heavy.

"I'm not either," Alden said, yawning.

The twins usually went down easily, so it was odd to hear them say they weren't tired. "What's going on, guys? Why don't you want to go to sleep?"

"I'm scared," Aubrey said, her little chin quivering.

"Of what, honey?"

"Jack's daddy died. My daddy died. My mommy died. Why do people have to die?"

Oh Lord...

"Dying is part of living," Nick said gently. "Everyone dies someday."

"Am I going to die?" Alden asked.

"Not until you're an old man," Sam said.

"My daddy wasn't an old man, and neither was Jack's daddy," Aubrey said.

"Most people live to be old," Nick said. "But others don't. We have no way to know who will and who won't, but what matters most is how much they loved you."

"I'm scared you're going to die," Aubrey said, her gaze encompassing Sam and Nick.

"We're not going anywhere, sweetheart," Nick said. "You're stuck with us."

"I don't want you to die," Alden said.

"I don't either," Jack added.

"We're fine, and we're going to be right here with you guys for years and years until you're sick of us telling you what to do," Nick said, giving Aubrey a little tickle that made her giggle.

Sam and Nick got up, and he picked up Jack, who cuddled into his embrace.

"I want you guys to have sweet dreams and not worry about anything," Sam said when she kissed the twins good night. "Okay?"

"Okay," Aubrey said, popping her thumb in her mouth.

At some point, they'd have to address the thumb-sucking, but not tonight or any time soon. If it gave her comfort, Sam couldn't see the point of taking that away from her.

"Come get us if you need us during the night," Nick said. "We love you."

"Night." Sam shut the light off but left the door open. She suspected they'd be asleep within minutes.

Nick delivered Jack to his bed and kissed him good night.

"I'll be just a minute," Sam said to Nick.

"Night, Jack."

"Night, Uncle Nick."

Sam tucked the covers up around the little boy. "How'd today go?"

"Everyone wanted to sit with me at lunch because my aunt is the president's wife."

Sam smiled. "I do what I can for the people."

Jack giggled. "I knew you'd say that."

"Your mom says you might be worried about something happening to her, too."

He shrugged. "Kinda. I mean, my dad... He was fine, and then he was just dead."

"It's very rare for that to happen, especially to young people like your dad."

"If it can happen to him, it can happen to anyone."

"That's true, but your mom doesn't want you to worry about that. I know it's easy for me to say. My dad didn't die when I was seven, but it's very rare for someone to die suddenly the way your dad did."

"It's hard not to worry about it happening to other people."

"I know, buddy, but all worrying does is upset you about something that's probably not going to happen."

"It's hard not to worry."

"You have to try, or you'll make yourself sick."

"I feel sick." He rubbed his belly. "Right here. All the time."

Her heart broke all over again. "I know, baby. One thing I've learned since Gramps died, is that I won't always feel as bad as I did when it first happened. People talk about how time helps to soothe the wound, and it's kind of true. It loses the sharp edges that make us feel sick inside, even if we'll always miss the person we lost."

"I'll be glad when I don't feel this sick anymore."

"I'm so sorry you're going through this, Jack Sparrow. I'm sad for everyone, but I'm saddest for you because of how close you guys were."

"We had a lot of fun."

"I want you to remember that. When you're sad or feel sick or lonely for him, think about the things you guys did together and the fun you had. Hold on to those memories during this difficult time."

"That's a good idea. Thanks, Uncle Sam."

Laughing, Sam hugged him tightly. "That was a good one."

"I know," he said, smiling. "I was saving it."

"I wish there was more I could do for you."

"It helps to be here with you guys and to have other kids to play with. Are we going to live here with you now?"

"For a while. Eventually, you'll go home again, but not until your Mommy is ready to."

"I don't want to go home. It'll be too hard to be there without Daddy."

"We offered our house on Ninth Street to your mom and you kids."

He seemed to brighten a bit hearing that. "Are we going to live there?"

"It's up to Mommy to decide that, but maybe."

"That would be good," he said, sounding relieved.

"You need to get some rest, little man. It's time to turn off that busy mind of yours, close your eyes and have sweet dreams."

"I'll try."

"Come get me if you need me. You remember where my room is, right?"

"Yeah, I memorized the way."

Smiling, Sam kissed his forehead and smoothed a hand over his hair. "Love you, Jackpot."

"Love you, too, Samsonite."

"Another good one," she said, laughing.

"I used Mommy's phone to Google some new ones."

"Shhh, don't give away your secrets." She kissed him again and tucked the covers around his tiny shoulders that held the weight of his world on them. "See you in the morning."

"Will you be here?"

"You bet."

"Okay."

Sam turned on his nightlight and left the door cracked open the way he liked it. For a long moment, she stood outside the door, head back, eyes closed as she breathed through the tsunami of emotions.

That's where Nick found her when he came looking for her.

His unmistakable scent washed over her, providing immediate comfort. He curled his hand around hers. "Let's go to bed, babe."

CHAPTER FIFTEEN

S am and Nick went downstairs to their suite and closed the door.

"I simply cannot stand this," Sam said, turning into his embrace.

"How's Jack?"

"He's sick with grief, the poor guy. And what the twins said..."

"I know, love. All our poor babies have seen too much, too soon."

"I hate that the twins are afraid of losing us, too. Maybe I should've taken the deputy chief's job so I could be off the streets and safer. I was only thinking of myself when I turned it down."

"If you're unhappy, you're no good to anyone."

"It kills me that they're worried about us when we both have jobs that put us in danger."

"We're as careful as we can possibly be, and we're surrounded by world-class security."

"Still, the older they get, the more they'll realize they have good reason to be worried."

"I'll mention this conversation to the therapist before their next appointment," Nick said.

"She must cream her jeans every time she hears from you."

"Ew."

Sam laughed at the face he made.

"Thanks for putting that image in my head."

"I do what I can for the people."

"Speaking of doing what we can, I've given considerable thought to our loft not being currently available to us."

"Have you?" she asked.

"I have, and if you're in the mood to shed all your worries for a bit, I'd be happy to show you."

She had work to do, but when he looked at her that way, nothing else mattered. "Definitely in the mood to think about something besides death and murder for a while."

"In that case, if you'll come this way, I'll demonstrate the many ways this suite can be useful to us."

Sam took his hand and followed him into their large, marble bathroom. He positioned her in the middle of the long vanity, so she was looking into the mirror as he stood behind her.

"I want you to watch," he said, kissing the side of her neck before raising her sweater up and over her head.

Sam shivered at the hungry way he gazed at her breasts, contained in a lacy bra that she'd recently bought online and had sent to Tracy's house. Nick hadn't seen it yet, but judging by the way he studied it, he approved.

His hands moved from her hips to slide up over her ribs to cup her breasts. "Someone has been doing some shopping."

Her nipples tightened in anticipation of his touch, but he was in no hurry. "Maybe."

"I'm digging it."

"I thought you might." She sighed when she realized he was going to torture her and enjoy every second of it.

He touched her everywhere but where she most wanted him to, making her squirm against the tight press of his body against her back. Her knees felt weak, like they might give out at any second, but he'd never let her fall.

She knew that with a certainty she'd never experienced with any boyfriend or lover before him.

"Is my baby feeling eager tonight?" The heat of his breath on her neck sent a shiver through her that landed as a tight ache between her legs.

"Your baby is feeling murderous."

Chuckling, he said, "Nah, you'd never murder me. Too much paperwork."

Sam laughed and then gasped when he cupped her breasts,

holding her breath in hope that he might touch her nipples. But he denied her again. "Nick!"

"What, honey?"

"Come on."

"All in good time, my love."

She wanted to tell him she didn't have time. She had a murderer to catch. But he wouldn't want to hear that. Not now, anyway. And besides, it wouldn't compel him to move things along. When he was in this sort of mood, he took his own sweet time.

"You need to relax and let it all go for a few minutes," he whispered.

"Not sure I can."

"You can. Just look at me. Look at us. Let it all go."

He was good. She'd give him that. He always knew what she needed to hear and was the only person alive who could truly distract her when her mind was occupied with murder, especially one that had struck so close to home. With a twist of his fingers, he released the front clasp on her bra and pushed the straps down her arms until the garment fell onto the floor.

Sam's inclination was to look away from her own nudity, but he wasn't having that.

"Watch us," he said a little more sternly this time. "Don't look away."

Her breasts were too big, at least in her opinion. He said they were perfect, and as he held them and caressed them, she trembled from the need for more.

"Easy," he whispered, setting off goose bumps on her fevered skin. "Keep looking." His thumbs brushed over her nipples in a lightning-quick caress that was gone before it started, but it was nearly enough to make her come.

His hand slid down the front of her to unfasten the button on her pants, which were soon around her ankles, along with the panties that matched the bra. "My wife is the sexiest wife in the world."

That wasn't true, but he made her believe he thought so, and he was the only one who mattered.

She pressed back against his rock-hard erection, drawing a sharp gasp from him.

He pulled back only long enough to remove his pants and

underwear, and then his arms were around her again, one moving to her breast while the other cruised south to caress between her legs. "Mmm," he said when he encountered the evidence of her desire, "is someone enjoying this?"

"Not at all."

His laughter transformed his handsome face from sexy to sinfully so. "Liar."

All he'd need to do was brush against her clit to make her come, but of course he knew that, so he touched her everywhere but there. She was on the verge of begging when he pushed into her from behind, forcing her to lean forward on the vanity.

"Don't look away."

He met her gaze in the mirror as he moved in her, driving her crazy one deep stroke at a time. "What do we think of alternative-location sex?"

"We like it, but you already knew that."

"Doesn't hurt to be sure."

Sam prided herself on being the kind of woman who never begged a man for anything, but she was about to start begging when he suddenly tweaked her nipple with one hand and her clit with the other. The orgasm took her completely by surprise, thundering through her with power and heat that made her head spin from the impact.

"Now that's what I'm talking about," he said as he moved his hands to her hips to hold her still while he rode her release into his own.

Flat on the vanity, demolished, her mind was clear of all thoughts as her body vibrated with pleasure. He'd achieved his goal—and then some.

"Earth to Sam, come in, Sam."

"She's left the building."

His low rumble of laughter made her smile. She loved his laugh. She loved everything about him, which was funny in and of itself. Usually, she could find something not to like about everyone. But not him. Never him.

"What's happening in that pretty head of yours?"

"I was just thinking that there's not a single thing about you I don't like, and how odd that is because I can almost always find something I dislike about people."

"I'm oddly complimented by that."

"You should be. I hate people. But I love the hell out of you."

Nick pressed a kiss to the center of her back. "You loving the hell out of me has made my whole life. I hope you know that."

"Is it better than being president?" she asked with a coy smile.

"That had better be a rhetorical question," he said, giving her a light slap to the ass that made her gasp from the charge it sent through her body.

"Oh, my baby liked that." He did it again and again, until she was writhing beneath him as he moved in her.

If you'd asked her if she had a round two in her a few minutes ago, she would've said no way, but leave it to him.

The second orgasm was even more epic than the first, and as she came down from the highest of highs, she felt like a bowl of Jell-O.

Nick withdrew, cleaned her up and helped her to bed.

She felt like she could sleep for a week. So much for getting some work done.

He followed her into bed and curled up to her back. "What do we think of being creative while our loft is off-limits?"

"Mmmmmm."

"I'll take that as a positive review."

"Uh-huh."

"Love you, Samantha. Forever and ever."

"Love you more."

"No way."

"Yes way."

She fell asleep with a smile on her face and a persistent ache in her heart for Angela, Spencer, their children and all that had been lost.

AT NINE THE NEXT MORNING, Jake made the call to the 504 number he'd been given by the bar manager.

"Rosa residence."

"Hi there, my name is Jake Malone, and I'm an old friend of Tom's from the DC police department. I'm in town for a few days and wondered if it might be possible for me to see him?"

"Let me get Mrs. Rosa. She decides who gets in and who doesn't. Please hold."

Jake waited five minutes.

"This is Amanda Rosa. Who's this?"

He went through the introduction once again. "I know it's a lot to ask, but Tom and I are old friends, and when I heard he was ill, I came down hoping to see him." That was only a slight white lie.

"He's never mentioned you."

"We worked together a long time ago, but those were good years. Very good years." He winced as he poured it on thick, hoping it would help to sway her.

"Let me have your number, and I'll speak to Tom when he's awake."

Jake recited his number.

"I'll get back to you when I can."

"Thank you."

The line went dead.

He wondered how long he'd have to wait to hear from her and whether Tom would want to see him. If he didn't, he might die with information they badly needed, a thought that spiked Jake's anxiety. That happened whenever he thought about the absolute mess Stahl had left for them. He suspected they'd seen only the start of it, and with the U.S. Attorney reviewing past convictions tied to Stahl's shoddy investigations, he expected things to get much worse before they got better.

While he waited, he took a walk around the Quarter, had a couple of beignets with a strong cup of chicory coffee and people-watched. Bourbon Street was booming that Saturday morning, but he suspected this city was a lot like New York in that it never shut down.

He was contemplating a tour when his phone rang with a call from the 504 area code.

"Jake Malone."

"It's Amanda Rosa. Tom will see you at two. Let me give you our address." She recited the address as he scrambled to type it into his phone.

"Thank you both so much."

"See you then."

Again, the line went dead. Mrs. Rosa didn't screw around. She probably had no time for anything other than caring for her husband.

He put the Belle Chasse address into his phone to find out how far it was from the Quarter. About thirty minutes. He could grab an Uber. With time to spare, he returned to his hotel room to make a list of the most pressing questions he had for Rosa, such as:

Did you help Stahl archive reports of investigations he didn't actually conduct?

Did Stahl have something on you? Because why else would you do such a thing?

What else do you know about Stahl and his activities around that time?

Anything else you shouldn't take to the grave with you?

As Jake reviewed the list of questions, he hoped the wife wasn't planning to be in the room, because she'd probably shut it down as soon as she figured out that this was much more than a friendly deathbed visit.

AFTER VERNON DROPPED Sam at the morgue entrance, she stopped to see Lindsey. "Anything new on Mary Alice Albright?"

"Same as Spencer. Morphine in her brain. I'm ruling her death as suspicion of opioid toxicity."

Sam let out a low swear. "Did you do recent exams on Morgan Newell and Angelo Diaz?" As a matter of course, autopsies were performed on any potentially suspicious deaths that occurred in their jurisdiction.

"Let me check."

What did it say about the number of suspicious deaths in their jurisdiction that Lindsey did so many autopsies, she didn't immediately recall all the names?

"Byron did Morgan's." She clicked around on her computer, calling up the reports. "She had morphine in her brain, too, and was ruled as accidental overdose. Angelo's family declined the autopsy. I'll send you the full report on Morgan."

"How much you want to bet they're related to Spencer and Mary Alice?"

"I don't take bets I can't win."

"We have to find these people."

"You will. Work the case. Follow the leads. Do what you do. You'll get him."

Sam nodded. "That's what I needed to hear. Thank you."

"It never happens as fast as we'd like it to."

"No, it doesn't. We're issuing an alert to the public today that we suspect someone is selling laced Oxy, which will send our suspect deep under."

"But it'll save lives."

"Yeah, it will. I just hope it doesn't ruin any chance we have of catching them."

"Stay focused and pull the threads."

"Thank you for always knowing what I need to hear."

"I got you, boo."

Sam gave her a quick hug. "You're the best."

"Go kick some ass and take some names."

"I'm on it."

Energized by the pep talk from Lindsey, Sam exited the morgue and headed for the pit, determined to make some serious headway before her shift ended. "Everyone—conference room in five."

She went into her office to stash her coat and fire up her computer to review the full report on Mary Alice's autopsy. Other than the morphine, no other abnormalities were found during the exam. Just like Spencer.

In her email, she also found the report for Morgan Newell's autopsy that Lindsey had sent. Newell had morphine in her brain plus signs of liver damage, which Byron noted could be the result of a prolonged addiction.

She printed all the reports as well as the photos from the Newell and Diaz obituaries and brought them with her when she joined her team in the conference room. While they watched her from the table, she pulled a fresh murder board toward the head of the table and pinned up the photos of Spencer, Mary Alice, Morgan and Angelo.

CHAPTER SIXTEEN

"I now believe we have at least four victims." Sam pointed to each one as she introduced them to her detectives. "Three were found with morphine in their brains postmortem, which can only get there through opioids. In the case of Morgan Newell, Dr. Tomlinson also noted liver damage that could be the result of prolonged addiction. The family of Angelo Diaz declined the autopsy, but according to the report on the 911 call, his mother could give no known reason for his sudden death. As a result, I'm operating under the assumption that he may be a fourth victim. I believe these cases may be connected to one dealer. We need to find that person as quickly as possible. Our job has been made more difficult by the warning the department is issuing this morning, making the public aware that someone is selling laced pills to unsuspecting opioid addicts." She glanced at her sergeant. "Gonzo, did you hear back from the dealer you contacted yesterday?"

"Not yet, and that's not uncommon. If they don't have what you're looking for, they don't call back."

Sam absorbed that info with a growing sense of frustration and panic. Once the alert went out, this case would become a thousand times more difficult than it already was. "Cruz and I will visit the Newell and Diaz families this morning. I want the rest of you working on the leads that came from the dump of Spencer's phone. Green, check with Archie to see where we are with Mary Alice Albright's phone, and let's keep working on the info from

Spencer's. We'll see if we can get the phones of Newell and Diaz and get them processed as quickly as possible."

When someone knocked on the door, they turned to find their new deputy chief, Jeannie McBride, in the doorway. "Is this a private party, or can anyone come?"

"Come in, Chief," Sam said, smiling at her friend.

"I saw the alert about the Oxy and figured you guys would be hard on it. I'm having a bit of FOMO."

"Fear of missing out," Freddie translated for Sam.

"We're dividing up the work for the day," Sam said. "You're welcome to join us."

Matt O'Brien pushed the box of doughnuts he'd brought in toward Jeannie, who chose one from the box and sat next to Gonzo.

"What've you got?" Jeannie asked, eyeing the murder board.

As they brought her up to speed, she listened intently as she ate her doughnut and sipped from the bottle of water she'd brought with her. "Do we know whether there might be others?"

"That's on the list," Sam said. "O'Brien, go through all the autopsy reports from the last month and look for morphine in the brain, suspected opioid overdose or anyone who is especially young and died for no apparent reason."

"I thought you might want to check in with Roberto," Gonzo said of her longtime informant and friend. "He's often in the know about this stuff."

"Good idea. Cruz and I will stop at City Hall to see him. Any questions?" Sam's gaze took in each of the detectives and Jeannie. "Before we go, I want to let you know I've asked Officer Neveah Charles to join our squad to attempt to fill the very large shoes left by Deputy Chief McBride. As you know, I was deeply impressed with Officer Charles's attention to detail when she planned my dad's funeral, and I think she'll be an awesome addition to our team."

"That's a wonderful choice," Jeannie said. "I'll do what I can to expedite the paperwork."

"It's nice having friends in high places," Sam said, smiling at her.

"I do what I can for the people," Jeannie said with a grin.

"Hey! That's trademarked."

The others cracked up laughing.

"She outranks you, Lieutenant," Cruz said with a smirk. "You might have to let her use your lines."

"I suppose I can make an exception for you, Chief," Sam said. "But the rest of you have to ask first. Cruz, let's roll. Everyone else, keep me posted on any developments."

She went into her office to grab her coat and locked the door, since Ramsey would probably be back before long and might be tempted to ransack it again.

They walked out to the SUV, where Vernon waited to open the door for her. How did he know when she was coming? Did he have some sort of bug attached to her? She got in and slid over to make room for Freddie and then gave the Glover Park address for Morgan Newell's parents that had been listed in the incident report.

"I hate going to bother people who are grieving," Sam said when they were on the way.

"A necessary evil of the job," Cruz said as he downed a six-pack of powdered doughnuts and chased them with a Coke—after eating two in the conference room. Life wasn't fair for many reasons, but his ridiculous metabolism was at the top of her life-is-unfair list.

"When I show up, it causes a circus in addition to the grief."

"You know how to handle that."

"What's up with you today?" Sam asked, suddenly realizing her partner was lacking his usual sparkle and unfettered joy for powdered doughnuts.

"Nothing."

"Don't say nothing when it's clearly something."

"I don't want to talk about it."

"Too bad. Start talking."

"For God's sake, Sam. I said I don't want to talk about it."

Sam saw Vernon glance in the rearview mirror, as if he, too, was concerned about young Freddie. "Talk to me. You know you want to."

"I don't want to."

She was alarmed to see the starting of tears in his eyes. "Freddie... Now you're scaring me."

"Elin had a miscarriage, okay? Are you happy now?"

"Not at all. I'm so sorry."

"We said we weren't going to tell anyone."

"I'm not just anyone. I'm your best friend, and you needed to tell someone."

"Now Vernon and Jimmy know, too."

"We won't breathe a word of it," Vernon said, "and I'm sorry for your loss."

"Yeah, man," Jimmy said. "Very sorry."

"Thank you. Can we drop it now?"

"Yeah, we can." Sam dropped it, but she rode the rest of the way to the Newell's house with her hand on top of Freddie's. A new ache took up residency in her heart for a loss she understood far too well.

When they reached the address, Vernon pulled up to the curb. "Jimmy, stay with the car."

"Yes, sir."

Sam and Freddie went up the walk to a black front door bearing a wreath left from Christmas. Something about that wreath added to her sadness, as the occupants' lives had changed dramatically since someone hung the festive wreath. She rang the doorbell and stepped to the side to wait.

She was about to ring the bell again when the door opened.

A middle-aged man stuck his head out the storm door. "Help you?"

Sam showed her badge as Freddie did the same. "Lieutenant Holland and Detective Cruz, MPD, looking for the family of Morgan Newell."

His expression changed at the mention of Morgan's name. "What about her?"

"We're investigating a recent string of suspicious deaths and wondered if we might have a word with you about Morgan."

"Right now?"

"Right now."

"Um, sure. I guess."

"We're very sorry to disturb you and to intrude at such a difficult time. We wouldn't ask if we didn't feel it was urgent."

He stepped aside to admit them to a tidy, well-kept house. "What could be urgent about Morgan? She's dead." His voice quivered on the word *dead*.

Sam and Freddie sat together on a sofa.

"Are you her father?" Sam asked.

Nodding, he said, "Stepfather technically, but I raised her."

"And your name?"

"Jim Newell."

"We're very sorry for your loss, Mr. Newell."

"Thank you. It's been..." Sighing, he sat across from them. "It's been rough. My wife... She's not doing well at all."

"Can you tell us the circumstances of Morgan's death?"

"We, ah, we found her in her bed. She'd been gone for a while by the time we found her. Been three weeks now, but we're still as shocked as we were that first day. Doesn't go away." He paused, glanced at her, seeming to blink her into focus. "You're the first lady."

"Yes, sir."

"Wow. My daughter... She really admired you. She would've loved to have met you." He turned away when his eyes filled with tears. "She'd had some struggles, Morgan did. But she was doing so much better. So much better. Just landed a nice new job, was getting ready to move into her own place. It was all coming together for her. Finally."

He brushed at tears as if they infuriated him.

"We're so sorry for your loss. You mentioned she had some struggles... Would you mind telling us more about that?"

"What's the point of this?"

"We're investigating a string of sudden deaths among people in their twenties and thirties that may or may not be related."

"Related to what?"

"We'll get to that if you're able to give us some more info about Morgan."

He took a deep breath and then sighed. "She was a good kid, you know? Didn't give us any trouble. None of that typical teenager crap. Then she went to college at Mason, met some kids who ran a little faster than she did and caught the party bug. We thought it was a stage, and for the most part, it was, but they introduced her to Molly and X. From there, she moved on to Oxy."

There it is, Sam thought. "Was she addicted to Oxy?"

Nodding, he said, "For a couple of years. She went to rehab twice, and she'd been clean for four years."

"Do you think it's possible she relapsed?"

He leaned forward, elbows on his knees. "My wife and I... We've been round and round about that, and we just can't imagine she'd do that after being clean for so many years."

"Could someone have slipped her something?"

"I mean, sure, but she didn't hang with that crowd anymore. She had a nice group of friends who were more likely to be found at book club than a dance club." His face lifted into a small, sad grin. "That was how she described them."

"Where did she work?"

"She was the assistant manager of a trendy restaurant in Georgetown called Zénitude, which is a French word for calm and serene. She said it was a good word to describe her new life these last few years."

Sam had a thought. "Did she work with or know someone named Angelo Diaz?"

"There was a waiter named Angelo at the restaurant that she mentioned a few times, but we didn't know him. I'm not sure what his last name was."

Sam felt a tingle of sensation attack her backbone, which happened whenever she felt like she'd had a breakthrough in an investigation. "Can you think of anything from the last few weeks of her life that was suspicious or worrisome in any way?"

"There was one night, about a week before she died, when she didn't come home, didn't call or text to let us know she was staying out. That was wildly out of character for her since her last time in rehab. She knew how her mother worried about her and would never have given her reason."

"Did you find out where she was?"

"She said she ran into an old friend and lost track of the time. She was all apologies for making us worry. I was a little hard on her that next morning. I let her have it for worrying her mother, and she broke down into tears. I felt bad about that for days, but she needed to understand how we felt."

He glanced up at them. "Part of me couldn't believe I was still having that conversation with my thirty-two-year-old daughter. They say parenting never ends, but I was ready to be done with that part of it. All our friends' kids... They're married with big careers and kids and mortgages. Morgan was so far behind them, but she was catching up. At least we thought she was."

"Did her behavior change at all after the night she didn't come home?"

He seemed to give that some considerable thought. "Now that you mention it, she did become a bit withdrawn. We figured she was upset with us for making a big deal about that night and that she'd snap out of it eventually."

"And that lasted for the final week of her life?"

"Yes," he said, tearing up, "and I'll always regret that one of our last interactions was me screaming at her about being irresponsible and how sick I was of her bullshit." He swiped at a tear. "I'm going to have to live with that for the rest of my life."

"You said what any parent would after what you'd been through in the past," Sam said.

Freddie stood. "Excuse me."

Surprised by his sudden departure, Sam watched him go.

"My wife says the same thing you did about having every right to get after her, but still…"

"You couldn't have known what would happen a few days later. Can you tell me about that?"

He blew out another deep breath. "Morgan was a night owl. That's why restaurant work was good for her. She didn't have to be there until four and often worked until after midnight. She was usually up and about by late morning, but that day, my wife got home from doing some errands and found it odd that Morgan wasn't up yet. So she went to check on her…" He lowered his head. "I'll never forget that phone call at work. She couldn't get Morgan to wake up. EMS was on the way. She was completely hysterical."

Sam was struck by the similarities to Spencer's case and Mary Alice's. It had to be drugs from the same lot. "Would you mind if we took Morgan's phone to be examined?"

"When do you need it?"

"Now would be good."

He gave her a strange look as he got up to see to her request.

While she waited, Sam texted Freddie. *Are you ok?*

Yeah, just needed some air. Sorry.

Don't be. It's fine.

No, it isn't, but thanks for understanding.

I do understand—better than most would.

I know.

Her heart broke for Freddie and Elin, and she hoped they wouldn't end up in a protracted infertility battle like she'd endured. She wouldn't wish that on anyone, especially her best friend and his wife.

Jim returned and handed her the phone. "My wife says the code is Morgan's birthday, zero-two-one-five."

Sam made a note of the code.

"We'll get it back, right?"

"As soon as possible. I have to ask something else of you. Something deeply disruptive and invasive, but we need to search Morgan's room to make sure that whatever substance killed her isn't still in your home."

"For real?"

"I'm afraid so. We have four sudden deaths of twenty- and thirtysomething people in the last couple of weeks that may be linked to the same batch of laced Oxy. If those pills are still in your home, we'd need them for evidence in the case we're building against the dealer. Not to mention your safety."

He rubbed the back of his neck as he tried to process what she'd said. "You really think she OD'd? I just can't imagine that."

"Have you seen the autopsy report?"

"We have it, but neither of us can bring ourselves to look at it."

"Morphine was found in her brain. The only way that happens is through opioids. They might still be in your house, Mr. Newell."

He sighed with weary acceptance. "Okay. Fine. You can look."

"Is there somewhere you and your wife could go while we conduct the search?"

He seemed shocked to hear that they'd be required to vacate the premises. "Ah, yeah, we have friends down the street."

"Maybe you could call them and let them know what's going on and get your wife situated before our Crime Scene detectives arrive?"

"I'll do that."

"I'm sorry again about all of this."

"I am, too. Will you let us know if you discover something about Morgan's death?"

She held out her notebook to him. "Please write down your name and phone number for me, and I'll keep you posted."

He took the pad from her, wrote the info and handed it back to her.

"I really appreciate your help."

"If you can find some answers, that might help my wife. And me, too."

"I'll be in touch."

After he left the room, Sam called Haggerty and requested he and his team come to the Newell home to conduct a search for the pills that killed Morgan. While she waited for them, she walked out into the frigid winter air and zipped her coat against the stiff breeze that made it feel even colder than it was.

Freddie was leaning against the SUV, checking his phone. When he saw her coming, he stashed the phone. "What's our next stop?"

"Do you need to go home?"

"No, it's fine."

"Freddie. Does your wife need you?"

"She's really upset."

"Go home. I'll take it from here. Take tomorrow, too."

"I want to work on Spencer's case."

"I know you do, but you need to take care of your wife." Sam could see that he was seriously torn. "Go, Freddie, and let me know if I can do anything."

"You've got enough going on."

"I'm never too busy for you and Elin." She gave him a quick hug. "Go ahead, and don't worry about work."

"Tell me the truth…"

"Always."

"Will we get through this?"

"You will. I promise. It'll suck for a while, but you're young and healthy, and the good news is that she got pregnant in the first place. That's huge."

"We weren't even really trying, or well, not for long."

"Miscarriage happens far more often than anyone realizes until it happens to them. Please give Elin my love and tell her I'm here if she needs to talk to someone who understands."

"Thank you."

Sam hugged him again. "Go to her. That's where you need to be right now."

"In case I forget to tell you, you're the best."

"Duh. I know. Do you want us to take you to the Metro?"

"I can walk. Thanks again."

"Check in later."

"Will do."

He jogged off and disappeared around the corner.

Sam wasn't worried about him getting home. He had the Metro grid memorized, or so it seemed to her.

Vernon approached her. "Did you send him home?"

"I did. He's of no use to me today when his heart and mind are elsewhere."

"You're a very good supervisor."

"My dad used to say it doesn't cost anything to be human."

"No, it doesn't. What's next?"

"I have Crime Scene headed here to search for the pills that killed their daughter. After I get them started, we're heading to Georgetown and a restaurant called Zénitude. You'll have to look up the address. My smartphone access left with Freddie."

"I've got it," Jimmy said.

"Thanks."

CHAPTER SEVENTEEN

W hile Vernon drove them to Georgetown, Sam called Gonzo.
"Hey, what's up?"

"I just sent Cruz home. Elin had a miscarriage, which isn't for public consumption. His head wasn't in the game."

"So sorry to hear that. Is she okay?"

"She will be, and so will he. Just not today. I'm only telling you what's up because you're one of his supervisors."

"No one will hear it from me."

"Anything new on your end?"

"I'm working on trying to track down some people I'd like to talk to. They don't make it easy to find them, especially when a cop is looking for them."

Sam was about to reply to that when the SUV was hit head-on by a speeding car in a crash so loud it made her ears ring. "What the fuck?" Sam's body was jolted by the impact that deployed airbags in the front seat. "We just got hit hard head-on. Are you guys okay?" she asked Vernon and Jimmy.

"Yeah," Vernon said.

"Where are you?" Gonzo asked, sounding frantic.

"Wisconsin Ave."

"I'll get Patrol over there, and I'm on my way."

Sam bent to look out the window and couldn't believe who she saw sitting in the driver's seat of the other car. "Gonzo..."

"What?"

"It's Ramsey."

"Are you kidding me?"

"It's him."

"I'm coming."

Sam leaned over the seat. "Are you sure you're okay?" she asked Vernon and Jimmy.

"Took a hit from the airbag, but I'm fine," Jimmy said. "Vernon has a cut on his forehead."

"I want to get out," Sam said.

"Stay right where you are until backup arrives," Vernon said sternly as he accepted a tissue from Jimmy to tend to the cut.

"Are you okay?" Sam asked Vernon.

"I'm fine. It's a scratch."

Sam wanted to scream from the delay this would cause right when she was starting to make some headway. She took a call from the chief.

"What happened?" he asked.

"I'm on Wisconsin with my detail and we got hit head-on. Ramsey hit us."

"I'm on my way."

"Cavalry is coming," Sam told Vernon and Jimmy.

"From our house, too," Jimmy said.

Sam silently raged as half an hour became an hour, statements were taken, and Ramsey was arrested, screaming that they'd hit him, not the other way around.

"Maybe this will help me get rid of him once and for all," Farnsworth said to Sam.

"We can only hope."

"Do you need to be seen at the ER?" the chief asked.

"Absolutely not, but Vernon might."

"I'm fine," Vernon said.

As media vehicles began to arrive, Sam said, "Let's get out of here." She handed Morgan Newell's phone to the chief along with the piece of paper containing the code. "Would you please give this to Archie when you get back to the house?"

"Yes, I'll take care of it."

Vernon, Jimmy and Sam were transferred to a different Secret Service SUV after they assured their supervisors that they were fine.

Gonzo jumped into the back seat with Sam. "I'll stick with you since you sent Freddie home."

"I'm perfectly capable of going it alone, you know."

"I know. Where're we headed?"

Sam brought him up to speed on what she'd learned from Morgan Newell's father. "Angelo Diaz worked there, too, and I want to interview their work friends. After that, I want to talk to Diaz's family."

"I'm with you, LT," Gonzo said before taking a call. "Gonzales." He listened for a long time. "Where can I find him?" More listening. "Can you text me that info?" Another pause. "It won't come back on you. I'll make sure of it." He ended the call and glanced at Sam. "Getting closer to some of the bigger dealers in the area. People are reluctant to share the info, for obvious reasons."

"Since I might not make it to City Hall today, I'll try calling Roberto."

The friend she'd made two years ago while undercover with the Johnson family answered on the second ring. "Is this my lady cop first lady?"

Sam smiled, amused by him as always. "The one and only."

"Well, this is truly an honor. How you doin'? I still can't believe your old man is the president."

"Neither can I."

"Hey, I'm real sorry about your brother-in-law."

"Thank you. I need a favor."

"Anything for you." After Roberto was paralyzed in the shooting at the Johnsons' drug house, Sam had helped him get a job at City Hall in support of his effort to go straight. For the most part, anyway. "What can I do?"

"We think someone's selling laced pain pills. You heard anything about that?"

"Give me a minute," he said to someone else. "I'm talking to the first lady."

Sam winced. She didn't bother to remind him that she wasn't the first lady on the job.

"She don't believe me," Roberto said. "Will you tell her?"

"Sure," Sam said, rolling her eyes at Gonzo, who was trying not to laugh.

"Who is this?"

"Sam Holland Cappuano. Who's this?"

"You're really the first lady?"

"That's what my husband tells me."

"And you know Roberto?"

"We're old friends. Could I please speak to him again?"

"Told ya," Roberto said to the woman as he came back on the line.

"Back to my question..." She was becoming more frustrated by the minute by the delays that kept popping up. And she wasn't telling anyone that her neck was starting to hurt, probably from the crash. "Have you heard anything about laced pills on the streets?"

"A rumbling here and there. My pal Dino had a friend who turned up dead outta nowhere. He had an issue with Oxy a while ago, but he'd been doin' better. They don't want to believe he relapsed, but hearing there might be bad shit out there, I guess it's possible."

"Can you get me the name of the guy who died and your friend's contact info, too?"

"Yeah, I'll send it over by text."

"And you'll let me know if you hear anything else on this subject?"

"You got it."

"How's Angel?" she asked of his longtime girlfriend, who'd figured into a case of hers a while back when Angel had been kidnapped and raped.

"She's pregnant, Sam. Can you believe it? I did it. I got her pregnant."

"That's amazing. I'm so happy for you guys."

"We're gonna tie the knot one of these days. I'd invite you, but you're too fancy for us now."

"No, I'm not, and you'd better invite me."

"For real?"

"Hell yes. I'll even bring my old man."

"Shut up. Angel will die, and so will my mom."

"You know where to send the invite, right?"

"Yeah, lady cop," he said with a low laugh. "I know where to send it."

"Mark it personal. I hear that helps things get through the mailroom quicker."

"I'll drop it off at HQ to make sure you get it."

"That works, too. Good to talk to you, Roberto. Glad to hear you guys are doing well."

"That's thanks in large part to you, boss lady. You set me straight. Wouldn't be here without you."

"You set yourself straight. Don't give anyone else the credit for that. I'm proud of you and Angel."

"Means a lot to us. I'll be in touch soon."

"Take care."

"You, too. Stay safe out there."

Sam closed her phone to end the call and then reopened it to wait for the text from Roberto with the information about Dino and the friend who'd died.

"You're really going to his wedding?" Gonzo asked.

"I'm really going. I'm so proud of them both for surviving it all to get to this point."

"You're a good friend, Sam."

"I'm a crap friend who gets it right once in a while."

"You don't give yourself enough credit."

"We agree with the sergeant," Vernon said.

"You're not allowed to take anyone else's side but mine, Vernon."

"Duly noted, ma'am, but I still agree with him."

Gonzo laughed. "You're still working on getting them trained, huh?"

"Young Jimmy is coming along quite nicely, but the old guy is stubborn."

"Who you calling old?" Vernon asked, glancing at her in the mirror. "Ma'am."

"Just had to add that last part, didn't you?"

"Yes, ma'am."

Sam rolled her eyes at Gonzo. "They ma'am me to death."

"This is the place, *ma'am*," Vernon said as they pulled up to the restaurant.

"You see what I deal with?" Sam asked Gonzo.

"I love that they have you figured out."

"They do not."

"Do, too, ma'am," Vernon said with a cheeky grin.

"I'm reporting this to your supervisor. We're on a first-name basis after the accident."

"Knock yourself out, ma'am. Jimmy, stay with the car."

"Yes, sir."

As Sam, Gonzo and Vernon approached the Zénitude restaurant, Sam noted the exterior façade was painted black, and the name of the establishment was carved into a sign above the door that had been painted in gold foil. Bright red window boxes were still full of holiday greenery, which gave the place a festive appearance.

"Classy joint," Gonzo said as he held the door for her to go in ahead of him.

The young woman working the hostess desk did a double take when she saw Sam, who held up her badge to nip that in the bud. "Lieutenant Holland, Sergeant Gonzales, Metro PD. We'd like to speak to the owner or manager, please."

"Y-yes, ma'am. I'll get him."

"Another ma'am," Gonzo said with a snicker after the woman took off to find the guy they needed.

"Makes me feel like I'm seventy or something." Sam put her hand on the back of her neck and did a couple of stretches, hoping to address the ache. Just what she needed was another freaking injury.

"Do you have whiplash?" Gonzo asked.

"Nope."

"And you know that how?"

"Because I said so."

"The four mom words everyone says they'll never say to their own kids—or subordinates. You should get that looked at before it becomes a thing."

"I'll get right on that."

"How's Ang doing?"

"She's hanging in there but dreading the wake and funeral and all that. We had to wait for his brother's family to get home from Italy. She'd like to get it over with."

"What a nightmare."

"That it is." Sam continued to stretch her aching neck as she looked for the hostess. "Where the hell did she go to find this guy?"

"What if he's our guy?"

The second that registered with Sam, she took off running,

with Gonzo and Vernon chasing after her. She burst into the kitchen, startling the staff. "Where's the manager?"

"He went out the back."

"Gonzo, get the front."

Sam nearly bowled over the young hostess as she went through the back door to an alley. "Where is he?"

The woman recoiled from her shouted question.

"Tell me right now, or I'll arrest your ass and toss you in jail!"

"He heard you were looking for him, and he ran. I tried to follow him, but he was too fast."

"What's his name?"

"Richard Day."

"What's he wearing?"

"Black shirt, black pants."

"What's he look like?"

"White guy about six feet tall with blond hair."

"When I come back, I want every bit of information you have about him. If you need to call the owners, do it." Sam took off, realizing he had a five-minute head start on her and the chances of her catching up to him with a bum hip were slim. She went anyway, aware of Vernon following her as she jogged around the corner and down the block. She checked every storefront on the block, every alley, nook and cranny, but didn't see any sign of a man dressed in all black.

Dejected, she turned around to head back to the restaurant while using her portable radio to call in a description of the suspect to get Patrol officers looking for him.

Vernon walked along with her. "How's the hip?"

"Not great."

"You took off like a shot."

"Wasn't thinking about the hip." She'd pay for that later.

They met up with Gonzo outside. "Run Richard Day and see if he's in the system."

While he did that, she went into the restaurant. Sam was in pain from her hip and neck, but she pressed on, looking for the hostess. She was waiting for them at her post and handed Sam a piece of paper with Richard's name, address and phone number on it.

"Thank you. Do you know why he'd run from cops?"

"I don't," she said, her eyes big and spooked. "I haven't worked here long."

"Who has?"

She pointed to the bartender, and Sam went to talk to him. She showed her badge and took a seat, looking to give her hip a break. "What's your name?"

"Tim Child."

"You've been here awhile?"

"Five years."

"Why would Richard run from cops?"

"I don't know."

"Are you lying?"

"Nope."

"If I find out you lied to me, I'll be back for you."

"I know how it works. I was on the job in Baltimore for a decade."

She tipped her head to look at him more closely. He had dark hair and eyes and a neatly trimmed goatee with some silver sprinkled in. "Why'd you leave?"

"Blew out my knee and was gonna be stuck on desk duty if I stayed."

"I would've done the same. Has Richard been in any trouble?"

"Not that I know of, but something must be up if he ran from you."

"I tend to have that effect on people."

"It's pretty cool that you're still on the job with everything else going on."

"The White House stuff, you mean."

"Yeah, that," Tim said, grinning as he put ice waters on the bar in front of her and Vernon.

"I'd be bored senseless without the job." As soon as she said that she winced. "Sorry."

"It's okay. I've gotten used to the boredom. Nothing can compare to the rush."

"Very few things." Sex with her husband was a bigger rush. But nothing else was, that was for sure.

"Any idea where we might find Richard, besides his place, now that he's bolted?"

Tim pulled a pad from his pocket and made a note before pulling the page out and handing it to her. "A couple of places he's known to frequent. If you find him, be sure to tell him I sent you. He's a dick."

"Will do. Did Angelo Diaz work here?"

"Yeah, he did." Tim's smile faded. "He was a waiter. A good kid."

"What can you tell me about him?"

"He was young and still figuring things out. Lived with his mother in Kingman Park. I think he was an only child, which is so sad. He was just a goofy kid trying to find his way, you know?"

"Who was he close to here?"

"He was friendly with everyone. No one will have a bad word to say about him."

Sam wished there was a former cop waiting to help her everywhere she had to go on the job. "You must've known Morgan Newell, too, then."

"I did. Two of them a week apart. It was rough."

"Did Angelo have any drug issues that you knew of?"

"Something was off with him. He'd be totally fine for weeks, and then he'd show up whacked out on something."

"What about Morgan?"

"She was a great worker and colleague. Everyone loved her. The last week or so before she died, she seemed different, but I couldn't say why."

Sam took notes as he spoke, starting to wonder if Richard was the common denominator. "Were either of them close to Richard?"

"No one is close to him. He's highly unlikable. But we all have to deal with him as the general manager. I've told the owner—repeatedly—that he's making a mistake leaving him in charge here, but he hasn't been inclined to make any changes. Maybe he will after this."

"Have him give me a call, will you?" She slid her business card across the bar to him. "And tell him to make it snappy."

"I will."

"If you see or hear anything that might be of interest, give me a call."

He nodded. "Sure thing."

"Appreciate the professional courtesy."

"Feels good to be back in the mix, even for just a few minutes."

"Did you have any IT training on the job?"

"Lots of it. I worked with our IT squad for five of my ten years."

"Give me your contact info. I'll pass it on to our IT LT, who's always looking for tech-savvy people. You don't have to have a good knee to work on a computer."

He wrote down his info and gave it to her. "Thank you."

"Appreciate your help. Vernon, let's go."

"That was a very nice thing you did just now, ma'am," Vernon said as they walked out together.

"I'm a nice person."

"Won't hear me arguing."

"You'd better not tell people that, you hear me?"

His snort of laughter followed her out the door.

CHAPTER EIGHTEEN

Gonzo was on the sidewalk talking on the phone. "Did you issue a description of our guy?" he asked Sam.

"I did. Patrol is looking for him. Our next stop is his apartment."

"I gotta go," Gonzo said into the phone. "Talk to you later." He stashed the phone in his pocket as they got back in the SUV. "That was one of my informants. He might be on to something. He'll get back to me if he has anything."

"This case is making my head hurt."

"They all do."

"True, but this one is worse than most."

"Because it involves your sister's family."

"What did you find on Day?" Sam asked.

"The name Richard Day is an alias. He's also known as Richard Kent, which is his legal name. Under that name, he has numerous priors, including DUI and intent to distribute cocaine, heroin and meth. He did three years at Jessup on the drug charges and was released on probation eighteen months ago."

"I wonder if his probation officer knows he's using an alias."

"I highly doubt it. Call your probation officer friend Brendan Sullivan and ask."

"I'll send a text." *What can you tell me about a Richard Kent, out on parole after three years at Jessup for dealing? Also goes by Richard Day.*

Not one of mine, but I'll see what I can find out and let you know if I have anything. Might not be one of ours.

Thanks.

"He's going to get back to me if he's in their system."

Sam checked her phone and found a message from Haggerty. *Same white packet, same S20 pills found at Newell home, zipped into a pocket in her purse. HazMat is coming and will get them to the lab. Moving to Diaz home.*

Thank you for the update and the great work. Appreciate you.

He sent back a thumbs-up.

"CSU found the same pills at Morgan Newell's home," Sam said. "That makes three from the same batch."

"That right there is called progress," Gonzo said.

"If you say so."

"I say so."

Sam called HQ and asked for the Patrol commander.

"Dawkins."

"Hey, it's Holland. Just making sure you got the word that we're looking for Richard Day along with the description. Last seen in Georgetown."

"Yep, we got it, and we're on it."

"He's also known as Richard Kent, with a long list of priors, including a stint at Jessup. Please give me a call if you find him."

"Will do."

"Thanks." She slapped her phone closed. "Is it my imagination, or is Lieutenant Dawkins a little chilly?"

"I haven't noticed that."

"Maybe it's just me. I have that effect on people."

Gonzo laughed. "They're all just jealous of your success."

"If you say so."

"I do."

"Get the rest of the squad up here to help look for Day."

Gonzo sent a text conveying her orders to the rest of their team.

"What's the word on Ramsey and the ramming?" Sam asked.

"I heard Hill is involved."

"Really?"

"The chief called him and asked them to handle the case."

"I love that."

"I thought you might."

"What did he think was going to happen when he intentionally rammed a Secret Service vehicle?"

"I don't think he gave much thought to potential consequences."

"Is it weird that despite everything he's put me through, I feel a little sorry for the guy?"

"Yes, that's very weird."

"Hear me out."

"I'm listening."

"The guy clearly has issues. We know that. But to lose his son the way he did after finding out the kid was a violent, raping felon... I have no idea how any parent handles something like that, especially one who's given his entire adult life to Special Victims."

"I'm surprised you can feel an ounce of empathy for him."

"Well, I do. Not that I've forgotten what a nasty asshole he is, but I still feel for what he's going through after losing his son. He needs someone to blame, and he decided I was handy, as usual."

"He's a dangerous criminal, Sam."

"And he's a father who lost his son in the worst way possible."

"Yes, he's that, too, but don't let your guard down where he's concerned."

"I agree with the sergeant," Vernon said. "I don't want that guy anywhere near you. Ma'am."

Sam smiled at Vernon when he glanced at her in the mirror. "I hear you. I'm not so far gone with the empathy that I've forgotten who he really is."

"Glad to hear it," Vernon said.

"If the Feds are involved, his days of tormenting us at HQ are possibly over," Gonzo said.

"We can only hope."

FREDDIE ARRIVED home to a silent apartment. He stashed his weapon, badge and cuffs in the kitchen drawer where he kept them and hung up his coat. As he'd never been through anything like this, he took a full minute to prepare himself to be whatever his wife needed before he went looking for her in their bedroom.

He found her curled up on her side on the bed, eyes open but unfocused, like they'd been since the night before when she realized she was losing the baby they'd only just realized they were expecting. With her bent in unbearable pain, he'd rushed her to the ER and held her hand during the D&C she'd had early that morning.

She'd sent him to work, telling him she needed to sleep, but he hadn't felt right about leaving her.

He crawled onto the bed and snuggled up to her.

"What are you doing home?"

"Couldn't keep my head in it. I told Sam what happened, and she sent me home to be with you."

"That was nice of her."

"I hope you don't mind that I told her."

She shrugged. "What does it matter?"

"I wanted to tell her because I knew she'd understand how we're feeling, and she does. She said to call her if you need to talk to someone who's been through it."

"I don't want to talk about it."

"Even with me?"

"At all. It happened. We'll deal with it and go on."

"How do we deal with it if we don't talk about it?"

She turned onto her back, staring up at the ceiling. "What do you want me to say, Freddie?" Her stunning blue eyes flooded with tears that gutted him. "That I feel like a failure because I couldn't have our baby?"

"Don't say that, sweetheart. You know as well as I do how often pregnancies end in miscarriage. This baby wasn't meant to be. That doesn't mean the next one won't be."

"What if I'm like Sam? What if I can't ever have a baby?"

"Then we'll adopt like they did. One way or another, we'll have a family."

"I want you to have a baby that's ours," she said, sobbing. "I want to give you that."

"You've given me everything, Elin. Every single thing that I could ever want. If it was only you and me forever, I'd be more than satisfied. Please don't put that kind of pressure on yourself. This terrible, sad thing happened to us, but we'll be okay because we have each other." He reached for her and was relieved when she moved into his embrace and let him hold her. "It's going to be okay. I promise."

He held her for a long time, until he felt her finally relax into sleep.

Freddie hurt like he never had before, for her, for him, for the child they'd wanted so badly who was gone now. For as long as he'd worked with and been friends with Sam, he'd been aware of her ongoing fertility struggles, but until it had happened to him, he hadn't really understood how painful her journey must've been.

Exhaustion tugged at him after the sleepless night and emotional firestorm. As he gave in to the pull to sleep, he vowed to do whatever he could to get Elin through this and to try again as soon as possible.

JAKE MALONE PULLED up to Tom Rosa's home right at two o'clock. He'd watched enough HGTV with his wife to recognize the house as a craftsman style. The cozy porch was decorated with white wicker furniture and red floral pads on the chairs. He walked up the stairs and was about to knock when the inside door opened.

A blonde woman greeted him.

He figured she might want to see his badge, so he showed it to her. "Jake Malone, Metro PD."

"Come in. Tom was excited to hear you were in town and coming by." She stepped aside to admit him to the house. "I'm Amanda. It's nice to meet an old friend of Tom's."

Jake shook her hand. "Nice to meet you, too." He noted dark circles under her eyes and a pinched, strained set to her mouth.

"I'm not sure what they told you at the bar, but Tom... He's really sick. I just wanted you to be prepared... He doesn't look like himself anymore."

"I understand but thank you for the concern."

"Right this way."

Her warning in no way prepared Jake for the sight of Tom, shriveled and diminished in the hospital bed in what had probably once been a dining room. That reminded him of Skip, who'd been relegated to the former dining room at his house after the shooting.

Tom's eyes lit up at the sight of Jake. "This is a nice surprise," he said softly. "A blast from the past." It seemed to take all his strength to hold out his hand to Jake, who shook it gently.

"Good to see you, old friend."

"You, too. What brings you to NOLA?"

"I came to see you. Heard you were hanging your hat down this way these days."

"Been here almost twelve years now. Since right after I retired. You and Joe..." He coughed and tried to sit up a bit.

Amanda raised his bed.

"Thanks, hon." He glanced at Jake. "You and Joe... They're gonna carry you two dinosaurs outta there in pine boxes at this rate."

Jake laughed. "Still going strong."

"Fools."

He laughed again. "So we're told. Frequently."

"Heard about Skip. Awful sorry about that."

"Thanks. It was a tough one."

"And his daughter, the first lady..." He coughed again. "That's something."

"Sure is."

"What're they like? Her and the husband?"

"Good people. What you saw from him with the State of the Union... That's who he really is."

"He's been obsessed with the coverage of them," Amanda said. "That his old friend's daughter is now the first lady has given him something to look forward to every day when he watches the news."

"They'll like hearing that."

"Are they as nice as they seem?" Tom asked.

"Very much so. Our country is in good hands with them in the White House."

"She's a heck of a detective, too."

"One of the best I've ever worked with, tied for first place with her dad."

"You must miss him. You two and Joe were tight."

"We do miss him. Even after he was so grievously injured, he was still sharp as a tack and a huge part of our lives."

"And Conklin..."

"Don't get me started on that bastard."

"I couldn't believe when I heard he'd sat on info in Skip's case. I was shocked for days."

"We all were."

"Lenny Stahl, too. What the heck is wrong with him, trying to kill Skip's daughter—*twice*?"

"So many things are wrong with him. We've reopened some of his cases and are finding all kinds of irregularities."

"What do you mean?"

"Did you hear about the Carisma Deasly case? A missing teenager who was believed kidnapped by a family friend eleven years ago? That was Stahl's case when it first happened, and he filed in-depth reports that were pure fiction. They were found archived separate of the case files. Detective Jeannie McBride, who was recently named our new deputy chief, dug into the case, found Carisma in Richmond living in absolute filth along with ten other children. It's led to a massive human trafficking ring."

"Holy crap," Tom said.

"I read about that," Amanda added. "It made the national news."

Jake nodded. "Only took a couple of days to find her once someone bothered to care. Now we're reopening all his cases, even the successful prosecutions, to see what other corners he cut."

"He was always a bit of a creep," Tom said, "but I never thought he'd do something like that—or be convicted of attempted murder."

"None of us did." Jake paused as he tried to find a delicate way to pose the question he'd come to ask. "You don't remember anything about his reports being archived, do you?"

"I can't say that I do. Doesn't that require a captain or above?"

"It does."

"I never had much to do with him. I tried to steer clear. He was just one of those people we had to put up with, you know?"

"I sure do." Jake was relieved that Tom seemed to know nothing about the archiving of reports, but that left him with only one other captain from that time to ask, and with hindsight, he realized he probably should've started with Conklin.

"Your kids must be all grown up by now," Tom said.

"They are. Mel is practicing family law in Pittsburgh. She's married to a great guy. Chris is in LA, working for a company that provides support services to the film industry. He's been dating someone for a while but doesn't seem to be in any rush to make it official."

"Wow, they were in high school the last time I saw them."

"Time flies, doesn't it?"

"Sure does, especially when you're almost out of it."

"I was so sorry to hear you're ill."

"Came outta nowhere. Had a pain right about here." He placed his hand on his abdomen. "Was diagnosed with stage four stomach cancer a few weeks later."

"God, what a shock that had to be."

"Indeed, it was." He reached out to Amanda. "I finally found my true love five years ago and didn't get near enough time with her." Tears filled Tom's eyes and Amanda's.

"We've made the best of it," she said.

"Not enough time," Tom said, gazing up at her.

Jake was unbearably sad for them. "I won't take up any more of your time," he said, standing. "It sure was good to see you, old friend."

"You as well. Thanks for coming down." Tom held out his hand, which Jake shook. "If I think of anything that might help figure out who archived for Stahl, I'll let you know."

"I'd appreciate that. I wish you peace and Godspeed in your journey, Tom."

"Thank you."

Jake forced himself to leave Tom with a smile, even as he was filled with sadness for his old friend.

Amanda walked him to the door. "Thanks for coming. Your visit made his day."

"Thanks for having me at such a difficult time." He handed her his business card. "If there's anything our department can do for either of you, don't hesitate to reach out. The blue family takes care of its own."

"I appreciate that."

"Please keep me posted on how Tom is doing."

"I will."

"Take care of yourself, Amanda."

"I'm trying."

Jake walked down the block to summon an Uber back to the Quarter. On the ride to his hotel, he called Joe. "It wasn't Tom. He said he kept his distance from Stahl, like most people did. He was disgusted when he heard what he'd done with the Deasly case and asked what was with him trying to kill Sam twice."

Joe's deep sigh came through loud and clear. "Who does that leave us with?"

"Skip and Conklin, who I probably should've started with."

"Son of a bitch. It must be him. There's no way it was Skip."

"I would've said there was no way it'd be Paul either. He hated Stahl."

"Stahl must've had something on him," Joe said, sounding as disgusted as Jake felt. "Can you talk to him when you get back to town?"

"Yeah, I'll take care of it."

"In the meantime, Forrester is pressuring me for a full investigation into all of Stahl's cases, starting with the successful convictions. I'm going to divide that up among the various squads that investigated the cases. Deputy Chief McBride is going to oversee it for me."

"That's an excellent plan. She'll do a great job."

"I fear this situation is going to get a whole lot worse before we see the end of it."

"I agree."

"When are you coming home?"

"Going to try to get a flight tonight."

"Keep me posted, and tomorrow, I'm going to work on getting you back here where you belong."

"Hey, Joe..."

"Yeah?"

"Seeing Tom so sick has me thinking about a lot of things."

"Such as?"

"Life after the MPD."

"Don't you do this to me."

"We need a plan to exit together before too much longer. Tom was living his best life, happily married for the first time, then lightning struck, and now he's got months to live, if that. I don't want to see that happen to either of us."

"I don't either, but we've got to clean up this mess Stahl left us with before we go anywhere."

"Agreed, but after that, we need to have a conversation."

"I'll talk to you then."

"It's a date."

CHAPTER NINETEEN

While the others looked for Richard Day/Richard Kent, Sam went to see Angelo Diaz's mother in the Kingman Park neighborhood, feeling the usual dread about intruding on grieving people.

On the way, she received a text from Roberto. *Friend of the friend is Cory White. Died two weeks ago. No one knows why. You can find the family in Columbia Heights off 16th. Well-to-do peeps. My guy knew him thru work at MedStar. My friend is an orderly. White was a PA.*

Very helpful, Sam replied. *Thanks so much. Let me know if you hear of anything else on people dying suddenly who are otherwise fine. And make sure I get that wedding invite.*

You got it, lady cop. You da best.

I know! I tell everyone that.

He responded with an LOL.

Sam told Gonzo what Roberto had told her. "We'll hit them up after this."

Since she had a few minutes, she composed a text to Archie. *Met a guy today who used to be on the job in Baltimore. A bad knee sent him into early retirement, but he has a lot of IT experience and is sharp. He's bartending in Georgetown. I told him I'd pass along his info to you if you have any openings. He might be an asset to your team.* Sam included Tim's name and phone number and sent the text. With that, she'd done her good deed for the day.

Archie responded a few minutes later. *Thanks. I'm always looking for good people. I'll give him a call.*

That'd be awesome. I think you'll like him. He helped me a lot just now with valuable insight.

You getting anywhere?

SLOWLY

I'm hearing some rumblings that Narcotics is making noise about you working this case without them.

For F's sake. I'm investigating homicides, and last I heard, that was my job. Besides, if they hadn't dropped the ball on reporting OD deaths, we might not be in this boat, and I might not be attending my BIL's wake on Sunday.

Don't shoot the messenger. Cooper was hot about it earlier.

Thanks for the heads-up.

Sure thing.

"What is it with men and their egos?" Sam asked. "I'd really like to know why they have to get all hot under the collar when a woman is doing something they think they'd be better at."

"What now?" Gonzo asked.

"Cooper is making noise about our investigation and how it should include his team."

"We're investigating possible homicides."

"As you heard me say. Not to mention, it's been brought to my attention that Narcotics was several weeks behind in collecting OD data from the local hospitals, data that might've been instrumental in stopping my brother-in-law and others from buying laced pills. And PS, can I do anything without people getting riled up about me?"

"It doesn't seem so."

Sam rubbed her neck, which hurt almost as much as her hip did after chasing after Day. "It's not enough that I've got Ramsey coming for me in traffic, and Offenbach wants to shoot me for outing his affair. Now I gotta deal with Cooper, too?"

"You should've taken the deputy chief's job when you had the chance," Gonzo said with a laugh. "Then you'd be their boss."

"Bite your tongue. I wanted nothing to do with that, as you know."

"Did you hurt your neck in the crash?" Gonzo asked again.

Sam pulled her hand down from her neck. "No."

"Are you lying?"

"No."

"Yes, you are."

"Bite me. I'm not injured."

"I'll pass on the biting, but if you hurt yourself, ignoring it won't make it go away. Exhibit A is your hip."

Sam turned on him. "Whose side are you on, anyway?"

Gonzo held up his hands, as if to fend her off. "Yours. Always yours. I don't want to see you have permanent injury from whiplash."

"You can't get permanent injury from whiplash."

"Yes, you can."

"No, you can't."

"Vernon?" Gonzo asked with exasperation.

"Yes, you can," Vernon said.

"Another reminder that as *my* agent, you're supposed to always be on *my* side."

"I am, ma'am," he said with a grin in the mirror.

"My neck is fine, but I've got a pain in the ass where Cooper is concerned that I don't need right now."

"Just ignore him and keep doing what you're doing."

"Spinning my wheels?"

"Working the case. Pulling the threads. Doing what you do."

"Still nothing from your contacts?"

"Nothing solid. I'm working every angle."

Sam sighed. "Give me a nice shooting or knifing or strangulation over drug ODs any day."

Gonzo sputtered with laughter. "There is so much wrong with that sentence, I don't know where to begin."

Vernon and Jimmy laughed.

"Well, it's true! I feel like we're hunting ghosts in the night or something."

"We are."

"I rest my frustrating case."

The Diaz family lived in an apartment complex off C Street Northeast. As they trooped to the third floor, Sam ignored her aches and pains to stay focused on the case. With Narcotics wanting in on the investigation, she had to step up the pace to close it before they forced their way in.

She knocked on the door to apartment 3F and stepped to one side while Gonzo stood on the other. Vernon hung back as he always did, there if needed, but out of the way.

A heavyset middle-aged woman answered the door, her mouth falling open when she realized who was there.

Sam held up her badge while Gonzo did the same. "Lieutenant Holland, Sergeant Gonzales, Metro PD. Could we have a moment of your time, please?"

"Is this about my Angelo?" she asked tearfully.

"It is."

"Come in." She led them to a living room full of religious items. Mass was playing on the TV, and rosary beads sat on an easy chair. She picked up the beads and muted the TV. "What's happened?"

"Before we get to that, could we have your name?"

"Evelyn Diaz."

"Can you tell us what happened to Angelo?"

Her eyes immediately filled with tears. "He went to bed one night after work and didn't wake up the next morning." Her chin quivered as she relived the horror. "The doctor said he probably had an undiagnosed heart condition."

"Was there an autopsy?"

"No. I didn't want that done to his body."

"Even if it would give you answers about what happened to him?"

"What does it matter what happened? My only child is gone forever. That's the only detail that matters."

"Was he friends with Richard Day, the restaurant manager?"

"He couldn't stand that guy."

"What if I told you we have evidence that his death might've been a crime?"

"What evidence do you have?" she asked warily.

"Several young, healthy people have died in recent weeks. We believe their deaths might be tied to laced pills purchased illegally on the streets."

"My Angelo would never buy illegal drugs."

"Maybe he didn't buy them. Maybe someone gave them to him and told him they were regular headache pills or something. Anything could've happened, but without an autopsy, we can't say for sure that Angelo is one of our victims."

"He's already been buried."

"We have several things we'll need to do to decide whether he was one of our victims."

"What things?"

"We'd like to search your home to see if the pills he might've taken are still here. If they are, they're highly toxic and would be a danger to you and anyone else who might encounter them."

"What else?"

"We'd like to examine his phone, and if none of that gives us the information we need, we might ask you if we can exhume his body and have him tested to determine if he's one of our victims."

Evelyn recoiled. "I'll never allow that. His resting place is sacred."

"I understand that, but if someone is responsible for his death, don't you want them brought to justice?"

"What would it matter? My son is still dead. I'll never give consent to have him exhumed."

"Are you aware that another of his coworkers also died suddenly around the same time Angelo did?"

"I am," she said sadly. "He went to her funeral two days before he died."

"We believe their deaths might be connected."

Evelyn looked shocked. "How can that be?"

"It's possible that someone gave them both laced pills that killed them. We want to get that person off the streets before this tragedy happens to another family. You and Angelo could help us do that if you allow us to fully investigate his death."

"It goes against everything I believe in to disturb his final resting place."

"I understand and apologize for asking you for such a thing. I hope it won't come to that."

"If I agree to this, will everything be done with the utmost care and respect?"

"You have my word."

Tearfully, she said, "All right, then."

"May we take his phone for examination?"

Sighing, Evelyn got up to get it. "This is very precious to me, as you might imagine."

"We'll get it back to you the minute we're finished with it. Do you have the code?"

"It's eight-one-eight-zero. Please don't make me regret helping you."

"I promise you won't."

"I'll hold you to that."

"May we have your permission to search Angelo's room for evidence and to make sure there aren't lethal pills still in your home?"

"The thought of strangers in my home, going through his things..."

"They're police officers, ma'am. They do this all the time and will be respectful of your home and Angelo's possessions."

"You really think this is necessary?"

"I'm sorry, but I do. If we find the pills, we may not need to exhume him."

"That would be a blessing, I suppose. Okay, you can do it."

"Thank you, and I'm sorry again to put you through this on top of losing your son." Sam stepped into the hallway to make the call to Haggerty. "I've got another possible crime scene."

GONZO ARRANGED for Patrol to take Mrs. Diaz to her sister's home in New Carrollton, Maryland.

"What the hell is happening?" Haggerty asked Sam when he and three of his officers arrived at the Diaz home. "I left the rest of my team at the Newells', making sure there weren't more pills to be found."

"We're up to five sudden ODs that I know of, and I expect to find more before we're done."

"Is one of them your brother-in-law?"

"Yeah, but that's not public knowledge."

"I understand. We'll get going and let you know what we find in both places."

"There might be more after this."

"Argh. You're killing me."

Sam laughed. "Sorry."

"It's all right. We'll get it done."

Back in the car, Sam gave Vernon the address for the White family and then called Captain Andrews. "It's Holland," she said when he answered with a terse, "Andrews."

"What's up?"

"We might need a body exhumed, and I've never had to do that before. I'm not sure what the steps are."

"I'll have to look into that and get back to you."

"Thanks." The phone line went dead. "Wow. Everyone is so happy to hear from me." She made a joke, but inside, it pained her to realize her colleagues resented her for whatever reason. It could be any number of reasons. Such as her successful case close rate, her personal relationship with the captain and chief, her new role as first lady, the fact that she was a woman in a job still considered male territory. Who knew?

Each person with a beef probably had a different reason. Such as Offenbach, who blamed her for outing his affair—and the ensuing demise of his marriage—when he was the one having sex with someone who wasn't his wife when he was supposed to be at a work conference. So, yeah, that was her fault.

Whatever.

People needed to grow the fuck up and get over themselves. She opened her messages and composed a text to Malone. *When are you coming back?*

Soon, I hope.

Good. I need you.

What's up?

I might need to exhume a body and have no clue what's involved.

Get a warrant to cover your ass.

How do I do that? You always do it for me...

He replied with the eye roll emoji. *I'm at the airport about to get on a flight back to DC from NOLA. I'll fill out the form for you and send it to your email. What's the name of the deceased?*

Angelo Diaz.

Got it. Will shoot it over shortly. You'll need to fill in the narrative justifying the request.

Can do. You're the best.

I know.

Haha. Get your ass back here. I need you!

Working on it.

"Malone said we need a warrant to exhume. He's filling out the form for me and sending it to my email."

"That's good of him," Gonzo said.

"Yeah, because God forbid I ask Andrews for that. What the hell am I going to do when Malone and Farnsworth retire? The whole department will turn against me."

"You've got a very powerful ally in the deputy chief's office now,

don't forget, and if Webster is still mayor when Farnsworth retires, she'll promote Jeannie in a heartbeat."

"That does make me feel a little better," Sam said, "but I get so sick of jackass men hating me because I'm good at my job and refuse to stroke their fragile little egos."

"I'm sure it gets old after a while."

"It does, and it's only gotten worse since the recent developments."

"You mean your husband becoming president, making you the first lady?"

"Yeah, that."

"People resent success, Sam. You know that. They're jealous."

"So that means they're abrupt and even nasty with me when we're forced to interact?"

"That's their issue, not yours."

"It becomes my issue when I have to deal with it."

"I hate to say you might have to get used to it, because the higher your profile rises, the more out of joint they'll get."

"Awesome. Something to look forward to."

"Try to ignore it," Gonzo said. "What do you care if they're resentful? They'd all like to *be* you."

"It bugs me because I've worked hard my entire career to be a team player. I've always got the backs of my colleagues, even if they're stabbing me in mine."

"The people who matter know that. The rest can go fuck themselves."

Sam laughed.

"Who cares what they think? You're great at your job, and now the whole world knows it. You're a superstar, and they're not. It's that simple."

"And that complicated."

"Just keep doing your job and try not to sweat what other people think."

"I'll work on that."

"Here we are," Vernon said when he pulled up to a brick house that took up at least half the block.

"Wow," Sam said when she looked out at the palatial home. "Fancy."

"Says the lady who lives at the White House," Gonzo said.

"Not because I want to!"

Gonzo laughed.

"But don't tell Nick I said that."

"Your secret is safe with us," Gonzo said.

Vernon gave a thumbs-up to agree with him.

"I really hope you guys don't decide to write a tell-all or something."

"You've got enough worries without adding that to the list," Vernon said as he helped her out of the car.

"Yes, I do."

"We will never speak a word of what goes on with you, and Jimmy knows I'll cut his tongue out if he ever talks about you to anyone."

"He means it, too," Jimmy said, wide-eyed.

Sam laughed. "Excellent mentoring, Vernon."

"I do what I can for the people."

"*Everyone* is using my lines lately."

"They're good lines," Vernon said as he followed her and Gonzo up a flight of stone stairs.

"I know. That's why I trademarked them."

CHAPTER TWENTY

S am rang the doorbell, which chimed loudly inside the house. "Another day, another doorbell that would scare the crap out of me if I lived here. Why do people want doorbells like that?"

"Um, so they can hear them?" Gonzo replied.

"There's hearing them and then there's being attacked by them."

A woman came to the door. "May I help you?"

Sam showed her badge while Gonzo did the same. "Lieutenant Holland, Sergeant Gonzales, Metro PD, to see the family of Cory White."

"What's this about?"

"I just told you what it's about."

"They're not taking visitors."

"We're not visitors. We're cops."

"Wait here." The woman slammed the door in their faces.

"Was it something I said?" Sam tried to peek into the side windows to see where the woman had gone.

"Do you think she'll be back?" Gonzo asked.

"She'd better be. I'm giving her five minutes to produce a person named White, or I'll be ringing that air raid siren doorbell again and again and again until I drive them out."

"And you wonder why your charm is lost on people," Gonzo said.

"I don't wonder."

Four minutes and thirty seconds later, the door opened. A man with a thick shock of white hair glared at them. "What's this about?"

Sam held up her badge and introduced them. "We're investigating the death of Cory White. Are you a relative?"

At that, his expression softened ever so slightly. "He was my son. Why are you investigating it? We already know what happened. He overdosed."

"May we come in for a moment? We have some questions and would appreciate your cooperation."

"This is not a good time."

"I understand, and we're very sorry to intrude, but this is a Homicide investigation, so it needs to be now."

They engaged in a staring contest until he blinked and stepped aside to admit them.

"What do we have to do with homicide? Cory overdosed. He was an addict for years." The man led them into an elegant sitting room, the type reserved for company that never came.

"Could we please have your name?" Sam asked.

"Gerald White."

She and Gonzo sat across from him on a settee so delicate, Sam feared it would break under their combined weight.

"Can you tell us about the day Cory died?"

His erect posture sagged a bit. "He... He lived in our pool house."

"How old was he?"

"Twenty-five as of Christmas." With a small smile, he added, "He was our Christmas baby, the youngest of our six children."

"We're so sorry for your loss."

"Thank you. It's been..." He looked up at them with tears in his eyes. "You think you've seen everything life can throw at you until you lose a child." Shaking his head, he wiped away tears. "I wouldn't wish it on anyone."

Sam tried to be patient with him as she waited for him to continue.

"As I said, he lived in the pool house, but he was in and out of here all the time. That day, my wife, Kathy, thought it was odd that he didn't come in for coffee before leaving for the hospital. He was finishing his training as a physician's assistant, had just signed a lease on his first apartment and was doing so much better than he had been."

"You said he'd been an addict for years?"

Gerald nodded. "He did four trips to rehab. The last one seemed to have finally worked, but he was under a lot of pressure at work. The last stages of PA training are rigorous, and he wasn't sleeping much. We were concerned that the stress would threaten his recovery, but when we brought that up with him, he didn't want to hear it. He said he had things under control and that we had to learn to trust him."

His expression was a cross between a grimace and a grin. "That was hard for us after what he'd put us through over the years."

"What was his drug of choice?"

"Oxy and then heroin when the Oxy became too expensive." He cleared his throat. "We... We had to cut him off from all resources, but somehow, he still found a way to score. I hope you can appreciate... It was just a fucking nightmare of never knowing when we were going to wake up to cops at our door telling us he was dead. And we were so, so hopeful after this last rehab. He was different after that. More determined than we'd ever seen him to stay sober and finish his training. He was regularly drug tested at work, and that gave him the incentive to stay clean. We were so encouraged by his progress." He sighed as his eyes filled again. "Sorry, it's so hard to talk about this."

"We appreciate you sharing it with us."

"So that day, when he didn't come in for coffee, Kathy went to check on him. He was... He was on the floor next to his bed, like he'd been crawling and just collapsed or something. She could tell by his coloring that he was dead, but she called 911 anyway. She called me at work and was so hysterical, she couldn't breathe, and I knew. I just knew he was gone. It was like I'd been waiting all this time for that news or something. I'm not sure if that makes sense, but that's how it was. It was like a self-fulfilling prophecy or something."

Sam's heart broke for him and his family and the terrible ordeal they'd endured. "We believe someone is selling laced Oxy. Cory would be the sixth person that we know of who's overdosed recently. We expect there could be more."

"You're saying that someone is deliberately killing people with laced pills?"

"Yes, we think so."

"Why would they do that? Dead addicts are bad for business."

"We aren't sure how or why, but we've attributed five recent sudden deaths to possible fentanyl poisoning in people who sought Oxy illegally."

While he struggled to process this information, she pressed on. "Was there an autopsy performed on Cory?"

He shook his head. "We didn't see the point. We knew what killed him."

Sam was afraid he would say that. "Would you allow us to search Cory's room and phone to try to determine if his death is related to our case?"

"How would you know if it is?"

"That would depend on the evidence. In several instances, we've found pills in small white envelopes that came from the same batch. You also should know that if those pills are still in your home, they present a danger to everyone who lives here."

That seemed to get his attention as he sat up straighter. "You can search the pool house. That was the only place they'd be."

"And his phone?"

"I'll get it for you."

While he was gone, Sam glanced at Gonzo, who was looking somewhat paler than usual. "Are you okay?"

"Yeah, it's just, you know, hard to hear this stuff and to realize it could've been me who was given laced pills. Any time you procure illegally, it's a crapshoot."

"We're all very thankful it wasn't you."

"I feel so bad for him and his wife. They did everything they could to save their son, and it wasn't enough. I think about Alex and what I'd ever do..."

"You'll be so vigilant. Extra vigilant because of your own history."

"But will that be enough?"

Before Sam could reply, Mr. White returned with an iPhone that he handed over to her along with a slip of paper containing the code to open it. "Will we get it back?"

"As soon as possible. Are we authorized to bring in Crime Scene detectives?"

He nodded.

"Thank you for your cooperation."

"If it turns out that Cory was murdered... As strange as it sounds, that might provide some comfort to my wife and the rest of our family. To know it wasn't his fault. I'm not sure if that makes sense."

"It does," Gonzo said. "It makes sense."

"Let's see if we can get you some answers," Sam said.

WITH THE CSU pushed to the limit, Haggarty said the soonest they could get to the White home would be the following morning. Sam asked Mr. White to keep the pool house off-limits to everyone in the household until the detectives could do the search.

On the way back to HQ, Sam received a text from Haggerty. *White packet of pills sitting right on Diaz's desk, same S20 marking. HazMat on the way.*

Thanks for the update. No need to exhume him now.

You were gonna?

If I couldn't find the pills.

Damn. On to the Whites' house in the AM.

Thank you.

When they arrived back at HQ, Sam stopped at the morgue to speak to Lindsey while Gonzo took White's phone up to Archie. "Tell me something, Doc," Sam said. "How is it that twenty-or thirtysomething people can die under suspicious circumstances, and they're not automatically autopsied?"

"Could be for any number of reasons, such as the family refusing it or us not having the staff to perform every autopsy that ought to happen as a matter of course. If I had my way, anyone who died under suspicious circumstances would come through my office. But unfortunately, I don't live in that world."

"I see, and no judgment. I was just wondering how that works."

Lindsey sighed and sat at her computer station. "I'm sorry. My frustration isn't with you. It's with the budget constraints we're all forced to work under. Many families pay for private autopsies if they aren't done by us. If we could examine everyone, maybe we would've caught on to the fact that someone was selling laced pills before your brother-in-law—and the others—became victims of this person."

"Yeah." Sam sat at another computer station, feeling defeated on several levels. "That would've been good."

"I'm really sorry I couldn't stop it from happening to your family."

"It's not your fault, Linds. Don't take that on. Most of us do what we can."

"I hate when all we can isn't enough."

"Did you hear about Narcotics dropping the ball on the OD reports?" Sam asked.

"I did, and it's outrageous. Something like that should never be postponed."

"No, it shouldn't."

"What happened with Ramsey today?"

"He rammed my Secret Service SUV in a moment of utter stupidity, because now the Feds are involved."

"Which could turn out to be a good thing in our campaign to be rid of him."

"Let's hope so."

"Are you hurt?"

"Not really."

"What does that mean?"

"My neck is kinda hurting, but it's nothing I can't handle."

Lindsey got up and came over to Sam. "Hold still."

Sam did as she was told while Lindsey performed an in-depth examination of her neck and upper back that more resembled a massage than an exam. "If you could keep that up for an hour or two, I'd appreciate it."

Lindsey laughed. "I wish I had the time. Everything feels okay, but if it's still hurting in a day or two, you should have it checked more thoroughly."

"I will."

"No, you won't, so I'll stay on you about it."

"Whose idea was it to have doctor friends?"

"Haha, very funny. We're very convenient to have around. I bet you could even get an X-ray right at the White House."

"They sent me to the hospital for the hip thing."

"Because everyone but you knew that thing was fractured."

"Whatever."

"Blame the ice, not the doctors."

"The doctors are more convenient, and they don't melt." Sam glanced at her friend. "Can I tell you something else?"

"Anything."

"It's getting to me a bit that everyone here seems to hate me unless they're in my squad or one of my close friends."

"Who could blame you when your former LT tried to kill you —twice—and now all this nonsense with Ramsey?"

"It's not just them, though. I've had contact with Dawkins and Andrews this week that was chilly at best, and now I hear Cooper is coming for me because I haven't brought Narcotics in on the investigation after they dropped the ball in the first place. It gets exhausting after a while."

"I'm sure it must, but here's what I know. You're the best at what you do, and when you're the best, everyone else is less than the best. That burns their asses, so they take it out on you, which is totally unfair. But that doesn't stop them."

Sam tipped her head as she studied her friend. "It sounds like you've experienced some of this yourself."

"Damn straight, I have. I'm the first female ME this department has ever had, and if you think that's been without its challenges, think again."

"I guess you would know what it's like."

"I know all too well, but it's even worse for you now that Nick is president. People are jealous, Sam."

"Gonzo said the same thing."

"It's true. Their ordinary lives are never going to be anything more than they are right here and now, but yours... Yours is extraordinary, and they resent that."

"I've never understood jealousy. I don't have a jealous bone in my body. If someone else does well, I'm happy for them. I don't get the point of envying them their success."

"So, you'd be fine if another woman came on to Nick?"

Sam's gaze narrowed. "Absolutely not."

Lindsey smiled. "Which means you have at least one jealous bone in your body."

"He's off-limits, but I don't suffer from professional jealousy. I don't understand that concept."

"Roll with me here, but who in this department is more professionally successful than you are?"

"There're people. Like Jeannie."

"She's had a good month, but overall, she can't touch you. No one can, and they know it."

"Hmm, well, I guess I hadn't thought of it that way."

"I hate to say you have to suck it up, deal with their shit and try not to let it bother you. They're not worth it."

"I'm so thankful for you and my other true friends in this place. I'd be lost without you all."

"We love you. We're proud of you—and Nick—and we want only the best for both of you. That's called true friendship."

Sam got up and hugged her. "I really needed this. Thanks, Doc."

"I'm here any time you need me."

"That's very comforting. I've got to get back to figuring out who's killing people in my town."

"Keep me posted on how I can help."

"Will do."

CHAPTER TWENTY-ONE

After Sam left the morgue, she went upstairs to find Archie, relieved that there was no chance she might run into Ramsey. The SVU office was across the hall from IT, which had made coming up there risky for her when Ramsey was underfoot. She walked past the IT cubicles where officers were hard at work on computers and knocked on Archie's door.

"You received Morgan Newell's phone?"

"Delivered by the chief himself, and thanks for the heads-up that he'd be popping in." The IT lieutenant was a handsome, dark-haired man with a quick grin.

"Oops."

Archie laughed. "Good thing I made them clean up yesterday."

"Good thing indeed." She handed him phones belonging to Angelo Diaz and Cory White, along with the paper containing the codes. "I'm looking for commonalities with Spencer, Mary Alice, Morgan, Angelo and now Cory White."

"Got it. It's been slow going. Spencer had more than sixty thousand calls, texts and messages on his phone."

"Damn. He used it for work. That's probably why."

"Yep, but it's been a slog. We're running his dump against Mary Alice's now, looking for common numbers. I'm not sure you'll find anything, though. These guys are smart. They know what we look for and how to avoid detection."

"Burner phones."

"That and blocking caller ID and other tricks."

"Thanks for trying," she said, feeling dejected. "Why does it have to be so hard to find a dealer who's killing people?"

"Is that a rhetorical question?"

"No, it's a real question. You'd think the public would want to help us find this guy before someone else has to die."

"They're afraid of being charged with buying drugs in the first place."

"I guess."

"Anything more from Cooper?"

Sam shook her head. "I'm ignoring him and his hell-raising since his team failed to keep up with the OD reports that might've alerted us to this situation much sooner—in time to save my brother-in-law and others, so he can fuck right off."

"Wow, I hadn't heard that."

"I'm trying not to be bitter about the failings around here, but sometimes it's damned hard not to be."

"I don't blame you. This is a case that involves multiple squads within the department, but you had it first."

"Yes, I did, and Cooper is going to have to claw it out of my cold dead hands."

"Let's hope it doesn't come to that."

Sam walked away laughing, as she often did when she talked to Archie.

She returned to the pit, feeling fortified by the chats with Archie and Lindsey. It was a relief to have good friends and helpful to know she wasn't the only one chafing against the old boys' network within the department, not that she would wish that nonsense on anyone, especially someone as great as Lindsey. In her office, Sam tossed her coat over the chair and fired up her computer.

While she waited, her gaze shifted to the photo of her and her dad that she kept on the desk. A pang of longing for him swept over her. He always knew just what she needed to hear whenever her spirits were low. She could almost hear his voice telling her to shake it off and fuck the bastards who gave her crap. That put a smile on her face because it was exactly what he'd say, along with "build a bridge and get over it" or "kill 'em with kindness."

Good advice, Skippy.

Avery Hill appeared in her doorway. "Got a second?"

"Sure. Come in."

He stepped in and shut the door. "Talk to me about what happened earlier."

"There's not much I can give you other than one minute we were cruising along, and the next minute, we were hit hard. Vernon probably had a better view of it than I did from the back seat."

Avery took a couple of notes. "I'm talking to him next. Give me a little background on your history with Ramsey, other than recent events."

"Ah, jeez. How much time do you have?"

"As much as it takes."

Sam went through a recitation of various altercations with Ramsey. "One time, I tried to get away from him by pushing him away and sent him down the stairs. He ended up with a fractured wrist and concussion. For a time, I worried about being charged, but Forrester took it to a grand jury, which declined to indict. I realize that was a lucky break, but it only added gas to Ramsey's fire when I wasn't charged."

"Has he threatened you?"

"Numerous times. Malone and Gonzales witnessed the most recent two times. We were also able to prove that he tossed my office, but he said his fingerprints being in there was because we work together, which we most assuredly do not. I go out of my way to avoid him. Every time we think we've seen the last of him around here, the union intercedes on his behalf."

"After today's stunt, he's facing three federal felony counts of assault with a deadly weapon, as well as three additional counts of assaulting federal agents and a police officer."

Sam's entire day immediately improved. "Wow."

"This is serious, and he knows it, so be careful. I'll tell your detail the same. He's locked up for now, but he'll make bail and be released in the next day or two."

"Ugh, why can't you keep him locked up? He's repeatedly proven he's dangerous. Many people here can attest to that."

"Who else besides you and your squad?"

"Detective Erica Lucas. She works with him in SVU and has been on the receiving end of his vitriol on many an occasion."

"I'll talk to her. While I have you, I wanted to update you on our investigation into your mother-in-law."

Sam sat up a little straighter. "Don't tell me you haven't found any dirt on her."

"Quite the opposite. I asked some of our Ohio-based agents to investigate her, and it seems she's running a high-end escort service for clients aged sixty and older."

For a second, Sam's brain went blank with shock. "Are you kidding me?"

"I wish I was. They've worked meticulously to make their case, and they're taking it to a grand jury this week. I wanted to let you —and Nick—know that she could be indicted."

"Oh damn," Sam said on a long exhale as her stomach gave a twinge of anxiety. What would Nick think of Sam sending the Feds to investigate his mother and getting her in big trouble? Hopefully, he'd see it as a good thing... "Keep me in the loop on that?"

"I will, but you should give Nick a heads-up."

"Yeah." *Jeez, be careful what you wish for.* Sam had wanted Nicoletta out of their lives, which was why she'd asked Avery to take a low-level look at her. She'd expected him to find something, but this... This would be a huge embarrassment to Nick. Damn it.

"I'll be in touch," Avery said as he left her office.

"What was that about?" Gonzo asked when he came in.

Sam updated him on the Ramsey situation and how he was facing federal felony charges. "Close the door." When the door was closed, Sam told him about Nicoletta.

"Yikes. Does Nick know you asked Avery to investigate her?"

She shook her head, eager to get out of there for the night. "I didn't want to bother him with it if it turned out to be nothing."

"I think you'd better bother him with it—sooner rather than later."

"I was afraid you'd say that."

WORK KEPT Nick busy late into the night, so Sam never got a chance to talk to him about what Avery had told her. After a restless night, Sam received word at six a.m. from Detective Matt O'Brien that they'd located Richard Day/Kent and were bringing him in. "Pleasant sort of guy," Matt said, sounding aggravated.

"Aren't they all?"

"This one is more so than most."

"Thanks for working all night to track him down."

"Glad to have found him."

After breakfast with Nick and the kids, Sam left for HQ, calling the U.S. Attorney's Office on the way and asking to speak to an assistant USA.

"Please hold."

The hold music was hideous. She needed to talk to Nick about providing funding to the U.S. Attorney's Office to improve their music. That was better than telling him she'd sent the FBI after his mother, and she might be facing indictment for prostitution. That was just what they needed with everything on the upswing after his State of the Union address. She would make sure to get some time with him later to discuss that with him.

"Faith Miller."

"Hey, it's Sam Holland. Can you come by to witness an interrogation?"

"Which case?"

"A new one that I need to brief you on beforehand."

"I'll be there shortly."

"Thanks."

She'd no sooner put down the phone than it rang with a call forwarded from her extension at HQ. Freddie must've set that up. "Holland."

"This is Kyle Atkins, the owner of Zénitude. I understand you came by yesterday, asking about Morgan and Angelo."

"Yes, I did." Since she wasn't sure what his angle was, she said as little as possible.

"I was out on a boat offshore all day yesterday and only just heard about your visit. Can you tell me more about what you're looking for?"

"We recently issued an alert about fentanyl-laced pain medication being sold illegally."

"I saw that. Is that what you think happened to Morgan and Angelo?"

"We're looking into their deaths and the sudden deaths of numerous other local residents with a possible connection to the same dealer."

"And you think that's tied to my place somehow?" he asked, sounding slightly hysterical now.

"We don't know anything yet, other than that two young people who worked for you died recently under suspicious circumstances. We suspect that Morgan most likely died from fentanyl poisoning."

"Fentanyl? My God. Tim said Richard ran off when he heard you wanted to speak to him."

"Are you aware that Richard Day isn't his real name?"

"What? No."

"His real name is Richard Kent, and he's on probation for dealing cocaine, heroin and meth. He did three years at Jessup and was released late last year."

"Oh my fucking God," he said on a moan. "He had an outstanding résumé and sterling references."

"I believe you were had by a career criminal, Mr. Atkins."

"What kind of liability am I looking at if he sold laced pills that killed my employees?"

"I'm not sure, but you might want to check with your attorneys."

"This cannot be happening. Do you have any idea how much goes into getting a restaurant off the ground, let alone making it profitable? We're just starting to make real progress, and now this."

Sam wasn't sure what she was supposed to say to that.

"Will you keep me informed of the investigation?"

"Probably not. You're not a person of interest currently, and you're not a victim."

"Two of my employees are dead. I'd say that makes me a victim."

"Give me your number. If I have time to update you, I will." She wrote down the number he recited.

"Thank you."

"Sure." Sam put down the phone and made a note of the info he'd provided, not that it was much of anything. She really did feel for the guy. He was right. It wasn't easy to get a business off the ground or to make a success of it.

Faith Miller came in, wearing a sharp black suit, closed the door and took a seat. "Today has already been a day and a half, and it just started."

"Sorry to hear it."

"Your friend Stahl and his shenanigans are causing a lot of trouble. I've got lawyers filing requests for new trials left and right."

"That didn't take long."

"Nope. I wanted to tell you how sorry I was to hear about your brother-in-law."

"Thank you."

"I've been thinking of your sister and family. What a shocking thing."

"It was, and it's why I asked you to come by."

Faith tilted her head, eyeing Sam with trepidation. "Okay..."

"Here's what I know." She went through the details of the cases involving Spencer, Mary Alice Albright, Morgan Newell, Angelo Diaz and Cory White. "Each of them died unexpectedly in the last three weeks. The first three were found to have morphine in their brains during autopsy. Diaz's family refused the autopsy, but we found pills in his home. Crime Scene is headed to the home of Cory White, whose parents also declined the autopsy. If we can find pills that came from the same batch as the others, we can make some conclusions without autopsies for Diaz and White."

Faith took notes as Sam went through the facts of the case.

"The manager of the restaurant where Newell and Diaz worked is a convicted drug dealer who did three years at Jessup and is on probation. His name is Richard Kent. The people at the restaurant knew him as Richard Day. When we stopped by to talk to the staff, he ran from us. We tracked him down, and he's on his way in now. I thought you might want to watch the interrogation."

"You thought right, but Sam... Should you be investigating this one?"

"Gonzo is signing the paperwork. My name won't be on it."

Faith seemed to give that some thought. "I suppose that could work but be careful. We don't want to compromise the prosecution."

"Trust me. That's the last thing I want."

Her phone chimed with a text from Haggerty. *Found the white packets and S20 pills strewn about in the Whites' pool house. The mother said she hasn't been in there since she found him dead. Too painful. Good thing because possibly lethal powder was all over the place. HazMat on the way.*

Another one tied to the same batch that had killed Spencer. *Good work*, she replied to Haggerty. *There are probably going to be more. Will let you know.*

Standing by.

Sam appreciated the sort of cooperation Haggerty and his CSU team provided on most of her cases.

Gonzo appeared in the doorway. "We've got Richard in interview two. Figured you'd want to take the lead."

"You figured right." Sam put her hair up in a clip, grabbed her pad, pen and a bottle of water and followed Gonzo to the room.

They were almost there when Detective Cameron Green came running into the pit looking freaked out. "I can't find Gigi."

CHAPTER TWENTY-TWO

S am pivoted and walked toward Cam. "What do you mean?"

"I was out all night helping to look for Kent. Gigi texted that she was going home from my place this morning." His voice was as shaky as his hands. "I texted her a while ago, but she didn't reply, which is weird because she always replies. I've tried calling her a couple of times, and I just went by her place. Her car is out front, but she didn't answer the door. I don't have a key." He ran his hands through his hair as if trying to keep his head from blowing off his neck. "We haven't gotten there yet, and I don't know what to do. I feel like something is wrong, because she'd never let me worry this way after everything with Jaycee."

No one could miss the underlying hysteria in his voice. "Are you able to track her phone?"

"It's off. It's never off. I feel like I'm coming out of my skin."

"What about Jaycee? Are you able to track her phone?"

He shook his head. "I deleted her out of my phone after she slashed my tires."

To Gonzo, Sam said, "Let's get Jaycee's mother on the phone and find out where she is."

He went to see to that while Sam guided Cam into the conference room.

"This is exactly what I was afraid of. I told Gigi we should take a break, but she wouldn't have it. She said we're cops, and we can take care of ourselves. But what if Jaycee hurts her?" His voice caught. "I don't know what I'd do."

Sam kept a hand on his shoulder while she put through a call to Gigi's partner, Dani Carlucci.

"Hey, LT, what's up?"

"Cameron is here and says he can't get in touch with Gigi. He said her phone is off."

"We never shut off our phones."

"He's worried. Do you have a key to her place?"

"No, but her mother would. Should I call her?"

"I think so. Gonzo and Cam will meet you there."

"I'm on it."

"Keep me posted."

"Will do."

Gonzo came back from calling Jaycee's mother. "She hasn't seen her since last night. She can't track her phone."

"Go with Cam to Gigi's place. Dani is calling Gigi's mother to get keys and meeting you there."

"Should we get SWAT over there to ram the door?" Gonzo asked.

Sam thought about that for a second. "Yeah, do it."

"Address?" Gonzo asked.

Cameron gave it to him.

Gonzo made the call

"You don't really think..." Cameron swallowed hard.

Sam put a hand on his shoulder. "Try not to think the worst."

"Right, why would I do that?" He seemed to realize who he was talking to. "Sorry."

"Don't be. Go with Gonzo and keep me in the loop."

As they took off, Sam hoped and prayed that Gigi was okay. Then she had to get herself together and force her head back into the interrogation of Richard Kent.

Captain Dawkins came into the pit. "What's up with you guys calling SWAT?" He was tall and thick, with reddish-gold hair and broken blood vessels in his face.

"It's possible that Detective Dominguez is in some sort of trouble, and we need their help breaching her residence."

"What makes you think she's in trouble?"

Summoning patience she didn't have, she quickly recapped the trouble Detective Green's ex-girlfriend had caused since he'd begun seeing Detective Dominguez, including throwing a rock through Detective Green's window and narrowly missing them.

"Lotta drama in your squad, huh?"

"Pardon me?"

"Always something happening with some member of your team."

"How is being harassed by an ex who can't take no for an answer drama on our part?"

"Just saying. Seems like a lot."

"Are you here to help? If not, I have work to do."

When he didn't reply, she opened the door to interview two, went in and shut the door, sitting across from Richard Kent, who was still wearing the black shirt with the restaurant's logo. His wispy blond hair was standing on end, and he looked terrified.

Good. She wanted him afraid.

"Why'd you run from us?"

"I didn't. I had somewhere to be."

"And you just happened to have somewhere to be when you heard cops were asking for you?" She leaned in, making eye contact with him. "Here's what I know, Richard. Innocent people don't run from cops."

"I didn't do anything."

"I just talked to Kyle Atkins."

Richard flinched.

"You know what he was surprised to hear? That your real name is Richard Kent, and you're on probation after doing time for dealing drugs. He was positively shocked to learn you lied to get the job at his restaurant."

Richard dropped his head into his hands. "I need that job. I have kids to support."

"Tell me what you know about the bad dope sold or given to Morgan Newell and Angelo Diaz."

His head whipped up. "What?" He looked and sounded genuinely shocked, or he was doing a good impression of shock. "I don't know anything about that. I had nothing to do with it."

"Here's the thing, Dick, I don't believe you. Consider the facts. We've got a convicted drug dealer working with two people who turn up dead within a week of each other due to overdoses, and you expect me to believe you had nothing to do with that?"

"I didn't!"

Sam sat back and crossed her arms, staring at him without blinking.

He stared right back, also not blinking.

"Why'd you run from us?"

"Because I'm on probation, and any time cops show up, it freaks me out."

"When have cops shown up before today?"

"After Morgan and Angelo died."

"Who was it?" Sam asked, flabbergasted to hear that someone else had investigated their deaths, but she'd heard nothing about that.

"I can't remember who it was. Some big, bald dude."

"Cooper?"

"Yeah, that was it."

Sam was outraged to hear that the Narcotics lieutenant had investigated their deaths and did nothing to alert the public or the department that someone was possibly selling laced pills. That information could've saved Spencer's life—and Mary Alice's, among others. She felt sick all over again as she processed that news.

"Can I go?"

"Do you know anything at all about where those laced pills came from?"

He squirmed in his seat. "No."

"You're lying." She leaned in again. "This is a Homicide investigation. You can be charged for obstruction if you don't tell us what you know. Do you want to end up back at Jessup? What good will you be to your kids then?"

To her immense frustration, he began to cry. "I'm trying so hard to go straight. Do you know what that's like when you're used to making the kind of money I made before? It's really, really difficult."

Sam stayed quiet, hoping he would say more.

"The people in that world... They're bad dudes."

"I assume they must be if they're selling pills that they know will kill people."

"They don't always know that. Sometimes, they get stuff from others and only find out it's bad when they hear someone dies."

"Am I supposed to feel sorry for them?"

"No, I'm just saying... It's not always the fault of the frontline dealer."

"If you give me something that helps, I might consider letting you go. After I fully investigate the lead, that is."

Once again, he dropped his head into his hands. "If I tell you anything, they'll kill me. They might kill me just because they know I'm in custody."

"We have ways we can protect you."

"And my family?"

"Yes."

His deep sigh echoed through the small room. "There's a guy named Riggs Lawton. Lives in a penthouse in Shaw. If you want insight into the drug business in this town, he's your guy."

"Is he a customer at the restaurant?"

"I've seen him there a few times."

"What's he look like?"

"Handsome white guy. Drives a Bugatti and lives large."

Sam wrote down the name and other details. "Stay here."

"For how long?"

"As long as it takes."

She met Faith in the hallway outside the interrogation and observation rooms. "I tend to believe he didn't know where the pills came from—or he's putting on a good show for us."

"I agree."

Sam put through a call to Gonzo, anxious to know what was up with Gigi. "Anything?" she asked when he answered.

"SWAT is getting ready to go in. I'm this close to cuffing Green to keep him from jumping the gun. He's out of his mind."

"Can't say I blame him. Keep me posted."

"Yep."

After the line went dead, Sam glanced at Faith. "What do you think about Cooper sitting on the fact that two workers from the same restaurant died under suspicious circumstances in the same week?"

"I think he's going to wish he'd done something about that before you're through with him."

"Right you are. Why can't people just do their fucking jobs? Do your job and my brother-in-law isn't dead."

"That was my thought, too. I can't imagine how you must feel."

"I'm pissed and outraged and all the things."

"What're you going to do about it?"

"Normally, I'd take it right to Malone, but I'm not sure I can trust Dawkins, the captain on duty."

"Call Malone and ask what he'd do."

"That's a good idea."

"People are on edge around here since the FBI report hit and the Stahl stuff. It's been a lot. I'd recommend treading carefully."

Sam eyed her longtime colleague warily. "Are you giving that advice to everyone or just me?"

"Just you, so far, but it applies universally. People have a lot of 'feelings' about Ramsey's son being killed."

"I was there. He was going to kill that woman if we didn't take him out."

"Still... There's a sense that more could've been done to keep it from getting to that point."

Sam laughed, but it had a bitter edge to it. "I love a good Monday-morning quarterback. Anyone who was there will say the same thing. He wasn't going to let her go, and there was no way she was getting out of there alive if we hadn't taken him. If you don't believe us, ask her."

"I have."

That shocked Sam. "Are you investigating it as a crime?"

"I'm investigating it in conjunction with IAB's inquiry."

"The involvement of the USA gives a routine inquiry a different level."

"I understand. We're being thorough. I expect it will go the way you want it to in the end, but in the meantime, tread lightly. People are on edge."

"Over me being first lady, too?"

"I've heard some of that."

"Do you have a problem with it?"

Faith held up her hands. "Not at all. Don't shoot the messenger."

"I'm not really sure what message it is you're trying to convey."

"Look at it from an outside perspective. You have a long-running beef with Ramsey, and you're standing next to Malone, your father's close friend, when the order is given to take his son."

"I had nothing to do with giving that order, Faith. The captain did what needed to be done to defuse the situation before we added another victim to Shane Ramsey's list. I'll take whatever flack that comes my way if it means saving that innocent woman's life. And I have no doubt the captain would say the same thing."

"He would," a voice said behind them.

Sam spun around to find Captain Malone in uniform. "You're back." She'd never been so happy to see him in her life.

"I am. Is there a problem, Faith?"

"No problem," Faith said. "I need to get back to the office. Sam, keep me in the loop on the investigation."

"I will."

"What was that about?" Malone asked when they were alone.

"I have no idea. I feel like she was giving me some sort of warning, but I can't say for sure. And she let on that the USA is investigating the Ramsey shooting."

That clearly shocked him as much as it had her. "Why?"

"IAB brought them in on it."

"What the hell? Why would they do that unless they thought a crime had been committed?"

"I have no idea. Are there Ramsey allies in IAB?"

"He doesn't have a lot of allies. Wait... Walcott."

"Who?"

"His first partner, Doug Walcott, is in IAB now. I think he might've been Shane's godfather. Damn, I never even thought of that."

"Well, that explains a lot." Sam gestured for him to come to her office with her. When he closed the door, she updated him on the situation with Gigi and Cameron's fear that his ex might be involved.

"I would've thought that two felony charges would've scared her straight."

"Or it made her think she has nothing left to lose."

CAMERON GREEN WAS LOSING his mind one minute at a time as it seemed to take forever for the SWAT team to get into position to breach Gigi's townhouse.

"They aren't going to break the windows, are they?" the super asked.

Cam wanted to punch his teeth out. Despite Gigi's hysterical mother arriving with a key, SWAT had decided to go in through all points of egress at the same time.

"If they do," the super said, "I hope she's got good insurance."

"Will you please shut up and go away?" Cameron gave him his most sinister look until the guy did what he asked and moved away from Cam, saving the guy's teeth. Right about now, he was capable of that and much worse.

He'd known something terrible was going to happen, but he'd let Gigi talk him into going forward with their relationship despite his fear that Jaycee wasn't done with them yet.

A hand landed on his shoulder.

He startled and then turned to see Jeannie. "I came as soon as I heard. What's the latest?"

"Waiting on SWAT. They're taking their own sweet time."

"They want to get it right."

Cam knew that, but in this case, all he cared about was Gigi and making sure she was safe. He had a terrible, sick feeling in his gut. If she was hurt, he didn't know how he would cope with knowing his ex was the one who'd harmed her. His knees buckled, and only Jeannie's hands on his arm kept him from falling.

"Come sit," she said.

"I don't want to."

"Don't make me order you, friend," she said with a kind smile.

Cameron let her lead him to a bench in a common area within sight of Gigi's front door. Thanks to Jeannie's radio, he could hear the chatter of the SWAT commander communicating with his team.

Gigi's partner, Detective Dani Carlucci, came over to be with him, bringing Gigi's sobbing mother with her.

"Everyone is in place," the SWAT commander said over the radio. "Can we get the order to go in?"

"So ordered," Jeannie said as the senior officer on the scene.

Cameron held his breath as the SWAT team blasted through windows and doors. What if he was wrong and she wasn't in there? What if he'd overreacted and caused massive damage to her home all for nothing?

It wasn't nothing. His gut was telling him it was definitely *something*. Gigi didn't just fall off the grid. None of them did that. Their job required they be accessible all the time. The only time they checked out was when they were on vacation, and she wasn't on vacation.

"Clear."

"Clear."

"Clear."

Every report was like a knife to his heart.

"Captain! Up here."

Cameron took off running toward the front door.

Jeannie and Dani were right behind him, holding him back.

He fought against them with everything he had, desperate to get to Gigi.

"Call EMS. Tell them to hurry."

Cameron's knees buckled under him. "Oh my God. Gigi..."

Dani attended to Gigi's hysterical mother while Jeannie kept her arms around Cameron.

"Breathe," Jeannie said. "They called for EMS, not the ME."

"Please, Jeannie. Let me go to her." He pulled his arm free of her grip and ran for the door, flashing his badge at the officer who met him. "She's mine. Please..."

"You need to prepare yourself..."

Cameron died a thousand deaths as he raced up the stairs to Gigi's bedroom where the activity was centered. In the doorway, he stopped short at the sight of her, bruised and bloody, sitting on the bed, wearing a robe. Her big dark eyes shifted to him, but she barely reacted to him. Her service weapon was in her lap.

Jaycee was on the floor in a pool of blood.

"Possible DOA," one of the SWAT officers said, using his chin to point to Jaycee.

Relieved beyond measure that Gigi was alive, Cameron sat next to her and put his arm around her.

Every muscle in her body stiffened.

"Baby..." He couldn't speak or breathe. "It's me, Cam. I'm here, and I love you. I love you so much." He would be forever thankful that she'd survived whatever had happened.

Gigi trembled violently as he held her.

"We need to take your weapon, Detective Dominguez," Jeannie said as one of the others called for the ME. That meant Jaycee was dead. All he felt was relief that she couldn't hurt either of them ever again. If that made him a monster, then so be it.

"She... She said she was going to k-kill me..." Gigi said.

"You're safe now," Cameron said as he blinked back tears. "I've got you."

CHAPTER TWENTY-THREE

D ani came to the doorway with Gigi's mother, who collapsed into hysterics when she saw the blood.

"She's okay," Dani said. "Look. She's okay."

Mrs. Dominguez's wails seemed to shock Gigi out of the stupor she'd been in.

"Mama. I'm okay." She held out a hand to her mother, who sat on the other side of her on the bed.

"We'll need a statement, Detective," Jeannie said, following the steps required in a situation like this.

"She needs medical treatment first," Cameron replied. "Let's get the EMTs up here to tend to her."

Jeannie called for paramedics.

"I'm okay," Gigi said, even though she was bleeding from multiple cuts on her face, neck and arms.

Cameron held her until the paramedics arrived. He kissed her cheek and got up so they could gain access to her. While they tended to her, he called Sam.

"Did you find her?"

"Yeah, she's okay, but banged up. There was an altercation in her bedroom. She shot Jaycee, who's DOA."

"Oh God."

"I think it was a close call, LT. She might've... She could've killed Gigi."

"I can't imagine what's going through your mind right now but focus on whatever Gigi needs. Malone is back. I'll ask him to come with me."

"Jeannie's here, too."

"That's good. It's a clear case of self-defense, Cam. She did what was needed to stay alive. That's how this will go."

"I hope so."

"Stay calm and be there for her. I'm on the way."

When the line went dead, Cameron stashed his phone in his pocket.

Dani came over to him. "This is so fucked up."

"She looks wrong in the eyes."

"Probably will for a while. She's never fired her weapon on the job."

Cameron took a deep breath and released it slowly, the implications multiplying so rapidly, he barely had time to process one before another needed his attention. This was going to wreck her—and them.

And it was all his fault.

ON THE RIDE TO Gigi's place, Sam filled Captain Malone in on the latest with the fentanyl investigation. "Not only did Narcotics totally drop the ball on the weekly OD reports, but Cooper knew that two employees at the same restaurant had overdosed and didn't sound any kind of alarm or investigate any further as far as I can tell. If he had, Spencer and the others who died recently might still be alive."

"Maybe he was in the process of investigating?"

"I don't know what he was doing, but he sure as hell didn't put out an alert that perfectly healthy people were turning up dead, and the likely culprit was fentanyl."

"I know this is super personal to you, Sam."

"It's super personal to everyone who's lost someone because of these laced pills. We need to find this guy. I got a good lead from the restaurant's manager, and I'm going there after I see what's up at Gigi's."

"What's your thought on what happened there?"

"Jaycee somehow got into Gigi's house, and Gigi went into survival mode."

"That's gonna be complicated."

"Everything is complicated in my world." She leaned around the seat to check the time on the dash. Six twenty already. At this rate, she would miss seeing the twins before bed, but she was determined to find this Riggs Lawton guy before she called it a day.

The parking lot at Gigi's complex was swarming with public safety vehicles, including the medical examiner's van.

Sam and Malone made their way to the front door, showed their badges to the officer minding the entrance, even though he obviously recognized them, and headed upstairs to the scene of the crime.

"Thanks for your good work," Malone said to the SWAT commander. "You can remove your team now."

"Yes, sir."

After the SWAT officers filed out, they were able to move toward the bedroom where all the activity was centered, overseen by Deputy Chief McBride.

Sam took one look at Gigi, and her heart sank as she realized her detective was deeply traumatized and seriously injured because of the day's events. Gigi had only recently come back to work on limited duty after suffering a ruptured spleen and other injuries at the hands of her now-ex-boyfriend.

Cameron Green didn't look much better than his new girlfriend. The expression "cat on a hot tin roof" came to mind as he paced the room while paramedics tended to Gigi.

"Does she need to be transported?" Cam asked.

"No, I don't," Gigi said.

Cameron looked to the paramedics for the final verdict.

"She lost some blood, but nothing requires sutures. If she won't be alone tonight, I don't think we need to take her in."

"She won't be alone," Cam said.

"I've already taken photos and processed the scene." Jeannie held up an evidence bag containing Gigi's weapon. "If you agree, I'm going to authorize Byron to remove the body."

"Go ahead," Malone said to Byron Tomlinson, the deputy ME.

"Someone needs to notify her family," Sam said.

"I'll take care of that," Dani said.

"I'll go with you," Jeannie said. "I've been to her mother's house before."

Gigi stared straight ahead, seeming removed from the activity happening around her.

Sam stepped out of the room and put through a call to Dr. Anthony Trulo, the department's psychiatrist.

"Hi there," he answered.

"I need you at the home of Detective Dominguez. She shot and killed Detective Green's ex-girlfriend, who's been harassing them." She gave him the address.

"I'll be right there."

"Thanks." She slapped her phone closed. "Trulo is coming."

"That's good." Malone eyed the bloodstained carpet. After the paramedics left, Malone squatted before Gigi. "I'm sorry to have to ask you this now, but you know how this stuff works. I need to know what happened while it's still fresh in your mind."

Gigi nodded and seemed to summon the strength she needed to get through this. "I, um, I left for a minute to go get my mail at the other end of the parking lot. It was my fault. I left the door unlocked. I know better."

"It's not your fault, Gigi." Cam sat next to Gigi on the bed and put his arm around her. "None of this is your fault."

"What happened then?" Malone asked.

"When I came back in... She was standing in the foyer with a knife. I was so shocked that I couldn't move for a second. She started screaming at me to get upstairs. 'Take me to the bedroom where you fuck my boyfriend,' she said. She pushed me up the stairs."

Cameron closed his eyes and went very still.

Sam was almost as concerned about him as she was about Gigi.

"She took me by the hair and dragged me down the hallway. Wh-when we came in here, she cut my clothes off me." She gestured to the pile of shredded clothes on the floor. "She said she wanted to see what was so special about me that he wanted me and not her." Gigi's hands shook as she folded them in her lap. "She said she wanted to know if my pussy was tighter than hers." Gigi swallowed hard. "She... She put her fingers in me."

"Fucking hell," Cameron whispered.

"I let her do what she wanted while I waited for an opportunity to get away from her. She touched my breasts and my bottom. She said she didn't understand what he saw in me when she was so much prettier and sexier than me."

"No," Cameron said. "*No.*"

"She told me to get on the bed, and that's when I grabbed my gun from the bedside table drawer. When she saw that I had it, she laughed and said, 'You wouldn't dare shoot me.' I said, 'You don't think so?' She came at me with this crazy look in her eyes and the knife in her hand, and I realized she was going to kill me unless I killed her first. I fired and hit her in the chest."

"You did what you had to do, Gigi." Dani wiped away tears. "You survived."

Cameron got up suddenly and left the room.

Sam went after him. "Wait. Cam. Stop." She grabbed his arm and spun him around to face her. "This is not your fault."

"How is it not my fault? I tried to tell her we should take a break because Jaycee wouldn't let it go, and now..."

"It's not your fault, Cameron," Gigi said from behind them.

"How can you say that?" Cam's eyes filled with tears as he returned to her. "You were assaulted and had to fight for your life, all because you're with me."

"You're worth it," Gigi said softly, as she looked up at him. "*We're* worth it."

Tears rolled down his face. "She hurt you." He ran a gentle hand over one of the wounds on her face.

"She can never hurt us again."

He reached for her, and she stepped into his arms.

Sam felt like she was intruding, so she gestured for the others to follow her downstairs to give them a minute alone. "Let's call for Crime Scene detectives to do a full workup and relocate them to Cameron's for the night," Sam said to Dani.

"I'll take care of that and then go with Deputy Chief McBride to notify Jaycee's mother," Dani said.

Sam sent Dr. Trulo a text directing him to Cameron's place rather than Gigi's. *They'll be there within the hour.*

Got it, he replied.

Dani went back upstairs to help Gigi pack a bag.

Mrs. Dominguez came down the stairs, wiping away tears. "Is she in trouble, Lieutenant? Tell me the truth."

"It appears to be a clear case of self-defense, but we'll have to let the investigation play out."

"That woman... She'd been tormenting my Gigi. She didn't want Cameron to know, but Jaycee had left notes for her and said terrible, hateful things."

Sam was shocked to hear that. "Did she keep them?"

"She has them all in case she needed them."

Sam squeezed her arm. "Thank you for letting me know that." She went back upstairs and gestured for Malone to come to her. "Her mom tells me that Gigi had been receiving hateful notes from Jaycee and kept them all."

"Got it."

"Also, Cam doesn't know about the notes."

"Right. Okay." Malone went back into the bedroom.

Sam followed him.

"Gigi, could I have a moment, please?" he asked. "Alone?"

"Why alone?" Cameron asked.

"Give us one minute," Malone said, ushering Gigi and Sam into the attached bathroom and closing the door.

"Your mother told us you've been receiving notes from Jaycee and Cameron doesn't know that."

"Yes."

"We're going to need you to turn them over to us as evidence."

She went to a closet in the bathroom, opened the door and removed a plastic evidence bag containing pieces of paper.

"How long has this been going on?" Sam asked.

"Weeks. Since right after she slashed Cam's tires."

"Why didn't you report it?"

"I figured she was in enough trouble with multiple charges pending. I was being careful, until I made one mistake and gave her the opportunity to get at me. That was my fault."

"No, it wasn't, Gigi," Sam said. "It wasn't your fault."

"I knew she was blaming me for 'stealing' Cam from her and all the troubles she's had since he ended things. I shouldn't have left my door unlocked for even a minute."

"These will help," Malone said. "It should be a slam-dunk case of self-defense."

Gigi eyed him warily. "I guess we'll see."

. . .

"WHERE TO?" Vernon asked when Sam got back in the SUV with Captain Malone. She gave him the Shaw address for Riggs Lawton.

"What's in Shaw?" Malone asked.

"An alleged drug dealer named Riggs Lawton."

Malone startled as he looked over at her. "How does he factor into this?"

"Richard Kent, the manager at the restaurant where two of my victims worked, told me I should talk to him."

"He's setting you up, Sam. No one gets near that guy. Narcotics has been after him for years."

"Kent told me he's a regular at the restaurant where he worked until recently and where two of our victims worked."

"Is that so?" Malone thought about it for a minute and then made a call. "This is Malone. Put me through to Cooper."

"No," Sam hissed. "Don't involve him."

Malone held up his hand. "I've got a lead on Lawton. Meet me at the Homicide conference room in fifteen minutes." He listened for a minute. "You'll need to cancel your plans." He ended the call in a huff. "What's with people telling me they've got plans when I'm handing them a guy they've been after for years?"

"Am I expected to answer that? Because if I was, I'd say it's because he's a slacker. And why am I being forced to deal with him?"

"Because the two of you are on the same side and you both want Riggs. Let's make that happen together."

"I don't wanna."

"Your objection has been noted."

"Back to HQ, then?" Vernon asked.

"Yes," Malone said. "Do you have the contact info for the owner of the restaurant?"

Sam nodded even as she fumed.

"Call him and tell him we want him to invite his buddy Lawton to come in, and we'll nab him."

"What if Lawton has heard that Kent got arrested?"

"He doesn't know him as Kent, right?"

"No, but..."

"Let's try it. Or better yet, ask the owner if he knows Lawton and if he'd be willing to help us get him to come in for some reason."

Sam reluctantly made the call to Kyle Atkins. "This is Lieutenant Holland with the MPD."

"Did you find Richard?"

"We did, and he mentioned a frequent customer of yours that we're very interested in speaking to."

"Which one?"

"Riggs Lawton. Would you be able to invite him to come in so we could speak to him?"

"What's going to happen to me when he finds out I invited him to an ambush?"

"Are you aware of Mr. Lawton's line of business?"

"I'm not, but if I invite him to my place and he's surrounded by cops, that's not going to be good for me or my business."

"If you don't help us with this, I'm sure we can find another reason to shut you down, such as two of your employees dying suddenly under mysterious circumstances and the only thing they had in common was your restaurant."

"Are you blackmailing me, Lieutenant?"

"Not at all. I'm asking you to cooperate in a Homicide investigation."

She let that land and gave him a minute to decide whether he would help them.

"I need to know why you want to talk to him before I lure him in."

"I'm afraid I can't share that with you, as it would compromise our investigation."

"And you think he had something to do with what happened to Morgan and Angelo?"

"We don't know that. We simply want to talk to him."

"Why does it have to happen in my place?"

"Because it does."

"Do I need a lawyer?"

"I don't know. Do you?"

"I haven't done anything but work my ass off for years to make my restaurant successful. This will ruin me."

"I'm sorry about that, but I want justice for your dead employees."

"I do, too! Of course I do!"

"Then you'll help us?"

"You ask that like you've given me a choice."

"When can you call Mr. Lawton?"

"He'll suspect something is up if I call him. I'll ask the hostess to call to let him know the chef is making his favorite dish tonight. That's when he usually comes."

"Get back to me when you know for sure he'll be there."

"All right."

Sam slapped the phone closed before he could tell her again how fucked up this entire thing was. She couldn't agree more, but that wouldn't stop her from using him to get what she needed.

Malone called Cooper and put it on speaker so Sam could hear. "It's on for tonight. Get your team together. We'll be there in five minutes." He ended the call before Cooper could say a word.

"This ought to be fun."

"Unless you want a ding on the 'plays well with others' portion of your yearly evaluation, I'd suggest you get on board with this plan."

"Yes, sir." She said what he wanted to hear even as she seethed on the inside at having to play nice with the buffoon who led Narcotics.

CHAPTER TWENTY-FOUR

Cooper was, indeed, a buffoon. Sam had had limited contact with him in the past, but she'd heard rumors about him being a blowhard. The rumors had been correct. He started talking the minute he walked into the conference room and had barely taken a breath in the ensuing ten minutes. While he ranted about her taking over his investigation, Sam tuned him out while she checked her email on her laptop, hoping for news from Haggerty on the search taking place at the White home.

Nothing yet.

"Did you hear what I said?" Cooper asked, his round face red with exertion.

Sam wondered if he was in danger of having a heart attack or a stroke. "No, I wasn't listening."

"You're every bit the piece of work people say you are."

"Thank you."

"That wasn't a compliment."

"And yet, I feel strangely complimented." She glanced up at him. "I'm not engaging in a pissing contest with you. I'm looking for a murderer. That's my only goal and my only focus. I couldn't care less who gets credit for the bust or whose toes I might be stepping on. I want this guy off the streets before he kills someone else."

At that, Cooper softened ever so slightly. "That's my goal, too."

"Good, then we're on the same page."

"I, uh, I heard about your brother-in-law. I'm sorry."

Sam had so much she'd like to say to him about that, but recalling Malone's warning, she simply said, "Thank you."

"We've been after Lawton a long time," Cooper said as Gonzo and O'Brien joined them in the conference room.

"Tell me more."

Cooper took a seat across the conference room table from her. "He's a kingpin. We've had eyes on him for years, but he's slick, surrounded by top-level security. Impenetrable."

"Did you know he regularly eats at Zénitude in Georgetown?"

Cooper seemed surprised by that. "No, we didn't."

"If you've had eyes on him for years, how is it possible you don't know that?"

He sighed. "Like I said. He's slick. We can't afford twenty-four-hour surveillance, and he knows that. His security knows when we're watching and when we aren't."

"What's his drug of choice?"

"Heroin, but he dabbles in many other varieties, not that we've been able to pin any of it on him. We've arrested a few lower-level lieutenants, but they won't turn on him, even when they're looking at decades in prison."

"So, he's threatened to kill them if they talk and has the reach, inside and out, to get to them."

"That's our theory."

"What do you suppose the odds are that he had something to do with two employees at Zénitude overdosing during the same week?"

"The odds are high that even if he didn't personally provide the product, it was tied in some way to his operation."

"Why would he sell laced pills, knowing that's going to bring even more scrutiny down on him?"

"That's a good question. My only guess is he didn't know it was laced, which means someone double-crossed him."

"Do you have a phone number for Lawton?"

"It changes all the time, but I can give you the most recent numbers we have for him."

"That would help." While he used his phone to gather that information, Sam called Gonzo into the room. "Cooper has some numbers for Lawton. Can you check them against the dumps of the victims' phones?"

"Yep."

"It doesn't work that way," Cooper said. "You won't find Lawton's numbers on your vics' phones. It'd be one of his people using a burner. That's why it's so hard to find them. They're mostly off the grid."

"Let's check anyway," Sam said to Gonzo, who nodded and took the list of numbers from Cooper.

A handsome dark-haired officer appeared at the conference room door.

Cooper waved him in. "Sergeant Merrick heads up our fentanyl task force. I asked him to come in and brief you on the particulars."

"It's good to meet you all," Merrick said as he took a seat at the table. "I'm sure you guys have questions, and I'm happy to answer them, but a few things to start with. First, it's a misconception that you can die from touching fentanyl or fentanyl-laced pills. That said, we still take full precautions when we think there's fentanyl on a scene. For the most part, it's replaced heroin as the street drug of choice."

"How can that be," Gonzo asked, "when people know it's so lethal?"

"Believe it or not," Merrick said, "that's part of the attraction. People describe the total brain-numbing high of fentanyl as far superior to the quick high they get from coke or heroin, and the dealers brag about how many people their drugs have killed. It's like a badge of honor in their world."

"What the fuck?" Sam asked. "How does that make sense when they're killing their own customers?"

"There're plenty of others," Merrick said. "It makes no sense to people who aren't addicted to it, but people describe the brain fog that comes with fentanyl as highly addictive. There's a false sense of security for addicts, too, because of the prevalence of Narcan, which can quickly reverse the effects of the drug. Our officers have brought the same people back from the brink three or four times with Narcan. Some of them are furious after we give them Narcan because it kills their high."

"That's crazy," Matt O'Brien said.

"It is," Merrick agreed. "The kicker is that the street form of fentanyl has made it harder for people who really need it—like cancer patients in hospice—to get it. Doctors are very reluctant to prescribe it for its intended purpose."

"We're finding pills with a distinctive S20 stamp on them," Sam said.

Merrick nodded. "The street pills have become much more sophisticated with markings like the ones you describe that make them look like they came from a pharmacy. That provides a false sense of security for people buying them on the street."

"This has been very helpful, Sergeant," Sam said. "And horrifying."

"I hear you. It's the most lethal street drug I've seen in my career and getting worse all the time."

"Thank you for the info, Sergeant," Malone said. To Sam, he asked, "What's our plan for tonight?"

"I'm waiting to hear back from the owner about whether he was able to convince Lawton to come in for dinner," Sam said.

"How long are we waiting?" Cooper asked, checking his watch.

"Do you have something more important to do, Lieutenant?" Malone asked, sounding annoyed.

"In fact, I do. It's my twentieth wedding anniversary, and I'm supposed to be taking my wife to dinner at eight. I intentionally made it later so it wouldn't interfere with work."

"You should go do that," Sam said. "Lawton knows you and all your people. My team is new. We can handle this."

Cooper glanced at Malone.

"Go ahead," Malone said.

"Are you sure? I don't want you to be mad."

"It's fine," Malone said.

"Thank you so much. Both of you. You're saving my ass with my wife."

"We do what we can for the people," Sam said as Cooper beat feet out of the conference room.

"I swear to God," Malone said, sighing as he took a seat. "No one wants to work anymore."

"I don't think that's true, sir," Sam said. "It's just that people are trying to do a better job of balancing their work with the rest of their lives."

"I guess. It's aggravating sometimes."

"Yes, it is, but if it keeps people from hating us, their jobs and the department, I suppose it's worth the hassle."

"I heard you sent Cruz home today. What's up with that?"

"I'm not at liberty to say. Suffice to say he was of zero use to me due to what was happening at home."

"I hope he's okay."

"Me, too." Sam sent him a text while hoping her phone would ring with a call from Kyle Atkins. *How's it going?*

Terrible. She's heartbroken. I don't know what to do for her.

Just be there. I know it seems trite to say, but the initial heartbreak will eventually fade, and you can try again in a month or two. Tell her I said this baby wasn't meant to be born for some reason.

I'll tell her.

And tell her I'm here if she wants to talk.

I will. Thanks.

Take tomorrow off. Be with her. Come back when you're ready.

Thank you.

Sure thing.

"I gave Cruz tomorrow off, too."

"We're a mess."

"Nah, the days of acting like the job is all there is are over. We need to acknowledge that and roll with it."

"If you say so."

"I say so." Sam put her feet on the table, exhausted from days of frenetic activity. "How'd you make out in New Orleans?"

"Not so great. Rosa is dying of cancer and had nothing good to say about Stahl. He's not our guy."

"So, who does that leave?"

"Your father and Conklin."

"It's got to be Conklin. My dad wouldn't have done anything for Stahl, no matter what he had on him."

"I agree. I'm going to see Conklin in the next day or two."

"Ugh."

"I know. I just can't believe the things he was hiding. In the meantime, Deputy Chief McBride is triaging Stahl's cases to determine where we'll start with that review."

"Can't wait for that."

"It's going to be intense for all of us. We'll have to double and triple up on investigations—new and old at the same time."

Sam sighed, exhausted already. "Reminder that I'm leaving early Sunday for the wake and taking all day Monday for the funeral."

He nodded. "I'll be at both."

"Thanks."

"How's Ang?"

"Terrible."

"You should go home to your family. We can take this from here."

"You and who else?"

"I'll find someone to help me."

Sam was torn between seeing this through and going home to be with her sister. "Is it wrong that I'm finding it hard to be around her right now? All I can think about is what I'd do if it happened to me, which isn't helping her at all."

"It's normal to go to worst-case when something awful happens to someone close to you."

"I'd never survive it."

"Yes, you would."

"No, I really wouldn't, and I'm not sure Angela will either. They were crazy in love."

"She'll survive it because she has to for her kids. They need her, and she'll rally for them."

"I sure hope so, but right now... I'm not so sure."

Sam's phone rang. "It's Kyle," she said to Malone as she took the call. "What's up?"

"He'll be here at eight. He usually sits at the left side of the bar."

"What's he look like?"

"Blond, handsome, well dressed. You can't miss him. He stands out."

"Thank you."

"Sure, no problem." His tone dripped with sarcasm. "If you're going to make a scene, I only ask that you make it as quickly and quietly as possible. My reservations are down twenty percent from before Morgan and Angelo died."

"We'll be in and out so quickly, you won't even know we were there."

"Right. Is there anything else?"

"Nope. That's it."

"Great. Bye."

"Was it something I said?" Sam asked Malone, who laughed. "I'll see this through, and then I'll go home."

"I'll see it through with you."

. . .

CAMERON DROVE Gigi to his place, feeling sick to his soul over what Jaycee had put her through. He'd died a little more inside every time she'd been forced to retell the story before everyone was satisfied that they had the necessary details and told her she was free to go.

Malone had said she'd be suspended with pay while the incident was investigated, but he'd assured her she had nothing to worry about, as it was a clear case of self-defense.

Cameron was worried for her anyway. These things had a way of blowing up into a much bigger deal than initially expected, and if that happened to her because of his ex... God, he was going to be sick if he didn't get himself together.

"It's not your fault," she said after a painfully long silence.

"Whose fault is it?"

"Jaycee's. She's the one who couldn't handle being rejected by a man and chose to make his life—and mine—a nightmare. That has nothing to do with you."

"How can you say it has nothing to do with me?"

"Because it doesn't. She made her choices, and I will never blame you for them. She was mentally unbalanced, and you were wise to end it with her when you did."

Cameron's eyes watered to the point that he could barely see to drive. He pulled off the road and put the car in Park, staring straight ahead as he battled out-of-control emotions.

Gigi turned to him and put her hand on his arm. "It is *not* your fault."

"This is what I tried to tell you was going to happen, but you convinced me that she couldn't get near us."

"I let down my guard for one minute. That's on me."

"If I can't blame myself, then you can't either."

She smiled for the first time, but it was a faint smile, not her usual dazzling affair. "We're going to have to agree to absolve ourselves of guilt, or she'll succeed in driving us apart. That's what she wanted. We can't give her that."

"I keep thinking about what she did to you..."

"The only thing that matters is that I survived it."

"That's not all that matters, Gigi. She sexually assaulted you."

"And I survived."

"Not to mention the consequences of firing your weapon. That'll be a permanent entry in your jacket."

"I survived. I have no regrets, and I refuse to be made a victim by her or anyone, even you."

"I don't see you as a victim."

"Please don't. I'm all done with that after everything with Ezra and now her. They can fuck right off."

"I hate that I brought her into your life."

"You didn't, Cam. She brought herself into my life because she couldn't accept that you want me and not her. That's the simple fact of this situation, and no one, not even you, could've stopped her from doing what she was determined to do."

"She was determined to kill you."

"And who stopped her?"

"You did."

"That's right, and I'd do it again a thousand times if it meant she's out of our lives forever."

"Once was more than enough."

"I don't want you to think I'm a heartless bitch. I hate that I had to take her life to save my own, but I did what I had to."

"I'll be thankful you saved yourself every day for the rest of our lives."

"If you continue to blame yourself for this, we're going to have a problem. Do you understand me?"

"I do. And I'll do my best not to."

"I'd feel the same way if the roles were reversed and Ezra had come for you, but people make their own choices. All we can do is control how we react to them. I refuse to give her one more minute of the limited time I have left. She's already gotten too much of my time and yours."

"Yes, she has. Why did Malone want to talk to you alone before?"

Gigi sighed. "Jaycee had left some notes for me over the last few weeks."

"What? Why didn't you tell me?"

"Because I was afraid you'd go after her and end up in jail. I saved them all as evidence that I've now turned over to the captain."

He blew out a deep breath. "Don't keep stuff from me."

"I did that to protect you—and us. You know you would've

gone looking for her and gotten yourself in big trouble. I was trying to prevent that." Leaning her head on his shoulder, she added, "I know you're sick over this, and I am, too, but we did everything we could to rid ourselves of her before it came to this."

"We did, but there's likely to be an uproar over it in light of who we work for."

"Yeah," she said with another sigh. "Hopefully, it won't be too big of a deal."

Cameron wanted to believe it wouldn't be that bad, but he wasn't optimistic. As he drove them the rest of the way to his place, his only hope was that their new relationship would survive the scrutiny.

CHAPTER TWENTY-FIVE

At ten after eight, Sam and Malone walked into Zénitude, which seemed to be doing robust business, despite what Atkins would have her believe. Heads turned as they always did when she went anywhere these days. She noted Tim was behind the bar.

He nodded to her.

She approached the blond man sitting right where she'd been told to look for him. "Riggs Lawton?"

"Who wants to know?" he asked without looking up from his dinner.

Sam stuck her badge under his nose and was gratified to see his body go stiff. "Here's how we're going to do this. You're going to get up and come with us without making a scene."

"That's not going to happen."

"Then we'll make a scene. The choice is yours."

"If you think you're going to get me past my security people, you're insane."

"We've got an army outside prepared to do battle with them if it comes to that. Again, your choice."

"You're the one married to the president."

"Am I? I had no idea. What's it going to be?"

He put down his fork, wiped his mouth with the cloth napkin and glanced at Tim. "Tell Kyle he's a dead man."

"Was that a threat?" Sam asked as she slapped cuffs on him so fast, he never saw them coming. "Let's go, you fucking scumbag."

Malone had his weapon drawn as he helped her drag him out of the restaurant while stunned patrons and staff looked on.

"That's the first lady!" Sam heard someone say.

She ignored everything as she and Malone moved him toward Malone's SUV and jammed him in the back before his so-called security people had gotten their heads out of their asses to realize something was up.

Two guys in black suits came running.

"Sorry, boys," Sam said, smiling at them. "You're too late."

"You're going to be sorry," one of them said.

"Are you threatening a police officer by any chance?"

He wisely took a step back.

Sam conferred with Malone. "Do you mind getting him processed while I run home for thirty minutes?"

"Go ahead."

"I'll be back."

"I could handle the interrogation, you know."

"I know, but I want to be there."

"Fine. I'll call Faith, too."

"What do you think about protective custody for Kyle Atkins and his family?"

"I'll arrange it."

"I'm very glad to have you back where you belong."

"I'm sure you are," he said with a huff of laughter. "See you back at the house."

"I'll be there." Sam got into her SUV. "Let's go home for a quick minute," she said to Vernon.

"Yes, ma'am."

"Do you guys have another shift you could hand me off to? It could be a late night."

"Don't worry about us, ma'am," Vernon said. "We're fine."

She took advantage of the short break to call Tracy.

"Hey," her sister said. "How's it going?"

"Making some progress. I think. How are things with Ang?"

"About the same. I took care of getting the clothes they need for the next few days from the house and brought some more of the kids' toys and things to them. She was saying she should go home, that you guys have enough to deal with without having them underfoot."

"I'm on my way home now. I'll talk to her and let her know it's no problem."

"She's spinning," Tracy said with a sigh. "Changing her mind about everything from one minute to the next."

"I guess it'll take a while for that to stop. I just can't imagine what she's going through."

"Me either, and I don't want to."

"It's like watching my greatest fear happen to my closest friend —well, one of them."

"I know. Same here. It's awful. At times, I wanted to tell him to shut the fuck up, but I never once doubted that he was crazy about her and the kids."

"Yes, he certainly was."

"I'm worried about Jack. He isn't saying much, but he's devastated."

"It's so crushing to see him that way. I hate this so much."

"I want to wave a magic wand and be done with the funeral and stuff."

"Me, too. She'll be all right eventually, won't she?"

"We'll make sure of it."

"I've been hiding in the case because her grief is unbearable. I feel bad about that."

"You're doing what you can to get justice for him, for her and the kids. Keep doing that. It'll matter someday that his death wasn't for nothing. You're saving other people by finding the person selling that poison."

"That makes me feel a little better."

"There's nothing any of us can do or say to make this less of a staggering blow for her and Jack. It's just going to take some time for them to pick themselves up and get back to some semblance of normalcy."

"Their normal will never be what it was again."

"No, it won't, but it also won't always be this awful."

"Thanks for all you're doing for her."

"Thanks for all *you're* doing. It helps them to be surrounded by your family."

"I guess I'll see you tomorrow."

"Yes, you will."

"Love you, Trace."

"Love you, too, kid."

Sam closed her phone and held it to her chest, thinking about Tracy, Angela and the tight bond the three of them had shared all their lives. Sure, they'd fought as kids, the way siblings always did, but when push came to shove, they were always there for each other. She recalled the fateful night, now nine years ago, when she met Nick after accompanying Angela to a party Spencer had invited her to. While Angela and Spencer's relationship had taken off after that night, Sam and Nick hadn't seen each other again for six long years.

Her eyes filled with tears when she thought of Angela, Jack and the tragic loss of Spencer's young life. Days after his shocking death, it was still impossible to believe he was really gone.

If Riggs Lawton was in any way responsible for taking him from Angela and her kids, Sam would make him sorry he was ever born.

WHEN SHE ENTERED the White House residence, she heard the twins laughing and followed the joyful noise to their bedroom, where Nick was seated between them on the bed, reading them a story.

"What's so funny in here, and why is everyone up so late?" At least it wasn't a school night.

"Sam, Nick is being silly," Aubrey said.

"My Nick is never silly."

"Yes, he is!" Alden said.

Sam stretched across the foot of the bed. "This I need to see."

Nick gave her a warm smile that immediately helped to alleviate some of the anxiety she'd brought home with her. The voices he gave the characters in the book were, in fact, very silly, sweet and funny. The twins' laughter was the best thing she'd heard all day. After they tucked them in with kisses and love, Sam and Nick left them to sleep.

"You're a wonderful daddy," she said, kissing him.

"Aw, thanks. It's the most fun I've ever had, except, you know, naked fun and all other fun with you."

"It's okay to say they're the most fun."

"You're all tied for first. They were wound up and playing with Jack, so I let them stay up a little later. Let's check on the big boy." He knocked on Scotty's door, making Skippy bark.

"Enter!"

They stepped into a wild wrestling match between dog and boy.

"I think she might be winning," Scotty said, breathless.

Skippy was on top of him, killing him with kisses.

"That dog tongue is lethal," he said, wiping his face with his T-shirt.

"She's getting big," Nick said, as if he'd just noticed the growth spurt.

"How was your day?" Sam asked Scotty.

"Eh, two hours of algebra homework that's not due until next week."

"Wait," Sam said. "You did algebra homework early? Nick, take his temperature."

"We've got the wake and funeral, so I figured I'd get it done."

"Good call, buddy," she said.

"Next year, I get to take geometry. I hear that's not much better."

"I hated it."

"Sam!" Nick said.

"What? I did."

"You don't have to tell him that before he even tries it."

"Why not?" She gave Scotty a look that made him laugh. "Don't you want him to be prepared?"

"I want him to go into it with a good attitude."

Sam rolled her eyes at Scotty. "As if that's even possible."

"I'm putting you in time-out," Nick said to Sam as Scotty laughed.

"Yes, please," Sam said with a sultry look for her husband.

"Gotta make it dirty, don't you?" Scotty said, groaning.

"I'm just saying a time-out would be very nice right about now."

"Have you found the dealer of the laced pills?" Scotty asked, all signs of amusement now gone.

"Not yet, but I think we might be getting closer. I have to go back to HQ tonight to talk to a guy who may have some info." Sam scratched Skippy behind the ears when the puppy sidled up to her. "You've got your clothes ready for the next two days?"

"Yeah, Celia and I did that earlier. She made me iron my own shirts."

"Good for her," Nick said. "That's a valuable skill to learn."

"Like algebra?" Scotty asked, eyebrow raised.

"Much more useful than algebra," Nick said.

"So, you admit algebra is useless and ought to be outlawed by the president?"

"I never said that!"

Sam and Scotty lost it laughing.

"That's what I heard," Scotty said. "How about you, Mom?"

"Yep, I heard it, too."

"Just what I need is you guys double-teaming me when the whole world is coming for me."

"What now?" Sam asked, alarmed to hear that.

"Eh, the usual nonsense. Nothing to worry about."

They said good night to Scotty and left him and Skippy watching the end of the Caps game.

She glanced at the stairs to the third floor. "Have you seen Ang?"

"She was at dinner with the kids and said she was going to bed."

"How'd she seem?"

"About the same. Very anxious about the next few days."

"Aren't we all?" Sam asked with a sigh. "I need a minute with you before I go back to work."

"I need a minute with you, too. Something about a car accident yesterday?"

"Oh crap. There's so much going on that I forgot to tell you. I'm sorry."

"I heard about it from the tattletales."

"We can't live with the Secret Service, and we can't live without them."

He chuckled as he guided her into their suite with a hand on her back, closing the door behind them. "That's a fact. They said it was Ramsey?"

"It was, and now the FBI is involved, which is actually a relief. We haven't had any luck getting rid of him. Maybe they'll get it done for us."

"We can only hope." He gave her that penetrating look of his, the one that saw all the way through her. "You weren't hurt at all?"

"My neck is aching a bit, but Lindsey checked it for me, and she said everything seems okay. I'll get it looked at more thoroughly if it gets worse."

"Yes, you will." He held out his arms to her, and she walked into them with relief and gratitude for his steady presence. "Now, what can I do for you, love?"

"Well... You're either going to be really happy with me or super pissed. I'm not sure which."

"You have my attention."

Sam took him by the hand and led him to the sofa, sitting next to him. "A while back, before all this happened," she said, gesturing to their White House sitting room, "I asked Avery to take an informal look at what your mother is up to."

"Wait... You asked a top-ranking FBI agent to informally investigate my mother?"

Did he sound mad or shocked or both? Definitely both.

"After that horrible interview she gave, I was looking for a way to get her out of your life permanently—and I sensed it was possible she was up to no good. Turns out I was right."

"How so?" he asked warily. The topic of his mother always had that effect on him.

"It seems she's running some sort of high-end escort service in Ohio for the over-sixty crowd."

His face went flat with shock. "*What?*"

"Avery said they don't have all the info yet, but it's not looking good for her, and he thought I ought to let you know before the shit hits the fan in the form of a possible indictment."

Nick exhaled and sat back against the sofa. "This is just great. My mother is going to be indicted on prostitution charges—by my Justice Department."

"I'm sorry. I never expected anything like that when I asked Avery to investigate her."

The look he gave her was one she'd never seen directed her way before—pure fury. "What did you expect when you asked the FBI to investigate my mother without telling me?"

Sam was so surprised by his outrage that she was speechless for a full minute. "You... You weren't president then, and—"

"I was vice president, which would still make it a huge story. Jesus, Sam. What the fuck were you thinking?"

For the first time in their otherwise blissful relationship, she was afraid she'd gone too far. "I wanted her out of your life so she couldn't hurt you anymore."

"Which I totally understand, but do you have any idea what a massive scandal this will be?"

"I'll ask Avery to drop it."

"They've uncovered a crime and taken it to a grand jury. It's too late to drop it." Nick got up and went to use the phone. "I need to see you. Yes, right now. Thank you."

"Who was that?"

"Terry. We need to figure out how we're going to get in front of this, so it doesn't derail our entire agenda."

"I'm sorry, Nick. I should've told you about this when I did it."

"Yes, you absolutely should have."

"I thought you'd be glad to hear that she'd done something that would get her out of our lives once and for all."

"Well, I'm not. I know your intentions were good, but this will be a shitstorm of epic proportions—and right when I've finally convinced the country that I can handle the job I wasn't elected to do."

Sam swallowed around the lump of fear in her throat. He'd never been this angry with her, and she'd given him lots of reason to be before now.

He headed for the door. "I've got to go meet Terry and figure out a plan to deal with this."

"Nick, wait. Don't leave like this."

For the first time ever, he walked away from her and slammed the door on the way out.

Sam's entire body trembled with anxiety and another thing she'd never experienced when it came to him and their relationship—fear.

CHAPTER TWENTY-SIX

Nick went downstairs and headed for the West Wing in a rage of disbelief directed at both his wife and his mother. How could Sam have done something like that and not even told him about it? What the hell was she thinking sending the FBI after his mother? Talk about crossing the lines of personal and professional with Avery Hill.

Nick's feelings for the woman who'd given birth to him were complicated, especially since she'd done nothing but cause him grief his entire life. Naturally, Sam felt protective of him and wanted her gone, but this...

Motherfucker.

He couldn't begin to wrap his head around the potential disaster this would bring down on his fledgling administration.

Since Terry had Secret Service protection as his chief of staff, and they got him where he needed to be quickly, he arrived in the Oval Office fifteen minutes after Nick called.

"What's up?"

Sitting behind the Resolute desk, Nick put his feet up. "You aren't going to believe it."

"Try me."

"A while back, Sam asked Avery to take an 'informal' look at what my mother might be up to."

"And..."

"How do you think operating a high-end escort service for the senior set in Ohio will be received?"

"Are you kidding me?" Terry asked in disbelief as he sat in a chair next to the desk.

"I so wish I was."

"Holy. Fuck."

Nick could see that, like him, Terry was struggling to process the news and the impact it would have on everything they'd been working so hard to accomplish.

"I don't even know what to say," Terry finally said.

"Me either."

"Is there any chance Avery would back off the investigation?"

"Doubtful. The FBI isn't known for turning a blind eye to crime."

"Perhaps if the request came from the president himself?"

"I'm not doing that, Terry. That could cause an even bigger scandal if it got out. If she's arrested, I suppose I can simply say once again that I have no relationship and have never had any relationship with her, and I fully support any prosecution the FBI and U.S. Attorney choose to pursue."

"That could work," Terry said. "It immediately separates you from her—and it's also consistent with past statements you've made about your nonrelationship with her."

"But it'll still be a fucking circus if the mother of the sitting president gets arrested for prostitution—and a circus my own wife brought down on me."

"Were you the president when she asked Avery to take a look at your mother?"

"No, but still... Even me being VP would've made this big news."

"I'm sure Sam's only goal was to remove her from your life."

"It was, but I'm pissed that she did this without telling me."

"Maybe that was because she was hoping it wouldn't amount to anything."

"Yeah, probably."

"There's no sense getting pissed at her, Mr. President."

Nick scowled at him. "Call me Nick when it's just us."

"Nick... Don't let this come between you and Sam. She was trying to help you get rid of your mother, which has long been your goal."

"I suppose having her locked up in a federal prison accomplishes that goal."

"We'll set up a network interview, if it comes to that, for you to once again tell the story of how she's barely been part of your life."

"I really hope it doesn't come to that."

SAM WAS sick to her stomach and everywhere else as she left the White House to return to HQ. He'd never been so enraged with her. Even when she'd pushed him out of the way of a woman with a gun in Eastern Market the first week they were together, it hadn't been like this.

He was furious—and with good reason.

Her phone rang with a call from Freddie. "Hey, how's Elin?"

"She's sleeping, but I heard about Gigi shooting Cam's ex, and I'm wondering if they're okay."

"As far as I could tell, they're shocked, but it was a clear-cut case of self-defense since Jaycee got into her home and threatened her with a knife, among other things."

"What other things?"

"She sexually assaulted her."

"Oh my God."

"Yeah, but Gigi kept her wits about her and survived against a crazy woman with a knife."

"Thank God she's okay. I texted them but haven't heard back. I hope they're okay."

"They will be. In time."

"Why do you sound weird?" Freddie asked.

"It's been one hell of a day."

"How so besides that?"

"I just had a big fight with Nick."

"Wait. What? You guys don't fight."

"Sometimes we do, but not like this. He's furious with me."

"How come?"

"A while ago," Sam said, sighing, "I asked Avery to take an informal look at Nick's mother on a hunch she was up to no good since she hadn't tried to shake Nick down for money lately. They found she's running a high-end escort service in Ohio."

"No way."

"Yes way. Just when Nick is making progress in getting people to talk about something other than his inexperience or his age or all the other reasons he shouldn't be president, this will undercut everything."

"You couldn't have known that would happen when you asked, or that he'd end up being president."

"No, but now he has a mess to clean up that I created, and he's mad, Freddie. Really, really mad."

"He'll get over it. He loves you and knows you had only his best interest in mind when you asked Avery to get involved."

"I hope you're right about that."

"Come on, Sam. This is you and Nick, the most stupidly in-love couple any of us has ever met."

"Stupidly, huh?" she asked with a small smile.

"So stupidly. He might've been surprised and upset, but he'll get over that. You know he will."

"I guess we'll see. In the meantime, I'm on my way back to HQ to talk to a drug kingpin that Narcotics has been after for years who may or may not factor into our case."

"Do you need help? I can come in. Elin's asleep for the night."

"That's okay. Captain Malone is back and will be there."

"I'm glad he's back. That's a relief."

"It is, but Faith said something today about the USA looking into the Ramsey shooting just to make sure all the bases are covered in light of the department's history with Sergeant Ramsey."

"Oh damn."

"It won't come to anything. Everyone who was there can attest that it was either him or the woman he was holding hostage. We chose to save her. It was a no-brainer."

"What about Gigi shooting Jaycee? Will that be a no-brainer, too?"

"I really hope so."

"Me, too. I'll be back in the morning. Elin wants to go to work and get back to normal, so that's what we're doing."

"I'll see you then and remind her I'm here if she wants to talk."

"She appreciated that offer earlier. I don't think she's ready to talk about it yet, even to me."

"She'll get there. It'll take some time."

"That's what I hear. Thanks for the support. It helps."

"Any time. I'm almost back to HQ. I'll see you in the morning."

"See you then—and don't worry about this thing with Nick. You guys are as solid as it gets. He'll get over it."

"I sure hope so."

"He will."

"Thanks. See you."

Sam closed her phone and tried to find her calm to get back into work mode after the upsetting encounter with Nick. But there was no calm to be had when things were unsettled with him. They were so rarely out of sync that it came as a shock to her entire system to realize he was seriously—and legitimately—furious with her.

She made a quick call to Avery.

"Hey," he said. "What's up?"

"Sorry to call so late."

"It's fine."

"So, this thing with Nick's mom. Any chance I can call you off the scent?"

"I've got field agents in Ohio who've dedicated hundreds of hours to what's turning out to be a very big deal. Calling them off now would be almost impossible—and it would be a bigger stink than the indictment if it got out that you made this phone call in the first place."

Sam's heart sank at hearing that. "Nick wasn't president when I asked you to investigate her, and now... The timing is horrible for him."

"I'm sorry about that, Sam. I really am, but this train left the station quite some time ago, and there's no getting it back."

"I thought you might say that. What kind of charges is she looking at?"

"I'm not at liberty to discuss an active investigation—and it's in your best interest to be able to say you had no idea of the particulars. I'm sure you understand."

"I do."

"I'm sorry if this will cause heartburn for you guys, especially right now, but you were right to point me in her direction. That's all I can say."

Sam felt sicker by the minute. "Understood. Have a good night, Avery."

"You do the same."

There was no chance she'd have a good night as long as Nick was upset with her.

"We can go to the main entrance at this hour," Sam said to Vernon.

"Sounds good."

They pulled up to the curb a few minutes later, and Vernon held the door for Sam.

"I'll try to make this quick."

"Take your time."

As she made her way inside, her hip and her neck ached like a bitch.

She knocked on the door to Malone's office. "Ready?"

"Yep. He's in interview one."

"Is Faith here?"

"Waiting in observation."

As they made their way to the interview rooms, Faith came toward them.

"Stand down," she said. "He took something. EMS is on the way, but he was foaming at the mouth and convulsing."

"How in the hell did this happen?" Malone asked.

"I assume he had something with him just in case he needed it," Faith said.

EMS arrived a short time later and declared Lawton dead.

Fucking hell. Just when they were getting somewhere.

Sam and Malone interviewed the Patrol officers who'd been assigned to guard Lawton after he entered the interview room.

Officers Keeney and Watts were familiar to Sam and had earned her respect in earlier investigations.

"We uncuffed him as we always do once they're in the room," Keeney said, "and a minute later, he was convulsing."

"You did a thorough search on the way in?" Sam asked.

"We did," Watts said, seeming rattled. "Pockets were emptied, his wallet and phone confiscated. All the usual stuff."

"Let's get a warrant to dump the phone," Sam said.

"I'll take care of that," Malone said as the EMTs wheeled Lawton to the morgue. "First thing tomorrow, I need you to brief the media on what happened with Dominguez earlier and now this."

"Okay. I need some time to figure out how losing Lawton impacts the case."

"Yeah, that's fine, I guess. Brief when you're ready. Go ahead home. I'll take care of updating Cooper and Farnsworth on what happened with Lawton."

Sam didn't need to be told twice. She hadn't even removed her coat, so she headed for the main door and was in the warm back seat of the SUV in a matter of minutes. "Our guy took his own life. Let's go home." Frustration beat through her like a bass drum. Spencer had been dead nearly a week, and she was no closer to answers than she'd been when it first happened.

She called Gonzo.

"Hey," he said, sounding sleepy.

"Lawton just offed himself in interview one—before we talked to him."

"Whoa, really?"

"We're back to square one with nothing more than we had a week ago."

"I've got a few things that may come to fruition."

"When?"

"Soon, I hope. It's tough, Sam. These people operate in the shadows. Their whole goal is to steer clear of us, not to grab our attention."

"I wanted to be able to tell Spencer's family, when I see them at the wake, that we got the people who poisoned him."

"We'll get them, but it might not happen as quickly as we'd like it to."

"We both know there's a big chance we'll never get them. This isn't like other cases. We need criminals to help us, and how likely is that to happen?"

"Everyone is working their sources. Something will pop."

"Any time now."

"I know it's hard to be patient when this strikes so close to home. It's hard for me to be patient, and Angela is only my friend. I can't imagine how you must feel."

"I'm outraged that someone is selling fucking poison in my town to super vulnerable people. I want that person stopped."

"We're on it. Working it from every front. It might be time to involve Narcotics more seriously. They might have better intel than we do."

"I guess. I'll talk to Cooper in the morning and make it clear he isn't taking over my investigation."

"This might be time to not care who gets the credit. Whatever it takes."

"Let's reconvene in the AM and do what we always do when things stall out," Sam said.

"Start over."

"Yep. I'll be here until two tomorrow. Let the others know that we're starting at eight, and it isn't mandatory, but OT is on the table if they want it."

"Will do. Try to get some rest, Sam."

She didn't tell him there was no way that was happening unless she worked things out with Nick, and that didn't seem likely. "You, too," she said before closing the phone.

"May I make a suggestion?" Vernon asked.

"Always."

"Bring DEA in on this one. They might be able to help."

It went against everything she believed in to ask the Feds for help, but Vernon was right. Sometimes they could do things she couldn't. "That's a good idea, and I should've done it sooner."

"No time like the present."

"I need to remind people about the tip line, too," Sam said. "Someone knows who's selling laced pills. We just need one tip to blow the whole thing wide open."

When she got home, LeRoy greeted her at the door.

"Can you tell me where the president is, LeRoy?"

"I believe he's in the Oval, ma'am."

"Thank you." She turned to Vernon and Jimmy, who'd followed her inside. "Go home and get some sleep. I'm in for the night." If she got called out overnight, she could request another detail.

"Yes, ma'am," Vernon said. "We'll be back to take you to work in the morning."

"See you then."

CHAPTER TWENTY-SEVEN

S am made her way to the West Wing, realizing that at some point over the last month she'd figured out her way around the vast campus they now called home. Not that long ago, she'd have had to ask for directions to her husband's office. Now she went right there and paused outside the closed door, hoping she'd be welcome.

That feeling was so foreign to her that it briefly left her breathless with fear and anxiety that she'd made a crucial, unforgivable error in the most important relationship in her life. Before him, the thought of making a romantic partner mad wouldn't make her knees feel weak or her stomach hurt like it did now. But with Nick... Everything was different with him, and she couldn't stand that she'd upset him.

She knocked on the door and opened it to poke her head in. "May I interrupt?"

Terry stood. "Of course. I was just leaving. I'll speak with you in the morning, Mr. President."

"Thanks for coming in, Terry."

"No problem."

He nodded to Sam as he went by, which made her stomach clench again. No doubt Nick had filled him in, and he was probably angry with her, too.

She stepped into the Oval Office, but none of the trappings interested her. Only the gorgeous man on the sofa had her attention, and she went right to him.

"I'm so sorry, Nick. I feel sick over this. I shouldn't have done it, but it was after she gave that awful interview, and all I could think about was getting rid of her in any way I could. I didn't think it all the way through and—"

Nick held out his hand to her. "Come here."

She went, taking hold of his hand as she sat next to him.

"I don't want you to be sick over it."

"I am. You're so upset, and rightfully so. I never meant—"

He rested a finger over her lips. "It's okay. I was shocked before, and I took it out on you, when I should be focused on her."

"Still... If I hadn't asked Avery to investigate her, this wouldn't be happening."

"Or it might have happened with no warning to us, which Terry pointed out."

"I was wrong not to tell you I'd talked to Avery about her. I apologize for that."

"Thank you."

"I was so fired up after she gave that outrageous interview, it was all I could do not to go to Ohio and strangle her with my own hands."

He smiled, and everything in her settled after hours of uncertainty. "Please don't do that. I need you here with me, not in prison."

"It'd be worth it to be rid of her. I talked to Avery earlier and asked him what the chances were of them backing off the investigation. He said it was too far gone."

"I figured as much. Part of the reason I was so upset earlier was directed at her. You know how I get whenever *she* rears her ugly head."

"I do, and I'm sorry this is happening when you have so many bigger things to contend with."

"Like you said, if it gets rid of her once and for all, it might be worth whatever dustup it causes."

"What did Terry think you should do?"

"We're talking about a number of preemptive strikes, including another interview reminding people she's not in my life, has never really been in my life and has caused only hell and heartache for me since the day I was born."

"That's a good idea."

"No matter how we play it, though, if it happens, the image of the president's mother in handcuffs will dominate the news cycle for a while."

"I'm sorry about that. I feel awful about this."

"You're not the one running the escort service, Samantha."

"But I'm the one who sent the Feds after her."

"You were trying to protect me. I get that."

Sam rested her head against his shoulder. "I was so scared."

"Of what?"

"That you were really, really mad and wouldn't forgive me for this."

"That's never going to happen, Sam. I was upset and shocked and a little mad. I can't deny that. But with a minute to calm down and think it through, I blame her, not you. I mean, if there wasn't anything for the FBI to find, we wouldn't even be having this conversation."

"True."

"I know what you were doing and why, and I appreciate you looking out for me."

"I'm sorry it blew up in our faces."

"We'll deal with it and move on." He turned toward her. "Is there anything else you haven't told me?"

"No! I swear. And the only reason I didn't tell you about asking Avery to investigate her is that there was nothing to tell. Until there was."

He cuffed her chin. "Thanks for looking out for me."

"I never want to do anything that makes this job harder for you than it already is."

"I know that, babe. How'd you make out with the suspect tonight?"

"He killed himself before we could talk to him."

Nick's eyes went wide. "Jeez."

"Yeah, so our most promising lead is gone, and we're back to having jack shit almost a week after Spence died."

"Angela wasn't doing well tonight. The kids were weepy, and it was all too much for her. Celia and I did what we could, but I can't for the life of me imagine what she's going to do with a newborn on top of the two she already has."

"I know," Sam said, sighing. "The GoFundMe will give her the money to hire help, but that's no substitute for having her husband."

"I'm having a hard time thinking about anything but them and the shock of it all."

"Me, too." Sam curled her hand around his. "I never got to tell you what else happened today." She filled him in on the incident at Gigi's house.

"Oh my God, Sam. Is she okay?"

"As okay as she can be. She knows she did what she had to, but it's still shocking and upsetting."

"Will she be in trouble at work?"

"There'll be a standard investigation, but it seems like obvious self-defense."

"Wow. They must both be so upset."

"They were, but they'll get through this. At least I hope they will."

"You'll get them through it. Let's go to bed. I'm beat, and we get to have all this fun to look forward to again tomorrow."

"And then the wake on Sunday," she said with a sigh.

"Ugh, that, too. I'm dreading that."

"Same. It's all so fucking awful. I can't bear it."

"Neither can I."

SAM and her team spent all day Saturday with their heads down, interviewing informants, working the streets, talking to people of interest, and got absolutely nowhere as the press went wild with speculation about the death of Riggs Lawton in police custody and the incident at Detective Dominguez's house the day before. Sam would brief them on all of it, eventually, but she wasn't ready to deal with that yet.

That night, she slept fitfully as the stress of the week followed her into disturbing dreams that included Gigi, Cameron, Jaycee, Riggs Lawton, Nick's mother, Avery, Angela and Spencer. She awoke feeling as if she hadn't slept at all, which was the last thing she needed with so much to contend with before the wake. That would require all her fortitude on its own.

Her neck hurt like hell, but she wasn't telling anyone that. She had no time for doctors with a shortened workday before the wake.

"I thought we might leave here together at three thirty," Nick said as he pulled on a gray V-neck sweater over a dress shirt.

Sam was still trying to get her eyes to stay open, and he was ready for world domination. "Sure, that's fine. I'll try to be home by three. What's the plan for the twins while we're at the wake?"

"Shelby will go first and then come here so Celia can attend the wake."

"Thanks for thinking ahead about that." She flattened her hands on his chest. "What's on the docket for you this morning?"

"Security briefing followed by a couple of interviews on the Sunday shows touting my domestic agenda."

"I wish I could see you."

"You can watch online after." He kissed her forehead and then her lips. "I'll see you for breakfast after your shower?"

"I'll be there."

Sam dragged herself into the shower and stood under the water for much longer than she should have, nearly falling back to sleep at one point. She was stepping out when Nick appeared with a towel, which she'd forgotten, and a cup of coffee.

"Bless you, my love."

"I'm worried about you, Samantha."

Surprised to hear that, she glanced up to find him studying her in that all-knowing way of his. "Why?"

"You're convinced that you're the only one who can get justice for Angela and Spence, and you're running yourself ragged—while grief-stricken for your sister and her family and still recovering from a major injury."

"I'm not sure what else I'm supposed to do but try to catch the person who did this to them. It's already been a week, and we're no closer than we were when it first happened."

"You are closer. You know much more than you did a week ago, and it doesn't have to be you who catches these people, Sam."

"I need to be doing this. I know everyone must think I've got some sort of savior complex, but that's not it. This is the one thing in this whole world I'm really good at, and my sister needs me to give this everything I've got. I know it doesn't matter to her right now that we find the person who did this to them, but someday it'll matter to her—and to her kids—that we got justice for him and them."

"It will matter, but you can't sacrifice yourself in the process. You were tossing and turning all night."

"Sorry if I kept you awake."

"You know I don't sleep much anyway. I just hate to see you so agitated."

"I'm frustrated more than anything. We're no closer to closing this case than we were the day it happened."

"And that is sitting on your shoulders." He massaged the tension from them. "You're tight as a drum and as stressed as I've seen you in a long time, and that's saying something in light of recent events."

Sam hoped he didn't get too close to her sore neck. "Probably because I thought you were going to divorce me for a while last night."

His eyes widened. "You did not."

"For a second or two."

"Samantha... How could I divorce you when I can't bear to be away from you for a single day?" He took the mug from her, set it on the vanity and drew her into his warm embrace. "Do you know what most presidents do right after they give the State of the Union speech?"

"No. What?"

"They hit the road to promote the agenda they've just laid out. They go to factories to promote their job programs. They tour plants and shake lots of hands with lots of people."

"Why didn't you do that?"

"Because I want to be here, with you and our family, more so than ever since we lost Spencer. But mostly because I want to be where you are, and you're here."

"I like having you here with me."

"Don't ever worry about me leaving you. I can't believe you actually thought that last night."

"It was scary to have you so upset with me."

"I'm sorry. I never want you to be scared like that. I reacted badly, like I always do when my mother is involved. All the blame belongs with her, not you." He held her for another minute. "I hate to say I have to go do the briefing in about ten minutes. But there's breakfast ready for you in the kitchen."

"Thanks for taking such good care of me."

"Nothing I love more than taking care of my gorgeous wife." He kissed her. "Take care of her for me today. She's my whole world, and she's under a lot of strain."

"I will. I promise. I'll try to be home by three."

"See you then. Love you."

"Love you, too."

Sam thought about what he'd said about her feeling like she had to personally find the person who'd directly or indirectly killed Spencer. With that thought in mind, she called Captain Malone.

"Morning."

"I hate people who are peppy in the morning, especially when I didn't sleep worth a damn."

"Thanks for giving me a preview of how my day is going to unfold."

Sam laughed. "I do what I can for the people, and with that in mind, I want to call in help on this case. We're getting nowhere. We need Narcotics and DEA and anyone else who might be able to move things along. I'm going to give Kevin Kavanaugh a call. I know him a little through his brother, Derek."

"Is this Sam Holland? Lieutenant Sam Holland?"

"Very funny. I'm serious. This is a world I don't understand, and I need help navigating it, especially since our very promising lead with Lawton went tits up."

"I sent Patrol to the address we had on record for him last night to notify his family that he'd passed away, but no one was there. We'll need to track them down today."

"Great. Something else I don't have time for."

"I'm hoping we're not in for an uproar about him dying in custody."

"The proof of what happened will be in the autopsy."

"Let's hope so."

CHAPTER TWENTY-EIGHT

While Vernon drove her to work, Sam called Agent Kevin Kavanaugh. She'd met him a few times through Derek and had taken Kevin's number in case she ever needed his agency for anything.

"Kavanaugh."

"This is Lieutenant Sam Holland with the MPD."

"Oh. Hey, how's it going?"

"Not so great, if I'm being honest."

"Heard about your brother-in-law. I'm so sorry."

"Thank you. That's why I'm calling. We believe he died from fentanyl poisoning, and we're having no luck tracking down the source. I was hoping we might bring you all in on the investigation."

"I heard Riggs Lawton died in your custody last night."

"He did."

"We've been after him for years. His death is a huge setback to us on several fronts."

"I'm sorry to hear that. We brought him in for questioning, and he took something he had hidden on his person."

"Why wasn't he stripped of everything he came in with?"

Sam felt like she was being interrogated. "He was. We emptied his pockets, took his phone and wallet, as we always do when we bring someone in for questioning."

"I see."

"Look, I'm sorry if you're pissed about Lawton, but I need help. Are you able to assist?"

"Sure. I can get a team together and meet with you tomorrow morning?"

"I'm attending my brother-in-law's funeral tomorrow, but I'm here for a few more hours today."

"I can be there within the hour, but it'll just be me on a Sunday."

"I'll take what I can get. Thank you."

"Sure."

She arrived at her office with a queasy feeling in her gut. The DEA was furious with them about Lawton. Narcotics probably was, too, and she needed both teams to figure out this baffling case.

"Awesome."

"What is?" Malone asked when he came to her door.

"The people I need help from are all pissed that Lawton died on our watch."

"Yeah, I've already gotten an earful from Cooper."

"How was his anniversary dinner?"

"Shockingly, I forgot to ask."

"I want to know what Lawton took," Sam said.

"It was fentanyl," Lindsey said when she appeared in the office doorway.

Frustrated, Sam blew out a deep breath. "Is there a way to know if it was from the same batch that killed Spence and the others?"

"No," she said, "but he had twice the amount of morphine in his brain that Spencer and Mary Alice had, so he took a particularly potent amount."

"How did we miss that he had fentanyl on him?" Sam asked.

"That's a good question," Lindsey said. "I sent the full report to your email."

"Thanks, Doc."

"You got it."

After Lindsey left, Sam looked to Malone. "Does this tie him to our case?"

"Only if we believe he's the only fentanyl dealer in town, which we don't."

"We've got Haggarty's team working at multiple homes, and now we've got another with Lawton's place."

"Believe me. I know. I've already talked to him this morning about CSU being stretched thin by this case. I authorized OT for them."

"Thank you."

"DEA Agent Kevin Kavanaugh is meeting me here in an hour. Can you notify Cooper and his team that we've brought in the DEA?"

"Will do. In the meantime, the media is ravenous."

"That's next on my to-do list."

Sam grabbed her coat and headed for the main door to brief the media, which always put her hackles up. She steeled herself for whatever they might throw at her and pushed through the door to the outdoor area where they gathered seven days a week—and in much greater numbers since Nick became president.

"I have a statement for you about several matters, and then I'll take some questions. The first question about my husband or his administration will be the last one I take. We're actively investigating the sudden and suspicious deaths of several District residents that we believe are the result of fentanyl poisoning. Per the alert that we issued recently, anyone who procures OxyContin illegally is at risk for certain death.

"While in our custody last night, Riggs Lawton, a person of interest in the investigation, ingested fentanyl, which he'd apparently brought in with him, and died instantly. We are continuing to investigate his ties to our case while we seek any information on the person or people who are distributing this toxic substance to unsuspecting customers.

"Often, the people who seek out this medication have suffered some sort of injury, after which they become addicted to the Oxy they were initially prescribed. After doctors stop prescribing it for them, they often procure the product illegally. People in the throes of addiction to a medication they can no longer obtain legally are particularly vulnerable in this instance. If you know of someone who fits this description, please make them aware of the very high risk they're taking by procuring this medication illegally.

"If you have any information at all about where this toxic medication is originating, we ask that you call our tip line." Sam recited the phone number twice. "If you suspect that someone in your home has already procured this medication, please note that it's incredibly lethal and you shouldn't handle it. Please call for law enforcement assistance.

"In other news, on Friday, the Secret Service SUV I was riding in was intentionally struck by a vehicle driven by my colleague Sergeant James Ramsey. Thankfully, neither myself nor the two agents with me were seriously injured. As you will recall, Sergeant Ramsey's son was recently killed by a department sharpshooter in Rock Creek Park after he took a woman hostage and was tied to several other rapes and murders. Since then, Sergeant Ramsey has been escalating his attacks on me and other officers who were on the scene when his son was killed. After yesterday's incident, he was taken into federal custody and is facing charges of attempted murder of federal agents and a police officer. The FBI will have the most up-to-date information about Sergeant Ramsey's case going forward.

"Also Friday, the home of Detective Giselle Dominguez was invaded by a woman named Jaycee Patrick, who came in wielding a knife, threatening the life of Detective Dominguez. Ms. Patrick assaulted Detective Dominguez with the knife. Detective Dominguez used her service weapon to defend herself, killing Ms. Patrick with a single shot to the chest. Detective Dominguez has been suspended with pay pending an internal investigation.

"That's all I have at the moment. I'll take a few questions."

"Is your brother-in-law one of the fentanyl victims?"

"I'm not authorized to provide any further information about his death, beyond what's already been released."

"But is it a safe leap to conclude he died from a fentanyl overdose?"

"It would be irresponsible to leap to any conclusions. My brother-in-law and my sister are not public figures, and as such, they retain a right to privacy regardless of who their brother-in-law and sister are."

"What was the connection between Ms. Patrick and Detective Dominguez?"

"Ms. Patrick is the former girlfriend of Detective Cameron Green, who is now romantically connected to Detective Dominguez. And yes, we knew of their relationship and had no concerns with it as neither of them reports to the other and they work separate shifts. Ms. Patrick had been charged with vandalism after slashing Detective Green's tires and with felony assault of police officers after throwing a brick through Detective Green's window, narrowly missing both detectives."

"And they report to you?"

"They do." Sam pointed to Darren Tabor, her favorite reporter. "What's up, Darren?"

"Were you aware of the possibility that Ms. Patrick might go after Detective Dominguez?"

"We were aware that she was unhappy that her ex-boyfriend had moved on to someone new. Detectives Dominguez and Green had been vigilant, of course, but with multiple felony charges looming, we'd hoped that Ms. Patrick might decide to leave them alone. Sadly, she chose to confront Detective Dominguez in her home."

"Will Ramsey lose his job with the MPD after this latest incident?"

"I have no information about his status with the department."

"Was Riggs Lawton suspected of dealing the laced Oxy?"

"Not specifically, but we hoped he'd have information that would be useful in the investigation. He died before we could question him."

"Are you concerned about the chaos swirling around your department? In this briefing alone, you mentioned three officers embroiled in scandals or criminal activity."

"I'm not responsible for the conduct of my fellow officers or that of a former girlfriend who is unable to accept that a man no longer wishes to be with her. I fully support Detectives Green and Dominguez, who are outstanding police officers and detectives."

"Your brother-in-law was stricken at Camp David. Does that make his death a federal matter?"

"Not necessarily," Sam said. "As I mentioned, I have nothing else to say about his death. That applies now and into the future. I need to get to work. Thank you all."

Sam walked away as they yelled more questions at her. She yanked the door to the lobby open and disappeared inside as quickly as possible. As she went in, Vernon and Jimmy rushed toward her.

"We just heard you were outside," Vernon said, seeming perturbed. "We should've been there with you."

"I'm sorry. I forgot."

"It's okay this time, but try to remember in the future," Vernon said. "We try to leave you alone when you're in the building, but we need to know when you go outside."

"I'll do better. Sorry again."

"It's okay." He gave her a side-eyed look and a smile. "This time."

As they returned to the pit, Sam picked over the infuriating details of a case that had been more baffling than most from the outset. These dealers were like ghosts, operating on the fringes of society, always available when someone wanted their product, but impossible to find otherwise.

She stopped short in her tracks. "We need to send someone out looking to buy pain pills." Entering the pit, she called for Freddie.

He popped up in his cubicle. "You bellowed?"

"Come with me."

He followed her into her office.

"One of us needs to go looking for Oxy on the street."

"You're not asking me to do that, are you?"

"Get Gonzo on the phone, and let's make a plan."

For the first time since Spencer's untimely death last weekend, she felt like maybe she had an idea that might work.

When Gonzo answered his phone, Freddie told him, "The LT has a big idea she wants to run by you."

"What's that?"

"One of us needs to go undercover to score street Oxy."

"And you're bringing me in on that because I know how it's done?"

"Maybe," Sam said, "but it's not going to be you who does it."

"I might be the best one. You know, the former junkie who's relapsed. I could sell that."

"I'm not risking your sobriety for this, Gonzo."

"There'd be no risk. I have zero desire to go back to that life."

"Won't they question the timing?" Freddie asked. "We're making pleas for info about people dealing laced Oxy, and suddenly our sergeant is off the wagon and looking to score?"

"That's a good point," Gonzo said.

"It needs to be someone they don't know is a cop," Freddie said.

"I have a thought," Sam said. "Officer Charles. No one would attach her to me or us or even the department if we play this right."

"I assume you'll bring Narcotics in on this," Gonzo said.

"Definitely. I want every base covered if I send her into this hornet's nest."

"I think it could work," Gonzo said. "I'll give her some of my contacts, and she can reach out, since none of them got back to me."

"I've got to clear this with Malone—and with her—so hold off until you hear back from me. DEA Agent Kevin Kavanaugh is coming in to meet with us in an hour if you want to join us."

"I'd like to," Gonzo said, "but I forgot Alex has a tumbling class this morning. I've missed the last two, so I was hoping to catch this one."

"Go do it. No problem."

"We'll see you at the wake."

"Sounds good. I'll let you know if we get the green light from Malone."

"Okay. I'll put together some phone numbers for her."

"Thanks."

After they ended the call with Gonzo, Sam said, "I feel like I'm flailing blind in this investigation."

"Because it's unlike anything we've ever done, and it's personal."

"It's personal as fuck. I want to be able to tell my sister, niece and nephew that I found the person who sold poison to their husband and father."

"We'll get them, one way or the other. It doesn't have to be you who makes it happen."

"I don't care how we get them, as long as we do."

"We will."

Sam wanted to believe him, but she wasn't anywhere near as confident as he was.

CHAPTER TWENTY-NINE

S am figured she owed Gigi a heads-up that she'd briefed the press, so she called her.

"Morning, Lieutenant."

"Morning. How're you holding up?"

"Didn't sleep much, but I'm okay. It's still surreal, you know? I'm still trying to accept that I had to take her life to save my own."

"The day you don't feel awful about that is the day it's time to hang up your hat as a police officer."

"That's what Cam said, too."

"He's right, and so am I. You did what you had to. There was no other alternative. I wanted to let you know that I've briefed the media about what happened yesterday."

"Thank you for taking care of that."

"Did you see Dr. Trulo last night?"

"We did. He was wonderful, as always. We'll both be seeing him again this week."

"That's good. Stick with him. He's good at what he does."

"Yes, he is. I was going to call you because Jaycee's mom is blowing up Cameron's phone, telling him he's going to pay for this and that she blames him."

"I'll ask Jeannie if she has time to take another ride out to speak to Mrs. Patrick on behalf of both of you and the department."

"That might help."

"Hang in there, Gigi. This, too, shall pass, even though it's hard to believe that today."

"I will. I appreciate you checking in."

"Of course."

"I was hoping to attend the wake and funeral for your brother-in-law, but I don't want to draw any attention away from the family."

"You're more than welcome to come if you feel up to it." Sam had put her entire squad and several other close colleagues on the guest list. "Don't worry about us."

"Then I'll see you there."

"If you need anything, you know where I am," Sam said.

"I do. Thanks again for checking in."

"You got it."

Sam ended the call feeling confident that Gigi was handling a horrible situation as well as could be expected. Next, she picked up her desk extension and called Captain Malone.

"Can you come over to my place?" Sam asked him.

"Sam, we're both married."

"Very funny. I need you."

"Coming."

He came into her office a minute later. "You rang?"

"I have an idea."

"I'm listening."

"I'd like to send Officer Charles, who's going to take Jeannie's spot on my squad, by the way, out to procure some Oxy."

As Malone listened, his expression never changed. "Have you asked her yet?"

"No, I wanted to clear it with you first."

"This is above my pay grade. Let's talk to the chief."

"Is he here?"

"For a few hours."

Sam told Freddie she'd be right back and went with Malone to the chief's suite, passing Helen's desk, which was unoccupied since it was Sunday. "It's weird not having to go through Helen to get to him."

"I know. I bet she's watching us from home."

Sam laughed as he knocked on the door.

"Come in."

Since it was Sunday, the chief was wearing civilian clothes. "What's up?" he asked.

"Holland has an idea that needs to go through you."

"What idea?"

Sam filled him in.

"So you've succeeded in officially stealing my Officer Charles?" Neveah had been helping the chief with administrative work, and he'd resisted Sam's earlier attempts to lure the young officer to the Homicide squad.

"Can a grown adult be stolen? Sir?"

"Is she being cheeky with me?" Farnsworth asked Malone.

"I believe she is, sir."

"What do you think of the idea?"

"I want this saved as an 'if all else fails' plan," Farnsworth said. "As you know, Officer Charles is near and dear to my heart."

"And to mine," Sam said. "I think the world of her. If we decide to go this route, I'll make sure she's fully supported in her mission."

"If she's willing and if all other investigative avenues have been exhausted, you have my permission to try it, provided you cover every base to keep her safe."

"Thank you, sir."

"I'll see you at the wake."

"Thank you for coming."

"Of course. Marti and I want to be there for Angela."

"She'll appreciate it. I'll see you then."

"I heard you're consulting with the DEA."

"I'm desperate enough to ask the Feds for help."

"Whatever it takes."

"Yes, sir. I'm going back to work. I'm a short timer today."

"Keep me in the loop on the operation with Officer Charles."

"I will." Sam walked out of the chief's office and headed back to the pit.

Freddie stood when he saw her coming. "Lawton's wife is in your office."

"Come with me, will you?"

They walked into Sam's office, where a gorgeous blonde woman sat waiting for them in one of Sam's visitor chairs. When they came in, she jumped up. "I want to know what happened to my husband."

"Please have a seat," Sam said.

"I don't want to sit. I want answers."

"I want them, too, Mrs. Lawton. Your husband is with the medical examiner now, and she's determined he died from a likely fentanyl overdose."

"He'd never touch that stuff."

"The proof is in the autopsy."

"Riggs... He was perfectly fine when he left for dinner last night."

"You didn't want to go with him?"

"I don't like that restaurant, so he goes there alone."

"I need to back up and ask for your name," Sam said.

"It's Leslie. Leslie Lawton."

"And how long have you been married to Riggs?"

"It would've been ten years this fall." Her eyes filled. "Riggs would never take that stuff or end his own life. He loved his life and me..."

"I'm sorry to have to confirm that he did, in fact, take his own life."

"He couldn't have done that."

Sam chose to let her silence speak for her.

"Where did it come from?"

"He had it hidden on his person and was dead in a matter of minutes."

Suddenly, Leslie reached for her necklace. "Oh my God... He wears a pendant. He never took it off, and when I asked him what it was, he told me it was for emergencies. I had no idea what that meant." She looked stricken. "You don't think...."

Sam nodded to Freddie to notify Lindsey.

He got up and left the room, closing the door behind him.

"What do you know about your husband's business, Mrs. Lawton?"

"He... He was involved in so many things."

"Was he involved in dealing drugs?"

She recoiled from the question. "No! He would never do something like that!"

Sam tipped her head. "Are you certain of that?"

"He... He was so health conscious. I can't for the life of me picture him involved with drugs."

"What other businesses did he own or manage?"

"It was all online stuff. I don't really know."

Sam wanted to ask how she could be so oblivious, but she bit her tongue. "Could we have your permission to search his computers and phone as well as your home?"

"What? No. Absolutely not."

"We believe your husband was possibly overseeing a vast criminal empire that included drug dealing. Unless you'd like to be charged as an accessory, it would be in your best interest to allow us to fully investigate him." Charging her would be a long shot, but whatever it took to convince her to help them.

"He... He wouldn't want that. He was so private."

"He's dead, Mrs. Lawton, and he's left you to deal with the fallout. I'd suggest you cooperate with us, if for no other reason than to prove he wasn't involved in any of this." He absolutely was, but that, too, didn't need to be said right then.

"I... I'm not sure what to do. Should I talk to a lawyer?"

"You're not currently facing any charges, so you don't need a lawyer."

"Not currently facing charges? What does that mean? I didn't know anything about what he was doing."

"Which will help you if you help us." Sam stared her down, hoping to make her understand the position she was in. "What's it going to be? Can we have your permission to search your home and his electronics?"

She took a deep breath as tears slid down her cheeks. "He promised he'd never leave me."

Sam handed her a tissue. "I'm very sorry for your loss."

Leslie wiped away her tears. "He was distrustful of police."

"If he was dealing drugs, he had good reason to be."

"Is it possible that's not what he was doing?"

"I don't think so, but if it is, you'll be the first person I tell."

"How could I not have known this?"

"I'm sure he went to great lengths to keep it hidden from you."

She blew her nose and looked up at Sam with red, watery eyes. "I'll allow the search. I want to know the truth."

"Thank you. Could you please give me the address?"

When she had confirmed the location and retrieved the keys to the Lawton home, Sam picked up the phone and called Lieutenant Haggerty from Crime Scene to ask for a team at the Lawton residence.

"Got it. We're on it."

Next, she called Lieutenant Archelotta to notify him that she needed a deep dive on Lawton's computers and devices that would be coming from the scene.

"I was just going to call you about something I found on the phones of everyone involved in this case."

"Can you come down?"

"Yep, on the way."

To Leslie, Sam said, "Is there somewhere you can go while we conduct the search?"

"I can go to my friend's house."

"Was she a friend of Riggs's, too?"

Leslie nodded. "She and her husband are our closest friends."

"Until we know more about your husband's business and who else was involved, I think you should steer clear of mutual friends. In fact, I think we should put you in one of our safe houses, just in case."

Shocked, she said, "In case of what?"

"In case there are people who'd kill you to keep you from letting us into your husband's business."

ARCHIE CAME INTO THE PIT, holding up a thumb drive.

"Everyone in the conference room," Sam said. "Give me five, and I'll be right there." She called Officer Charles. "Are you in the building?"

"Yes, I am."

"I need a favor. Can you come to my office?"

"On my way."

When Officer Charles arrived, Sam briefed her on the situation with Leslie. "I need you to get her into a safe house and arrange for round-the-clock security."

"I'll take care of it."

"Thank you. I need to talk to you about something else when you get back. Will you find me?"

"Yes, ma'am."

Sam gave her a playful glare over the ma'am thing and then introduced her to Mrs. Lawton. "Officer Charles will get you settled somewhere safe while we conduct the search of your home."

"I can't go there to get my things?"

"We don't think that would be wise right now. We can get you anything you need elsewhere."

"Can I call my family to tell them where I am?"

"You can notify them you're in protective custody, and then we need you to turn off your phone."

"Why?"

"So no one can track you. Our goal is to keep you safe, which means no one can know where you are."

"I'll go crazy without my phone."

"I'm sorry, but it has to be powered down, and we'll take possession of it so you aren't tempted to turn it back on."

"You're asking an awful lot of me."

Sam was starting to be seriously annoyed by this woman, but since she needed her, she kept her tone conciliatory. "I'm trying to keep you alive."

Leslie seemed to deflate somewhat after hearing that.

"Please go with Officer Charles and do exactly what she tells you to do."

"How long will I have to stay there?"

"Until we're sure it's safe." Sam decided she needed to level with the woman. "If we're able to prove that your husband was who we think he was, there's a good chance you might never be able to return to your home or your previous life."

Her face turned ghostly pale in an instant. "*What?*"

"We'll know more in a day or two. In the meantime, please do what you're told, and if you think of anything you might've heard about your husband's business, we'd like to know that."

Chastened by the reality of her situation, Leslie nodded and went with Officer Charles.

Sam texted Haggerty to give him the details of the search needed at the Lawton home. *I have the keys and the code for the elevator to their high-rise apartment.*

Will come get it in a few.

CHAPTER THIRTY

"What's the latest?" Deputy Chief McBride asked when she came to the door to Sam's office.

Sam filled her in on what was happening with Leslie. "I'm glad you came by. I need a favor."

"What's that?"

"Jaycee Patrick's mother is blowing up Cam's phone, accusing him of being responsible for her daughter's death, even though we know the truth. I wondered if you might be able to have another talk with her."

"Sure, I can try. Not sure what good it'll do. She was out of her mind when we were there last night."

"It may not do any good, but it's worth a try to get her to leave Cameron alone."

"I'll pay her a visit. The reason I came by was to let you know that Lenore Worthington and LaToya Deasly are planning to hold a press conference in the next week or two to call out the MPD and law enforcement in general for allowing their children's cases to languish."

"Crap," Sam said.

"Yeah, it's not great news for the department, but they have every right to air out their grievances with the way their cases were handled. I've been working on triaging some of Stahl's other cases, beginning with successful prosecutions, and I have a few that we need to look at very soon. One is a man convicted of rape and murder sixteen years ago who has sworn every minute since he was arrested that he didn't do it. I'm asking Erica Lucas to take a hard look at that one and told her you and your team would be available to assist."

"Yes, of course. Detective Green is my point person on the cold cases."

"I'll ask Erica to coordinate with him."

"Sounds good." Sam smiled at Jeannie. "That uniform looks good on you, friend."

"Thanks. I appreciate your support. It's been a little... weird."

"How so?"

"The usual bullshit. People who used to be friendly toward me have nothing to say now. That kind of thing."

"They're jealous."

Jeannie shrugged. "Whatever. I tell myself I don't care."

"That's the way to be. In a few months, people will forget about how it happened."

"You think so?" Jeannie asked, seeming skeptical.

"I know so. Things happen fast around here. Something else will come up that will make them forget all about you. In the meantime, you keep your head down and do the job. That's what will win them over, when they realize how lucky they are to have you in a leadership role."

"I hope you're right."

"When have you known me not to be?"

Jeannie rolled her eyes. "I walked right into that one. I'm going to see Mrs. Patrick. Pray for me."

"Will do, Chief."

At the door, Jeannie turned back. "None of this would've happened for me without you. I'll never forget that."

"I'm so proud of you, and I can't wait to see you shine."

"Thanks, Sam. Your support means the world to me."

"You have it. Always."

"I'll report back after I see Mrs. Patrick, and Michael and I will be at the wake later."

"Thank you for coming."

"If there's anything you need over the next few days, just ask."

"If you could find the person who sold my brother-in-law poison, that'd help."

"I heard you're bringing in Narcotics and the DEA. I think that's wise."

"I'm way out of my league on this one. I need help."

"There's nothing wrong with admitting that."

"If you say so."

"I do, and I'm the deputy chief now."

"Haha, don't let it go to your head, boss."

"I'll try not to. See you later."

"See you."

Freddie came in as Jeannie went out. "We're in the conference room. Are you coming?"

"Yeah, sorry." As she stepped out of her office, Haggerty entered the pit. Sam handed him the keys to Lawton's place and the piece of paper with the elevator code written on it.

The entire transaction occurred silently. They were like two ships passing in the night, hopefully headed for a successful resolution to this case sooner rather than later.

ARCHIE HAD a presentation ready to go with lists of numbers highlighted. When Sam entered the room, he dove right in. "These are numbers found on the phones of all our victims, each of them untraceable, which means they're burner phones. Even though the numbers are all different, that doesn't mean they aren't going to the same person. Each of them also had the Burner app on their phones, which is another way dealers communicate without being traceable."

"Why can't we stop the sale of burner phones?" Sam asked.

"It wouldn't matter at this point with so many in circulation," Archie said. "I've heard of cases where they have a phone for each kind of drug they deal, so they can keep their customers separated. I've also heard of dealers selling their burners for top dollar when they want out of the business. They're a hot commodity to the next dealer, looking to step into an already established business."

"Isn't it bad for all of them when someone sells something that kills people?" Sam directed the question to no one in particular.

"I would think so," Archie said. "It makes all their customers hesitant, because how do they know their guy isn't the one selling the laced pills?"

"Sergeant Merrick mentioned how death is a badge of honor to some of them," O'Brien said.

"Which is sick," Archie said.

"Wouldn't it be in all of their best interest to help us find the one who's selling the lethal stuff?" Sam said. "Maybe we can work that angle."

Freddie came into the room, catching the tail end of that comment. "Which angle?"

"Turning them against each other," Sam said. "It's bad for business for someone to be selling lethal drugs, so we ask them to help us figure out who's doing it."

"We might have something from the tip line," Freddie said. "A caller said to look at a guy named Sal Vincent."

"Did they say anything else?"

"No, only that."

DEA Agent Kevin Kavanaugh came to the door. Sam noted his resemblance to his brother, Derek, with the same coloring, but Kevin had a hard edge to him that Derek lacked.

"Come in, Agent Kavanaugh." Sam stood to shake his hand and introduced him to the other officers in the room. "Thanks for coming in."

"No problem."

To Freddie, she said, "Will you see what's keeping Lieutenant Cooper?"

"I'm here," Cooper said, entering the room with a large cup of coffee and what looked to be an egg sandwich.

For fuck's sake.

"What'd I miss?" Cooper asked. "Other than Lawton offing himself in our custody."

"Does the name Sal Vincent mean anything to either of you?" Sam asked.

Cooper nodded since his mouth was full.

"He's well known to us," Kevin said. "We've been after him for years."

Nodding, Cooper pointed to Kevin. "What he said."

Sam wanted to tell him to chew with his mouth closed. "Freddie, can you do a run on him?"

"Already did, and nothing popped on a Sal Vincent or a Salvador Vincent or an S. Vincent."

"I'm not surprised," Kevin said. "He flies well below the radar."

"Where do we begin to look for a dealer who isn't in our system?" Sam asked.

"You take to the street and talk to your informants," Kevin said. "Someone will know him."

"We're shorthanded today," Sam said to Cooper. "Can we get your team on that for us?"

"Yep." A piece of egg fell out of his mouth and landed on the conference table. He gave a sheepish grin and scooped up the egg and popped it back into his mouth.

Revolting.

"I'll get my team started on that and keep you informed," Cooper said, grabbing the other half of his sandwich, which he stuffed into his face as he left the room.

"Charming fellow," Kevin said.

"I assume you've met him before."

"I've had the pleasure many times, unfortunately."

Sam laughed. "What are the odds that his team will come back with some info?"

"Fairly good. The rest of them are well connected, as are my people. I'll put them on it right away and keep you informed of any developments. I understand this case is personal to you, but the frustration you're feeling is common in these investigations. You're looking for people who know how to stay hidden and have tremendous incentive to operate off the grid. It takes a lot of old-school gumshoe detective work to find them."

"That makes me feel a little better," Sam said. "I feel like we've been spinning our wheels for a week now."

"Because you have. We'll do what we can to help."

"Before you go, I want to run an idea by you." She outlined the plan to have Officer Charles go looking for street Oxy. "What do you think of that?"

"It's worth a try, but make sure she's well protected. If these guys sniff a cop, they won't hesitate to end her."

His warning landed like an arrow of fear to her gut. "I hear you."

"Before you do that, give us twenty-four hours to try to find Vincent."

"Will do."

"I'll be in touch."

"Thank you, Kevin."

"Sure thing."

Sam returned to her office and made a call to her friend Roberto.

"Lady cop, twice in one week. To what do I owe the pleasure?"

"I'm looking for a guy who goes by Sal Vincent. You know anything about him?"

"The name isn't familiar to me, but I can poke around a bit, if you'd like."

"I would as long as you aren't endangering yourself by doing it."

"Nah, it's fine. The people I'd ask are loyal to me."

"Let me know if you hear anything about him or Riggs Lawton, okay?"

"I will. How you holding up?"

"I'm frustrated to be no closer to answers for my sister than I was a week ago."

"You'll get there, lady cop. You always do."

"Thanks for your help. I appreciate it."

"Girl... I'm friends with the bad-ass first-lady cop. You have no idea what that does to my street cred."

Sam laughed. "I'm sure it does wonders."

"You know it. I'll be back to you if anything pops."

"Thanks, Roberto."

"Any time."

Sam slapped her phone closed and thought about what he'd said about how she'd get them eventually because she always did. But how many more people would have to die before they got a break?

Freddie came to the door. "Dispatch got a call from a hotel downtown about three people OD'd. Two DOA. One still alive, but in critical condition on his way to GW. Pills and white powder all over the room. The maid who entered the room is being treated for potential fentanyl exposure."

"What about the EMTs?"

"They suited up before they went in."

"So, it's gotten to the point where they have hazmat protection in the buses?" she asked, using law enforcement slang for ambulances.

"I think it got to that point quite some time ago."

Sam jumped up and grabbed her coat. "Did they call in a team to deal with the drugs?"

"They're on their way along with the ME, who'll go in after HazMat clears the scene."

"Let's go."

"Where to?"

"GW to talk to the guy who survived."

GIGI WOKE from a nap late on Sunday morning, feeling slightly better than she had earlier. The events with Jaycee ran through her mind on repeat. She expected to feel regret, but she didn't. All she felt was relief that she'd survived the encounter with someone who'd come to kill her.

Did feeling no regret make her heartless? Maybe so, but gratitude outweighed the regret.

"How long have you been awake?" Cam asked.

"Not long."

"Are you okay?"

"I'm wondering if it makes me heartless to have no regrets about shooting her."

"Why should you have regrets? She came into your home intending to kill you and then assaulted you. She got what she deserved."

"Did she deserve to die, though?"

"Let's turn that around to ask if, God forbid, she'd succeeded in killing you, do you think she'd be asking that question?"

"No. She'd be glad I was out of her way so she could get you back."

"Which was never going to happen. She wouldn't have given you another thought, which means you shouldn't give her one either."

"I wish it was that simple."

"She forced the standoff. You defended yourself. End of story."

"Is it, though? Are we naïve enough to think it's going to be that simple?"

"That's the truth of what happened, Gigi. That's what you have to cling to."

Their phones chimed with a text.

"It's from Sam," Cam said after he grabbed his phone and read the text to her. "Jeannie is going to talk to Mrs. Patrick about her outrageous accusations. I think it'll mean a lot that the deputy chief is representing us there. Gigi, we need you to file your report on the incident first thing this morning so the internal investigation can get started."

"Tell her thank you from both of us, and I'll get the report done right away."

Cameron typed the message and put the phone on the bedside table before turning toward her. "I'll help you write it."

"She offered OT today. You ought to go grab a few hours."

"I'm not going anywhere, babe. I'm staying right here with you."

"Are we still going to the wake for Sam's brother-in-law today?"

"I think we should."

"Yes, I agree."

He leaned in to kiss her. "Let's get that report done so we can move on to other things."

"You really don't have to help me."

"Yes, I really do."

"Are you still blaming yourself?"

"Not like I was, but I feel responsible for the fact that she came for you in the first place. I can't believe I spent so much time with her and never knew she was a psycho."

"She kept that hidden from you."

"Can you imagine what my life would've been like if I'd married her?"

"No, I can't, and I don't want to imagine that."

He shuddered. "Me either. I mean, I feel bad that she obviously had serious issues, but that doesn't excuse what she did to you."

"Or to you."

"I'm far more concerned about you."

"And I'm far more concerned about you."

He smiled. "I'm so damned glad you survived, Gigi. One thing I can be certain of is that I never would've survived losing you. Not like that, anyway."

"I'm here, and you're stuck with me."

"Never been so happy to be stuck with anyone."

"Same goes, love."

CHAPTER THIRTY-ONE

Jeannie drove to the Patrick home in the department SUV that had been made available to her as deputy chief.

Deputy chief.

She still couldn't wrap her head around the amazing turn of events that had led to a promotion she'd never seen coming. Jumping three ranks from detective to deputy chief was unheard of, which was why she'd sensed the unspoken pushback coming from many of her colleagues.

Half of her wanted to tell them to fuck off. The other half quaked inside at the realization that people deeply resented her for being promoted to the second-highest rank in the department, a heartbeat away from the top job. In reasoning with herself, she was quick to think that she'd earned the position through hard work and tenacity, especially after being kidnapped and raped on the job.

She'd come back from that—somehow—and had helped to bring down a massive human trafficking organization when she found missing District resident Carisma Deasly. That bust had gotten national coverage and elevated her standing within the department, which was one reason why the mayor had asked her to take the job.

Yes, Sam had turned it down—twice—before she pushed the mayor in Jeannie's direction, and yes, the Black mayor had loved the idea of a Black woman in the role. Jeannie loved that, too, as she'd long wished for better representation and diversity in the department's top ranks.

If only she could shake the feeling that her big promotion was more about her sex and her race than her work, no matter how big the Deasly bust had been or how hard she'd worked in her time on the job.

Ugh, she hated thinking that way. She was going to bust her ass and prove herself to every doubter, even if it took the rest of her career. She'd be the best deputy chief the MPD had ever had. As she had that thought, she issued a silent apology to Skip Holland, whom she'd admired and respected, but she was going to put even him to shame before she was done.

Fired up, she pulled into the driveway at the Patrick home, prepared to do battle on behalf of Detectives Dominguez and Green as well as the MPD. Badge in hand, she rang the bell and peeked through the glass next to the door.

The door flew open, surprising her, as did the large handgun Mrs. Patrick pointed at her.

"Do come in." Mrs. Patrick's eyes were wild, her appearance unkept. "I've been hoping you might come by again."

Fuck, Jeannie thought as she rested her hand on her own weapon and stepped inside.

"I'll take that," Mrs. Patrick said, using her chin to point at Jeannie's gun.

"I don't think so."

She directed her gun at Jeannie's chest. "I have absolutely nothing left to lose, so don't fuck with me. Give me your gun. Now!"

Because she had a lot to live for, especially her husband and the child she was carrying, Jeannie handed over her weapon and went to sit in the chair the woman directed her to.

"My team knows I'm here. They'll come looking for me." As she said that, Jeannie wondered how long it would be before she was missed. As a detective, she'd carried a side piece strapped to her leg. She'd stopped doing that after her promotion, which had been a big mistake.

"Good. I hope they do come looking for you."

Jeannie glanced into the dining room, where a veritable arsenal of weapons was laid out on the table and swallowed hard.

Fuck.

. . .

SAM CALLED AHEAD to Dr. Anderson. "I need to talk to the OD guy coming in with EMS. It's absolutely critical."

"Let us get him stable, and I'll do what I can for you."

"Thanks, Rob. Appreciate it."

"Sure thing. I'll call you when you can see him."

"We'll be outside the ER waiting."

"Got it."

While Vernon drove them to GW, Sam called Lindsey. "Are you with the two vics at the hotel?"

"Not yet. We're waiting on HazMat. It's going to be a while before it's safe for us to go in there."

"We need names and addresses of the victims ASAP."

"I'll get them for you when I can."

Sam glanced at the clock on the dashboard, which was inching closer to noon. She had two more hours, three at the absolute most, before she had to head home and get ready for the wake. "Thanks, Linds."

"How are you doing?"

"I'm pissed that more people had to die while we spin our wheels trying to find ghosts."

"You're doing everything you can, Sam."

"And yet, it's nowhere near enough."

"How's Gigi?"

"She's holding up okay, but I'm sure she's still struggling to wrap her head around it all."

"Such an awful thing. My heart goes out to her and Cam—and strangely to Jaycee's family."

"I know. You feel for them because it's not their fault that she did what she did, but they're left to deal with the fallout."

"Exactly. Let me know if there's anything I can do to help you besides the obvious autopsy reports."

"We know exactly what they'll show."

"I'm afraid you're right. We'll see you at the wake."

"Unfortunately, I'll be there."

She ended the call with Lindsey and tried to cool her jets while she waited to hear from Anderson. "I hate waiting."

"No kidding," Freddie said. "I had no idea."

Vernon coughed to hide a laugh.

"Don't be a smart-ass."

"My apologies," Freddie said.

"And don't apologize when you're not actually sorry."

"I know this totally sucks, and I'm sorry it's so frustrating."

"I keep thinking back to last Sunday when we were hanging out in our cabin at Camp David with no idea whatsoever that a bomb was about to go off in our lives."

"It's so awful. I can't stop thinking about him playing with Jack on Christmas morning and how good he always was with him."

"Yeah." When tears filled her eyes, Sam turned to look out the window. "Ella won't remember Spence, and the baby will never get to meet him. I can't imagine Angela facing that on her own."

"She'll be surrounded by family and friends. She'll never be on her own."

"I feel so guilty because all I can think about since it happened is that I'd die if anything like that ever happened to Nick. I would simply cease to exist."

"No, you wouldn't."

"I really would, and what kind of sister does it make me that I'm thinking of myself at a time like this?"

"You're the best sister and friend anyone could ever ask for," Freddie said, "and it's only natural to think that way when disaster strikes close to home this way."

"Makes me feel like a selfish asshole to be worried about my own husband when my sister has just been widowed."

"It's normal, Sam. Ask Vernon. Isn't it normal?"

"It is," Vernon said. "When my wife's father and brother died of lung cancer within two years of each other, I worried for years that it was coming for my wife, too. It's what people do, Sam. They worry about lightning striking them after it's hit someone close to them."

"That makes me feel a little better. Thanks, you guys." She glanced at the clock again. "Not sure how much longer I can wait."

"I can stay if you have to go."

"You need to get home to your wife."

"She's seeing her sister after work, so it's fine. I can stay awhile longer."

Sam was about to leave when the phone rang with a call from Anderson. She pounced on it. "Hey."

"He's conscious and alert if you want to come talk to him."

"Coming in now."

Vernon had the door open before Sam finished the call.

"Thank you," she said to him.

"Sure thing."

He followed them into the waiting room, where, predictably, everything came to a stop when people realized who'd come in.

Sam pressed forward, showing her badge at the reception desk. "Dr. Anderson is expecting me."

"Yes, ma'am, Mrs. Cappuano, and if I may say—"

"Please get the doctor."

He came around the corner and gestured for them to follow him.

"You need to tell her that when I show up, I'm Lieutenant Holland, and I don't have time for nonsense."

"I'll take care of it." He stopped outside a cubicle. "Bryan Smith, age thirty-two and very lucky to be alive."

"Why did he survive, and the others didn't?" Sam asked.

"Hard to say. Could be he took less than they did, or the pills he took had a less lethal amount of fentanyl. It's not like the people lacing the pills are pharmacists who ensure that every pill is the same as the last one, you know?"

"Yeah, true. Okay, here we go." Sam stepped into the room where nurses were tending to a man with brown hair. His blue eyes were wide with fear, or maybe it was the aftereffects of the drugs. What did she know about such things? She'd never even smoked pot because the thought of being altered by drugs of any kind freaked her out, especially after everything she'd seen on the job.

Sam showed him her badge. "I'm Lieutenant Holland with the MPD, Mr. Smith."

"Am I under arrest?"

"Not at this time, but I'd like to know where you got the pills that you and your friends took."

"There was this guy in the bar at the hotel. He sold them to us."

"Which hotel was it?"

"The W."

Sam glanced at Freddie. "Get there right away and get the security film for the bar."

He took off to see to her order, while Sam hoped the film might finally provide a break they badly needed.

"Did you catch his name?"

"He said it was Craig something. I told Tommy we shouldn't do it, but he said I didn't know what I was missing. No one will tell me where they are."

"I'm sorry to have to tell you they're deceased."

"What?" His eyes instantly filled with tears. "No. They can't be."

"They are, Mr. Smith, and you're very lucky you aren't, too. Can you tell me their full names?"

"Ah, Tommy O'Donald and Jesse Myer. We grew up together in Shaw." He looked up at her, eyes watery. "They're really dead? Tommy and Jess..."

"They are. I'm sorry."

He covered his face with his hands and moaned. "Oh my God." His heartbroken sobs echoed through the room.

"You need to stay calm, Mr. Smith," one of the nurses said, giving Sam a disapproving look.

"I know this is a terrible shock to you, but I need you to tell me everything you can remember about the person who sold you the pills."

Bryan wiped tears from his face with the tissue a nurse handed him. "He came up to us at the hotel bar, and we got to talking."

"What'd he look like?"

"Dark hair, well dressed."

"White guy?"

"Yeah."

"How old?"

"Mid-thirties maybe. He bought us a round of drinks and invited us to a party upstairs, said they had all the good stuff for free."

"And you weren't at all suspicious that he was willing to give you drugs for free?"

"Nah, he seemed like a cool dude."

Sam pulled out her phone and texted Freddie to find out who had reserved the hotel room. *Looking for a dark-haired white guy, midthirties, well dressed, approaching three guys at the bar. He invited them upstairs to party.*

Got it.

"What happened when you got to the room?"

"There were women there. They were there to play, you know?"

She didn't know. "Did Craig stay to hang out?"

"Yeah, he was there, too. It got kinda wild," he said, looking sheepish. "Everyone was doing something with someone."

"When did the pills enter the picture?"

"He started handing them out after the sex. He and the women took some, too, so we figured it was okay."

"Did the three of you actually discuss whether you should take the pills, or did you just take them?"

"We kind of looked at each other and shrugged as if to say hey, they're doing it, so why not?"

Idiots, she thought, but being stupid didn't mean they deserved to die.

"Why did I live when they died?" he asked as tears ran down his face.

"Hard to say," Sam replied. "You could've gotten a lesser dose than they did."

"Of what?"

"Fentanyl, probably."

"Jesus. I've heard about that stuff. We never would've gone anywhere near something like that."

It was too late to tell him that by taking anything provided by a stranger, they were risking much more than they bargained for.

"I'll be right back." She stepped into the hallway and called Captain Malone.

"What's up?"

"This investigation just took a turn. I think someone is deliberately poisoning people with fentanyl-laced pills."

"Why do you say that?"

Sam told him about how Smith and his friends were lured to a hotel room with a promise of a party and free drugs. "They had women waiting to seduce them, and when everyone was well satisfied, they started handing out free pills."

"What's in it for the dealer?"

"I'm not sure yet, but this latest incident was deliberate. He lured them upstairs to give them laced pills."

"It sure sounds that way."

"Cruz has gone to the hotel to get the security film from the bar and to get the name of the person who reserved the room. I'm hoping for a break. Finally."

"Cruz asked me to get a warrant for the security film, which I'm working on now, and Haggerty's team is on their way to the hotel to work the scene."

"Thanks. I have to head home after this to get ready for the wake, but I want to be kept in the loop."

"I'll keep you posted."

"Thanks, Cap."

"See you at the wake."

"Thanks for coming."

"Of course I'm coming. I've known Angela since she was a baby."

"Means a lot to us."

Sam ended the call and went back into the room. "Can you give me contact info for the families of Tommy and Jesse?"

He reached for his phone on the tray and poked around his contacts. "Tommy's wife is Catherine with a C." He recited her address and phone number. "Jess was single. His mom still lives in Shaw." He gave her the contact info. "Will you tell them I'm so sorry?" he asked, his eyes filling again. "Tell them I'm so damned sorry."

"I will."

Sam needed to get home to prepare for the wake, but someone needed to notify the families of the latest victims, so she set out for the O'Donald home in Kalorama, asking Vernon to use the lights to save time. She pulled out the BlackBerry to call Nick.

"Hey, are you on the way home?"

"Not yet. I have two stops to make, and then I'll be there."

"Tracy and Mike are here to take Angela to the funeral home."

"Tell them I'll be home in time to go with them."

"Will do."

"How does she seem?"

"Not so good. She's barely functioning, and Jack had a meltdown because he wants to go. We tried to explain to him that wakes aren't for kids, but he wasn't having it. Angela told him he can come to the service tomorrow, and that seemed to pacify him."

"My heart aches."

"I know. Mine, too.

"Before I come home for my brother-in-law's wake, I've got to tell a wife and a mother that their husband and son overdosed in a hotel room last night."

"Can't someone else do that?"

"It's fine. I'll take care of it and be home soon."

"We'll be here."

"Love you."

"Love you, too, babe."

CHAPTER THIRTY-TWO

"Here we are, ma'am," Vernon said when they arrived at the O'Donalds' home.

A blonde woman was in the yard supervising two little ones on tiny bikes.

Sam summoned the courage she would need to shatter the woman's world with the news she'd come to deliver.

When she emerged from the SUV, the woman's eyes got big with recognition that quickly morphed into fear. If the first lady was at her house, she wasn't bringing good news.

"No," she said. "*No.*"

"Is there someone you could call to come be with you and your kids?" Sam asked.

"How can you be here already? I just called the police to say I couldn't find my husband."

"I wasn't aware of that call, but I do have information about your husband."

The kids, aware that something terrible was happening, toddled over to their mother and began to cry along with her.

"Please don't tell me he's dead. Please."

"I'm so sorry," Sam said.

The three of them wailed in perfect harmony that broke Sam's already shattered heart all over again.

A woman came running across the street. "What's going on? Cath... What's wrong?"

"Tommy's dead. She's come to tell me he's dead."

"Oh my God."

"How?" Cath asked, looking up at Sam with utter devastation.

"He overdosed."

Her face lost all expression. "No. He doesn't do drugs."

She decided not to tell her about the sex. She'd find out about that soon enough. "His friend Bryan Smith survived. He told us they were approached by a man in a bar at a hotel downtown and invited to a party upstairs. Once they were there, they were given the pills that killed Mr. O'Donald and Mr. Myer."

"Oh God, Jesse, too? Tommy didn't do drugs. There's no way he would've taken those pills willingly."

Sam decided to let her hold on to her illusions for as long as she could. "I'm very sorry for your loss."

"What am I supposed to do now?"

"If you can give me your number, the medical examiner will be in touch after the autopsy is performed. She'll want to know what funeral home you'd like to use."

Cath's friend kept her arms around her when her knees would've buckled as she recited the phone number that Sam wrote down.

"Here's my card. My cell number is on there."

"I'm surprised they send the first lady to do things like this," the neighbor said.

"I'm not the first lady right now," Sam said, annoyed by the comment when there were bigger concerns to be dealt with for her friend. "I'm the lieutenant who oversees the Homicide division for the MPD, and this is my job." To Cath, she said, "Please let me know if there's anything I can do for you."

"Thank you," Cath said.

Having done what she could, Sam left to head to the Myer home, where she had to break the news all over again, this time to Jesse's mother.

"I just called to report my son missing," Mrs. Myer said when she saw Sam on her doorstep, immediately on the alert for impending disaster. "Why'd they send you?"

Sam had that effect on people. "May I come in for a moment?"

Hesitantly, she opened the door and stepped back to admit Sam.

"Tell me what's going on."

"Mrs. Myer, I'm very sorry to have to tell you that Jesse was found dead of a drug overdose this morning."

The woman collapsed against Sam, who held her up as best she could while she wailed.

"There's no way! He would never take drugs."

"I'm sorry to have to tell you that's what happened."

"It can't be. It simply cannot be."

"Is there someone you could call to be with you?"

"My other son... He'll come."

"Could I call him for you?"

Sam helped her reach out to her other son, said the words for her when she couldn't and was told he'd be there in fifteen minutes, so she waited until he arrived. "Can I get you a glass of water?" Sam asked.

She shook her head. "How could this have happened?"

Sam went through what they knew so far about what had transpired the night before. "Tommy is also dead, but Bryan survived. That's how we know what happened."

"Not Tommy, too. My God, they've been friends since elementary school. The three of them."

When Mrs. Myer's other son arrived, Sam took down a contact number, gave him her business card and notified him that the ME would be in touch after the autopsy was completed. Emerging from the stuffy house into the cool air was such a welcome relief.

"Worst fucking part of the job, hands down," Sam said to Vernon as he held the door for her.

"I can't imagine having to do that."

"It sucks, and now I get to go home to prepare for my brother-in-law's wake."

"A crap day all around," Vernon said.

"For sure." She checked her phone and found a still photo from the hotel's security video that she forwarded to Malone to be further investigated. After she sent the photo, she called him because that was quicker than typing a text.

"That's the guy we're looking for. He lured our three vics upstairs at the hotel, plied them with sex and laced pills."

"I'll do a reverse-image search to see if we can get a name and go from there."

"Let me know if anything pops."

"Yep."

Next, Sam called Lindsey and left a message on her voice mail with the phone numbers for Catherine O'Donald and Mrs. Myer so they could be notified when the autopsies were completed.

She slapped the phone closed, hoping they might be on the verge of finally catching a break in this baffling case. When she got home, she went upstairs as quickly as her hip would allow and encountered Elijah and his new wife, Candace, in the hallway. He wore a dark suit, and she had on a black wrap dress. "It's good of you guys to be here," she said as she hugged them.

"We wanted to be here for you and your family," Eli said.

"That's very nice of you."

"How's Angela?" Eli asked.

"Not so great, but that's to be expected. It's been such an awful shock for everyone."

"I know what that's like," Eli said grimly. His father and stepmother had been brutally murdered in a home invasion. That incident had brought him and his young twin siblings into their lives last fall.

"Yes, you do. I really appreciate you being here, and Angela will, too."

"No problem."

"Will you guys do me a favor?"

"Anything you need," Candace said.

"Will you keep an eye on Scotty at the wake and get him out of there if it's too much for him?" To Candace, she added, "We just lost my father in October, and he took that hard."

"Of course," Eli said. "We'll take care of him."

"Thank you. I need to change and get myself together."

"Go ahead. We're going to spend some time with the twins before we go."

"I'll see you in a few." Sam went to the end of the hallway and ducked into the suite she shared with Nick as he stepped out of the closet, knotting his tie as he walked.

"Hey," he said.

"Hey yourself."

"How'd it go today?"

"We might've made a bit of progress, but we added two more bodies to the tally. I know I say they're all frustrating, but this case is next level. These people slither in to distribute their poison and then disappear. This latest one feels deliberate, like they intentionally set out to find people they could kill with their laced pills."

"What would be the point of that? Isn't it counterproductive to kill the customers?"

"We've heard that some of these dealers wear the deaths like a badge of honor."

"That's so fucked up."

"Sure is." Sam's phone rang, and she took the call from Malone. "What's up?"

"I'm not sure. Michael Wilkinson just called me. He's been trying to get in touch with Jeannie, and her phone has been going right to voice mail for some time now."

"She went to see Jaycee Patrick's mother hours ago," Sam said as panic overtook her. "We need to get people out there right now."

"Give me the address."

Sam tried to remember it, but her mind went blank. "Dani would have it. She went there with her yesterday. You don't think..." Her knees buckled, and she had to sit before she fell. "Cap..."

"I'm on it. Calling Dani now, and we'll send the cavalry."

"Please."

"Breathe, Sam. She knows how to take care of herself."

"I sent her there and never even checked on her when I didn't hear from her."

"It's not like you've been twiddling your thumbs. I'm calling Dani. I'll keep you posted."

The line went dead.

"Oh my God," Sam whispered.

Nick sat next to her and put his arm around her. "What's going on?"

"Jeannie went to talk to Jaycee Patrick's mother, and now she's not answering her phone. Michael was worried enough to call Malone."

"I'm sure she's fine."

"What if the mother is as unhinged as the daughter was, and I sent her into an ambush?"

"You didn't send her anywhere. She outranks you now, remember? If she didn't want to go, she wouldn't have."

"Still... She went to try to defuse the situation on our behalf."

Sam blew out a deep breath. "If anything happens to her... I don't know what I'll do."

"She'll be fine. She's savvy and has been in far worse situations than this and survived."

"Keep telling me that, will you?" Sam wanted nothing more than to go right back to work to help find her friend, but that wasn't an option. At times like this, the push-pull of the professional and personal was so strong, she didn't know whether she was coming or going.

She moved through the motions of changing her clothes and making herself somewhat presentable. Then she went upstairs to find Angela, knocking on the door to her room.

"Come in."

She stepped into the room where Angela was seated on an office chair, wearing a smock while Ginger and Davida saw to her hair and makeup.

Sam had asked Gideon to send the White House hair and makeup team up to tend to Angela, after asking her sister if she'd like a little pampering. "How's it going?"

"This is some nice service you provide at the White House," Angela said, looking slightly better than she had in days.

"These ladies are my miracle workers."

"Which is what I needed today," Angela said. "A miracle."

"You're beautiful," Davida said. "We just enhanced what you already had."

"You're too kind," Angela said. "I know how awful I looked."

"Be kind to yourself, honey," Ginger said. "It's a difficult time."

"We're ready for you, Mrs. Cappuano," Davida said.

"I just need a quick once-over," Sam said.

"We can do that."

It went against everything Sam believed in as a cop to sit still for people to fuss over her, but in deference to her new role as first lady, she let them do their thing so she wouldn't embarrass Nick by looking feral in public. People would be watching them as they went through the motions of mourning—again. Far too soon after losing her father. When she needed to be focused on her sister, all she could think about was Jeannie and what she might be going through.

"How's the investigation?" Angela asked after she came out of the bathroom dressed in black.

"We might be getting somewhere—finally." On a hunch, she said, "Grab my phone, will you?"

After Angela handed Sam the phone, she opened it to find the photo Freddie had sent of the man from the hotel bar. "Do you know this guy?" She held up the phone.

Angela leaned in for a look at the grainy photo. "I've seen him somewhere, but I'm not sure where."

"Try to think if you can."

Angela stared at the photo until Sam's arm began to prickle from blood loss.

"I can't remember where I know him from. He might be a friend or colleague of Spencer's."

"Who among his friends was invited to the wake?"

"I sent the email to his high school and college friends, former coworkers, the organizers of his softball and basketball leagues and some of his former roommates. I'm not sure who among them is coming. I gave them the link from the Secret Service to RSVP."

Sam's backbone tingled the way it did when she was on to something. Hearing that their mystery man might be among the guests, she'd be on the lookout for him at the wake. Would he be so brazen as to show his face there?

She sure as hell hoped so.

SHACKLED to a chair with her own handcuffs, Jeannie kept a careful eye on Mrs. Patrick as she moved around the house, rifle clutched to her chest, muttering about revenge and retribution and how her daughter had been slaughtered. She talked more to herself than she did to Jeannie, which was fine with Jeannie. By now, Michael would be wondering why she hadn't come home to get ready for the wake. Her phone had been ringing incessantly. He would sound the alarm when she didn't take his calls.

She wasn't sure how she'd remained so calm when she was in grave danger, being held captive by an unhinged woman who was in possession of an arsenal. But she figured if Mrs. Patrick planned to kill her, she would've done it by now.

"Can we talk?" Jeannie asked when the woman came back into the kitchen.

"About what?"

"About what happened to Jaycee?"

Mrs. Patrick's brows narrowed. "You mean how your colleagues *murdered* my daughter?"

"They didn't want that to happen. You must know that."

"Why do I have to know that?" she asked in a mocking tone. "They wanted her out of the way, and now she is."

"Believe it or not, police officers never want to have to use their weapons to defend themselves. That's the last thing any of us wants to do. We need this job to pay our bills and take care of our families. An incident like this puts our careers in jeopardy."

"Don't act like that department of yours isn't full of corrupt characters who'd happily shoot someone who got in their way."

"Every organization has people of questionable character. Detective Dominguez isn't one of them, and neither is Detective Green."

"Save it. They're your friends. I've done my research. I know how cozy you all are and how you think you're special because the first lady is your boss."

"We don't think we're special. We work very hard on behalf of the citizens of the District. Our goal is to keep people safe. That's what we show up to do every day, and Detective Dominguez is an exemplary detective and person."

"That exemplary person *murdered* my daughter, and she's going to pay for that."

"Your daughter entered her home uninvited, wielding a knife, and attacked Detective Dominguez physically and sexually."

Mrs. Patrick recoiled from that news. "How did she attack her sexually? How is that even possible?"

"She forced Detective Dominguez to disrobe and then Jaycee pushed her fingers into Detective Dominguez's vagina to find out why Detective Green wants her and not Jaycee."

"She would never do that!"

"Why would Detective Dominguez make up such a thing?"

"Because she wants to discredit my daughter."

"Mrs. Patrick," Jeannie said as gently as possible, "your daughter discredited herself, first by slashing Cameron's tires and then by throwing a brick through his window and narrowly missing him and Detective Dominguez. She was facing two felony counts of attempted assault of police officers, not to mention the vandalism charges. All this because her boyfriend broke up with her, which was his right to do."

"He made promises to her."

"He promised her nothing, and she knew it."

"They were getting married!"

"He never once considered marrying her. Not once."

"So you say."

"I got that right from him. He wasn't going to marry her. He'd known for quite some time before they broke up that he wasn't in love with her."

"That's not true! I saw them together. He was in love!"

"No, he wasn't, and I'm sorry if that hurts you to hear or if it hurt her, but he was under no obligation to her and was honorable in his dealings with her. She's the one who couldn't take no for an answer and turned this into a nightmare for herself and him." Jeannie hoped she wasn't going too far, but these were things the woman needed to hear—again. "He had every right to end his relationship with Jaycee and move on to someone else."

"He had no right to treat my daughter like garbage."

"He didn't treat her that way, and you know it."

That led to a stare-down.

Jeannie refused to blink. "Let me tell you how this will go. By now, my husband has reported to my colleagues that I'm not answering my phone. We have a wake to go to this afternoon, and he'll be wondering where I am. The minute my team finds out I've gone off the radar, this place will be surrounded by officers who will do whatever it takes to save me, even if that means killing you. I don't want you to end up dead. Your family needs you to guide them through the loss of Jaycee. There's no need for anyone else to die."

"I want retribution for my daughter's death! I want them to pay!"

"File a lawsuit. Have your day in court. But if you hurt me or detain me any longer, you'll end up in jail. You won't get retribution if you're in jail."

Her gaze darted toward Jeannie. "If I let you go, will I still go to jail?"

"We can chalk this up to a misunderstanding, and you can pursue your retribution through legal channels. But you need to let me go now, or I can't help you."

She was wavering.

Jeannie could see that.

Her eyes filled with tears. "My daughter didn't deserve what happened to her."

Jeannie didn't agree, but she kept her mouth shut, hoping Mrs. Patrick would see the error of her ways and let her go.

"I want justice for her."

"I understand."

"Will you help me get it?"

"Our department will do a thorough investigation of the incident that took place at Detective Dominguez's home. She's been suspended while that plays out. However, I expect she'll be fully exonerated because your daughter entered her home uninvited, threatened her life, assaulted her with a knife, sexually assaulted her and forced Detective Dominguez to defend herself with lethal force. We're deeply sorry for your loss, but we're not responsible for the choices Jaycee made that led to her death."

"That doesn't sound like justice to me."

"That's the truth of what happened, and the sooner you accept that, the sooner you can deal with your grief and move on with your life."

"Have you ever lost a child?"

"No, I haven't."

"There's no 'moving on' from this. My child was *murdered*."

"Your child attacked someone who defended herself."

Another stare-down ensued.

Again, Jeannie refused to blink.

Time seemed to slow to a crawl as Mrs. Patrick raised the rifle and pointed it at Jeannie. "I could end you right here and now. Since there's no chance for true justice for my daughter, that would make me feel a whole lot better."

Jeannie forced herself to remain calm. "How so?"

"An eye for an eye."

"I didn't kill your daughter."

"No, but you sit in my house and defend the cunt who did."

"She's not a cunt. She's a dedicated police officer, an excellent detective and a wonderful human being who never would've hurt your daughter if Jaycee hadn't threatened her life."

She cocked the rifle.

Jeannie's heart nearly stopped.

A shot rang out.

Jeannie screamed as Mrs. Patrick toppled forward onto the table, which collapsed under her weight.

Doors crashed open as officers in armored gear rushed in.

"Chief McBride is safe," one of them said over the radio. The announcement echoed through the house on the radios of the other officers.

Someone removed the cuffs that had locked her to the chair.

Jeannie flexed her wrists, which ached. "Those are my cuffs."

The officer handed them to her.

"Who's here from my house?" she asked the Fairfax County officer.

"Chief and captain."

"Am I free to go?"

"We'll need you to file a report."

"I'll do that later today." Jeannie took the card he handed her. "Thank you." She glanced at Mrs. Patrick, dead on the floor from a gunshot wound to the head and felt a pang of sadness for the senselessness of it all. Two people were dead because a man had chosen to end a relationship that was no longer making him happy.

She grabbed her phone and service weapon off the counter where Mrs. Patrick had tossed them, walked outside and took a deep breath of the cold air, relieved to be out of that house.

Captain Malone and Chief Farnsworth rushed over to her.

"Are you all right?" Malone asked.

"I'm fine."

"Took five years off my life, Chief," Farnsworth said.

"Sorry about that."

"All that matters is that you're safe."

"Call your husband," Malone said. "He's out of his mind."

Jeannie called Michael. "I'm fine," she said when he answered.

"What the hell, babe? I was scared shitless. Are you hurt?"

"No, I'm fine. I'll tell you about it when I get home."

"Thank God you're all right."

"I'm all right," she said, but her knees were weak after another close call.

CHAPTER THIRTY-THREE

S am immediately regretted the heels she knew she shouldn't have worn. Her hip was on fire, and the wake hadn't even officially started yet.

The family had been invited to come in early, to have a moment alone with Spencer before the doors opened to guests.

Seeing her husband laid out in the coffin had made Angela hysterical. Sam and Tracy had held her up as best they could, but it had been a scene none of them would soon forget. Sam was deeply rattled by it all, agonized for her sister and wishing to be anywhere but in a room with her dead brother-in-law's waxy remains on display.

It was brutal and wrong and horrible and every other terrible word she could think of. How she longed for her dad and his steady presence to make sense of this for Angela and the rest of them. He would've known what to say and do, and Sam ached from missing him.

Tracy's daughter Brooke came in with Nate, the Secret Service agent she'd been seeing for quite some time, though the family had only recently learned of their relationship. This was the first time the family had seen them together. Brooke took one look at her uncle in the coffin and completely lost it. Mike and Tracy went to her, and Nate kept an arm around her while she sobbed helplessly.

"It's all so awful," Nick said.

"So awful."

Sam's mother, Brenda, came in and stopped short at the sight of Spencer in the coffin, as if it was too much for her.

Sam knew how she felt. She went over to greet her mother with a hug.

"This is unbelievable," Brenda said, "even a week later."

"I know. I still can't wrap my head around it."

"Do you know any more about what happened?"

"Just that he took laced pills. We're still working on figuring out where he got them."

"I'm glad you're on the case. If anyone can find these people, you can."

"I wish I was as certain. It's been extremely frustrating as the bodies continue to pile up. Two more today, and another escaped a close call."

"It's so terrible. I read about your detective and what happened with the ex-girlfriend."

"Another nightmare I'm dealing with."

"I don't know how you do it. I really don't."

"I don't know how *not* to do it," Sam said with a shrug.

"You're just like your father," Brenda said with a small smile. "Always have been."

"Thank you."

"I know you must miss him so much."

"I do, never more so since Spence died. We're trying to get Angela through this, but it's the hardest thing ever. He'd know what to do."

"You know, too. I've been comforted knowing you and Tracy are there for her. You girls have always been so close."

"We'll be there for the long haul, but the idea of what she has to face on her own is daunting."

"We'll get her through it."

"Thanks for helping Celia with the kids this week."

"I was happy to. I guess I should pay my respects to Spence and his family." Brenda dabbed at her eyes with a tissue. "It's so unnatural to bury a child. I can't bear this for them either."

"I know. The whole thing is unbearable."

"It really is." She gave Sam another hug before she went to sit with Angela, avoiding the body of her son-in-law for now.

Sam reached for her phone, intending to check on the

situation with Jeannie, and saw a text from Jeannie that filled her with relief.

Mrs. Patrick took me hostage. The Fairfax County sniper team took her out. I'm fine. Will see you at the wake.

God, Jeannie. Are you sure you're ok?

Other than the senselessness of it all... You know.

I do. But I'm so, so thankful you're safe.

Sorry to add drama to an already crappy day.

Not your fault. Don't feel obligated to come if it's too much.

We'll be there.

Sam went to share the news with Nick.

"Well, that's a relief, huh?"

"Huge relief."

Brooke approached Sam, her face red and puffy from crying. Sam hugged her.

"I still can't believe this. How can he be dead?"

"I know, honey."

"I'm sorry." Brooke tried to pull herself together. "I'm making this about me. It's not about me."

"It's about all of us who loved him."

Brooke's eyes flooded with tears again. "How's Ang?"

"She's holding up as well as can be expected."

"And the kids... God, they're so young. I was a mess at school this week. They were all I could think about."

"We'll get them through it. Somehow."

"Do you know any more about why this happened?"

"We're working on tracking down the dealer, but it's slow going."

"I'm glad you're working the case. That makes me feel better."

Sam glanced at Nate, who was speaking to Tracy and Mike. "How are things going with Nate?"

"So good. He's been wonderful this week. We've spent hours on the phone, and I was so happy to hear Eli was coming to the services so I could see Nate." Nate was Eli's lead Secret Service agent and was stationed with him in Princeton, New Jersey, while Brooke attended the University of Virginia in Charlottesville.

"I'm glad you have him to support you through this. I'm so happy for you, Brooke. Truly."

Her niece hugged her again. "That means so much to me.

Thank you." She glanced over her shoulder to see where her mother was. "Don't tell Mom, but—"

"Ack! Don't ask me to keep things from your mother."

"I'm going to tell her before I go back to school, but I've applied to transfer to Princeton for the fall."

"That's a big move. Are you sure?"

She glanced at Nate, who smiled at something Tracy said to him. "I'm very sure."

ANGELA HAD ASKED SAM, Nick, Tracy and Mike to be with her in the receiving line along with Spencer's parents, sisters, brother, sister-in-law and nephews. Despite her best intentions not to look, Sam kept shifting her gaze to the body in the coffin at the front of the room.

It was still surreal.

Spencer was dead.

How could Angela stand to be in a room with his dead body?

Sam would lose her mind if her husband was in that box.

Nick's hand landed on her back, almost as if he knew what she was thinking. "Why don't you take a break, babe?"

"Not until she does." If Angela could stand there and smile as she greeted friends, family, acquaintances and others who'd been invited to attend, so could she. Guests had to provide the invitation they'd received from the Secret Service to gain entrance so it wouldn't turn into a free-for-all of people wanting to meet the president and first lady. They'd had to provide lists of people who would want to attend so they could be issued invitations.

The Secret Service and Metro PD had formed a barrier around the building to ensure their protection and that of everyone else who attended.

Sam hated that she and Nick had complicated things for Angela and Spencer's family. But she was relieved that everyone entering the funeral home had been invited by some member of the family. Spencer's work colleagues and friends were numerous, and the line was endless, or so it seemed. Sam scanned every face that came through, looking for the man in the picture, although she didn't expect to see him.

How stupid would he have to be to show his face where he knew she would be one day after murdering two men and seriously injuring another? But if her experience had taught her anything, it was that criminals were rarely the sharpest tools in the shed.

Her entire squad came through with their significant others, as well as Captain Malone and his wife, Val, Joe and Marti Farnsworth, Lieutenant Archelotta and others from the department.

Elin Cruz hugged Sam. "I'm so sorry. Spencer was such a good guy."

"Yes, he was. Thank you for coming. I've been thinking of you this week. How're you doing?"

"I'm okay."

"It's okay to not be okay. You're going through a very difficult thing."

"Today isn't about me."

"Let's talk soon. I might be able to help."

"I'd like that. Thank you."

Sam hugged her again. "Hang in there. It won't always hurt as badly as it does right now."

"That's good to know."

As Elin moved down the line to greet others, Sam's friend and White House communications director, Roni Connolly, came with Nick's friend and deputy chief of staff, Derek Kavanaugh.

Interesting. After noticing them talking to each other at the White House, Sam wondered if they were seeing each other, but this wasn't the time to ask.

Roni hugged her. "I'm so, so sorry, Sam."

"Thanks for being here."

"Of course. How's Angela doing?"

"Ugh, you know. Not great."

"Tell her to call me any time—day or night. I'm here for her."

"Thank you, Roni. It's nice of you to make that support available to her."

"Ours is a club no one ever wants to join, but it's been an incredible source of support to me to be around people who get it."

Sam glanced at Angela, who was in tears as she hugged Celia's sisters. "She'll need that when the shock wears off and reality sets in."

"Yes, she will. I can also relate to expecting my late husband's baby and having to get through that without him." Roni rested a hand on her protruding midsection to make her point.

"I'll make sure she reaches out to you." Sam glanced at Derek, who was talking to Nick. "Do you have a new friend?"

"I do." Her little blush only added to Sam's curiosity about their relationship. "It's so funny. We met in our neighborhood before I was working at the White House, and then I found out he's also a member of the Wild Widows."

"He's been through so much since his wife died. I'm glad he has that kind of support, too."

"He's like my Yoda, since he's about eighteen months ahead of me on this journey."

"We love him and Maeve. I'm glad you guys are friends."

"Me, too. I won't keep you any longer. There's a huge line outside."

Sam hugged her. "Thanks again for being here."

"I'm here if I can do anything for any of you."

"Appreciate that."

Derek came to hug Sam. "So sorry about Spencer."

"Thank you. I talked to your brother."

"I heard. Hope he can help."

"I hope so, too. Thanks for being here."

"It's so sad."

"It truly is."

After Derek and Roni moved on to speak with the others, Harry and Lilia came over to hug Sam.

"Thanks for coming."

"I'm so sorry for all of you," Lilia said.

Sam couldn't help but notice that Harry looked haunted as he stared at Spencer in the coffin. "Are you okay, Harry?"

"I just keep going over it and over it in my mind," he said.

"He's had a rough week," Lilia added, curling her hands around her fiancé's arm.

Sam rested a hand on Harry's chest, over his heart of gold. "There was nothing you could've done. We know now that he was already gone when Angela alerted us."

"Still... It just seems impossible that this could've happened." Keeping his voice down, he added, "The opioid epidemic is a scourge. A fucking scourge."

"I couldn't agree more."

Harry turned his intense gaze toward Sam. "Are you looking for them?"

"That's almost all I've done this week."

"Good."

Sam had never seen him so upset. She hugged him again. "Thank you for all you did for him. It matters to us."

"I wish it could've been more."

When Sam stepped back into the receiving line, Scotty approached them with bottles of water that he handed to each of them.

"Thanks, buddy," Angela said. "I needed that."

"How're you doing?" Scotty asked Angela, seeming to make the same effort Sam did not to look at Spencer.

"Doing my best to get through it."

"You're doing great," Tracy said.

"Thanks for being in the line with me."

"Of course we are."

Cameron and Gigi came with Dani, each of them hugging Sam and her sisters.

"How're you doing?" Sam asked Gigi.

"I'm okay. You've got enough to think about. Don't worry about me."

"I will worry about you." Her gaze took in Gigi and Cameron. "I want you both to keep talking to Trulo."

"We will," Cam said. "We heard about what happened to Jeannie. Is she okay?"

"She is." Sam lifted her chin toward the line. "She and Michael just came in."

They came right over to hug Sam.

Jeannie also hugged Gigi. "How are you holding up?"

"I was about to ask you the same thing," Gigi said.

"I'm fine."

"I am, too."

Jeannie's gaze shifted to Spencer in the coffin and then moved away just as quickly. She shook her head in disbelief. "We're so sorry, Sam."

"Thank you. I'm so thankful you're safe."

"Michael wants me to quit my job. He says we don't need the money, and he's either going to have a stroke or a heart attack before I retire."

"Is he serious?"

"Might be heat of the moment, but he sounded quite serious. He said the new job was supposed to keep me safer."

"He's not wrong. I feel bad that I sent you out there."

"Don't feel bad. It's not your fault. Someone needed to do it. Why not me?"

"Thanks for taking one for the team."

"I'd say it was no problem, but..."

Sam smiled. "You're the best."

"How're you all doing?"

"Minute to minute."

"Hang in there. Call if I can do anything for you."

"Thanks, Chief."

Roberto and Angel came through the line a short time later. Sam, who'd put them on her list knowing he'd want to come, introduced them to her family and leaned over to hug Roberto and then stood upright to hug Angel.

"I hear congratulations are in order," Sam said to the pretty young woman who'd shown remarkable courage and resilience during the sniper investigation the year before.

Angel smiled and patted her still-flat abdomen. "We're so excited."

"I'm excited for you."

Roberto crooked a finger to bring Sam down to him. "I hear Riggs Lawton's wife is up to her eyeballs in the business. For what it's worth."

Stunned, Sam said, "It's worth a ton. She played dumb with us."

"Take a closer look at her."

"If this pans out, I'm getting you a key to the city."

Roberto smiled. "Whatever I can do for my lady cop."

"Thank you."

"You got it, friend."

CHAPTER THIRTY-FOUR

M ore than a few people seemed starstruck to meet her and Nick, but they didn't accommodate that nonsense. They accepted condolences and moved on to the next person.

Sam continued to scan the line for the man from the video from the hotel as new people arrived. She was watching so intently that she did a double take when she saw him, chatting with others in the line as if he didn't have a care in the world. "Excuse me," she said to her family as she made a beeline for the man, moving as quickly as her healing hip and high heels would allow. When she reached him, she grabbed his arm and said, "Come with me without a fuss, or I'll take you down right here."

"Wait just a minute," a woman with him said.

Sam turned her furious gaze on her. "Shut up, or I'll arrest you, too."

Everything around them went quiet as Sam dragged the man out of the line and headed for the door, where MPD officers were positioned. "Take him in and book him on first-degree murder charges."

"*What the fuck?*" the man cried. "I didn't kill anyone!"

The officers had him cuffed and on his way to a squad car in a matter of seconds, while the woman with him continued to scream for them to let him go.

"Take her, too." Sam's hands shook from the adrenaline rush. "Charge her with obstructing a homicide investigation."

Freddie, Gonzo and Malone, who'd remained in the funeral home after greeting the family, came over to her.

"That's the guy from the hotel. Angela thought she might recognize him, but she wasn't sure from where. I was watching the line to see if he was stupid enough to show up. The woman with him raised such a stink, I took her into custody, too."

"I'll take it from here," Malone said, signaling to his wife that it was time to go.

"Thanks for coming." Sam desperately wanted to go with him to see this through to completion, but she couldn't leave Angela. "Let me know."

"I will. Good grab."

"Thanks." Sam returned to her place in the line and glanced at Angela. "Sorry about that."

"Who was that?"

"The guy from the photo I showed you."

"So he was someone Spence knew? Who is he?"

"I don't know anything yet. I recognized him from the picture."

"Go find out," Angela said fiercely. "If he had something to do with Spencer's death, I want to know."

"I need to be here with you."

"Go," Angela said with more fire in her eyes than Sam had seen since disaster struck. "And if it was him pretending to be Spencer's friend while giving him poison? Nail his ass."

Sam glanced at Nick. "Do you mind if I go?"

"Not at all. Just be careful."

"I will." She hugged Angela, Tracy and Mike and kissed Nick. "I'll be home as soon as I can."

"Do what you've got to do, babe."

She took a minute to speak with her mother, Eli, Scotty and Celia to update them before she left.

"You think it might be him, and he came here?" Scotty asked, wide-eyed. "That takes balls."

"Indeed." Sam knew she should tell him not to be vulgar, but how could she when she agreed with him?

"Are you leaving?" Freddie and Gonzo asked in unison.

"I am. Ang wants me to find out who this guy is and if he's responsible for Spencer's death."

"Can we come with you?" Gonzo asked.

"I wish you would."

. . .

WHEN THEY WERE LOADED into the Secret Service SUV with Vernon and Jimmy, she called Malone. "I'm on my way in with Cruz and Gonzo. Angela told me to go work the case, so that's what I'm doing."

"I'm almost there and will get him booked."

"Talk to the USA's office, but this should be two counts of first-degree murder and one count of attempted first-degree murder. He intentionally gave three men a lethal dose of fentanyl, and we've got a witness who can prove it was him. We'll have to get Bryan Smith to do a photo ID."

"I'll have someone take care of that to close the loop," Malone said. "Can you believe the audacity of him showing up at the wake knowing you'd be there along with other cops?"

"He came because he was sure we had nothing on him, which means he doesn't know that Smith survived. Let's keep that info in our back pocket and see how we might use it."

"Good plan."

"I also heard that Leslie Lawton is in the business up to her eyeballs. That's how it was described to me, so I'll be having another chat with her."

"This is all good news. See you in a few."

Sam closed the phone and looked out the window as the city whizzed by, thinking about her approach.

"That was pretty intense with Spencer in the coffin," Freddie said.

"Yeah," Gonzo said. "I couldn't bear to look at him."

"Me either," Freddie said. "What a nightmare. How's she doing, Sam? Really."

"Maybe a tiny bit better than she was now that the shock has worn off somewhat, but she's got a very long road ahead of her no matter how you look at it."

"Over and over, I keep thinking there but for the grace of God go I," Gonzo said, sounding shaken. "Could've been me. I got lucky."

"We're very thankful you never encountered fentanyl when you were using," Freddie said.

"Very thankful," Sam said. "A week later, and it's still

unbelievable that this happened. Even after seeing him laid out in that coffin, I'm still in disbelief."

"You will be for a while," Freddie said.

"Find out where Officer Charles stashed Lawton's wife, will you? Here's her number."

Gonzo punched in the digits and made the call. "Hey, the LT is asking where you stashed Leslie Lawton." He recited the address out loud, and Freddie took note of it. "Thanks."

"I want to see her before we interview this Craig character," Sam said.

Freddie gave Vernon the address, and he made a U-turn at the next intersection.

Sam called Haggerty. "How're you making out at the Lawtons' house?"

"Clean as a whistle. Not finding anything of interest, and we're almost done."

"Had a feeling you might say that. Thanks for the thorough work."

"We're moving on to the hotel after this. Will keep you posted."

"Thank you." Sam closed her phone. "Lawton's penthouse is clean. No drugs found, which means they're somewhere else. Haggerty and his team are earning their keep and then some with this case."

"No kidding," Gonzo said. "What's the plan with the missus?"

"I'm going to give her a chance to save herself by spilling the tea."

WHEN THEY ARRIVED at the safe house on Connecticut Avenue, Sam was out of the car before Vernon could get the door for her, which earned her a scowl from the agent.

"Sorry," she said to him as she headed for the door, where two Patrol officers stood watch. She showed them her badge, even though they knew who she was. Inside, another officer stood between her and Leslie. Sam went through the badge ritual again. "Where is she?"

"Living room," the officer said, using his chin to point the way.

Leslie was curled up on the sofa with a blanket over her lap. She brightened when she saw Sam. "Can I go home?"

"Not yet."

"You haven't finished searching our place yet?"

Sam sat on a footstool facing her. "We're almost done."

Leslie's gaze darted toward Freddie and Gonzo, who stood right inside the room. "What's going on?"

"I got an interesting tip from one of my informants."

"What tip?"

"That you're into your husband's business. 'Up to your eyeballs' was the way he described it."

She recoiled. "I am not! I know nothing about it! I told you that."

Sam leaned in. "Guess what? I believe him."

Leslie's mouth opened and then snapped shut. She was silent for a long moment before she said, "I want a deal."

"No deal."

"That's it? Just 'no deal'? Don't you want the info I have?"

"I want it, but I'm not dealing until I know what you've got. If you lead me to the person who's selling laced pills, I might consider a word to the U.S. Attorney on your behalf, but I want this person locked up tight before we talk about a deal."

"How do I know you'll keep your word?"

"You don't, but the alternative is that I make it known you're cooperating with us and accidentally mention where you're hiding out. After that, I expect you'd be alive for an hour, maybe two, if you're lucky."

"You'd feed me to the wolves if I don't help you?"

"I just came from my brother-in-law's wake. He bought your laced pills and left my sister alone to raise two kids and a baby due in June. I'd feed you to the wolves in a second if I thought you were responsible for his death."

"I'm not! Someone is trying to sabotage our business! They're doing this to us intentionally!"

Now they were getting somewhere. "Gonzo, please record this conversation."

When his phone was in place, Sam said, "Lieutenant Holland interviewing Leslie Lawton, wife of Riggs Lawton. Sergeant Gonzales and Detective Cruz witnessing. Start at the beginning, and don't leave anything out."

Seeming to realize the bind she was in, Leslie let out a deep sigh. "I didn't want any part of it. I told Riggs that from the beginning."

"You knew what he did for a living, and you married him anyway?"

"I loved him. I know it seems hard to believe, but it's true. Separate of his business, he was the most wonderful, devoted, loving husband."

Separate of his business, Sam thought, *dealing drugs to addicts. What a prince.* "Go on."

"The business... It grew exponentially. He asked me to help him, and at first, all I did was keep records of transactions, phone numbers of customers. That kind of thing. It sort of grew from there until we were running the whole thing together." She took a tissue from a box on a side table and dabbed at her eyes. "We tried to keep it separate, you know? The business and our marriage."

Sam had so much she'd like to say to that, but she stayed quiet, waiting for the rest of the story.

"About a month ago, one of our longtime customers OD'd on stuff we'd sold him."

"Who was that?"

"You want a name?" she asked. "Isn't that private information?"

"In a Homicide investigation, very little is private."

"Wait, you're accusing me of *homicide*?"

"Not yet. Give me the name."

She took another deep breath and held it for a few seconds. "Jackson Audette."

Sam glanced over her shoulder, made eye contact with Freddie, who nodded and left the room to get the lowdown on Audette.

"We were shocked to hear of his death," Leslie said. "He'd been buying product from us for years. He knew what he was doing and how to stay safe. And then it happened again—twice in a week with two employees of Riggs's favorite restaurant."

"Where'd they get the pills?"

"Through the general manager, Richard. He's one of our dealers."

Bam, Sam thought as the puzzle pieces started to come together. She'd be taking steps to have his probation revoked as soon as she could. "Who's Craig?"

"Craig who?"

"I don't know his last name." Sam showed her the photo of the man named Craig from the W security system.

"That's Matthias Foster."

Sam glanced at Gonzo. "Get the name to Malone, will you?"

"Yep." Since they were using his phone to record the interview, he went to find Freddie.

"We've got him in custody. He was a friend of my brother-in-law's, which is where Spencer got the pills, right?"

"Probably," Leslie said with another sigh. "Please try to understand. We prided ourselves on running a clean operation. Someone did this to us."

"You'll have to excuse my lack of empathy for you."

"I don't expect you to understand."

"Try me."

"Once they get addicted, people are desperate for Oxy and heroin. Have you ever been so desperate you thought you might die if you didn't get what you need?"

"No," Sam said.

"Yes," Gonzo said when he returned. "I have."

"Then you know," Leslie said to him. "After a while, it wasn't even about the money for us. It was about helping people get what they needed to stay alive. Riggs believed that one of our rivals was trying to run us out of the business by funneling laced pills into our operation. If word got out that our product was laced, we'd be finished. That was their goal."

"Who would've done that?"

"The only one we think would've had motive and capability is Sal Vincent."

Sam's backbone buzzed with sensation. "Who is he?"

"He runs an operation like ours, and he's been trying for years to buy us out, to make us go away, but we don't trust him, so we've refused numerous offers. About six months ago, Riggs stopped taking his calls. We heard some chatter about how we're going to be sorry we dissed him. We blew it off as nonsense until people started dying."

"And what was your plan when you realized what was happening?"

"Riggs recalled all our product, but not everyone heeded the call."

"How does Matthias figure into it?"

"He was one who hadn't returned the product yet. We think it's possible he's been working for Vincent, too, and maybe Richard as well as a couple of others that Vincent convinced to double-cross us. Riggs was trying to figure out what was going on when he was arrested."

"Why would Riggs take his own life rather than own up to what was going on?"

"He'd rather be dead than in prison."

"Did you know he'd take his own life if he was arrested?"

"I had a feeling he might, although I'd hoped and prayed that if it ever happened, he'd decide to stick around for my sake." She dabbed at her eyes. "He couldn't bear the idea of being locked up."

"Then why become a drug dealer?"

"He tried other businesses but didn't get anywhere until he started dealing. That's when he started making serious money. Finally."

"Where can we find Sal Vincent?"

"If I send you to him, I'll be dead within an hour, safe house or not."

"He won't get to you in our custody."

"You have no idea what that son of a bitch is capable of."

"Reminder—I just came from my dead brother-in-law's wake. I know what he's capable of, and you're going to help me ruin him."

CHAPTER THIRTY-FIVE

Coordinating an operation like this one involved a lot of people, as Sam soon discovered. According to Kevin Kavanaugh, the DEA had been pursuing Vincent for years, but had thus far been unsuccessful in locating his operation.

Leslie had told Sam where it was and other information that only an insider would have, such as where Vincent lived, where he ate breakfast and where his mother was buried, along with the info that he visited her resting place daily. Vincent traveled with a huge entourage of well-armed security, making it so no one could get near him without risking their lives.

As Sam laid out the details she'd gotten from Leslie, Kavanaugh stared at her without blinking. She wasn't sure if he was impressed or horrified by her. What did she care? She'd done her job and would be responsible for bringing down a kingpin who'd eluded law enforcement for years.

"We're going to need a few days to prepare for this," Kavanaugh said.

"And you'll coordinate with our team?" Farnsworth asked.

Sam had called the chief and captain to update them on what she'd learned from Leslie, and they'd both come to HQ for the meeting with Kavanaugh.

"We could take it from here," Kavanaugh said.

"That's not happening," Sam said. "This is our bust. We brought you in on it as a courtesy."

"So getting the credit is more important than getting the guy?" Kavanaugh asked.

"We don't give a rat's ass who gets the credit," Farnsworth said, "but you're not doing this without us. You wouldn't even have a mission to coordinate without Lieutenant Holland's excellent work."

"Granted, but the more people involved in a mission like this one, the greater the chance of something going sideways."

"Believe it or not, Agent Kavanaugh," Farnsworth said, "we've actually done this before."

Sam wanted to kiss the chief on the lips for saying all the things she was thinking.

"I need to get back to my team and coordinate with them, and then we'll circle back to you with a plan."

"I wouldn't recommend going rogue, Agent Kavanaugh," Farnsworth said.

The agent gave them a filthy look as he got up and left the room.

"Unreal," she said when he was gone. "I deliver this guy on a silver platter, and he wants to cut me out of it." She looked over at the chief. "Thank you for standing our ground."

"No problem. I'll check in with his supervisor to let her know what's going on so there's no chance he might decide to go it alone." He got up to leave the room but stopped short of the door. "Very fine work, as always, Lieutenant."

"Thank you, sir. We got lucky."

"It's not luck. It's never luck. I'll see you in the morning at the funeral."

"See you then."

"You did good, kid," Malone said when they were alone. "When I told Cooper you'd located Vincent's operation, his mouth fell open in shock."

"Was it full of food when that happened?"

Malone cracked up. "Thankfully not."

"You got lucky."

"You have everything locked and loaded with the USA and Leslie Lawton?" Malone asked. "Our case is riding on her."

Leslie had agreed to testify in exchange for immunity from prosecution. "Yes, Faith has coordinated with the FBI to move her to one of their safe houses. That's all set, and they're hammering out the immunity deal."

"As the chief said, very good work, Lieutenant."

"All thanks to my longtime informant, Roberto, who came through for me big-time. He's the one who told me to take another look at her."

"However it happened, you got it done for your sister, her husband and all the other victims. Getting these people off the street will be a huge public service."

"Let's just hope Vincent doesn't slip through our fingers before we can get this done."

"He won't. He thinks he's untouchable. We're about to show him otherwise. What's your plan for Matthias Foster?"

"Oh shit. I forgot about him. Is he still in interview one?"

"As far as I know."

"Let's go have a chat with him."

They burst into the room.

Matthias, who'd had his head down on the table, sat up so fast, he nearly toppled his chair.

"Hey there, Craig," Sam said. "Or is it Matthias Foster?" She glanced at Malone. "These people who use multiple names are so annoying."

"So annoying indeed, because they think we won't figure out who they really are or who they really work for."

"I don't know what you're talking about," Foster said. "Those hookers set me up! They gave us the pills!"

"Save it," Sam said. "We already know you were double-crossing Lawton and Vincent by working for them both. Vincent must've been upset when he found out you'd continued to work for your old boss after he hired you away from Lawton."

Foster's expression registered shock that she knew so much about him.

"How do you know Spencer Radcliffe?"

Sam was relieved to see a hint of remorse in his expression. "We played basketball together for years." There it was. The connection she'd been searching for. Too bad there was no pleasure in putting those pieces together as Spencer was still dead.

"Whose idea was it to sell Lawton's customers laced pills to try to run him out of the business?" Sam asked.

"I don't know anything about that!"

"Sure, you don't." Sam glanced at Malone. "Let's go. This guy is wasting our time."

They stood and turned to leave the room.

"Wait! I want a deal."

Sam turned back to him. "I'm listening."

"I'm not the only one working for both of them. There're others out there who have the laced pills."

"Who else?"

He shook his head. "I'm not saying anything until I have a deal on the table that keeps me out of jail."

Sam was tempted to walk away to call his bluff but knowing there were other dealers selling laced pills meant lives were in danger. She pulled a pad and pen out of her purse and opened it to a blank page. "Write down their names, addresses and phone numbers. If your information bears fruit, we'll talk to the USA about a deal."

"I want the deal first."

"That's not how this works. You help us, and then we help you. That's how it works."

He crossed his arms and gave her a bullish look.

"Going once, going twice..." She picked up the pad and started to leave the room again.

"Wait!"

Sighing, she turned to face him again. "I hate when people waste my time. What's it going to be?"

"I'd need my phone to give you the info you want."

"I'll be right back." Sam left the interrogation room and went upstairs to Archie's office, where he was still at work. "I need the phone for Matthias Foster."

He rifled through the bagged phones on his desk and found the one she needed. "Will you bring it back after? I haven't gotten to it yet."

"Yep. I need you to run it because he's a link between two rival drug organizations, one of whom decided to try to run the other out of business by selling laced product to the other's customers."

"Holy crap," Archie said. "Great job putting the pieces together on that. What's the plan?"

"Foster is going to give us the names of the other dealers working for both organizations, and we'll round them up before they can sell laced product to more unsuspecting customers."

"Won't that tip off the big boss when he suddenly can't get in touch with his people?"

"I guess it will, which means we can't wait another day to bring in the head honcho." She let out a sigh. "This is going to be a long night."

"Good luck, Sam. I know how much this one means to you."

"Thanks."

As she went back downstairs, she called the chief. "I know we just agreed to twenty-four hours with Kavanaugh, but Foster is willing to roll on the other double-crossing dealers in exchange for a deal, and Archie just made a good point. Rounding them up, which we have to do immediately since they're in possession of laced pills, will tip off Vincent that we've infiltrated his organization."

"That's true. What're you thinking?"

Sam was making this up as she went. "We send Narcotics after the dealers. My team goes after Vincent at home while the DEA takes down the operation. In a coordinated strike tonight."

"Kavanaugh won't go for that."

"It's this or nothing. We can't leave those pills on the street now that we know who has them."

"I'll call Kavanaugh," Farnsworth said, "and I'm coming back in."

"Okay, thanks for handling him."

"No problem."

Sam called her entire squad back to work with a 911 text message. *Need all hands on deck immediately. Please get here as soon as you can.*

Carlucci and Dominguez usually worked the late shift, but they were off that night, so no one was in the pit when she cut through to take the phone to Foster in the interview room.

She delivered it to him, and Malone stayed with him while she went to call Faith Miller. "I need to update you on what's going on. Foster is giving us the names of the other dealers who were working for both Vincent and Lawton in exchange for a deal that's yet to be negotiated. We believe most if not all of them are in possession of the laced pills they've been selling to Lawton's customers as part of Vincent's plan to run Lawton out of the business, which makes Foster critical to us. We believe it's imperative that we round up those dealers immediately, before someone else is killed."

"Agreed," Faith said.

"But rounding up his dealers will tip off Vincent that we've infiltrated his organization. The plan was to put the pieces together to go after Vincent in a day or two, but knowing there's more laced product out there, we can't afford to wait. We're coordinating a three-pronged raid that's going down tonight. Narcotics will take care of the dealers. My team is going after Vincent at home, and the DEA will raid his warehouse in Alexandria. The chief is notifying the DEA that we've moved up the timeline."

"I'm still with Leslie Lawton, going over her statement and filling in some gaps. We've moved her to a new safe location."

"It's coming together."

"Keep me posted."

"Will do."

Next, Sam used the BlackBerry to call Nick.

"Hey, babe. How's it going?"

"It's gonna be an all-nighter. We've blown this thing wide open, and we're going in for the kill tonight." She filled him in on the details. "Roberto tipped me off that Leslie Lawton was involved in her husband's business, and it's taken off from there."

"I'm glad you've figured out where the pills came from and why."

"Doesn't make me feel better about what's happened, but at least we know."

"That'll matter to Angela and her kids. Maybe not now, but eventually."

"I hope so."

"It will, Sam, and it'll matter to them that you were the one who got justice for him."

"We haven't gotten it yet, but we're close."

"Be safe out there. My wife means everything to me."

"I can't be as hands-on with this one as I'd like to be, so nothing to worry about where I'm concerned."

"I will always worry where you're concerned."

"Try to get some rest. I'll be home to change in the morning before the funeral."

"See you then. Love you."

"Love you, too."

She was about to return to the interrogation room when Kevin Kavanaugh came into the pit, loaded for bear.

"You're jumping the gun. We can't pull this together tonight."

"You have to, or we'll take care of it ourselves."

"You have no idea what you're getting into going after Vincent."

"All I know is that when I start rounding up his dealers, he'll be in the wind so fast, we'll never see him again. And I have to round up the dealers *now*, before some other innocent person is killed by these people."

Kavanaugh tugged at his hair in obvious frustration. "I've heard you're impetuous, but I never took you for a fool."

That stung, coming from Derek's brother. "If trying to save other families from going through what mine and many others are makes me an impetuous fool, then I can live with that."

Cruz, Gonzo and Green came into the pit, stopping short at the sight of her in a standoff with the DEA agent.

O'Brien and Carlucci, wearing more makeup than Sam had ever seen on her, came in next.

"I was on a date," Carlucci said with a grin and a shrug.

"We've got work to do," Sam said to Kavanaugh. "Are you in or out?"

"I need at least two hours to get my team in place."

"Go to it. I'll call you when we're ready."

He gave her another filthy look and then stormed off.

"Making new friends, LT?" Gonzo asked.

"Everywhere I go."

"What's going on?" Cruz asked.

"We've broken this thing wide open, and tonight, my friends, we're bringing down a murdering kingpin."

IT TOOK until four o'clock Monday morning before all the players were in place to execute their three-pronged operation.

Sam and her team were positioned outside Vincent's home, which was ironically two blocks from where Alden and Aubrey had lived with their parents. The house, which could only be called a mansion, was now surrounded by SWAT and Special Response Team officers, awaiting the word to go in.

They'd been surprised to find no sign of security outside the home, which had given her pause. Why wasn't he surrounded by a fortress?

When she posed that question to Malone, he said, "Hubris. He thinks he's untouchable. Who would look for a drug kingpin in a regular neighborhood?"

Narcotics detectives had begun to round up the dealers at the addresses Foster had provided. One after another, they were arrested. Knowing they—and the poison they were peddling on Vincent's behalf—were off the streets was a huge relief to Sam.

"Massive amounts of product found at each dealer's house," Malone reported. "HazMat will be busy."

Not only would that product now be off the streets, but it would help them build the case against Vincent. "How much you want to bet it's from the same batch that killed Spencer and the others?"

"I'd put everything I've got on that," Malone said.

"Let's do this." Sam hated that she had to stay back while the rest of her team followed SWAT and SRT into the home, but she wouldn't do anything to compromise the integrity of the investigation.

After Malone gave the order, the sound of glass breaking shattered the quiet in the neighborhood as one officer after another reported in.

"Clear."

"Clear."

"Clear."

"We've got Vincent."

Sam exhaled the breath she'd been holding.

"Security neutralized."

"We got him," Sam said, filled with overwhelming relief and anguish for the pain this man had caused her family and so many others.

"*You* got him," Malone said. "You did this."

"Any word from the DEA?"

"Not yet."

Cruz and Green escorted Vincent out of the house in handcuffs. He wore only a pair of boxer briefs and was much younger than Sam had expected him to be. His hair stood on end, and his eyes were wild as he seemed to realize his game was over.

Carlucci and O'Brien followed with a half-naked woman, who was equally disheveled and also in handcuffs.

They'd been instructed to arrest everyone in the house. They would sort out the details back at HQ.

Next came the security people in various states of undress, fighting the officers escorting them every step of the way.

Malone took a call from the chief. "DEA has taken control of the warehouse. No one was there."

Hubris, Sam thought. They hadn't banked on her.

"You should go home," Malone said. "Get some rest. Be with your family tomorrow. We'll take it from here."

"Don't worry about coming to the funeral. Angela would want you guys working the case."

"We'll do both."

CHAPTER THIRTY-SIX

W hile others dealt with the paperwork following the raid at Vincent's home, Jake Malone slipped out in the predawn to pay a visit to Paul Conklin. He was out on bail awaiting trial on charges related to Skip's homicide and that of Skip's former partner, Steven Coyne. For four years, Conklin had withheld information that could've solved both shootings while serving as the department's deputy chief and pretending to be Skip's good friend.

Normally, Jake wouldn't show up at someone's house at five in the morning, but he needed to get this done, and Conklin had lost the right to any sort of human decency. People like him and Stahl made Jake sick. Stahl was hideous, but Conklin was worse because he'd been their friend, or so they'd thought.

Jake swallowed his revulsion as he rang the bell and knocked on the door to the Northern Virginia townhome Conklin shared with his wife.

The man who came to the door bore no resemblance to the Paul Conklin that Jake had known for decades. He'd put on weight, his hair was messy, and he hadn't shaved in days. His face registered surprise at seeing Jake on his doorstep as he pushed open the storm door.

"This is a surprise," Conklin said.

"I need to talk to you."

Eyeing him suspiciously, Conklin said, "Come in."

The house was almost as much of a wreck as the man who

lived there. A stale, musty smell had overtaken the place. Dishes were piled in the sink and on the coffee table in the living room.

"Is your wife home?"

"She's long gone," Conklin said with a bitter edge to his voice.

"Oh. I'm sorry to hear that."

"What do you want, Jake?" He sat in a recliner that faced the television. "I'm sure this isn't a social call."

"I want to talk to you about Stahl."

"What about him?"

"As you've probably heard, we're reopening some of his old cases, which led to arrests in the Worthington and Deasly cases."

"What's that got to do with me?"

"We've discovered some irregularities."

"Ah, I see," Conklin said with a harsh laugh. "So you automatically came to me."

"You're the last one I came to."

"Last one what?"

"The last captain at the time Stahl's bullshit reports were archived that I haven't talked to."

"And you think I did it?"

"I'm here to ask if you did and if so, why."

"It wasn't me. You know I never had a thing to do with that son of a bitch if I could avoid it."

A sinking sensation overtook Jake. That left Skip Holland, and there was no way he would've done it. Jake would bet his very life on that. "Do you have any thoughts on how it might've happened?"

"I don't."

He stood to leave. "Thanks for your time."

"That's it? You come here and accuse me of yet another crime and go on your merry way?"

"Yeah, that's it."

"Good to see you, Jake."

"Uh-huh. Take care."

He walked to the front door, eager for some fresh air after the staleness of Conklin's home.

"Jake."

He stopped but didn't turn back.

"I'm sorry, you know. If I had it to do over, I would've done everything differently."

"That's the thing about life, Paul. There are no do-overs." Jake walked out feeling disgusted and dirty for having darkened the doorstep of a man who'd lied to them for years. After he took a few deep breaths of the cold fresh air, he called Joe. "Conklin says it wasn't him, and I believe him. That leaves Skip, and there was no way. Just no way."

"There had to be another path to archiving besides the captains," Farnsworth said. "Let's put Archie on a deep dive into the system at that time to see what workarounds Stahl might've uncovered."

"I'll talk to him in the morning." After a pause, Jake said, "Conklin apologized. Said if he had it to do over, he would've done everything differently."

"Whatever," Joe said on a huff. "I hope you told him to eff off with that crap."

"I told him there're no do-overs in life."

"Well said."

"His wife left him."

"Can't say I blame her."

"He's a wreck. The house is a pigsty."

"He's sitting in a mess of his own making. I hope he spends all day every day thinking about how he betrayed Skip, Steven and every officer who's ever honorably served this department. I hope the guilt keeps him awake at night and eats away at him."

Jake had never heard Joe speak so forcefully about anyone else, but he wasn't surprised. Conklin's deceit had rocked the very foundation under them. "I think it's safe to assume it's eating away at him."

"Good. That's the least of what he deserves."

"Even with months to wrap my head around it, I still can't believe he knew the whole time and said nothing. It's unfathomable."

"It certainly is, and he'll have decades behind bars to think about what he did."

"Decades won't be enough."

"You sound exhausted."

"I am. I'm on the way home now to change for the funeral."

"See you there, and thanks for taking one for the team."

"No problem," Jake said with a laugh.

. . .

AN AGENT NAMED Dalton drove Sam home to change for the funeral as the sun was rising over the capital city on the day they would lay Spencer to rest. At least she could tell Angela and Spencer's family why he'd been taken from them, not that it would matter much to them today. She looked forward to being able to call the other families to tell them they'd gotten the drug dealers who'd taken their loved ones from them.

She thought of them all on the way home, about the lives of vulnerable people that had been changed forever by a man determined to run a rival out of business any way he could. As usual, the senselessness of murder was what stayed with her in the aftermath of all her cases. The motives hardly ever justified the outcome.

Even at five thirty in the morning, an usher was at the door to greet her when she stepped inside the White House.

"Morning, Mrs. Cappuano," he said.

"Morning. I don't believe we've met."

"I'm Roger, ma'am."

Sam shook his hand. "It's nice to meet you, Roger."

"You as well, ma'am."

"Would you mind asking the kitchen to send up coffee and breakfast for myself and the president when they get a chance?"

"I'd be happy to."

"Thank you so much."

Sometimes living at the White House had its advantages, she thought as she trudged up the stairs, weary to her bones and with no time to rest before another emotional day. Despite being exhausted, she was also euphoric to know they had captured Vincent and shut down his operation. She'd done that. Not Narcotics or the DEA.

Her.

The next time she questioned what she was doing with her life, she would remember this moment and the lives she'd saved by rounding up Vincent's dealers before anyone else could be harmed by them. That thought led to another that had her calling Malone.

"We need to announce the arrests and name the dealers who were most likely in possession of laced pills, so anyone who might've bought from them knows not to take them."

"Good point. We'll put out a release."

"ASAP?"

"Yes, ma'am."

"Thanks, Cap."

Sam closed the phone without the usual slap that gave her so much satisfaction and stepped into the suite she shared with Nick, quietly closing the door behind her. She tiptoed into their bedroom and wasn't surprised to see Nick sitting up in bed with a huge binder on his lap and the sexy, dark-framed reading glasses he'd recently started wearing sitting at the end of his nose.

"There's my favorite first lady, home from running the streets all night."

Sam smiled. "We got him."

He returned her smile. "Never had a doubt you would."

"I'm glad you didn't, because I had tons of them."

He held out a hand to her. "Come see me."

"I need to pee and brush my teeth. They're furry."

"I'll be here."

After she used the bathroom and brushed her teeth, she changed into joggers and a T-shirt, determined to relax for a bit before she had to get ready for the funeral. When she returned to the bedroom, he'd put aside the briefing book and taken off the glasses. Sam crawled onto the bed and snuggled up to him. "They're bringing up coffee and breakfast in a few minutes."

"Why didn't you plan to sleep for a bit?"

"Because two hours isn't enough, and I'm better off waiting until I can sleep for hours."

"Tell me all about it."

While he held her, she told him about Vincent trying to run Lawton out of business by hiring his dealers to deliver laced product.

"Jeez, Sam. That's crazy. Did Lawton's dealers know the product was laced?"

"Maybe not at first, but when customers started turning up dead, you'd think they would've gotten a clue that something wasn't right."

"But they just kept selling the product?"

"Yeah, they did, because drug dealers don't care who dies, or at least that's how it seems to us. Or maybe Vincent threatened them or their families. Who knows? There's no honor among thieves. Spencer played basketball with the guy who sold the pills to him."

"Of all the drug dealers in town, Spencer was friends with one recruited by Vincent," Nick said with a sigh.

"I know."

"How do you feel now that you have answers?"

"Oddly elated from a professional point of view, as I did something Narcotics and the DEA haven't been able to do, but incredibly deflated from a personal standpoint. It's all so sad and senseless and infuriating. Why do the doctors cut people off when they know they're addicted? Why aren't there more programs for people who've become addicted to opioids to help them manage their addiction safely as they work to get clean? Cutting them off sends them to the streets, and this is what can happen."

"I'd love to tackle this issue from a federal level, but it would be hard to go all in on that if people don't know what happened to Spencer. That would basically be telling them."

"Yeah, it would. Maybe Ang will decide to go public with it at some point, because there's a lot of good we could do on this issue."

"Yes, there is."

A knock on the door sounded.

"That'll be my breakfast."

"I'll get it," he said.

Sam watched him get up and cross the room. What did it say about her that she loved him so much that even watching him move did it for her? It said she had a bad case of love for him, and it seemed to get worse all the time, which was fine with her.

When she started to get up, he said, "Stay put. I'll bring it to you."

"Bless you."

Knowing she was the only person in the world that the sexy president of the United States waited on also did it for her. Big-time.

He set her coffee on the bedside table and a plate of steaming eggs, bacon, toast and fruit on her lap. "Is there anything else I can get you, madam?"

"This will do for now. Thank you, sir."

He gave a gallant little bow and left to get his own plate and coffee, returning to the bed to eat with her.

"This is the life. Breakfast in bed with the president."

"I'm not the president here. I'm just your husband."

"Just my husband. I like that."

"I need one place in the world to be just Nick, husband and father."

"I'm happy to be your safe place, love."

"And before I forget to say it, I'm so damned proud of you for tracking down these murdering assholes so quickly while you were in shock and trying to be there for your sister and nephew and the rest of us. This is why I call you my Wonder Woman."

"Thank you but having to face Spencer's funeral today makes it a hollow victory."

"I know, but it's a victory, nonetheless. You've saved a lot of other families from tragedy."

"I just wish I could've saved my own from this nightmare."

BEFORE THEY LEFT for the funeral, Sam went upstairs to see Angela and Jack. Celia had taken Ella outside to play on the swings so she wouldn't see her mom and Jack leave for the funeral. A friend of Angela's was coming to pick up Ella so Celia could go to the funeral.

Sam knocked on the door.

"Come in."

Angela wore a black maternity dress with heels, while Jack sat next to her in a dark suit and tie. His hair had been combed into submission. He looked like a tiny man trying to be strong for his mother, which broke her heart all over again.

She took Angela aside while Jack watched TV. "I, um, I wanted to tell you that we got them, the dealers, the kingpin, all of them."

"Who was it?" Angela asked in a dull, flat tone.

"A dealer named Sal Vincent had decided to run a rival dealer named Riggs Lawton out of business by hiring Lawton's dealers to sell laced pills to unsuspecting customers. One of those dealers was Matthias Foster, the man we arrested at the wake."

"I figured out where I met him. He played basketball with Spencer. Before everything happened."

Sam nodded. "That's what he told us. Spencer went to someone he knew to get the pills, probably thinking it would be safer that way."

Angela nodded.

"I'm sorry. I know it's small comfort during such an unfathomable loss."

"Thank you, Sam," Angela said. "I know you ran yourself ragged this week chasing these people down, and it's not a small comfort to know they can't do this to anyone else's family. It's a big comfort."

"I wish we could've caught them before this happened. I'll always be sorry that we didn't."

SPENCER'S FUNERAL, in the same church where her father's service had been held, was everything Sam expected it to be—poignant, funny, sweet and utterly heartbreaking.

Per Angela's request, their brother-in-law Mike read a message from Angela to her husband. "Spencer, you were everything wonderful and good in my life. In all the years we spent together, not a day went by when you didn't tell me how much you loved me and our family. I'll take that love with me into an uncertain future. I don't know how to go on without you, but I'll find a way through for the sake of our three beautiful children. I will make sure they remember you with love and smiles and the comfort that comes from knowing they were well and truly loved by their wonderful father. Sleep in peace and comfort, my love. We'll remember you always." Mike's voice broke on those last words from a wife to her husband.

Sam wiped away tears as Nick held her hand a little tighter.

Next to her, Angela sobbed softly. Sam put her arm around her sister, who leaned her head on Sam's shoulder.

"On a personal note," Mike said, "I want to add that I'll remember how much Spencer loved Angela and their children, how much he was looking forward to the birth of their third child, how wonderful he was with Jack and Ella and how much fun we had together being part of the Holland family. I love you, Spence. We all love you, and we'll miss you."

When Mike returned to his seat, Tracy and Angela both hugged him.

"Thank you for doing that for me," Ang said.

"Anything for you, kid," Mike said.

Spencer's brother, Jed, spoke on behalf of the Radcliffe family. "There are moments in life you'll never forget, and one of them for me will be getting the call that my brother had died while my family and I were in Italy. I'm still trying to wrap my head around the fact that he's really gone. Like, how can that be? I just talked to him before I left on the trip, and he was fine, or so I thought. I've since found out he wasn't fine, but he'd chosen to keep his struggles private. Rather than talk about how he died, I'd rather focus on how he lived. I was five years older than Spencer, so I remember the day he was born and all the days since then. Spencer was a presence. If he was in the room, you knew it. If you didn't notice him, he'd do something that would give you no choice but to notice him."

Sam and her family laughed at how true that was.

"Some would say he had a big opinion of himself, but I saw it a little differently. He was definitely full of himself sometimes, but it was more that he was full of life, bursting at the seams to get where he was going. From the time he was the littlest kid until the last days of his life, his eye was always on the next goal or accomplishment or game that needed to be won. He was a fierce competitor, and most of the time, he won whatever game he was playing.

"On behalf of Angela and the kids, my parents, sisters, and the entire extended Radcliffe family, we thank you for the outpouring of love and support this week as we've mourned the loss of Spencer. We will remember him with love and laughter and a million memories that will have to sustain us until we see him again in the next life."

After the beautiful service concluded, Spencer was laid to rest in the same cemetery as Sam's dad, a few rows away from his late father-in-law.

For a long time after the other mourners left to attend the reception being held at a nearby restaurant, Sam, Nick, Tracy, Mike, Brenda and Celia stayed with Angela and Jack at the gravesite.

"I can't bring myself to leave him here," Angela said between sobs.

What could be said to that? Sam wouldn't have been able to do it either. Just when she thought this nightmare couldn't get any worse, Jack knelt on the ground next to his father's grave and begged him to come back to them.

"Please, Daddy. Please don't go."

Nick bent to pick the little guy up and held him as he sobbed even as tears slid down his own face.

They eventually convinced Angela to come with them and were loaded into several Secret Service SUVs that had been made available to transport the extended family that day.

Sitting next to Sam, Angela said, "I want you to tell people what happened to him and warn them that these people are out there, looking to prey on defenseless people who've become addicted to this stuff." Angela's voice was firm and resolute.

"Are you sure?"

She nodded as she wiped more tears from red, raw eyes that seemed more focused than they'd been in days. "I talked to Spencer's family about it, and we all agree that we want to use his story and your big platform to make people aware of what can happen when you buy this stuff illegally."

"Nick wants to do something from a federal level but was hesitant, as it would out Spencer's cause of death."

"He should do something. Someone needs to."

"We'll do everything we can."

"If telling our story stops one person from doing what Spencer did out of desperation, then maybe his death won't be for nothing."

"It won't be for nothing," Sam said. "We won't let it be."

THE NEXT DAY, Sam stood before the media outside HQ to make the statement that Angela and Spencer's family had approved for release. Sam had spent the previous evening on the phone with each of her victims' families, updating them on the resolution of the case.

"On behalf of the Radcliffe and Holland families, we thank you for the outpouring of love and support that followed the death of our beloved Spencer Radcliffe, who was my sister Angela's husband and the father of my nephew Jack and my niece Ella, as well as another child due in June. Our hearts are truly broken by this unimaginable loss. Angela and the Radcliffe family have asked me to share Spencer's cause of death in the hope that his story might save other lives.

"More than a year ago, Spencer suffered a back injury while playing football with friends. He was treated with OxyContin, to which he became addicted. When his doctors refused to prescribe more of the medication he needed to manage the pain he was still experiencing, Spencer went looking for it elsewhere, which led to him encountering fentanyl-laced street Oxy. That is what killed him.

"Prior to his death, Spencer had worked diligently to overcome his addiction, spending months in rehab and working on his recovery. He was due to return to rehab for a third time the Tuesday after his death. The back pain that continued to plague him was such that he was desperate enough to go looking for the pills that brought relief anywhere he could get them. He turned to a friend to provide the pills. That friend was arrested this week.

"Our family's story is no different from that of many families who have faced the scourge of opioid addiction with similar results. My sister is determined that her husband's death will help bring about change in our society, our laws and our compassion for addicts of all kinds.

"I'm also here to announce the arrests of Sal Vincent and numerous members of his team who were dealing the laced pills to unsuspecting customers, hoping to run a rival dealer out of the local business. Vincent and others, whose names will be released pending arraignments, have been charged with seven counts each of felony murder in the deaths of Spencer Radcliffe, Mary Alice Albright, Morgan Newell, Angelo Diaz, Tommy O'Donald, Jesse Myer and Jackson Audette, as well as the attempted murder of Bryan Smith. We expect to link Vincent and his dealers to numerous other overdose deaths in the coming days.

"Our team is working with the DEA to locate the remaining product that Vincent's team was selling, but we urge the public to use extreme caution in taking any medication that was not prescribed by a doctor and obtained through a pharmacy. We believe there are fentanyl-laced pills still in circulation. If you have acquired Oxy illegally in recent weeks, we urge you not to touch the medication and to call the Metro PD immediately. No charges will be filed against anyone who asks for our assistance in disposing of these pills."

When she finished reading the prepared statement, she looked up at the huge group of media that had turned up when they made it known she'd be releasing her brother-in-law's cause of death. "I'll take a few questions."

"How involved were you in the investigation that led to the arrest of Vincent and the others?"

"I was involved, but Sergeant Thomas Gonzales was the lead detective."

"No questions, Lieutenant," one reporter said. "Just sympathy to your family."

"Thank you."

"What led you to Vincent?" Darren Tabor asked. "And my condolences as well."

"Thank you. We were assisted by numerous informants who put us on the trail of Vincent and his plan to use laced pills to drive a rival dealer out of business."

"Is the rival dealer under arrest as well?"

"He's deceased, and his operation is being dismantled by the DEA."

"Is it Riggs Lawton?"

"I'm not at liberty to comment on that at this time. This is an ongoing investigation, and more updates will be coming soon. Thank you for your time and for helping us to spread the word about my brother-in-law's cause of death in the hope that it might save someone else. Have a good day."

She walked away from the podium, fighting back a swell of emotions as she recalled Jack at Spencer's graveside, an image that would stay with her for the rest of her life. Now the word was out about what'd happened to Spencer, and the people responsible for his death were in custody. Hopefully, the information and the arrests would help to achieve Angela's goal of making Spencer's death count for something.

EPILOGUE

After the longest two weeks of her life, Sam slept for what felt like days. When she awoke alone on the Saturday morning after the funeral, she stared up at the ceiling, picking over the last few days. She'd overseen reams of paperwork and reports on the Vincent case, participated in numerous meetings with U.S. Attorney Tom Forrester and most of his Assistant U.S. Attorneys. The case was ready to proceed with arraignments.

As their star witness, Leslie Lawton had been given full immunity from prosecution as well as witness protection ahead of and after her testimony. Immunity had been given only after she disclosed the whereabouts of their warehouse and named every dealer who'd worked for them. Richard Kent had been charged as an accessory to murder, his parole was revoked, and he'd been sent back to Jessup along with Matthias Foster and several other dealers who'd accepted payment from Vincent to sell laced pills to Lawton's customers.

They all claimed not to know the pills were laced, but the USA had called bullshit on that. "The minute the first person died, they knew what they were selling," Forrester had said.

Haggerty's Crime Scene detectives had done a masterful job of collecting evidence. Lab analysis proved the pills all came from the same lot, providing them with the evidence needed to connect Vincent's scheme to each of their victims.

Timing, Sam thought, was everything. If Spencer had bought

the pills a month earlier or a month later, he might've missed getting sucked into Vincent's nefarious scheme.

Nick came into the room, already showered and dressed in jeans and a sweater. "You're awake. I was starting to get worried."

"Sorry. I didn't sleep much this week."

"I know, babe." He sat on the bed next to her and leaned in to kiss her. "You feel better?"

"I think so."

Curling a strand of her hair around his finger, he said, "Why do you look so troubled? Other than the obvious."

"I was just thinking about timing and how Spencer might've avoided this whole thing if he'd bought the pills a month earlier or later. If only Narcotics hadn't gotten behind on their OD reporting, maybe an alert would've been sounded in time to save him."

"Or maybe it was just his time to go."

Sam gave him a skeptical look. "Do you believe that?"

"I believe we're all along for the ride. Some of us will get lucky and have long lives, and others won't. But we can no more control how it plays out than we can control the tides or the sunrise or the weather."

"I wanted to fix this for Ang and the kids."

"You did fix it for them, sweetheart, as much as anyone could."

"I go through this life and this job, trying to get justice for people whose lives will never be the same, and I tell myself that what we do makes a difference for them. But does it? Does it really? The person they lost is never coming back, no matter what I do."

"No, but the parties responsible for taking those lives are held accountable and can't do this to another family. That *does* matter, Sam. It absolutely does."

"I might need you to remind me of that once in a while."

"Any time you need it," he said, kissing her. "I wanted to let you know that Angela decided to pack up this morning and go home. The Secret Service took them a while ago."

"What brought this on?" Sam asked, surprised to hear that news because Angela hadn't mentioned leaving when Sam saw her the night before.

"She didn't say much, but she left this for you." He handed her an envelope that she tore open, holding the letter so Nick could read along with her.

Dear Sam,

Sorry for sneaking out while you were getting some much-needed rest, but I was afraid you'd talk me out of doing what needs to be done. It wouldn't take much to convince me to stay forever at the wonderful White House, where we've been cared for so beautifully by you, Nick, Scotty, Alden, Aubrey, Eli, Candace and even Skippy. The White House staff has been so good to me and the kids, tending to our every need, and I've left a separate note to thank them.

It would be so easy to get comfortable here, in your life, but I need to go back to my own. Thanks to the GoFundMe and the generosity of so many people, I can pay off my debt and live comfortably in our home while I figure out what's next. I'll never be able to tell you and Freddie what it means to me to have the resources to take a minute to breathe, or how much I appreciate Nick promoting the fundraiser, even if that got the media wound up. Thank you for the offer of Ninth Street. It helps to know that's an option if it's too painful to stay in our home.

I've decided to use most of the GFM money to start a foundation in Spencer's name that will have two purposes—to pay for rehab for people who can't afford it and to help families like mine that have been devastated by overdose deaths. I think we can do a lot of good that will make Spencer proud of us. I'm hoping I can call on you, Lilia, Roni and your amazing team for help on how best to get the word out about the foundation when we're ready.

I'll never have the words to tell you and Nick how much I appreciate the way you made us feel so welcome in your home and surrounded us with love and comfort at the most difficult time in our lives. Jack and I will always remember the weeks we spent at the White House with you all. Despite our devastation, there were moments of joy and magic mixed in that made all the difference for us at this difficult time.

One more thing... You said it wouldn't matter to me now that you caught the people who did this, but it does matter. It matters

*greatly that they aren't out there living their lives while I'm
forced to piece mine back together. It matters. You matter. Thank
you for making it your personal mission to get justice for
Spencer, for me and for his beloved children. You are amazing all
the time, but never more so than lately.*

*I love you and Nick and your kids so much. Thank you for
everything.*

Ang

Sam wiped away tears and wasn't surprised to see Nick do the same.

"She sounds a little like her old self," Sam said.

"I was thinking the same thing. The foundation is an amazing idea. We'll make sure it's a huge success when the time comes."

"I'll add it to my first lady platform and do everything I can to promote it. What a great way to use the money that was raised."

"Does it help you to hear what she had to say about the case?"

"It does. It's good to know that she's comforted." Sam folded up the letter and put it on her bedside table. "And it's great to see her picking herself up and making some plans."

"She's still got a long road ahead, but she's on the right path."

"I think so, too." Sam reached for him, and he came into her embrace, kissing her with the heat that flared between them so reliably, she'd come to count on it as much as she counted on oxygen and water.

"Thank you for being my strength through this nightmare," she whispered against his lips. "And for being there for Ang and her kids, too."

"All my life, I've wanted to be part of a family like the one I have now. It's an honor to be with you and your sisters and the rest of our family through the good times and the bad times."

"I'm so, so thankful to get to experience everything with you— the good, the bad, the ugly."

"Likewise, my love." He kissed her again and had her squirming under him, looking for more, in a matter of seconds.

"Where are my kids?"

Kissing her neck, he said, "Outside on the playground with Scotty."

"How do you feel about a quickie?"

He pressed his hard cock against her core. "I feel very, very good about it."

They moved fast to move clothes out of the way while kissing and laughing like two fools. "If the rest of the world could see us now," Sam said.

"Thank God they can't," he said, sinking into her in one deep thrust that took her breath away.

She gasped from the impact and the pleasure.

"Too much?" he asked.

She held him close. "Just enough."

Though they'd billed it as a quickie, he took his own sweet time, drawing out the pleasure for as long as he possibly could.

She was mindless with it, lost in a sea of sensation and fired up in a way that she could only achieve with him.

As he pressed his fingers to her clit, he made her come so hard, she saw stars. He surged into her, losing himself in her as she took everything he had to give.

It was perfection, Sam thought, her eyes as heavy as if she hadn't just slept for twelve hours.

Nick kissed her cheek and then her lips as he continued to throb inside her. "You okay in there?"

Her eyes refused to open. "Very okay."

Sam's phone rang, forcing her to resurface.

Nick reached for it on her bedside table and handed it to her. "It's Freddie."

"Hey, what's up?"

"I just saw on the news that Nick's mother has been indicted."

~

Ahhh, this was a tough one. I'm not sure where these story ideas come from but know that they mess with my emotions as much as they do with yours! The opioid epidemic has touched so many families and altered so many lives. From my small group of beta readers, I heard several stories of loss or struggle within their families. My daughter lost a close friend to an accidental fentanyl overdose in 2016. Kevin was just twenty-two. This book is dedicated to him.

Many of my early readers have asked if Angela will show up in the Wild Widows Series, and the answer to that is yes, she will. Her story will also continue to play out adjacent to Sam and Nick's.

Join the State of Shock Reader Group to discuss this book with spoilers allowed at *facebook.com/groups/stateofshock*. If you haven't yet joined the series group, you can find that at *facebook.com/groups/fatalseries*.

A HUGE thank you to my friend, Capt. Russ Hayes, (retired), Newport, RI, Police Department, who went the extra mile to help me make this story authentic from a law enforcement standpoint by gathering important information from the front lines of the opioid battle. I so appreciate him and his amazing contributions to every one of the Fatal and First Family books over the last thirteen years.

Also, my thanks to Dr. Sarah Hewitt, family nurse practitioner, for her input into the opening scenes of this book.

Thank you to my editors, Linda Ingmanson and Joyce Lamb, as well as my primary beta readers, Anne Woodall, Kara Conrad and Tracey Suppo, and continuity assistant Gwen Neff. And a big thank you to the Fatal/First Family beta readers: Jennifer, Kelly, Karina, Sarah, Irene, Gina, Ellen, Elizabeth, Mona, Kelley, Viki, Juliane, Jennifer, Phuong and Marti.

I'm so lucky to be supported by my husband, Dan, and an amazing team that takes care of so many things behind the scenes so I can write. Shout out to Julie Cupp, Lisa Cafferty, Jean Mello, Nikki Haley and Ashley Lopez as well as Dani Sanchez and the team at Wildfire Marketing.

To my amazing readers who've followed Sam and Nick from the Watergate to the White House, thank you so much for your devotion to their story. You make it so fun to continue writing it. More to come for Sam and Nick in the New Year. Until then, happy holidays to you and your families and all the best in 2023!

Much love,
Marie

Book 18: Kevin & Chelsea (Episode 2)

A Gansett Island Christmas Novella

Book 19: Mine After Dark *(Riley & Nikki)*

Book 20: Yours After Dark *(Finn & Chloe)*

Book 21: Trouble After Dark *(Deacon & Julia)*

Book 22: Rescue After Dark *(Mason & Jordan)*

Book 23: Blackout After Dark *(Full Cast)*

Book 24: Temptation After Dark *(Gigi & Cooper)*

Book 25: Resilience After Dark *(Jace & Cindy)*

Book 26: Hurricane After Dark *(Full Cast)*

The Green Mountain Series

Book 1: All You Need Is Love *(Will & Cameron)*

Book 2: I Want to Hold Your Hand *(Nolan & Hannah)*

Book 3: I Saw Her Standing There *(Colton & Lucy)*

Book 4: And I Love Her *(Hunter & Megan)*

Novella: You'll Be Mine *(Will & Cam's Wedding)*

Book 5: It's Only Love *(Gavin & Ella)*

Book 6: Ain't She Sweet *(Tyler & Charlotte)*

The Butler, Vermont Series

(Continuation of Green Mountain)

Book 1: Every Little Thing *(Grayson & Emma)*

Book 2: Can't Buy Me Love *(Mary & Patrick)*

Book 3: Here Comes the Sun *(Wade & Mia)*

Book 4: Till There Was You *(Lucas & Dani)*

Book 5: All My Loving *(Landon & Amanda)*

Book 6: Let It Be *(Lincoln & Molly)*

Book 7: Come Together *(Noah & Brianna)*

Book 8: Here, There & Everywhere *(Izzy & Cabot)*

Book 9: The Long and Winding Road *(Max & Lexi)*

The Quantum Series

Book 1: Virtuous *(Flynn & Natalie)*

Book 2: Valorous *(Flynn & Natalie)*

Book 3: Victorious *(Flynn & Natalie)*

Book 4: Rapturous *(Addie & Hayden)*

Book 5: Ravenous *(Jasper & Ellie)*

Book 6: Delirious *(Kristian & Aileen)*

Book 7: Outrageous *(Emmett & Leah)*

Book 8: Famous *(Marlowe & Sebastian)*

The Treading Water Series

Book 1: Treading Water

Book 2: Marking Time

Book 3: Starting Over

Book 4: Coming Home

Book 5: Finding Forever

Single Titles

Five Years Gone

One Year Home

Sex Machine

Sex God

Georgia on My Mind

True North

The Fall

The Wreck

Love at First Flight

Everyone Loves a Hero

Line of Scrimmage

Historical Romance Available from Marie Force

The Gilded Series

Book 1: Duchess by Deception

Book 2: Deceived by Desire

ABOUT THE AUTHOR

Marie Force is the *New York Times* bestselling author of contemporary romance, romantic suspense and erotic romance. Her series include Fatal, First Family, Gansett Island, Butler Vermont, Quantum, Treading Water, Miami Nights and Wild Widows.

Her books have sold more than 12 million copies worldwide, have been translated into more than a dozen languages and have appeared on the *New York Times* bestseller list more than 30 times. She is also a *USA Today* and #1 *Wall Street Journal* bestseller, as well as a Spiegel bestseller in Germany.

Her goals in life are simple—to finish raising two happy, healthy, productive young adults, to keep writing books for as long as she possibly can and to never be on a flight that makes the news.

Join Marie's mailing list on her website at *marieforce.com* for news about new books and upcoming appearances in your area. Follow her on Facebook at *www.Facebook.com/MarieForceAuthor*, Instagram at *www.instagram.com/marieforceauthor/* and TikTok at *https://www.tiktok.com/@marieforceauthor?*. Contact Marie at *marie@marieforce.com*.

CPSIA information can be obtained
at www.ICGtesting.com
Printed in the USA
LVHW030026141222
735142LV00002B/146